and other stories

Selected and edited by CHRISTOPHER BIGSBY

A Phoenix Paperback

This edition first published in Great Britain by Phoenix Paperbacks in 1998

Selection, introduction and other critical apparatus © Phoenix Paperbacks 1998

Orion Publishing Group
Orion House
5 Upper St Martin's Lane
London WC2H 9EA

Typeset by Deltatype Ltd, Birkenhead, Merseyside
Printed in Great Britain by
The Guernsey Press Co. Ltd, Guernsey, C. I.

British Library Cataloguing-in-Publication
Data is available upon request.

ISBN 0 75380 448 4

Contents

Note on the Author and Editor

JACK LONDON, born in San Francisco, California, on 12 January 1876, was the author of fifty-one books, nineteen of which were short story collections. His novels include *White Fang* (1906), *The Iron Heel* (1908), and *Martin Eden* (1909). By far his best known and most successful, however, was *The Call of the Wild* (1903). London died on 22 November 1916 at his Glen Ellen ranch in Sonoma Valley, California.

CHRISTOPHER BIGSBY, Professor of American Studies at the University of East Anglia, has published more than twenty books on aspects of American culture. He is a regular broadcaster with BBC radio and television and is the author and co-author of several radio and television plays. He is the author of three novels: *Hester* (1994), *Pearl* (1995) and *Still Lives* (1996). He is also the Director of the Arthur Miller Centre for American Studies. He lives in Norwich, England.

Introduction

Jack London was born illegitimate and poor. Rejecting the career of manual labour for which his background seemed to have prepared him, he set out to invent himself. His first act of self-invention was to turn oyster pirate in San Francisco Bay. Thereafter he sailed on a sealing ship, looked for gold in the Yukon (returning with $5 worth) and travelled restlessly across America. But at the age of seventeen he had won a newspaper competition for young writers and on his return from gold prospecting, in 1899, published a story in the *Overland Monthly*. A year later his first book appeared. It was an immediate success. He was twenty-four. By forty he was dead. The success he had sought was his but the price proved too great. Though his doctor entered uremia following renal colic on the death certificate, the fact is that his body was undermined by alcohol and his spirit by a career which had brought him success but never really contentment.

Jack London believed that the short story was likely to be the principal literary form of the twentieth century and certainly a sudden growth of magazines for a burgeoning middle class created a ready market. Believing this, he set out systematically to prepare himself for his career copying out Rudyard Kipling stories in longhand, hoping thereby to acquire his technique, and began, 'like a first year medical student . . . to dissect the stories in the current magazines, taking them apart, tracing their nerves and sinews, and striving to reproduce the articulation of their joints.'

The medical reference is revealing for his stories are often visceral. The tendons, the veins, the muscles all stand out. There are no Jamesian ambiguities, no Hemingwayesque understatements here. London's ironies, unlike Hemingway's, are deliberately unsubtle.

His stories are, for the most part, determinedly male. Women are either sentimentalized, absent or mere objects of acquisition, representatives of values abrogated by those who serve other necessities than those of a civilized coherence. Indeed, he frequently takes his reader where such values do not operate in order to explore the nature of man stripped of everything including fundamental necessities. We watch as his characters regress, slough off those attitudes, habits, values, conventions judged necessary to normal life and rediscover brute needs to be served by equally brutal strategies. There is something almost sadistic in the pleasure with which he describes the physical privations, the maiming, the violence suffered by his protagonists who, when they survive (as they often do not), do so only in so far as they surrender everything but an instinct for existence. They kill, they endure exquisite tortures, they willingly sacrifice everything they have previously valued, in order to survive, and only rarely is there a sense that anything of value can be said to redeem such suffering, beyond the manner in which they resist their fate. Sometimes, to be sure, as in 'The Mexican', sacrifice is sanctified by a transcendent faith, but more often it serves no more than the iron law of nature.

Despite his socialist convictions, and London regarded himself as such and was a member of the party, his view of history is not progressive. In his stories ancient races succumb without the consolation of believing that they submit to superior philosophies, cultures or convictions. The white man replaces the native, age bows to youth, but there is little sense that this process constitutes an advance. In 'Koolau the Leper', a native, whose body is ravaged with a disease introduced by the white man, picks off white police and soldiers sent to arrest him even as his body disintegrates. Like many other London characters, he sinks into a final unconsciousness a defeated man. Where victory is granted it often seems unconvincing, unfelt. 'Love of Life' is one such story, though it served to raise Lenin's spirits when his wife read it to him two days before his death. The only absolute rules are those implicit in a Darwinian view of experience: those who do not adapt will die, the fittest survive. And Darwin (or, rather, Herbert Spencer, his popularizing follower) was a major influence, as is clear from *The Call of the Wild* in which the animal analogy is taken literally.

Society is fragile, a competitive arena. The connection between individuals is loose and arbitrary. Mother and child, husband and wife, comrades, are, more often than not, essentially rivals whose alliances are temporary, easily broken by circumstance and time. All of this is difficult to reconcile with London's announced socialism, but his was an idiosyncratic socialism based on the idea of a sustaining and vivifying conflict, a drama of colliding forces which seems to have mattered as much to him as any utopian scheme.

There are few London characters permitted the luxury of abstract thought. In his socialist stories some of his characters do serve the interests of a submerged class but their power derives not so much from class-consciousness as from a natural superiority, an inborn quality of leadership which has Nietzschean overtones. In *The Call of the Wild* the pack becomes all powerful but the pack can only function because it is led by one of its number distinguishable from the rest by its physical and mental strength.

Viewed ahistorically, through the lens of twentieth-century brutalities, there is something chilling about this allegory and it is hard not to find much of London's work disturbing – its clinical detachment, its atavistic impulses, its determinism, its sometimes sympathetic, sometimes patronizing attitude to the non Anglo-Saxon, its crude presentation of individual psychology and social behaviour. Yet there is no denying the raw force of stories whose energies lie in their unrelenting description of physical experience, in their exploration of primal feelings and extreme situations. They have a vicarious power which often triumphs over deficiencies of character and simplicities of social analysis.

He wanted his stories, he explained, to 'live and spout blood and spirit and beauty and fire and glamor'. The language is revealing. There is, to be sure, little beauty, except in his vivid descriptions of a bleak but impressive nature, and no glamour, but such qualities as they do have are uncompromisingly physical.

To be sure, London was fascinated by ideas – not only those of Darwin and Spencer but also Jung and Freud – and those inform some of his stories. But they are not best read as exemplary texts, embodiments of theory, but as tactile and vivid explorations of an elemental world in which the self encounters the extent of its own possibilities.

London was, throughout his life, a man of contradictions. If he felt the power of Spencer's notion of the survival of the fittest, he also rebelled against it in a work such as *The Sea Wolf*. He could etherealize women yet relegate them to the margin, celebrate the individual but admire the solidarity of the masses. His own life, meanwhile, was an embodiment of the capitalist ethos which he

so distrusted. Naming his ranch the 'Wolf Lair' and himself 'Wolf'
he came close to entering the very myths he celebrated but
whose dangers he also acknowledged. Yet he wrote stories which
continue to fascinate an international readership more than
three-quarters of a century after his death, stories whose terrors
still make the pulse beat faster.

Note on the Text

The texts included in this volume are based on the book publication of the stories and not the magazine versions. However, in each case the date of magazine and book versions are indicated, in that order.

THE CALL OF THE WILD
and other stories

The Call of the Wild (1903)

1

Into the Primitive

'Old longings nomadic leap,
Chafing at custom's chain;
Again from its brumal sleep
Wakens the ferine strain.'

Buck did not read the newspapers, or he would have known that trouble was brewing, not alone for himself, but for every tide-water dog, strong of muscle and with warm, long hair, from Puget Sound to San Diego. Because men, groping in the Arctic darkness, had found a yellow metal, and because steamship and transportation companies were booming the find, thousands of men were rushing into the Northland. These men wanted dogs, and the dogs they wanted were heavy dogs, with strong muscles by which to toil, and furry coats to protect them from the frost.

Buck lived at a big house in the sun-kissed Santa Clara Valley. Judge Miller's place, it was called. It stood back from the road, half hidden among the trees, through which glimpses could be caught of the wide cool veranda that ran around its four sides. The house was approached by graveled driveways which wound about through wide-spreading lawns and under the interlacing boughs of tall poplars. At the rear things were on even a more spacious scale than at the front. There were great stables, where a dozen grooms and boys held forth, rows of vine-clad servants' cottages, an endless and orderly array of outhouses, long grape arbors, green pastures, orchards, and berry patches. Then there was the pumping plant for the artesian well, and the big cement tank where Judge Miller's boys took their morning plunge and kept cool in the hot afternoon.

And over this great demesne Buck ruled. Here he born, and here he had lived the four years of his life. It was true, there were other dogs. There could not but be other dogs on so vast a place, but they did not count. They came and went, resided in the populous kennels, or lived obscurely in the recesses of the house after the fashion of Toots, the Japanese pug, or Ysabel, the Mexican hairless – strange creatures that rarely put nose out of doors or set foot to ground. On the other hand, there were the fox terriers, a score of them at least, who yelped fearful promises at Toots and Ysabel looking out of the windows at them and protected by a legion of housemaids armed with brooms and mops.

But Buck was neither house-dog nor kennel-dog. The whole realm was his. He plunged into the swimming tank or went hunting with the Judge's sons; he escorted Mollie and Alice, the Judge's daughters, on long twilight or early morning rambles; on wintry nights he lay at the Judge's feet before the roaring library fire; he carried the Judge's grandsons on his back, or rolled them in the grass, and guarded their footsteps through wild adventures down to the fountain in the stable yard, and even beyond, where the paddocks were, and the berry patches. Among the terriers he stalked imperiously and Toots and Ysabel he utterly ignored, for he was king – king over all creeping, crawling, flying things of Judge Miller's place, humans included.

His father, Elmo, a huge St Bernard, had been the Judge's inseparable companion, and Buck bid fair to follow in the way of his father. He was not so large – he weighed only one hundred and forty pounds – for his mother, Shep, had been a Scotch shepherd dog. Nevertheless, one hundred and forty pounds, to which was added the dignity that comes of good living and universal respect, enabled him to carry himself in right royal fashion. During the four years since his puppyhood he had lived the life of a sated aristocrat; he had a fine pride in himself, was even a trifle egotistical, as country gentlemen sometimes become because of their insular situation. But he had saved himself by not becoming a mere pampered house-dog. Hunting and kindred outdoor delights had kept down the fat and hardened his muscles; and to him, as to the cold-tubbing races, the love of water had been a tonic and a health preserver.

And this was the manner of dog Buck was in the fall of 1897, when the Klondike strike dragged men from all the world into the frozen North. But Buck did not read the newspapers, and he did not know that Manuel, one of the gardener's helpers, was an undesirable acquaintance. Manuel had one besetting sin. He loved to play Chinese lottery. Also, in his gambling, he had one besetting weakness – faith in a system; and this made his damnation certain. For to play a system requires money, while the wages of a gardener's helper do not lap over the needs of a wife and numerous progeny.

The Judge was at a meeting of the Raisin Growers' Association, and the boys were busy organizing an athletic club, on the memorable night of Manuel's treachery. No one saw him and Buck go off through the orchard on what Buck imagined was merely a stroll. And with the exception of a solitary man, no one saw them arrive at the little flag station known as College Park. This man talked with Manuel, and money chinked between them.

'You might wrap up the goods before you deliver 'm,' the stranger said gruffly, and Manuel doubled a piece of stout rope around Buck's neck under the collar.

'Twist it, an' you'll choke 'm plentee,' said Manuel, and the stranger grunted a ready affirmative.

Buck had accepted the rope with quiet dignity. To be sure, it was an unwonted performance: but he had learned to trust in men he knew, and to give them credit for a wisdom that outreached his own. But when the ends of the rope were placed in the stranger's hands, he growled menacingly. He had merely intimated his displeasure, in his pride believing that to intimate was to command. But to his surprise the rope tightened around his neck, shutting off his breath. In quick rage he sprang at the man, who met him halfway, grappled him close by the throat, and with a deft twist threw him over on his back. Then the rope tightened mercilessly, while Buck struggled in a fury, his tongue lolling out of his mouth and his great chest panting futilely. Never in all his life had he been so vilely treated, and never in all his life had he been so angry. But his strength ebbed, his eyes glazed, and he knew nothing when the train was flagged and the two men threw him into the baggage car.

The next he knew, he was dimly aware that his tongue was hurting and that he was being jolted along in some kind of a conveyance. The hoarse shriek of a locomotive whistling a crossing told him where he was. He had travelled too often with the Judge not to know the sensation of riding in a baggage car. He opened his eyes, and into them came the unbridled anger of a kidnapped king. The man sprang for his throat, but Buck was too quick for him. His jaws closed on the hand, nor did they relax till his senses were choked out of him once more.

'Yep, has fits,' the man said, hiding his mangled hand from the baggageman, who had been attracted by the sounds of struggle. 'I'm takin' 'm up for the boss to 'Frisco. A crack dog-doctor there thinks that he can cure 'm.'

Concerning that night's ride, the man spoke most eloquently for himself, in a little shed back of a saloon on the San Francisco water front.

'All I get is fifty for it,' he grumbled; 'an' I wouldn't do it over for a thousand, cold cash.'

His hand was wrapped in a bloody handkerchief, and the right trouser leg was ripped from knee to ankle.

'How much did the other mug get?' the saloon-keeper demanded.

'A hundred,' was the reply. 'Wouldn't take a sou less, so help me.'

'That makes a hundred and fifty,' the saloon-keeper calculated; 'and he's worth it, or I'm a squarehead.'

The kidnapper undid the bloody wrappings and looked at his lacerated hand. 'If I don't get the hydrophoby –'

'It'll be because you was born to hang,' laughed the saloon-keeper. 'Here, lend me a hand before you pull your freight,' he added.

Dazed, suffering intolerable pain from throat and tongue, with the life half throttled out of him, Buck attempted to face his tormentors. But he was thrown down and choked repeatedly, till they succeeded in filing the heavy brass collar from off his neck. Then the rope was removed, and he was flung into a cagelike crate.

There he lay for the remainder of the weary night, nursing his wrath and wounded pride. He could not understand what it all meant. What did they want with him, these strange men? Why were they keeping him pent up in this narrow crate? He did not know why, but he felt oppressed by the vague sense of impending calamity. Several times during the night he sprang to his feet when the shed door rattled open, expecting to see the Judge, or the boys at least. But each time it was the bulging face of the saloon-keeper that peered in at him by the sickly light of a tallow candle. And each time the joyful bark that trembled in Buck's throat was twisted into a savage growl.

But the saloon-keeper let him alone, and in the morning four men entered and picked up the crate. More tormentors, Buck decided, for they were evil-looking creatures, ragged and unkempt; and he stormed and raged at them through the bars. They only laughed and poked sticks at him, which he promptly assailed with his teeth till he realized that that was what they wanted. Whereupon he lay down sullenly and allowed the crate to be lifted into a wagon. Then he, and the crate in which he was imprisoned, began a passage through many hands. Clerks in the express office took charge of him; he was carted about in another wagon; a truck carried him, with an assortment of boxes and parcels, upon a ferry steamer; he was trucked off the steamer into a great railway depot, and finally he was deposited in an express car.

For two days and nights this express car was dragged along at the tail of shrieking locomotives; and for two days and nights Buck neither ate nor drank. In his anger he had met the first advances of the express messengers with growls, and they had retaliated by teasing him. When he flung himself against the bars, quivering and frothing, they laughed at him and taunted him. They growled and barked like detestable dogs, mewed, and flapped their arms and crowed. It was all very silly, he knew; but therefore the more outrage to his dignity, and his anger waxed and waxed. He did not mind the hunger so much, but the lack of water caused him severe suffering and fanned his wrath to fever-pitch. For that matter, high-strung and finely sensitive, the ill treatment had flung him into a fever, which was fed by the inflammation of his parched and swollen throat and tongue.

He was glad for one thing: the rope was off his neck. That had given them an unfair advantage; but now that it was off, he would show them. They would never get another rope around his neck. Upon that he was resolved. For two days and nights he neither ate nor drank, and during those two days and nights of torment, he accumulated a fund of wrath that boded ill for whoever first fell foul of him. His eyes turned blood-shot, and he was metamorphosed into a raging fiend. So changed was he that the Judge himself would not have recognized him; and the express messengers breathed with relief when they bundled him off the train at Seattle.

Four men gingerly carried the crate from the wagon into a small, high-walled back yard. A stout man, with a red sweater that sagged generously at the neck, came out and signed the book for the driver. That was the man, Buck divined, the next tormentor, and he hurled himself savagely against the bars. The man smiled grimly, and brought a hatchet and a club.

'You ain't going to take him out now?' the driver asked.

'Sure,' the man replied, driving the hatchet into the crate for a pry.

There was an instantaneous scattering of the four men who had carried it in, and from safe perches on top the wall they prepared to watch the performance.

Buck rushed at the splintering wood, sinking his teeth into it, surging and wrestling with it. Wherever the hatchet fell on the outside, he was there on the inside, snarling and growling, as furiously anxious to get out as the man in the red sweater was calmly intent on getting him out.

'Now, you red-eyed devil,' he said, when he had made an opening sufficient for the passage of Buck's body. At the same time he dropped the hatchet and shifted the club to his right hand.

And Buck was truly a red-eyed devil, as he drew himself together for the spring, hair bristling, mouth foaming, a mad glitter in his blood-shot eyes. Straight at the man he launched his one hundred and forty pounds of fury, surcharged with the pent passion of two days and nights. In mid air, just as his jaws were about to close on the man, he received a shock that checked his body and brought his teeth together with an agonizing clip. He whirled over, fetching the ground on his back and side. He had never been struck by a club in his life, and did not understand. With a snarl that was part bark and more scream he was again on his feet and launched into the air. And again the shock came and he was brought crushingly to the ground. This time he was aware that it was the club, but his madness knew no caution. A dozen times he charged, and as often the club broke the charge and smashed him down.

After a particularly fierce blow, he crawled to his feet, too dazed to rush. He staggered limply about, the blood flowing from nose and mouth and ears, his beautiful coat sprayed and flecked with bloody slaver. Then the man advanced and deliberately dealt him a frightful blow on the nose. All the pain he had endured was as nothing compared with the exquisite agony of this. With a roar that was almost lionlike in its ferocity, he again hurled himself at the man. But the man, shifting the club from right to left, coolly caught him by the under jaw, at the same time wrenching downward and backward. Buck described a complete circle in the air, and half of another, then crashed to the ground on his head and chest.

For the last time he rushed. The man struck the shrewd blow he had purposely withheld for so long, and Buck crumpled up and went down, knocked utterly senseless.

'He's no slouch at dog-breakin', that's wot I say,' one of the men on the wall cried enthusiastically.

'Druther break cayuses any day, and twice on Sundays,' was the reply of the driver, as he climbed on the wagon and started the horses.

Buck's senses came back to him, but not his strength. He lay where he had fallen, and from there he watched the man in the red sweater.

'"Answers to the name of Buck,"' the man soliloquized, quoting from the saloon-keeper's letter which had announced the consignment of the crate and contents. 'Well, Buck, my boy,' he went on in a genial voice, 'we've had our little ruction, and the best thing we can do is to let it go at that. You've learned your place, and I know mine. Be a good dog and all 'll go well and the goose hang high. Be a bad dog, and I'll whale the stuffin' outa you. Understand?'

As he spoke he fearlessly patted the head he had so mercilessly pounded, and though Buck's hair involuntarily bristled at touch of the hand, he endured it without protest. When the man brought him water he drank eagerly, and later bolted a generous meal of raw meat, chunk by chunk, from the man's hand.

He was beaten (he knew that); but he was not broken. He saw, once for all, that he stood no chance against a man with a club. He had learned the lesson, and in all his after life he never forgot it. That club was a revelation. It was his introduction to the reign of primitive law, and he met the introduction halfway. The facts of life took on a fiercer aspect; and while he faced that aspect uncowed, he faced it with all the latent cunning of his nature aroused. As the days went by, other dogs came, in crates and at the ends of ropes, some docilely, and some raging and roaring as he had come; and, one and all, he watched them pass under the dominion of the man in the red sweater. Again and again, as he looked at each brutal performance, the lesson was driven home to Buck: a man with a club was a lawgiver, a master to be obeyed, though not necessarily conciliated. Of this last Buck was never guilty, though he did see beaten dogs that fawned upon the man, and wagged their tails, and licked his hand. Also he saw one dog, that would neither conciliate nor obey, finally killed in the struggle for mastery.

Now and again men came, strangers, who talked excitedly, wheedlingly, and in all kinds of fashions to the man in the red sweater. And at such times that money passed between them the strangers took one or more of the dogs away with them. Buck wondered where they went, for they never came back; but the fear of the future was strong upon him, and he was glad each time when he was not selected.

Yet his time came, in the end, in the form of a little weazened man who spat broken English and many strange and uncouth exclamations which Buck could not understand.

'Sacredam!' he cried, when his eyes lit upon Buck. 'Dat one dam bully dog! Eh? How moch?'

'Three hundred, and a present at that,' was the prompt reply of the man in the red sweater. 'And seein' it's government money, you ain't got no kick coming, eh, Perrault?'

Perrault grinned. Considering that the price of dogs had been boomed skyward by the unwonted demand, it was not an unfair sum for so fine an animal. The Canadian Government would be no loser, nor would its despatches travel the slower. Perrault knew dogs, and when he looked at Buck he knew that he was one in a thousand – 'One in ten t'ousand,' he commented mentally.

Buck saw money pass between them, and was not surprised when Curly, a good-natured Newfoundland, and he were led away by the little weazened man. That was the last he saw of the man in the red sweater, and as Curly and he looked at receding Seattle from the deck of the *Narwhal*, it was the last he saw of the warm Southland. Curly and he were taken below by Perrault and turned over to a black-faced giant called François. Perrault was a French-Canadian, and swarthy; but François was a French-Canadian half-breed, and twice as swarthy. They were a new kind of men to Buck (of which he was destined to see many more), and while he developed no affection for them, he none the less grew honestly to respect them. He speedily learned that

Perrault and François were fair men, calm and impartial in administering justice, and too wise in the way of dogs to be fooled by dogs.

In the 'tween-decks of the *Narwhal*, Buck and Curly joined two other dogs. One of them was a big, snow-white fellow from Spitzbergen who had been brought away by a whaling captain, and who had later accompanied a Geological Survey into the Barrens. He was friendly, in a treacherous sort of way, smiling into one's face the while he meditated some underhand trick, as, for instance, when he stole from Buck's food at the first meal. As Buck sprang to punish him, the lash of François's whip sang through the air, reaching the culprit first; and nothing remained to Buck but to recover the bone. That was fair of François, he decided, and the half-breed began his rise in Buck's estimation.

The other dog made no advances, nor received any; also, he did not attempt to steal from the newcomers. He was a gloomy, morose fellow, and he showed Curly plainly that all he desired was to be left alone, and further, that there would be trouble if he were not left alone. 'Dave' he was called, and he ate and slept, or yawned between times, and took interest in nothing, not even when the *Narwhal* crossed Queen Charlotte Sound and rolled and pitched and bucked like a thing possessed. When Buck and Curly grew excited, half wild with fear, he raised his head as though annoyed, favored them with an incurious glance, yawned, and went to sleep again.

Day and night the ship throbbed to the tireless pulse of the propeller, and though one day was very like another, it was apparent to Buck that the weather was steadily growing colder. At last, one morning, the propeller was quiet, and the *Narwhal* was pervaded with an atmosphere of excitement. He felt it, as did the other dogs, and knew that a change was at hand. François leashed them and brought them on deck. At the first step upon the cold surface, Buck's feet sank into a white mushy something very like mud. He sprang back with a snort. More of this white stuff was falling through the air. He shook himself, but more of it fell upon him. He sniffed it curiously, then licked some up on his tongue. It bit like fire, and the next instant was gone. This puzzled him. He tried it again, with the same result. The onlookers laughed uproariously, and he felt ashamed, he knew not why, for it was his first snow.

2

The Law of Club and Fang

Buck's first day on the Dyea beach was like a nightmare. Every hour was filled with shock and surprise. He had been suddenly jerked from the heart of civilization and flung into the heart of things primordial. No lazy, sun-kissed life was this, with nothing to do but loaf and be bored. Here was neither peace, nor rest, nor a moment's safety. All was confusion and action, and every moment life and limb were in peril. There was imperative need to be constantly alert; for these dogs and men were not town dogs and men. They were savages, all of them, who knew no law but the law of club and fang.

He had never seen dogs fight as these wolfish creatures fought, and his first experience taught him an unforgettable lesson. It is true, it was a vicarious experience, else he would not have lived to profit by it. Curly was the victim. They were camped near the log store, where she, in her friendly way, made advances to a husky dog the size of a full-grown wolf, though not half so large as she. There was no warning, only a leap in like a flash, a metallic clip of teeth, a leap out equally swift, and Curly's face was ripped open from eye to jaw.

It was the wolf manner of fighting, to strike and leap away; but there was more to it than this. Thirty or forty huskies ran to the spot and surrounded the combatants in an intent and silent circle. Buck did not comprehend that silent intentness, nor the eager way with which they were licking their chops. Curly rushed her antagonist, who struck again and leaped aside. He met her next rush with his chest, in a peculiar fashion that tumbled her off her feet. She never regained them. This was what the onlooking huskies had waited for. They closed in upon her, snarling and yelping, and she was buried, screaming with agony, beneath the bristling mass of bodies.

So sudden was it, and so unexpected, that Buck was taken aback. He saw Spitz run out his scarlet tongue in a way he had of laughing; and he saw François, swinging an axe, spring into the mess of dogs. Three men with clubs were helping him to scatter them. It did not take long. Two minutes from the time Curly went down, the last of her assailants were clubbed off. But she lay there limp and lifeless in the bloody, trampled snow, almost literally torn to pieces, the swart half-breed standing over her and cursing horribly. The scene often came back to Buck to trouble him in his sleep. So that was the way. No fair play. Once down, that was the end of you. Well, he would see to it that he never went down. Spitz ran out his tongue and laughed again, and from that moment Buck hated him with a bitter and deathless hatred.

Before he had recovered from the shock caused by the tragic passing of Curly, he received another shock. François fastened upon him an arrangement of straps and buckles. It was a harness, such as he had seen the grooms put on the horses at home. And as he had seen horses work, so he was set to work, hauling François on a sled to the forest that fringed the valley, and returning with a load of firewood. Though his dignity was sorely hurt by thus being made a draught animal, he was too wise to rebel. He buckled down with a will and did his best, though it was all new and strange. François was stern, demanding instant obedience, and by virtue of his whip receiving instant obedience; while Dave, who was an experienced wheeler, nipped Buck's hind quarters whenever he was in error. Spitz was the leader, likewise experienced, and while he could not always get at Buck, he growled sharp reproof now and again, or cunningly threw his weight in the traces to jerk Buck into the way he should go. Buck learned easily, and under the combined tuition of his two mates and François made remarkable progress. Ere they returned to camp he knew enough to stop at 'ho', to go ahead at 'mush', to swing wide on the bends, and to keep clear of the wheeler when the loaded sled shot downhill at their heels.

'T'ree vair' good dogs,' François told Perrault. 'Dat Buck, heem pool lak hell. I tich heem queek as anyt'ing.'

By afternoon, Perrault, who was in a hurry to be on the trail with his despatches, returned with two more dogs. 'Billee' and 'Joe' he called them, two brothers, and true huskies both. Sons of the one mother though they were, they were as different as day and night. Billee's one fault was his excessive good nature, while Joe was the very opposite, sour and introspective, with a perpetual snarl and a malignant eye. Buck received them in comradely fashion, Dave ignored them, while Spitz proceeded to thrash first one and then the other. Billee wagged his tail appeasingly, turned to run when he saw that appeasement was of no avail, and cried (still appeasingly) when Spitz's sharp teeth scored his flank. But no matter how Spitz circled, Joe whirled around on his heels to face him, mane bristling, ears laid back, lips writhing and snarling, jaws clipping together as fast as he could snap, and eyes diabolically gleaming – the incarnation of belligerent fear. So terrible was his appearance that Spitz was forced to forego disciplining him; but to cover his own discomfiture he turned upon the inoffensive and wailing Billee and drove him to the confines of the camp.

By evening Perrault secured another dog, an old husky, long and lean and gaunt, with a battle-scarred face and a single eye which flashed a warning of prowess that commanded respect. He was called Sol-leks, which means the Angry One. Like Dave, he asked nothing, gave nothing, expected nothing; and when he marched slowly and deliberately into their midst, even Spitz left him alone. He had one peculiarity which Buck was unlucky enough to discover. He did not like to be approached on his blind side. Of this offence Buck was unwittingly guilty, and the first knowledge he had of his indiscretion was when Sol-leks whirled upon him and slashed his shoulder to the bone for three inches up and down. Forever after Buck avoided his blind side, and to the last of their comradeship had no more trouble. His only apparent ambition, like Dave's, was to be left alone; though, as Buck was afterward to learn, each of them possessed one other and even more vital ambition.

That night Buck faced the great problem of sleeping. The tent, illumined by a candle, glowed warmly in the midst of the white plain; and when he, as a matter of course, entered it, both Perrault and François bombarded him with curses and cooking utensils, till he recovered from his consternation and fled ignominiously into the outer cold. A chill wind was blowing that nipped him sharply and bit with especial venom into his wounded shoulder. He lay down on the snow and attempted to sleep, but the frost soon drove him shivering to his feet. Miserable and disconsolate, he wandered about among the many tents, only to find that one place was as cold as another. Here and there savage dogs rushed upon him, but he bristled his neck-hair and snarled (for he was learning fast), and they let him go his way unmolested.

Finally an idea came to him. He would return and see how his own team-mates were making out. To his astonishment, they had disappeared. Again he wandered about through the great camp, looking for them, and again he returned. Were they in the tent? No, that could not be, else he would not have been driven out. Then where could they possibly be? With drooping tail and shivering body, very forlorn indeed, he aimlessly circled the tent. Suddenly the snow gave way beneath his fore legs and he sank down. Something wriggled under his feet. He sprang back, bristling and snarling, fearful of the unseen and unknown. But a friendly little yelp reassured him, and he went back to investigate. A whiff of warm air ascended to his nostrils, and there, curled up under the snow in a snug ball, lay Billee. He whined placatingly, squirmed and wriggled to show his good will and intentions, and even ventured, as a bribe for peace, to lick Buck's face with his warm wet tongue.

Another lesson. So that was the way they did it, eh? Buck confidently selected a spot, and with much fuss and waste effort proceeded to dig a hole for himself. In a trice the heat from his body filled the confined space and he was asleep. The day had been long and arduous, and he slept soundly and comfortably, though he growled and barked and wrestled with bad dreams.

Nor did he open his eyes till roused by the noises of the waking camp. At first he did not know where he was. It had snowed during the night and he was completely buried. The snow walls pressed him on every side, and a great surge of fear swept through him – the fear of the wild thing for the trap. It was a token that he was harking back through his own life to the lives of his forebears; for he was a civilized dog, an unduly civilized dog, and of his own experience knew no trap and so could not of himself fear it. The muscles of his whole body contracted spasmodically and instinctively, the hair on his neck and shoulders stood on end, and with a ferocious snarl he bounded straight up into the blinding day, the snow flying about him in a flashing cloud. Ere he landed on his feet, he saw the white camp spread out before him and knew where he was and remembered all that had passed from the time he went for a stroll with Manuel to the hole he had dug for himself the night before.

A shout from François hailed his appearance. 'Wot I say?' the dog-driver cried to Perrault. 'Dat Buck for sure learn queek as anyt'ing.'

Perrault nodded gravely. As courier for the Canadian Government, bearing important despatches, he was anxious to secure the best dogs, and he was particularly gladdened by the possession of Buck.

Three more huskies were added to the team inside an hour, making a total of nine, and before another quarter of an hour had passed they were in harness and swinging up the trail toward the Dyea Cañon. Buck was glad to be gone, and though the work was hard he found he did not particularly despise it. He was surprised at the eagerness which animated the whole team and which was communicated to him; but still more surprising was the change wrought in Dave and Sol-leks. They were new dogs, utterly transformed by the harness. All passiveness and unconcern had dropped from them. They were alert and active, anxious that the work should go well, and fiercely irritable with whatever, by delay or confusion, retarded that work. The toil of the traces seemed the supreme expression of their being, and all that they lived for and the only thing in which they took delight.

Dave was wheeler or sled dog, pulling in front of him was Buck, then came Sol-leks; the rest of the team was strung out ahead, single file, to the leader, which position was filled by Spitz.

Buck had been purposely placed between Dave and Sol-leks so that he might receive instruction. Apt scholar that he was, they were equally apt teachers, never allowing him to linger long in error, and enforcing their teaching with their sharp teeth. Dave was fair and very wise. He never nipped Buck without cause, and he never failed to nip him when he stood in need of it. As François's whip backed him up, Buck found it to be cheaper to mend his ways than to retaliate. Once, during a brief halt, when he got tangled in the traces and delayed the start, both Dave and Sol-leks flew at him and administered a sound trouncing. The resulting tangle was even worse, but Buck took good care to keep the traces clear thereafter; and ere the day was done, so well had he mastered his work, his mates about ceased nagging him. François's whip snapped less frequently, and Perrault even honored Buck by lifting up his feet and carefully examining them.

It was a hard day's run, up the Cañon, through Sheep Camp, past the Scales and the timber line, across glaciers and snowdrifts hundreds of feet deep, and over the great Chilcoot Divide, which stands between the salt water and the fresh and guards forbiddingly the sad and lonely North. They made good time down the chain of lakes which fills the craters of extinct volcanoes, and late that night pulled into the huge camp at the head of Lake Bennett, where thousands of gold-seekers were building boats against the break-up of the ice in the spring. Buck made his hole in the snow and slept the sleep of the exhausted just, but all too early was routed out in the cold darkness and harnessed with his mates to the sled.

That day they made forty miles, the trail being packed; but the next day, and for many days to follow, they broke their own trail, worked harder, and made poorer time. As a rule, Perrault traveled ahead of the team, packing the snow with webbed shoes to make it easier for them. François, guiding the sled at the gee-pole, sometimes exchanged places with him, but not often. Perrault was in a hurry, and he prided himself on his knowledge of ice, which knowledge was indispensable, for the fall ice was very thin, and where there was swift water, there was no ice at all.

Day after day, for days unending, Buck toiled in the traces. Always, they broke camp in the dark, and the first gray of dawn found them hitting the trail with fresh miles reeled off behind them. And always they pitched camp after dark, eating their bit of fish, and crawling to sleep into the snow. Buck was ravenous. The pound and a half of sun-dried salmon, which was his ration for each day, seemed to go nowhere. He never had enough, and suffered from perpetual hunger pangs. Yet the other dogs, because they weighed less and were born to the life, received a pound only of the fish and managed to keep in good condition.

He swiftly lost the fastidiousness which had characterized his old life. A dainty eater, he found that his mates, finishing first, robbed him of his unfinished ration. There was no defending it. While he was fighting off two or three, it was disappearing down the throats of the others. To remedy this, he ate as fast as they; and, so greatly did hunger compel him, he was not above taking what did not belong to him. He watched and learned. When he saw Pike, one of the new dogs, a clever malingerer and thief, slyly steal a slice of bacon when Perrault's back was turned, he duplicated the performance the following day, getting away with the whole chunk. A great uproar was raised, but he was unsuspected; while Dub, an awkward blunderer who was always getting caught, was punished for Buck's misdeed.

This first theft marked Buck as fit to survive in the hostile Northland environment. It marked his adaptability, his capacity to adjust himself to changing conditions, the lack of which would have meant swift and terrible death. It marked, further, the decay or going to pieces of his moral nature, a vain thing and a handicap in the ruthless struggle for existence. It was all well enough in the Southland, under the law of love and fellowship, to respect private property and personal feelings; but in the Northland, under the law of club and fang, whoso took such things into account was a fool, and in so far as he observed them he would fail to prosper.

Not that Buck reasoned it out. He was fit, that was all, and unconsciously he accommodated himself to the new mode of life. All his days, no matter what the odds, he had never run from a fight. But the club of the man in the red sweater had beaten into him a more fundamental and primitive code. Civilized, he could have died for a moral consideration, say the defense of Judge Miller's riding-whip; but the completeness of his decivilization was now evidenced by his ability to flee from the defense of a moral consideration and so save his hide. He did not steal for joy of it, but because of the clamor of his stomach. He did not rob openly, but stole secretly and cunningly, out of respect for club and fang. In short, the things he did were done because it was easier to do them than not to do them.

His development (or retrogression) was rapid. His muscles became hard as iron, and he grew callous to all ordinary pain. He achieved an internal as well as external economy. He could eat anything, no matter how loathsome or indigestible; and, once eaten, the juices of his stomach extracted the last least particle of nutriment; and his blood carried it to the farthest reaches of his body, building it into the toughest and stoutest of tissues. Sight and scent became remarkably keen, while his hearing developed such acuteness that in his sleep he heard the faintest sound and knew whether it heralded peace or peril. He learned to bite the ice out with his teeth when it collected between his toes; and when he was thirsty and there was a thick scum of ice over the water hole, he would break it by rearing and striking it with stiff fore legs. His most conspicuous trait was an ability to scent the wind and forecast it a night in advance. No matter how breathless the air when he dug his nest by tree or bank, the wind that later blew inevitably found him to leeward, sheltered and snug.

And not only did he learn by experience, but instincts long dead became alive again. The domesticated generations fell from him. In vague ways he remembered back to the youth of the breed, to the time the wild dogs ranged in packs through the

primeval forest and killed their meat as they ran it down. It was
no task for him to learn to fight with cut and slash and the quick
wolf snap. In this manner had fought forgotten ancestors. They
quickened the old life within him, and the old tricks which they
had stamped into the heredity of the breed were his tricks. They
came to him without effort or discovery, as though they had been
his always. And when, on the still cold nights, he pointed his
nose at a star and howled long and wolflike, it was his ancestors,
dead and dust, pointing nose at star and howling down through
the centuries and through him. And his cadences were their
cadences, the cadences which voiced their woe and what to them
was the meaning of the stillness, and the cold, and dark.

Thus, as token of what a puppet thing life is, the ancient song
surged through him and he came into his own again; and he
came because men had found a yellow metal in the North, and
because Manuel was a gardener's helper whose wages did not lap
over the needs of his wife and divers small copies of himself.

3

The Dominant Primordial Beast

The dominant primordial beast was strong in Buck, and under
the fierce conditions of trail life it grew and grew. Yet it was a
secret growth. His newborn cunning gave him poise and control.
He was too busy adjusting himself to the new life to feel at ease,
and not only did he not pick fights, but he avoided them
whenever possible. A certain deliberateness characterized his
attitude. He was not prone to rashness and precipitate action;
and in the bitter hatred between him and Spitz he betrayed no
impatience, shunned all offensive acts.

On the other hand, possibly because he divined in Buck a
dangerous rival, Spitz never lost an opportunity of showing his
teeth. He even went out of his way to bully Buck, striving
constantly to start the fight which could end only in the death of
one or the other. Early in the trip this might have taken place had
it not been for an unwonted accident. At the end of this day they
made a bleak and miserable camp on the shore of Lake Le Barge.
Driving snow, a wind that cut like a white-hot knife, and
darkness had forced them to grope for a camping place. They

could hardly have fared worse. At their backs rose a perpendicular wall of rock, and Perrault and François were compelled to make their fire and spread their sleeping robes on the ice of the lake itself. The tent they had discarded at Dyea in order to travel light. A few sticks of driftwood furnished them with a fire that thawed down through the ice and left them to eat supper in the dark.

Close in under the sheltering rock Buck made his nest. So snug and warm was it, that he was loath to leave it when François distributed the fish which he had first thawed over the fire. But when Buck finished his ration and returned, he found his nest occupied. A warning snarl told him that the trespasser was Spitz. Till now Buck had avoided trouble with his enemy, but this was too much. The beast in him roared. He sprang upon Spitz with a fury which surprised them both, and Spitz particularly, for his whole experience with Buck had gone to teach him that his rival was an unusually timid dog, who managed to hold his own only because of his great weight and size.

François was surprised, too, when they shot out in a tangle from the disrupted nest and he divined the cause of the trouble. 'A-a-ah!' he cried to Buck. 'Gif it to heem, by Gar! Gif it to heem, the dirty t'eef!'

Spitz was equally willing. He was crying with sheer rage and eagerness as he circled back and forth for a chance to spring in. Buck was no less eager, and no less cautious, as he likewise circled back and forth for the advantage. But it was then that the unexpected happened, the thing which projected their struggle for supremacy far into the future, past many a weary mile of trail and toil.

An oath from Perrault, the resounding impact of a club upon a bony frame, and a shrill yelp of pain, heralded the breaking forth of pandemonium. The camp was suddenly discovered to be alive with skulking furry forms – starving huskies, four or five score of them, who had scented the camp from some Indian village. They had crept in while Buck and Spitz were fighting, and when the two men sprang among them with stout clubs they showed their teeth and fought back. They were crazed by the smell of the food. Perrault found one with head burried in the grub-box. His club landed heavily on the gaunt ribs, and the grub-box was capsized on the ground. On the instant a score of the famished brutes were scrambling for the bread and bacon. The clubs fell upon them unheeded. They yelped and howled under the rain of blows, but struggled none the less madly till the last crumb had been devoured.

In the meantime the astonished team-dogs had burst out of their nests only to be set upon by the fierce invaders. Never had Buck seen such dogs. It seemed as though their bones would burst through their skins. They were mere skeletons, draped loosely in draggled hides, with blazing eyes and slavered fangs. But the hunger-madness made them terrifying, irresistible. There was no opposing them. The team-dogs were swept back against the cliff at the first onset. Buck was beset by three huskies, and in a trice his head and shoulders were ripped and slashed. The din was frightful. Billee was crying as usual. Dave and Sol-leks, dripping blood from a score of wounds, were fighting bravely side by side. Joe was snapping like a demon. Once, his teeth closed on the fore leg of a husky, and he crunched down through the bone. Pike, the malingerer, leaped upon the crippled animal, breaking its neck with a quick flash of teeth and a jerk. Buck got a frothing adversary by the throat, and was sprayed with blood when his teeth sank through the jugular. The warm taste of it in his mouth goaded him to greater fierceness. He flung himself upon another, and at the same time felt teeth sink into his own throat. It was Spitz, treacherously attacking from the side.

Perrault and François, having cleaned out their part of the camp, hurried to save their sled-dogs. The wild wave of famished beasts rolled back before them, and Buck shook himself free. But it was only for a moment. The two men were compelled to run back to save the grub, upon which the huskies returned to the attack on the team. Billee, terrified into bravery, sprang through the savage circle and fled away over the ice. Pike and Dub followed on his heels, with the rest of the team behind. As Buck drew himself together to spring after them, out of the tail of his eye he saw Spitz rush upon him with the evident intention of overthrowing him. Once off his feet and under that mass of huskies, there was no hope for him. But he braced himself to the shock of Spitz's charge, then joined the flight out on the lake.

Later, the nine team-dogs gathered together and sought shelter in the forest. Though unpursued, they were in a sorry plight. There was not one who was not wounded in four or five places, while some were wounded grievously. Dub was badly injured in a hind leg; Dolly, the last husky added to the team at Dyea, had a badly torn throat; Joe had lost an eye; while Billee, the good-natured, with an ear chewed and rent to ribbons, cried and whimpered throughout the night. At daybreak they limped warily back to camp, to find the marauders gone and the two men in bad tempers. Fully half their grub supply was gone. The huskies had chewed through the sled lashings and canvas coverings. In fact, nothing, no matter how remotely eatable, had escaped them. They had eaten a pair of Perrault's moose-hide moccasins, chunks out of the leather traces, and even two feet of lash from the end of François's whip. He broke from a mournful contemplation of it to look over his wounded dogs.

'Ah, my frien's,' he said softly, 'mebbe it mek you mad dog, dose many bites. Mebbe all mad dog, sacredam! Wot you t'ink, eh, Perrault?'

The courier shook his head dubiously. With four hundred miles of trail still between him and Dawson, he could ill afford to have madness break out among his dogs. Two hours of cursing and exertion got the harnesses into shape, and the wound-stiffened team was under way, struggling painfully over the hardest part of the trail they had yet encountered and for that matter, the hardest between them and Dawson.

The Thirty Mile River was wide open. Its wild water defied the frost, and it was in the eddies only and in the quiet places that the ice held at all. Six days of exhausting toil were required to cover those thirty terrible miles. And terrible they were, for every foot of them was accomplished at the risk of life to dog and man. A dozen times, Perrault, nosing the way, broke through the ice bridges, being saved by the long pole he carried, which he so held that it fell each time across the hole made by his body. But a cold snap was on, the thermometer registering fifty below zero, and each time he broke through he was compelled for very life to build a fire and dry his garments.

Nothing daunted him. It was because nothing daunted him that he had been chosen for government courier. He took all manner of risks, resolutely thrusting his little weazened face into the frost and struggling on from dim dawn to dark. He skirted the frowning shores on rim ice that bent and crackled under foot and upon which they dared not halt. Once the sled broke through, with Dave and Buck, and they were half-frozen and all but drowned by the time they were dragged out. The usual fire was necessary to save them. They were coated solidly with ice, and the two men kept them on the run around the fire, sweating and thawing, so close that they were singed by the flames.

At another time Spitz went through, dragging the whole team after him up to Buck, who strained backward with all his strength, his fore paws on the slippery edge and the ice quivering and snapping all around. But behind him was Dave, likewise straining backward, and behind the sled was François, pulling till his tendons cracked.

Again, the rim ice broke away before and behind, and there was no escape except up the cliff. Perrault scaled it by a miracle, while François prayed for just that miracle; and with every thong and sled lashing and the last bit of harness rove into a long rope, the dogs were hoisted, one by one, to the cliff crest. François came up last, after the sled and load. Then came the search for a place to descend, which descent was ultimately made by the aid of the rope, and night found them back on the river with a quarter of a mile to the day's credit.

By the time they made the Hootalinqua and good ice, Buck was played out. The rest of the dogs were in like condition; but Perrault, to make up lost time, pushed them late and early. The first day they covered thirty-five miles to the Big Salmon; the next day thirty-five more to the Little Salmon; the third day forty miles, which brought them well up toward the Five Fingers.

Buck's feet were not so compact and hard as the feet of the huskies. His had softened during the many generations since the day his last wild ancestor was tamed by a cave-dweller or river man. All day long he limped in agony, and camp once made, lay down like a dead dog. Hungry as he was, he would not move to receive his ration of fish, which François had to bring to him. Also, the dog-driver rubbed Buck's feet for half an hour each night after supper, and sacrificed the tops of his own moccasins to make four moccasins for Buck. This was a great relief, and Buck caused even the weazened face of Perrault to twist itself into a grin one morning, when François forgot the moccasins and Buck lay on his back, his four feet waving appealingly in the air, and refused to budge without them. Later his feet grew hard to the trail, and the worn-out foot-gear was thrown away.

At the Pelly one morning, as they were harnessing up, Dolly, who had never been conspicuous for anything, went suddenly mad. She announced her condition by a long, heart-breaking wolf howl that sent every dog bristling with fear, then sprang straight for Buck. He had never seen a dog go mad, nor did he have any reason to fear madness; yet he knew that here was horror, and fled away from it in a panic. Straight away he raced, with Dolly, panting and frothing, one leap behind; nor could she gain on him, so great was his terror, nor could he leave her, so great was her madness. He plunged through the wooded breast of the island, flew down to the lower end, crossed a back channel filled with rough ice to another island, gained a third island, curved back to the main river, and in desperation started to cross it. And all the time, though he did not look, he could hear her snarling just one leap behind. François called to him a quarter of a mile away and he doubled back, still one leap ahead, gasping painfully for air and putting all his faith in that François would save him. The dog-driver held the axe poised in his hand, and as Buck shot past him the axe crashed down upon mad Dolly's head.

Buck staggered over against the sled, exhausted, sobbing for breath, helpless. This was Spitz's opportunity. He sprang upon Buck, and twice his teeth sank into his unresisting foe and ripped and tore the flesh to the bone. Then François's lash descended, and Buck had the satisfaction of watching Spitz receive the worst whipping as yet administered to any of the teams.

'One devil, dat Spitz,' remarked Perrault. 'Some dam day heem keel dat Buck.'

'Dat Buck two devils,' was François's rejoinder. 'All de tam I watch dat Buck I know for sure. Lissen: some dam fine day heem get mad lak hell an' den heem chew dat Spitz all up an' spit heem out on de snow. Sure. I know.'

From then on it was war between them. Spitz, as lead-dog and acknowledged master of the team, felt his supremacy threatened by this strange Southland dog. And strange Buck was to him, for of the many Southland dogs he had known, not one had shown up worthily in camp and on trail. They were all too soft, dying under the toil, the frost, and starvation. Buck was the exception. He alone endured and prospered, matching the husky in strength, savagery and cunning. Then he was a masterful dog, and what made him dangerous was the fact that the club of the man in the red sweater had knocked all blind pluck and rashness out of his desire for mastery. He was pre-eminently cunning, and could bide his time with a patience that was nothing less than primitive.

It was inevitable that the clash for leadership should come. Buck wanted it. He wanted it because it was his nature, because he had been gripped tight by that nameless, incomprehensible pride of the trail and trace – that pride which holds dogs in the toil to the last gasp, which lures them to die joyfully in the harness, and breaks their hearts if they are cut out of the harness. This was the pride of Dave as wheel-dog, of Sol-leks as he pulled with all his strength; the pride that laid hold of them at break of camp, transforming them from sour and sullen brutes into straining, eager, ambitious creatures; the pride that spurred them on all day and dropped them at pitch of camp at night, letting them fall back into gloomy unrest and uncontent. This was the pride that bore up Spitz and made him thrash the sled-dogs who blundered and shirked in the traces or hid away at harness-up time in the morning. Likewise it was this pride that made him fear Buck as a possible lead-dog. And this was Buck's pride, too.

He openly threatened the other's leadership. He came between him and the shirks he should have punished. And he did it deliberately. One night there was a heavy snowfall, and in the morning Pike, the malingerer, did not appear. He was securely hidden in his nest under a foot of snow. François called him and sought him in vain. Spitz was wild with wrath. He raged through the camp, smelling and digging in every likely place, snarling so frightfully that Pike heard and shivered in his hiding-place.

But when he was at last unearthed, and Spitz flew at him to punish him, Buck flew, with equal rage, in between. So unexpected was it, and so shrewdly managed, that Spitz was hurled backward and off his feet. Pike, who had been trembling abjectly, took heart at this open mutiny, and sprang upon his overthrown leader. Buck, to whom fair play was a forgotten code, likewise sprang upon Spitz. But François, chuckling at the incident while unswerving in the administration of justice, brought his lash down upon Buck with all his might. This failed to drive Buck from his prostrate rival, and the butt of the whip was brought into play. Half-stunned by the blow, Buck was knocked backward and the lash laid upon him again and again, while Spitz soundly punished the many times offending Pike.

In the days that followed, as Dawson grew closer and closer, Buck still continued to interfere between Spitz and the culprits; but he did it craftily, when François was not around. With the covert mutiny of Buck, a general insubordination sprang up and

increased. Dave and Sol-leks were unaffected, but the rest of the
team went from bad to worse. Things no longer went right. There
was continual bickering and jangling. Trouble was always afoot,
and at the bottom of it was Buck. He kept François busy, for the
dog-driver was in constant apprehension of the life-and-death
struggle between the two which he knew must take place sooner
or later; and on more than one night the sounds of quarreling
and strife among the other dogs turned him out of his sleeping
robe, fearful that Buck and Spitz were at it.

But the opportunity did not present itself, and they pulled into
Dawson one dreary afternoon with the great fight still to come.
Here were many men, and countless dogs, and Buck found them
all at work. It seemed the ordained order of things that dogs
should work. All day they swung up and down the main street in
long teams, and in the night their jingling bells still went by.
They hauled cabin logs and firewood, freighted up to the mines,
and did all manner of work that horses did in the Santa Clara
Valley. Here and there Buck met Southland dogs, but in the main
they were the wild wolf husky breed. Every night, regularly, at
nine, at twelve, at three, they lifted a nocturnal song, a weird and
eerie chant, in which it was Buck's delight to join.

With the aurora borealis flaming coldly overhead, or the stars
leaping in the frost dance, and the land numb and frozen under
its pall of snow, this song of the huskies might have been the
defiance of life, only it was pitched in minor key, with long-
drawn wailings and half-sobs, and was more the pleading of life,
the articulate travail of existence. It was an old song, old as the
breed itself – one of the first songs of the younger world in a day
when songs were sad. It was invested with the woe of
unnumbered generations, this plaint by which Buck was so
strangely stirred. When he moaned and sobbed, it was with the
pain of living that was of old the pain of his wild fathers, and the
fear and mystery of the cold and dark that was to them fear and
mystery. And that he should be stirred by it marked the
completeness with which he harked back through the ages of fire
and roof to the raw beginnings of life in the howling ages.

Seven days from the time they pulled into Dawson, they
dropped down the steep bank by the Barracks to the Yukon Trail,
and pulled for Dyea and Salt Water. Perrault was carrying
despatches if anything more urgent than those he had brought
in; also, the travel pride had gripped him, and he purposed to

make the record trip of the year. Several things favored him in this. The week's rest had recuperated the dogs and put them in thorough trim. The trail they had broken into the country was packed hard by later journeys. And further, the police had arranged in two or three places deposits of grub for dog and man, and he was traveling light.

They made Sixty Mile, which is a fifty-mile run, on the first day; and the second day saw them booming up the Yukon well on their way to Pelly. But such splendid running was achieved not without great trouble and vexation on the part of François. The insidious revolt led by Buck had destroyed the solidarity of the team. It no longer was as one dog leaping in the traces. The encouragement Buck gave the rebels led them into all kinds of petty misdemeanors. No more was Spitz a leader greatly to be feared. The old awe departed, and they grew equal to challenging his authority. Pike robbed him of half a fish one night, and gulped it down under the protection of Buck. Another night Dub and Joe fought Spitz and made him forego the punishment they deserved. And even Billee, the good-natured, was less good-natured, and whined not half so placatingly as in former days. Buck never came near Spitz without snarling and bristling menacingly. In fact, his conduct approached that of a bully, and he was given to swaggering up and down before Spitz's very nose.

The breaking down of discipline likewise affected the dogs in their relations with one another. They quarreled and bickered more than ever among themselves, till at times the camp was a howling bedlam. Dave and Sol-leks alone were unaltered, though they were made irritable by the unending squabbling. François swore strange barbarous oaths, and stamped the snow in futile rage, and tore his hair. His lash was always singing among the dogs, but it was of small avail. Directly his back was turned they were at it again. He backed up Spitz with his whip, while Buck backed up the remainder of the team. François knew he was behind all the trouble, and Buck knew he knew; but Buck was too clever ever again to be caught red-handed. He worked faithfully in the harness, for the toil had become a delight to him; yet it was a greater delight slyly to precipitate a fight amongst his mates and tangle the traces.

At the mouth of the Tahkeena, one night after supper, Dub

turned up a snowshoe rabbit, blundered it, and missed. In a second the whole team was in full cry. A hundred yards away was a camp of the Northwest Police, with fifty dogs, huskies all, who joined the chase. The rabbit sped down the river, turned off into a small creek, up the frozen bed of which it held steadily. It ran lightly on the surface of the snow, while the dogs ploughed through by main strength. Buck led the pack, sixty strong, around bend after bend, but he could not gain. He lay down low to the race, whining eagerly, his splendid body flashing forward, leap by leap, in the wan white moonlight. And leap by leap, like some pale frost wraith, the snowshoe rabbit flashed on ahead.

All that stirring of old instincts which at stated periods drives men out from the sounding cities to forest and plain to kill things by chemically propelled leaden pellets, the blood lust, the joy to kill – this was Buck's, only it was infinitely more intimate. He was ranging at the head of the pack, running the wild thing down, the living meat, to kill with his own teeth and wash his muzzle to the eyes in warm blood.

There is an ecstasy that marks the summit of life, and beyond which life cannot rise. And such is the paradox of living, this ecstasy comes when one is most alive, and it comes as a complete forgetfulness that one is alive. This ecstasy, this forgetfulness of living, comes to the artist, caught up and out of himself in a sheet of flame; it comes to the soldier, war-mad on a stricken field and refusing quarter; and it came to Buck, leading the pack, sounding the old wolf-cry, straining after the food that was alive and that fled swiftly before him through the moonlight. He was sounding the deeps of his nature, and of the parts of his nature that were deeper than he, going back into the womb of Time. He was mastered by the sheer surging of life, the tidal wave of being, the perfect joy of each separate muscle, joint, and sinew in that it was everything that was not death, that it was aglow and rampant, expressing itself in movement, flying exultantly under the stars and over the face of dead matter that did not move.

But Spitz, cold and calculating even in his supreme moods, left the pack and cut across a narrow neck of land where the creek made a long bend around. Buck did not know of this, and as he rounded the bend, the frost wraith of a rabbit still flitting before him, he saw another and larger frost wraith leap from the overhanging bank into the immediate path of the rabbit. It was

Spitz. The rabbit could not turn, and as the white teeth broke its back in mid air it shrieked as loudly as a stricken man may shriek. At sound of this, the cry of Life plunging down from Life's apex in the grip of Death, the full pack at Buck's heels raised a hell's chorus of delight.

Buck did not cry out. He did not check himself, but drove in upon Spitz, shoulder to shoulder, so hard that he missed the throat. They rolled over and over in the powdery snow. Spitz gained his feet almost as though he had not been overthrown, slashing Buck down the shoulder and leaping clear. Twice his teeth clipped together, like the steel jaws of a trap, as he backed away for better footing, with lean and lifting lips that writhed and snarled.

In a flash Buck knew it. The time had come. It was to the death. As they circled about, snarling, ears laid back, keenly watchful for the advantage, the scene came to Buck with a sense of familiarity. He seemed to remember it all – the white woods, and earth, and moonlight, and the thrill of battle. Over the whiteness and silence brooded a ghostly calm. There was not the faintest whisper of air – nothing moved, not a leaf quivered, the visible breaths of the dogs rising slowly and lingering in the frosty air. They had made short work of the snowshoe rabbit, these dogs that were ill-tamed wolves; and they were now drawn up in an expectant circle. They, too, were silent, their eyes only gleaming and their breaths drifting slowly upward. To Buck it was nothing new or strange, this scene of old time. It was as though it had always been, the wonted way of things.

Spitz was a practised fighter. From Spitzbergen through the Arctic, and across Canada and the Barrens, he had held his own with all manner of dogs and achieved to mastery over them. Bitter rage was his, but never blind rage. In passion to rend and destroy, he never forgot that his enemy was in like passion to rend and destroy. He never rushed till he was prepared to receive a rush; never attacked till he had first defended that attack.

In vain Buck strove to sink his teeth in the neck of the big white dog. Wherever his fangs struck for the softer flesh, they were countered by the fangs of Spitz. Fang clashed fang, and lips were cut and bleeding, but Buck could not penetrate his enemy's guard. Then he warmed up and enveloped Spitz in a whirlwind of rushes. Time and time again he tried for the snow-white throat, where life bubbled near to the surface, and each time and every time Spitz slashed him and got away. Then Buck took to rushing, as though for the throat, when, suddenly drawing back his head and curving in from the side, he would drive his shoulder at the shoulder of Spitz, as a ram by which to overthrow him. But instead, Buck's shoulder was slashed down each time as Spitz leaped lightly away.

Spitz was untouched, while Buck was streaming with blood and panting hard. The fight was growing desperate. And all the while the silent and wolfish circle waited to finish off whichever dog went down. As Buck grew winded, Spitz took to rushing, and he kept him staggering for footing. Once Buck went over, and the whole circle of sixty dogs started up; but he recovered himself, almost in mid air, and the circle sank down again and waited.

But Buck possessed a quality that made for greatness – imagination. He fought by instinct, but he could fight by head as well. He rushed, as though attempting the old shoulder trick, but at the last instant swept low to the snow and in. His teeth closed on Spitz's left fore leg. There was a crunch of breaking bone, and the white dog faced him on three legs. Thrice he tried to knock him over, then repeated the trick and broke the right fore leg. Despite the pain and helplessness, Spitz struggled madly to keep up. He saw the silent circle, with gleaming eyes, lolling tongues, and silvery breaths drifting upward, closing in upon him as he had seen similar circles close in upon beaten antagonists in the past. Only this time he was the one who was beaten.

There was no hope for him. Buck was inexorable. Mercy was a thing reserved for gentler climes. He manoeuvred for the final rush. The circle had tightened till he could feel the breaths of the huskies on his flanks. He could see them, beyond Spitz and to either side, half crouching for the spring, their eyes fixed upon him. A pause seemed to fall. Every animal was motionless as though turned to stone. Only Spitz quivered and bristled as he staggered back and forth, snarling with horrible menace, as though to frighten off impending death. Then Buck sprang in and out; but while he was in, shoulder had at last squarely met shoulder. The dark circle became a dot on the moon-flooded snow as Spitz disappeared from view. Buck stood and looked on, the successful champion, the dominant primordial beast who had made his kill and found it good.

4

Who Has Won to Mastership

'Eh? Wot I say? I spik true w'en I say dat Buck two devils.' This was François's speech next morning when he discovered Spitz missing and Buck covered with wounds. He drew him to the fire and by its light pointed them out.

'Dat Spitz fight lak hell,' said Perrault, as he surveyed the gaping rips and cuts.

'An' dat Buck fight lak two hells,' was François's answer. 'An' now we make good time. No more Spitz, no more trouble, sure.'

While Perrault packed the camp outfit and loaded the sled, the dog-driver proceeded to harness the dogs. Buck trotted up to the place Spitz would have occupied as leader; but François, not noticing him, brought Sol-leks to the coveted position. In his judgment, Sol-leks was the best lead-dog left. Buck sprang upon Sol-leks in a fury, driving him back and standing in his place.

'Eh? eh?' François cried, slapping his thighs gleefully. 'Look at dat Buck. Heem keel dat Spitz, heem t'ink to take de job.'

'Go 'way, Chook!' he cried, but Buck refused to budge.

He took Buck by the scruff of the neck, and though the dog growled threateningly, dragged him to one side and replaced Sol-leks. The old dog did not like it, and showed plainly that he was afraid of Buck. François was obdurate, but when he turned his back Buck again displaced Sol-leks, who was not at all unwilling to go.

François was angry. 'Now, by Gar, I feex you!' he cried, coming back with a heavy club in his hand.

Buck remembered the man in the red sweater, and retreated slowly; nor did he attempt to charge in when Sol-leks was once more brought forward. But he circled just beyond the range of the club, snarling with bitterness and rage; and while he circled he watched the club so as to dodge it if thrown by François, for he was become wise in the way of clubs. The driver went about his work, and he called to Buck when he was ready to put him in his old place in front of Dave. Buck retreated two or three steps. François followed him up, whereupon he again retreated. After some time of this, François threw down the club, thinking that Buck feared a thrashing. But Buck was in open revolt. He wanted, not to escape a clubbing, but to have the leadership. It was his by right. He had earned it, and he would not be content with less.

Perrault took a hand. Between them they ran him about for the better part of an hour. They threw clubs at him. He dodged. They cursed him, and his fathers and mothers before him, and all his seed to come after him down to the remotest generation, and every hair on his body and drop of blood in his veins; and he answered curse with snarl and kept out of their reach. He did not try to run away, but retreated around and around the camp, advertising plainly that when his desire was met, he would come in and be good.

François sat down and scratched his head. Perrault looked at his watch and swore. Time was flying, and they should have been on the trail an hour gone. François scratched his head again. He shook it and grinned sheepishly at the courier, who shrugged his shoulders in sign that they were beaten. Then François went up to where Sol-leks stood and called to Buck. Buck laughed, as dogs laugh, yet kept his distance. François unfastened Sol-leks's traces and put him back in his old place. The team stood harnessed to the sled in an unbroken line, ready for the trail. There was no place for Buck save at the front. Once more François called, and once more Buck laughed and kept away.

'T'row down de club,' Perrault commanded.

François complied, whereupon Buck trotted in, laughing triumphantly, and swung around into position at the head of the team. His traces were fastened, the sled broken out, and with both men running they dashed out on to the river trail.

Highly as the dog-driver had forevalued Buck, with his two devils, he found, while the day was yet young, that he had undervalued. At a bound Buck took up the duties of leadership; and where judgment was required, and quick thinking and quick acting, he showed himself the superior even of Spitz, of whom François had never seen an equal.

But it was in giving the law and making his mates live up to it, that Buck excelled. Dave and Sol-leks did not mind the change in leadership. It was none of their business. Their business was to toil, and toil mightily, in the traces. So long as that were not interfered with, they did not care what happened. Billee, the good-natured, could lead for all they cared, so long as he kept order. The rest of the team, however, had grown unruly during the last days of Spitz, and their surprise was great now that Buck proceeded to lick them into shape.

Pike, who pulled at Buck's heels, and who never put an ounce more of his weight against the breast-band than he was compelled to do, was swiftly and repeatedly shaken for loafing; and ere the first day was done he was pulling more than ever before in his life. The first night in camp, Joe, the sour one, was punished roundly – a thing that Spitz had never succeeded in doing. Buck simply smothered him by virtue of superior weight, and cut him up till he ceased snapping and began to whine for mercy.

The general tone of the team picked up immediately. It recovered its old-time solidarity, and once more the dogs leaped as one dog in the traces. At the Rink Rapids two native huskies, Teek and Koona, were added; and the celerity with which Buck broke them in took away François's breath.

'Nevaire such a dog as dat Buck!' he cried. 'No, nevaire! Heem worth one t'ousan' dollair, by Gar! Eh? Wot you say, Perrault?'

And Perrault nodded. He was ahead of the record then, and gaining day by day. The trail was in excellent condition, well packed and hard, and there was no new-fallen snow with which to contend. It was not too cold. The temperature dropped to fifty below zero and remained there the whole trip. The men rode and ran by turn, and the dogs were kept on the jump, with but infrequent stoppages.

The Thirty Mile River was comparatively coated with ice, and they covered in one day going out what had taken them ten days coming in. In one run they made a sixty-mile dash from the foot of Lake Le Barge to the White Horse Rapids. Across Marsh, Tagish, and Bennett (seventy miles of lakes), they flew so fast that the man whose turn it was to run towed behind the sled at the end of a rope. And on the last night of the second week they topped White Pass and dropped down the sea slope with the lights of Skaguay and of the shipping at their feet.

It was a record run. Each day for fourteen days they had averaged forty miles. For three days Perrault and François threw chests up and down the main street of Skaguay and were deluged with invitations to drink, while the team was the constant centre of a worshipful crowd of dog-busters and mushers. Then three or four western bad men aspired to clean out the town, were riddled like pepper-boxes for their pains, and public interest turned to other idols. Next came official orders. François called Buck to him, threw his arms around him, wept over him. And that was the last of François and Perrault. Like other men, they passed out of Buck's life for good.

A Scotch half-breed took charge of him and his mates, and in company with a dozen other dog-teams he started back over the weary trail to Dawson. It was no light running now, nor record time, but heavy toil each day, with a heavy load behind; for this was the mail train, carrying word from the world to the men who sought gold under the shadow of the Pole.

Buck did not like it, but he bore up well to the work, taking pride in it after the manner of Dave and Sol-leks, and seeing that his mates, whether they prided in it or not, did their fair share. It was a monotonous life, operating with machine-like regularity. One day was very like another. At a certain time each morning the cooks turned out, fires were built, and breakfast was eaten. Then, while some broke camp, others harnessed the dogs, and they were under way an hour or so before the darkness fell which gave warning of dawn. At night, camp was made. Some pitched the flies, others cut firewood and pine boughs for the beds, and still others carried water or ice for the cooks. Also, the dogs were fed. To them, this was the one feature of the day, though it was good to loaf around, after the fish was eaten, for an hour or so with the other dogs, of which there were fivescore and odd. There were fierce fighters among them, but three battles with the fiercest brought Buck to mastery, so that when he bristled and showed his teeth they got out of his way.

Best of all, perhaps, he loved to lie near the fire, hind legs crouched under him, fore legs stretched out in front, head raised, and eyes blinking dreamily at the flames. Sometimes he thought of Judge Miller's big house in the sun-kissed Santa Clara Valley, and of the cement swimming-tank, and Ysabel, the Mexican hairless, and Toots, the Japanese pug; but oftener he remembered the man in the red sweater, the death of Curly, the great fight with Spitz, and the good things he had eaten or would like to eat. He was not homesick. The Sunland was very dim and distant, and such memories had no power over him. Far more potent were the memories of his heredity that gave things he had never seen before a seeming familiarity; the instincts (which were but the memories of his ancestors become habits) which had lapsed in later days, and still later, in him, quickened and become alive again.

Sometimes as he crouched there, blinking dreamily at the flames, it seemed that the flames were of another fire, and that as he crouched by this other fire he saw another and different man from the half-breed cook before him. This other man was shorter of leg and longer of arm, with muscles that were stringy and knotty rather than rounded and swelling. The hair of this man was long and matted, and his head slanted back under it from the eyes. He uttered strange sounds, and seemed very much afraid of the darkness, into which he peered continually, clutching in his hand, which hung midway between knee and foot, a stick with a heavy stone made fast to the end. He was all but naked, a ragged and fire-scorched skin hanging part way down his back, but on his body there was much hair. In some places, across the chest and shoulders and down the outside of the arms and thighs, it was matted into almost a thick fur. He did not stand erect, but with trunk inclined forward from the hips, on legs that bent at the knees. About his body there was a peculiar springiness, or resiliency, almost catlike, and a quick alertness as of one who lived in perpetual fear of things seen and unseen.

At other times this hairy man squatted by the fire with head between his legs and slept. On such occasions his elbows were on his knees, his hands clasped above his head as though to shed rain by the hairy arms. And beyond that fire, in the circling darkness, Buck could see many gleaming coals, two by two, always two by two, which he knew to be the eyes of great beasts of prey. And he could hear the crashing of their bodies through the undergrowth, and the noises they made in the night. And dreaming there by the Yukon bank, with lazy eyes blinking at the fire, these sounds and sights of another world would make the hair to rise along his back and stand on end across his shoulders and up his neck, till he whimpered low and suppressedly, or growled softly, and the half-breed cook shouted at him, 'Hey, you Buck, wake up!' Whereupon the other world would vanish and the real world come into his eyes, and he would get up and yawn and stretch as though he had been asleep.

It was a hard trip, with the mail behind them, and the heavy work wore them down. They were short of weight and in poor condition when they made Dawson, and should have had a ten days' or a week's rest at least. But in two days' time they dropped down the Yukon bank from the Barracks, loaded with letters for the outside. The dogs were tired, the drivers grumbling, and to make matters worse, it snowed every day. This meant a soft trail, greater friction on the runners, and heavier pulling for the dogs; yet the drivers were fair through it all, and did their best for the animals.

Each night the dogs were attended to first. They ate before the drivers ate, and no man sought his sleeping-robe till he had seen to the feet of the dogs he drove. Still, their strength went down. Since the beginning of the winter they had traveled eighteen hundred miles, dragging sleds the whole weary distance; and eighteen hundred miles will tell upon life of the toughest. Buck stood it, keeping his mates up to their work and maintaining discipline, though he, too, was very tired. Billee cried and whimpered regularly in his sleep each night. Joe was sourer than ever, and Sol-leks was unapproachable, blind side or other side.

But it was Dave who suffered most of all. Something had gone wrong with him. He became more morose and irritable, and when camp was pitched at once made his nest, where his driver fed him. Once out of the harness and down, he did not get on his feet again till harness-up time in the morning. Sometimes, in the traces, when jerked by a sudden stoppage of the sled, or by straining to start it, he would cry out with pain. The driver examined him, but could find nothing. All the drivers became interested in his case. They talked it over at meal-time, and over their last pipes before going to bed, and one night they held a consultation. He was brought from his nest to the fire and was pressed and prodded till he cried out many times. Something was wrong inside, but they could locate no broken bones, could not make it out.

By the time Cassiar Bar was reached, he was so weak that he was falling repeatedly in the traces. The Scotch half-breed called a halt and took him out of the team, making the next dog, Sol-leks, fast to the sled. His intention was to rest Dave, letting him run free behind the sled. Sick as he was, Dave resented being taken out, grunting and growling while the traces were unfastened, and whimpering broken-heartedly when he saw Sol-leks in the position he had held and served so long. For the pride of trace and trail was his, and, sick unto death, he could not bear that another dog should do his work.

When the sled started, he floundered in the soft snow alongside the beaten trail, attacking Sol-leks with his teeth, rushing against him and trying to thrust him off into the soft snow on the other side, striving to leap inside his traces and get between him and the sled, and all the while whining and yelping and crying with grief and pain. The half-breed tried to drive him away with the whip; but he paid no heed to the stinging lash, and the man had not the heart to strike harder. Dave refused to run quietly on the trail behind the sled, where the going was easy, but continued to flounder alongside in the soft snow, where the going was most difficult, till exhausted. Then he fell, and lay where he fell, howling lugubriously as the long train of sleds churned by.

With the last remnant of his strength he managed to stagger along behind till the train made another stop, when he floundered past the sleds to his own, where he stood alongside Sol-leks. His driver lingered a moment to get a light for his pipe from the man behind. Then he returned and started his dogs. They swung out on the trail with remarkable lack of exertion, turned their heads uneasily, and stopped in surprise. The driver was surprised, too; the sled had not moved. He called his comrades to witness the sight. Dave had bitten through both of Sol-leks's traces, and was standing directly in front of the sled in his proper place.

He pleaded with his eyes to remain there. The driver was perplexed. His comrades talked of how a dog could break its heart through being denied the work that killed it, and recalled instances they had known, where dogs, too old for the toil, or injured, had died because they were cut out of the traces. Also, they held it a mercy, since Dave was to die anyway, that he should die in the traces, heart-easy and content. So he was harnessed in again, and proudly he pulled as of old, though more than once he cried out involuntarily from the bite of his inward hurt. Several times he fell down and was dragged in the traces, and once the sled ran upon him so that he limped thereafter in one of his hind legs.

But he held out till camp was reached, when his driver made a place for him by the fire. Morning found him too weak to travel. At harness-up time he tried to crawl to his driver. By convulsive efforts he got on his feet, staggered, and fell. Then he wormed his way forward slowly toward where the harnesses were being put on his mates. He would advance his fore legs and drag up his body with a sort of hitching movement, when he would advance his fore legs and hitch ahead again for a few more inches. His strength left him, and the last his mates saw of him he lay gasping in the snow and yearning toward them. But they could hear him mournfully howling till they passed out of sight behind a belt of river timber.

Here the train was halted. The Scotch half-breed slowly retraced his steps to the camp they had left. The men ceased talking. A revolver-shot rang out. The man came back hurriedly. The whips snapped, the bells tinkled merrily, the sleds churned along the trail; but Buck knew, and every dog knew, what had taken place behind the belt of river trees.

5

The Toil of Trace and Trail

Thirty days from the time it left Dawson, the Salt Water Mail, with Buck and his mates at the fore, arrived at Skagway. They were in a wretched state, worn out and worn down. Buck's one hundred and forty pounds had dwindled to one hundred and fifteen. The rest of his mates, though lighter dogs, had relatively lost more weight than he. Pike, the malingerer, who, in his lifetime of deceit, had often successfully feigned a hurt leg, was now limping in earnest. Sol-leks was limping, and Dub was suffering from a wrenched shoulder-blade.

They were all terribly footsore. No spring or rebound was left in them. Their feet fell heavily on the trail, jarring their bodies and doubling the fatigue of a day's travel. There was nothing the matter with them except that they were dead tired. It was not the dead-tiredness that comes through brief and excessive effort, from which recovery is a matter of hours; but it was the dead-tiredness that comes through the slow and prolonged strength drainage of months of toil. There was no power of recuperation left, no reserve strength to call upon. It had been all used, the last least bit of it. Every muscle, every fibre, every cell, was tired, dead tired. And there was reason for it. In less than five months they had traveled twenty-five hundred miles, during the last eighteen hundred of which they had had but five days' rest. When they arrived at Skagway they were apparently on their last legs. They could barely keep the traces taut, and on the down grades just managed to keep out of the way of the sled.

'Mush on, poor sore feets,' the driver encouraged them as they tottered down the main street of Skagway. 'Dis is de las'. Den we get one long res'. Eh? For sure. One bully long res'.'

The drivers confidently expected a long stopover. Themselves, they had covered twelve hundred miles with two days' rest, and in the nature of reason and common justice they deserved an interval of loafing. But so many were the men who had rushed into the Klondike, and so many were the sweethearts, wives, and kin that had not rushed in, that the congested mail was taking on Alpine proportions; also, there were official orders. Fresh batches of Hudson Bay dogs were to take the places of those worthless for the trail. The worthless ones were to be got rid of, and, since dogs count for little against dollars, they were to be sold.

Three days passed, by which time Buck and his mates found how really tired and weak they were. Then, on the morning of the fourth day, two men from the States came along and bought them, harness and all, for a song. The men addressed each other as 'Hal' and 'Charles'. Charles was a middle-aged, lightish-colored man, with weak and watery eyes and a mustache that twisted fiercely and vigorously up, giving the lie to the limply drooping lip it concealed. Hal was a youngster of nineteen or twenty, with a big Colt's revolver and a hunting-knife strapped about him on a belt that fairly bristled with cartridges. This belt was the most salient thing about him. It advertised his callowness – callowness sheer and unutterable. Both men were manifestly out of place, and why such as they should adventure the North is part of the mystery of things that passes understanding.

Buck heard the chaffering, saw the money pass between the man and the Government agent, and knew that the Scotch half-breed and the mail-train drivers were passing out of his life on the heels of Perrault and François and the others who had gone before. When driven with his mates to the new owners' camp, Buck saw a slipshod and slovenly affair, tent half stretched, dishes unwashed, everything in disorder; also, he saw a woman. 'Mercedes' the men called her. She was Charles's wife and Hal's sister – a nice family party.

Buck watched them apprehensively as they proceeded to take down the tent and load the sled. There was a great deal of effort about their manner, but no businesslike method. The tent was rolled into an awkward bundle three times as large as it should have been. The tin dishes were packed away unwashed.

Mercedes continually fluttered in the way of her men and kept up an unbroken chattering of remonstrance and advice. When they put a clothes-sack on the front of the sled, she suggested it should go on the back; and when they had put it on the back, and covered it over with a couple of other bundles, she discovered overlooked articles which could abide nowhere else but in that very sack, and they unloaded again.

Three men from a neighboring tent came out and looked on, grinning and winking at one another.

'You've got a right smart load as it is,' said one of them; 'and it's not me should tell you your business, but I wouldn't tote that tent along if I was you.'

'Undreamed of!' cried Mercedes, throwing up her hands in dainty dismay. 'However in the world could I manage without a tent?'

'It's springtime, and you won't get any more cold weather,' the man replied.

She shook her head decidedly, and Charles and Hal put the last odds and ends on top the mountainous load.

'Think it'll ride?' one of the men asked.

'Why shouldn't it?' Charles demanded rather shortly.

'Oh, that's all right, that's all right,' the men hastened meekly to say. 'I was just a-wonderin', that is all. It seemed a mite top-heavy.'

Charles turned his back and drew the lashings down as well as he could, which was not in the least well.

'An' of course the dogs can hike along all day with that contraption behind them,' affirmed a second of the men.

'Certainly,' said Hal, with freezing politeness, taking hold of the gee-pole with one hand and swinging his whip from the other. 'Mush!' he shouted. 'Mush on there!'

The dogs sprang against the breast-bands, strained hard for a few moments, then relaxed. They were unable to move the sled.

'The lazy brutes, I'll show them,' he cried, preparing to lash out at them with the whip.

But Mercedes interfered, crying, 'Oh, Hal, you mustn't,' as she caught hold of the whip and wrenched it from him. 'The poor dears! Now you must promise you won't be harsh with them for the rest of the trip, or I won't go a step.'

'Precious lot you know about dogs,' her brother sneered; 'and I wish you'd leave me alone. They're lazy, I tell you, and you've got to whip them to get anything out of them. That's their way. You ask any one. Ask one of those men.'

Mercedes looked at them imploringly, untold repugnance at sight of pain written in her pretty face.

'They're weak as water, if you want to know,' came the reply from one of the men. 'Plum tuckered out, that's what's the matter. They need a rest.'

'Rest be blanked,' said Hal, with his beardless lips; and Mercedes said, 'Oh!' in pain and sorrow at the oath.

But she was a clannish creature, and rushed at once to the defence of her brother. 'Never mind that man,' she said pointedly. 'You're driving our dogs, and you do what you think best with them.'

Again Hal's whip fell upon the dogs. They threw themselves against the breast-bands, dug their feet into the packed snow, got down low to it, and put forth all their strength. The sled held as though it were an anchor. After two efforts, they stood still, panting. The whip was whistling savagely, when once more Mercedes interfered. She dropped on her knees before Buck, with tears in her eyes, and put her arms around his neck.

'You poor, poor dears,' she cried sympathetically, 'why don't you pull hard? – then you wouldn't be whipped.' Buck did not like her, but he was feeling too miserable to resist her, taking it as part of the day's miserable work.

One of the onlookers, who had been clenching his teeth to suppress hot speech, now spoke up:

'It's not that I care a whoop what becomes of you, but for the dogs' sakes I just want to tell you, you can help them a mighty lot by breaking out that sled. The runners are froze fast. Throw your weight against the gee-pole, right and left, and break it out.'

A third time the attempt was made, but this time, following the advice, Hal broke out the runners which had been frozen to the snow. The overloaded and unwieldy sled forged ahead, Buck and his mates struggling frantically under the rain of blows. A hundred yards ahead the path turned and sloped steeply into the main street. It would have required an experienced man to keep the top-heavy sled upright, and Hal was not such a man. As they swung on the turn the sled went over, spilling half its load through the loose lashings. The dogs never stopped. The lightened sled bounded on its side behind them. They were angry because of the ill treatment they had received and the unjust

load. Buck was raging. He broke into a run, the team following
his lead. Hal cried 'Whoa! whoa!' but they gave no heed. He
tripped and was pulled off his feet. The capsized sled ground over
him, and the dogs dashed on up the street, adding to the gayety
of Skagway as they scattered the remainder of the outfit along its
chief thoroughfare.

Kind-hearted citizens caught the dogs and gathered up the
scattered belongings. Also, they gave advice. Half the load and
twice the dogs, if they ever expected to reach Dawson, was what
was said. Hal and his sister and brother-in-law listened unwilling-
ly, pitched tent, and overhauled the outfit. Canned goods were
turned out that made men laugh, for canned goods on the Long
Trail is a thing to dream about. 'Blankets for a hotel,' quoth one
of the men who laughed and helped. 'Half as many is too much;
get rid of them. Throw away that tent, and all those dishes –
who's going to wash them, anyway? Good Lord, do you think
you're travelling on a Pullman?'

And so it went, the inexorable elimination of the superfluous.
Mercedes cried when her clothes-bags were dumped on the
ground and article after article was thrown out. She cried in
general, and she cried in particular over each discarded thing.
She clasped hands about knees, rocking back and forth broken-
heartedly. She averred she would not go an inch, not for a dozen
Charleses. She appealed to everybody and to everything, finally
wiping her eyes and proceeding to cast out even articles of
apparel that were imperative necessaries. And in her zeal, when
she had finished with her own, she attacked the belongings of her
men and went through them like a tornado.

This accomplished, the outfit, though cut in half, was still a
formidable bulk. Charles and Hal went out in the evening and
bought six Outside dogs. These, added to the six of the original
team, and Teek and Koona, the huskies obtained at the Rink
Rapids on the record trip, brought the team up to fourteen. But
the Outside dogs, though practically broken in since their
landing, did not amount to much. Three were short-haired
pointers, one was a Newfoundland, and the other two were
mongrels of indeterminate breed. They did not seem to know
anything, these newcomers. Buck and his comrades looked upon
them with disgust, and though he speedily taught them their
places and what not to do, he could not teach them what to do.
They did not take kindly to trace and trail. With the exception of

the two mongrels, they were bewildered and spirit-broken by the strange savage environment in which they found themselves and by the ill treatment they had received. The two mongrels were without spirit at all; bones were the only things breakable about them.

With the newcomers hopeless and forlorn, and the old team worn out by twenty-five hundred miles of continuous trail, the outlook was anything but bright. The two men, however, were quite cheerful. And they were proud, too. They were doing the thing in style, with fourteen dogs. They had seen other sleds depart over the Pass for Dawson, or come in from Dawson, but never had they seen a sled with so many as fourteen dogs. In the nature of Arctic travel there was a reason why fourteen dogs should not drag one sled, and that was that one sled could not carry the food for fourteen dogs. But Charles and Hal did not know this. They had worked the trip out with a pencil, so much to a dog, so many dogs, so many days, QED. Mercedes looked over their shoulders and nodded comprehensively, it was all so very simple.

Late next morning Buck led the long team up the street. There was nothing lively about it, no snap or go in him and his fellows. They were starting dead weary. Four times he had covered the distance between Salt Water and Dawson, and the knowledge that, jaded and tired, he was facing the same trail once more, made him bitter. His heart was not in the work, nor was the heart of any dog. The Outsides were timid and frightened, the Insides without confidence in their masters.

Buck felt vaguely that there was no depending upon these two men and the woman. They did not know how to do anything, and as the days went by it became apparent that they could not learn. They were slack in all things, without order or discipline. It took them half the night to pitch a slovenly camp, and half the morning to break that camp and get the sled loaded in fashion so slovenly that for the rest of the day they were occupied in stopping and rearranging the load. Some days they did not make ten miles. On other days they were unable to get started at all. And on no day did they succeed in making more than half the distance used by the men as a basic in their dog-food computation.

It was inevitable that they should go short on dog-food. But they hastened it by overfeeding, bringing the day nearer when underfeeding would commence. The Outside dogs, whose digestions had not been trained by chronic famine to make the most of little, had voracious appetites. And when, in addition to this, the worn-out huskies pulled weakly, Hal decided that the orthodox ration was too small. He doubled it. And to cap it all, when Mercedes, with tears in her pretty eyes and a quaver in her throat, could not cajole him into giving the dogs still more, she stole from the fish-sacks and fed them slyly. But it was not food that Buck and the huskies needed, but rest. And though they were making poor time, the heavy load they dragged sapped their strength severely.

Then came the underfeeding. Hal awoke one day to the fact that his dog-food was half gone and the distance only quarter covered; further, that for love or money no additional dog-food was to be obtained. So he cut down even the orthodox ration and tried to increase the day's travel. His sister and brother-in-law seconded him; but they were frustrated by their heavy outfit and their own incompetence. It was a simple matter to give the dogs less food; but it was impossible to make the dogs travel faster, while their own inability to get under way earlier in the morning prevented them from travelling longer hours. Not only did they not know how to work dogs, but they did not know how to work themselves.

The first to go was Dub. Poor blundering thief that he was, always getting caught and punished, he had none the less been a faithful worker. His wrenched shoulder-blade, untreated and unrested, went from bad to worse, till finally Hal shot him with the big Colt's revolver. It is a saying of the country that an Outside dog starves to death on the ration of the husky, so the six Outside dogs under Buck could do no less than die on half the ration of the husky. The Newfoundland went first, followed by the three short-haired pointers, the two mongrels hanging more grittily on to life, but going in the end.

By this time all the amenities and gentlenesses of the Southland had fallen away from the three people. Shorn of its glamor and romance, Arctic travel became to them a reality too harsh for their manhood and womanhood. Mercedes ceased weeping over the dogs, being too occupied with weeping over herself and with quarreling with her husband and brother. To quarrel was the one thing they were never too weary to do. Their irritability arose out of their misery, increased with it, doubled upon it, outdistanced it. The wonderful patience of the trail which comes to men who toil hard and suffer sore, and remain sweet of speech and kindly, did not come to these two men and the woman. They had no inkling of such a patience. They were stiff and in pain; their muscles ached, their bones ached, their very hearts ached; and because of this they became sharp of speech, and hard words were first on their lips in the morning and last at night.

Charles and Hal wrangled whenever Mercedes gave them a chance. It was the cherished belief of each that he did more than his share of the work, and neither forbore to speak this belief at every opportunity. Sometimes Mercedes sided with her husband, sometimes with her brother. The result was a beautiful and unending family quarrel. Starting from a dispute as to which should chop a few sticks for the fire (a dispute which concerned only Charles and Hal), presently would be lugged in the rest of the family, fathers, mothers, uncles, cousins, people thousands of miles away, and some of them dead. That Hal's views on art, or the sort of society plays his mother's brother wrote, should have anything to do with the chopping of a few sticks of firewood, passes comprehension; nevertheless the quarrel was as likely to tend in that direction as in the direction of Charles's political prejudices. And that Charles's sister's tale-bearing tongue should be relevant to the building of a Yukon fire, was apparent only to Mercedes, who disburdened herself of copious opinions upon that topic, and incidentally upon a few other traits unpleasantly peculiar to her husband's family. In the meantime the fire remained unbuilt, the camp half pitched, and the dogs unfed.

Mercedes nursed a special grievance – the grievance of sex. She was pretty and soft, and had been chivalrously treated all her days. But the present treatment by her husband and brother was everything save chivalrous. It was her custom to be helpless. They complained. Upon which impeachment of what to her was her most essential sex-prerogative, she made their lives unendurable. She no longer considered the dogs, and because she was sore and tired, she persisted in riding on the sled. She was pretty and soft, but she weighed one hundred and twenty pounds – a lusty last straw to the load dragged by the weak and starving animals. She rode for days, till they fell in the traces and the sled stood still. Charles and Hal begged her to get off and walk, pleaded with her, entreated, the while she wept and importuned Heaven with a recital of their brutality.

On one occasion they took her off the sled by main strength. They never did it again. She let her legs go limp like a spoiled child, and sat down on the trail. They went on their way, but she did not move. After they had traveled three miles they unloaded the sled, came back for her, and by main strength put her on the sled again.

In the excess of their own misery they were callous to the suffering of their animals. Hal's theory, which he practised on others, was that one must get hardened. He had started out preaching it to his sister and brother-in-law. Failing there, he hammered it into the dogs with a club. At the Five Fingers the dog-food gave out, and a toothless old squaw offered to trade them a few pounds of frozen horse-hide for the Colt's revolver that kept the big hunting-knife company at Hal's hip. A poor substitute for food was this hide, just as it had been stripped from the starved horses of the cattlemen six months back. In its frozen state it was more like strips of galvanized iron, and when a dog wrestled it into his stomach it thawed into thin and innutritious leathery strings and into a mass of short hair, irritating and indigestible.

And through it all Buck staggered along at the head of the team as in a nightmare. He pulled when he could; when he could no longer pull, he fell down and remained down till blows from whip or club drove him to his feet again. All the stiffness and gloss had gone out of his beautiful furry coat. The hair hung down, limp and draggled, or matted with dried blood where Hal's club had bruised him. His muscles had wasted away to knotty strings, and the flesh pads had disappeared, so that each rib and every bone in his frame were outlined cleanly through the loose hide that was wrinkled in folds of emptiness. It was heart-breaking, only Buck's heart was unbreakable. The man in the red sweater had proved that.

As it was with Buck, so was it with his mates. They were perambulating skeletons. There were seven all together, including him. In their very great misery they had become insensible to the bite of the lash or the bruise of the club. The pain of the beating was dull and distant, just as the things their eyes saw and their ears heard seemed dull and distant. They were not half living, or quarter living. They were simply so many bags of bones in which sparks of life fluttered faintly. When a halt was made, they dropped down in the traces like dead dogs, and the spark dimmed and paled and seemed to go out. And when the club or whip fell upon them, the spark fluttered feebly up, and they tottered to their feet and staggered on.

There came a day when Billee, the good-natured, fell and could not rise. Hal had traded off his revolver, so he took the axe and knocked Billee on the head as he lay in the traces, then cut the carcass out of the harness and dragged it to one side. Buck saw, and his mates saw, and they knew that this thing was very close to them. On the next day Koona went, and but five of them remained: Joe, too far gone to be malignant; Pike, crippled and limping, only half conscious and not conscious enough longer to malinger; Sol-leks, the one-eyed, still faithful to the toil of trace and trail, and mournful in that he had so little strength with which to pull; Teek, who had not traveled so far that winter and who was now beaten more than the others because he was fresher; and Buck, still at the head of the team, but no longer enforcing discipline or striving to enforce it, blind with weakness half the time and keeping the trail by the loom of it and by the dim feel of his feet.

It was beautiful spring weather, but neither dogs nor humans were aware of it. Each day the sun rose earlier and set later. It was dawn by three in the morning, and twilight lingered till nine at night. The whole long day was a blaze of sunshine. The ghostly winter silence had given way to the great spring murmur of awakening life. This murmur arose from all the land, fraught with the joy of living. It came from the things that lived and moved again, things which had been as dead and which had not moved during the long months of frost. The sap was rising in the pines. The willows and aspens were bursting out in young buds. Shrubs and vines were putting on fresh garbs of green. Crickets sang in the nights, and in the days all manner of creeping, crawling things rustled forth into the sun. Partridges and woodpeckers were booming and knocking in the forest. Squirrels were chattering, birds singing, and overhead honked the wild-fowl driving up from the south in cunning wedges that split the air.

From every hill slope came the trickle of running water, the music of unseen fountains. All things were thawing, bending, snapping. The Yukon was straining to break loose the ice that bound it down. It ate away from beneath; the sun ate from above. Air-holes formed, fissures sprang and spread apart, while thin sections of ice fell through bodily into the river. And amid all this bursting, rending, throbbing of awakening life, under the blazing sun and through the soft-sighing breezes, like wayfarers to death, staggered the two men, the woman, and the huskies.

With the dogs falling, Mercedes weeping and riding, Hal swearing innocuously, and Charles's eyes wistfully watering, they staggered into John Thornton's camp at the mouth of White River. When they halted, the dogs dropped down as though they had all been struck dead. Mercedes dried her eyes and looked at John Thornton. Charles sat down on a log to rest. He sat down very slowly and painstakingly what of his great stiffness. Hal did the talking. John Thornton was whittling the last touches on an axe-handle he had made from a stick of birch. He whittled and listened, gave monosyllabic replies, and, when it was asked, terse advice. He knew the breed, and he gave his advice in the certainty that it would not be followed.

'They told us up above that the bottom was dropping out of the trail and that the best thing for us to do was to lay over,' Hal said in response to Thornton's warning to take no more chances on the rotten ice. 'They told us we couldn't make White River, and here we are.' This last with a sneering ring of triumph in it.

'And they told you true,' John Thornton answered. 'The bottom's likely to drop out at any moment. Only fools, with the blind luck of fools, could have made it. I tell you straight, I wouldn't risk my carcass on that ice for all the gold in Alaska.'

'That's because you're not a fool, I suppose,' said Hal. 'All the same, we'll go on to Dawson.' He uncoiled his whip. 'Get up there, Buck! Hi! Get up there! Mush on!'

Thornton went on whittling. It was idle, he knew, to get between a fool and his folly; while two or three fools more or less would not alter the scheme of things.

But the team did not get up at the command. It had long since passed into the stage where blows were required to rouse it. The whip flashed out, here and there, on its merciless errands. John Thornton compressed his lips. Sol-leks was the first to crawl to his feet. Teek followed. Joe came next, yelping with pain. Pike made painful efforts. Twice he fell over, when half up, and on the third attempt managed to rise. Buck made no effort. He lay quietly where he had fallen. The lash bit into him again and again, but he neither whined nor struggled. Several times Thornton started, as though to speak, but changed his mind. A moisture came into his eyes, and, as the whipping continued, he arose and walked irresolutely up and down.

This was the first time Buck had failed, in itself a sufficient reason to drive Hal into a rage. He exchanged the whip for the customary club. Buck refused to move under the rain of heavier blows which now fell upon him. Like his mates, he was barely able to get up, but, unlike them, he had made up his mind not to get up. He had a vague feeling of impending doom. This had been strong upon him when he pulled in to the bank, and it had not departed from him. What of the thin and rotten ice he had felt under his feet all day, it seemed that he sensed disaster close at hand, out there ahead on the ice where his master was trying to drive him. He refused to stir. So greatly had he suffered, and so far gone was he, that the blows did not hurt much. And as they continued to fall upon him, the spark of life within flickered and went down. It was nearly out. He felt strangely numb. As though from a great distance, he was aware that he was being beaten. The last sensations of pain left him. He no longer felt anything, though very faintly he could hear the impact of the club upon his body. But it was no longer his body, it seemed so far away.

And then, suddenly, without warning, uttering a cry that was inarticulate and more like the cry of an animal, John Thornton sprang upon the man who wielded the club. Hal was hurled backward, as though struck by a falling tree. Mercedes screamed. Charles looked on wistfully, wiped his watery eyes, but did not get up because of his stiffness.

John Thornton stood over Buck, struggling to control himself, too convulsed with rage to speak.

'If you strike that dog again, I'll kill you,' he at last managed to say in a choking voice.

'It's my dog,' Hal replied, wiping the blood from his mouth as he came back. 'Get out of my way, or I'll fix you. I'm going to Dawson.'

Thornton stood between him and Buck, and evinced no intention of getting out of the way. Hal drew his long hunting-knife. Mercedes screamed, cried, laughed, and manifested the chaotic abandonment of hysteria. Thornton rapped Hal's knuckles with the axe-handle, knocking the knife to the ground. He rapped his knuckles again as he tried to pick it up. Then he stooped, picked it up himself, and with two strokes cut Buck's traces.

Hal had no fight left in him. Besides, his hands were full with his sister, or his arms, rather; while Buck was too near dead to be of further use in hauling the sled. A few minutes later they pulled out from the bank and down the river. Buck heard them go and raised his head to see. Pike was leading, Sol-leks was at the wheel, and between were Joe and Teek. They were limping and staggering. Mercedes was riding the loaded sled. Hal guided at the gee-pole, and Charles stumbled along in the rear.

As Buck watched them, Thornton knelt beside him and with rough, kindly hands searched for broken bones. By the time his search had disclosed nothing more than many bruises and a state of terrible starvation, the sled was a quarter of a mile away. Dog and man watched it crawling along over the ice. Suddenly, they saw its back end drop down, as into a rut, and the gee-pole, with Hal clinging to it, jerk into the air. Mercedes's scream came to their ears. They saw Charles turn and make one step to run back, and then a whole section of ice give way and dogs and humans disappear. A yawning hole was all that was to be seen. The bottom had dropped out of the trail.

John Thornton and Buck looked at each other.

'You poor devil,' said John Thornton, and Buck licked his hand.

6

For the Love of a Man

When John Thornton froze his feet in the previous December, his partners had made him comfortable and left him to get well, going on themselves up the river to get out a raft of saw-logs for Dawson. He was still limping slightly at the time he rescued Buck, but with the continued warm weather even the slight limp left him. And here, lying by the river bank through the long spring days, watching the running water, listening lazily to the songs of birds and the hum of nature, Buck slowly won back his strength.

A rest comes very good after one has traveled three thousand miles, and it must be confessed that Buck waxed lazy as his wounds healed, his muscles swelled out, and the flesh came back to cover his bones. For that matter, they were all loafing – Buck, John Thornton, and Skeet and Nig – waiting for the raft to come that was to carry them down to Dawson. Skeet was a little Irish setter who early made friends with Buck, who, in a dying condition, was unable to resent her first advances. She had the doctor trait which some dogs possess; and as a mother cat washes her kittens, so she washed and cleansed Buck's wounds. Regularly, each morning after he had finished his breakfast, she performed her self-appointed task, till he came to look for her ministrations as much as he did for Thornton's. Nig, equally friendly, though less demonstrative, was a huge black dog, half bloodhound and half deerhound, with eyes that laughed and a boundless good nature.

To Buck's surprise these dogs manifested no jealousy toward him. They seemed to share the kindliness and largeness of John Thornton. As Buck grew stronger they enticed him into all sorts of ridiculous games, in which Thornton himself could not forbear to join; and in this fashion Buck romped through his convalescence and into a new existence. Love, genuine passionate love, was his for the first time. This he had never experienced at Judge Miller's down in the sun-kissed Santa Clara Valley. With the Judge's sons, hunting and tramping, it had been a working partnership; with the Judge's grandsons, a sort of pompous guardianship; and with the Judge himself, a stately and dignified friendship. But love that was feverish and burning, that was adoration, that was madness, it had taken John Thornton to arouse.

This man had saved his life, which was something; but, further, he was the ideal master. Other men saw to the welfare of their dogs from a sense of duty and business expediency; he saw to the welfare of his as if they were his own children, because he could not help it. And he saw further. He never forgot a kindly greeting or a cheering word, and to sit down for a long talk with them ('gas' he called it) was as much his delight as theirs. He had a way of taking Buck's head roughly between his hands, and resting his own head upon Buck's, of shaking him back and forth, the while calling him ill names that to Buck were love names. Buck knew no greater joy than that rough embrace and the sound of murmured oaths, and at each jerk back and forth it seemed that his heart would be shaken out of his body so great was its ecstasy. And when, released, he sprang to his feet, his mouth laughing, his eyes eloquent, his throat vibrant with unuttered sound, and in that fashion remained without movement, John Thornton would reverently exclaim, 'God! you can all but speak!'

Buck had a trick of love expression that was akin to hurt. He would often seize Thornton's hand in his mouth and close so fiercely that the flesh bore the impress of his teeth for some time afterward. And as Buck understood the oaths to be love words, so the man understood this feigned bite for a caress.

For the most part, however, Buck's love was expressed in adoration. While he went wild with happiness when Thornton touched him or spoke to him, he did not seek these tokens. Unlike Skeet, who was wont to shove her nose under Thornton's hand and nudge and nudge till petted, or Nig, who would stalk up and rest his great head on Thornton's knee, Buck was content to adore at a distance. He would lie by the hour, eager, alert, at Thornton's feet, looking up into his face, dwelling upon it, studying it, following with keenest interest each fleeting expression, every movement or change of feature. Or, as chance might have it, he would lie farther away, to the side or rear, watching the outlines of the man and the occasional movements of his body. And often, such was the communion in which they lived, the strength of Buck's gaze would draw John Thornton's head around, and he would return the gaze, without speech, his heart shining out of his eyes as Buck's heart shone out.

For a long time after his rescue, Buck did not like Thornton to get out of his sight. From the moment he left the tent to when he entered it again, Buck would follow at his heels. His transient masters since he had come into the Northland had bred in him a fear that no master could be permanent. He was afraid that Thornton would pass out of his life as Perrault and François and the Scotch half-breed had passed out. Even in the night, in his dreams, he was haunted by this fear. At such times he would shake off sleep and creep through the chill to the flap of the tent, where he would stand and listen to the sound of his master's breathing.

But in spite of this great love he bore John Thornton, which seemed to bespeak the soft civilizing influence, the strain of the primitive, which the Northland had aroused in him, remained alive and active. Faithfulness and devotion, things born of fire and roof, were his; yet he retained his wildness and wiliness. He was a thing of the wild, come in from the wild to sit by John Thornton's fire, rather than a dog of the soft Southland stamped with the marks of generations of civilization. Because of his very great love, he could not steal from this man, but from any other man, in any other camp, he did not hesitate an instant; while the cunning with which he stole enabled him to escape detection.

His face and body were scored by the teeth of many dogs, and he fought as fiercely as ever and more shrewdly. Skeet and Nig were too good-natured for quarreling – besides, they belonged to John Thornton; but the strange dog, no matter what the breed or valor, swiftly acknowledged Buck's supremacy or found himself struggling for life with a terrible antagonist. And Buck was merciless. He had learned well the law of club and fang, and he never forewent an advantage or drew back from a foe he had started on the way to Death. He had lessoned from Spitz, and from the chief fighting dogs of the police and mail, and knew there was no middle course. He must master or be mastered; while to show mercy was a weakness. Mercy did not exist in the primordial life. It was misunderstood for fear, and such misunderstandings made for death. Kill or be killed, eat or be eaten, was the law; and this mandate, down out of the depths of Time, he obeyed.

He was older than the days he had seen and the breaths he had drawn. He linked the past with the present, and the eternity behind him throbbed through him in a mighty rhythm to which he swayed as the tides and seasons swayed. He sat by John Thornton's fire, a broad-breasted dog, white-fanged and long-furred; but behind him were the shades of all manner of dogs, half-wolves and wild wolves, urgent and prompting, tasting the savor of the meat he ate, thirsting for the water he drank, scenting the wind with him, listening with him and telling him the sounds made by the wild life in the forest, dictating his moods, directing his actions, lying down to sleep with him when he lay down, and dreaming with him and beyond him and becoming themselves the stuff of his dreams.

So peremptorily did these shades beckon him, that each day mankind and the claims of mankind slipped farther from him. Deep in the forest a call was sounding, and as often as he heard this call, mysteriously thrilling and luring, he felt compelled to turn his back upon the fire and the beaten earth around it, and to plunge into the forest, and on and on, he knew not where or why; nor did he wonder where or why, the call sounding imperiously, deep in the forest. But as often as he gained the soft unbroken earth and the green shade, the love for John Thornton drew him back to the fire again.

Thornton alone held him. The rest of mankind was as nothing. Chance travelers might praise or pet him; but he was cold under it all, and from a too demonstrative man he would get up and walk away. When Thornton's partners, Hans and Pete, arrived on the long-expected raft, Buck refused to notice them till he learned they were close to Thornton; after that he tolerated them in a passive sort of way, accepting favors from them as though he favored them by accepting. They were of the same large type as Thornton, living close to the card, thinking simply and seeing clearly; and ere they swung the raft into the big eddy by the saw-mill at Dawson, they understood Buck and his ways, and did not insist upon an intimacy such as obtained with Skeet and Nig.

For Thornton, however, his love seemed to grow and grow. He, alone among men, could put a pack upon Buck's back in the summer traveling. Nothing was too great for Buck to do, when Thornton commanded. One day (they had grub-staked themselves from the proceeds of the raft and left Dawson for the head-waters of the Tanana) the men and dogs were sitting on the crest of a cliff which fell away, straight down, to naked bed-rock three hundred feet below. John Thornton was sitting near the edge, Buck at his shoulder. A thoughtless whim seized Thornton, and he drew the attention of Hans and Pete to the experiment he had in mind. 'Jump Buck!' he commanded, sweeping his arm out and over the chasm. The next instant he was grappling with Buck on the extreme edge, while Hans and Pete were dragging them back into safety.

'It's uncanny,' Pete said, after it was over and they had caught their speech.

Thornton shook his head. 'No, it is splendid, and it is terrible, too. Do you know, it sometimes makes me afraid.'

'I'm not hankering to be the man that lays hands on you while he's around,' Pete announced conclusively, nodding his head toward Buck.

'Py Jingo!' was Hans's contribution. 'Not mineself either.'

It was at Circle City, ere the year was out, that Pete's apprehensions were realized. 'Black' Burton, a man evil-tempered and malicious, had been picking a quarrel with a tenderfoot at the bar, when Thornton stepped good-naturedly between. Buck, as was his custom, was lying in a corner, head on paws, watching his master's every action. Burton struck out, without warning, straight from the shoulder. Thornton was sent spinning, and saved himself from falling only by clutching the rail of the bar.

Those who were looking on heard what was neither bark nor yelp, but a something which is best described as a roar, and they saw Buck's body rise up in the air as he left the floor for Burton's throat. The man saved his life by instinctively throwing out his arm, but was hurled backward to the floor with Buck on top of him. Buck loosed his teeth from the flesh of the arm and drove in again for the throat. This time the man succeeded only in partly blocking, and his throat was torn open. Then the crowd was upon Buck, and he was driven off; but while a surgeon checked the bleeding, he prowled up and down, growling furiously, attempting to rush in, and being forced back by an array of hostile clubs. A 'miners' meeting', called on the spot, decided that the dog had sufficient provocation, and Buck was discharged. But his reputation was made, and from that day his name spread through every camp in Alaska.

Later on, in the fall of the year, he saved John Thornton's life in quite another fashion. The three partners were lining a long and narrow poling-boat down a bad stretch of rapids on the Forty-Mile Creek. Hans and Pete moved along the bank, snubbing with a thin Manila rope from tree to tree, while Thornton remained in the boat, helping its descent by means of a pole, and shouting directions to the shore. Buck, on the bank, worried and anxious, kept abreast of the boat, his eyes never off his master.

At a particularly bad spot, where a ledge of barely submerged rocks jutted out into the river, Hans cast off the rope, and, while Thornton poled the boat out into the stream, ran down the bank with the end in his hand to snub the boat when it had cleared the ledge. This it did, and was flying down-stream in a current as swift as a mill-race, when Hans checked it with the rope and checked too suddenly. The boat flirted over and snubbed in to the bank bottom up, while Thornton, flung sheer out of it, was carried down-stream toward the worst part of the rapids, a stretch of wild water in which no swimmer could live.

Buck had sprung in on the instant; and at the end of three

hundred yards, amid a mad swirl of water, he overhauled
Thornton. When he felt him grasp his tail, Buck headed for the
bank, swimming with all his splendid strength. But the progress
shoreward was slow; the progress down-stream amazingly rapid.
From below came the fatal roaring where the wild current went
wilder and was rent in shreds and spray by the rocks which
thrust through like the teeth of an enormous comb. The suck of
the water as it took the beginning of the last steep pitch was
frightful, and Thornton knew that the shore was impossible. He
scraped furiously over a rock, bruised across a second, and struck
a third with crushing force. He clutched its slippery top with both
hands, releasing Buck, and above the roar of the churning water
shouted: 'Go, Buck! Go!'

Buck could not hold his own, and swept on down-stream,
struggling desperately, but unable to win back. When he heard
Thornton's command repeated, he partly reared out of the water,
throwing his head high, as though for a last look, then turned
obediently toward the bank. He swam powerfully and was
dragged ashore by Pete and Hans at the very point where
swimming ceased to be possible and destruction began.

They knew that the time a man could cling to a slippery rock
in the face of that driving current was a matter of minutes, and
they ran as fast as they could up the bank to a point far above
where Thornton was hanging on. They attached the line with
which they had been snubbing the boat to Buck's neck and
shoulders, being careful that it should neither strangle him nor
impede his swimming, and launched him into the stream. He
struck out boldly, but not straight enough into the stream. He
discovered the mistake too late, when Thornton was abreast of
him and a bare half-dozen strokes away while he was being
carried helplessly past.

Hans promptly snubbed with the rope, as though Buck were a
boat. The rope thus tightening on him in the sweep of the
current, he was jerked under the surface, and under the surface
he remained till his body struck against the bank and he was
hauled out. He was half drowned, and Hans and Pete threw
themselves upon him, pounding the breath into him and the
water out of him. He staggered to his feet and fell down. The faint
sound of Thornton's voice came to them, and though they could
not make out the words of it, they knew that he was in his
extremity. His master's voice acted on Buck like an electric shock.

He sprang to his feet and ran up the bank ahead of the men to the point of his previous departure.

Again the rope was attached and he was launched, and again he struck out, but this time straight into the stream. He had miscalculated once, but he would not be guilty of it a second time. Hans paid out the rope, permitting no slack, while Pete kept it clear of coils. Buck held on till he was on a line straight above Thornton; then he turned, and with the speed of an express train headed down upon him. Thornton saw him coming, and, as Buck struck him like a battering ram, with the whole force of the current behind him, he reached up and closed with both arms around the shaggy neck. Hans snubbed the rope around the tree, and Buck and Thornton were jerked under the water. Strangling, suffocating, sometimes one uppermost and sometimes the other, dragging over the jagged bottom, smashing against rocks and snags, they veered in to the bank.

Thornton came to, belly downward and being violently propelled back and forth across a drift log by Hans and Pete. His first glance was for Buck, over whose limp and apparently lifeless body Nig was setting up a howl, while Skeet was licking the wet face and closed eyes. Thornton was himself bruised and battered, and he went carefully over Buck's body, when he had been brought around, finding three broken ribs.

'That settles it,' he announced. 'We camp right here.' And camp they did, till Buck's ribs knitted and he was able to travel.

That winter, at Dawson, Buck performed another exploit, not so heroic, perhaps, but one that put his name many notches higher on the totem-pole of Alaskan fame. This exploit was particularly gratifying to the three men; for they stood in need of the outfit which it furnished, and were enabled to make a long-desired trip into the virgin East, where miners had not yet appeared. It was brought about by a conversation in the Eldorado Saloon, in which men waxed boastful of their favorite dogs. Buck, because of his record, was the target for these men, and Thornton was driven stoutly to defend him. At the end of half an hour one man stated that his dog could start a sled with five hundred pounds and walk off with it; a second bragged six hundred for his dog; and a third, seven hundred.

'Pooh! pooh!' said John Thornton; 'Buck can start a thousand pounds.'

'And break it out? and walk off with it for a hundred yards?'

demanded Matthewson, a Bonanza King, he of the seven hundred vaunt.

'And break it out, and walk off with it for a hundred yards,' John Thornton said coolly.

'Well,' Matthewson said, slowly and deliberately, so that all could hear, 'I've got a thousand dollars that says he can't. And there it is.' So saying, he slammed a sack of gold dust of the size of a bologna sausage down upon the bar.

Nobody spoke. Thornton's bluff, if bluff it was, had been called. He could feel a flush of warm blood creeping up his face. His tongue had tricked him. He did not know whether Buck could start a thousand pounds. Half a ton! The enormousness of it appalled him. He had great faith in Buck's strength and had often thought him capable of starting such a load; but never, as now, had he faced the possibility of it, the eyes of a dozen men fixed upon him, silent and waiting. Further, he had no thousand dollars; nor had Hans or Pete.

'I've got a sled standing outside now, with twenty fifty-pound sacks of flour on it,' Matthewson went on with brutal directness; 'so don't let that hinder you.'

Thornton did not reply. He did not know what to say. He glanced from face to face in the absent way of a man who has lost the power of thought and is seeking somewhere to find the thing that will start it going again. The face of Jim O'Brien, a Mastodon King and old-time comrade, caught his eyes. It was as a cue to him, seeming to rouse him to do what he would never have dreamed of doing.

'Can you lend me a thousand?' he asked, almost in a whisper.

'Sure,' answered O'Brien, thumping down a plethoric sack by the side of Matthewson's. 'Though it's little faith I'm having, John, that the beast can do the trick.'

The Eldorado emptied its occupants into the street to see the test. The tables were deserted, and the dealers and game-keepers came forth to see the outcome of the wager and to lay odds. Several hundred men, furred and mittened, banked around the sled within easy distance. Matthewson's sled, loaded with a thousand pounds of flour, had been standing for a couple of hours, and in the intense cold (it was sixty below zero) the runners had frozen fast to the hard-packed snow. Men offered odds of two to one that Buck could not budge the sled. A quibble arose concerning the phrase 'break out'. O'Brien contended it was Thornton's privilege to knock the runners loose, leaving Buck to 'break it out' from a dead standstill. Matthewson insisted that the phrase included breaking the runners from the frozen grip of the snow. A majority of the men who had witnessed the making of the bet decided in his favor, whereat the odds went up to three to one against Buck.

There were no takers. Not a man believed him capable of the feat. Thornton had been hurried into the wager, heavy with doubt; and now that he looked at the sled itself, the concrete fact, with the regular team of ten dogs curled up in the snow before it, the more impossible the task appeared. Matthewson waxed jubilant.

'Three to one!' he proclaimed. 'I'll lay you another thousand at that figure, Thornton. What d'ye say?'

Thornton's doubt was strong in his face, but his fighting spirit was aroused — the fighting spirit that soars above odds, fails to recognize the impossible, and is deaf to all save the clamor for battle. He called Hans and Pete to him. Their sacks were slim, and with his own the three partners could rake together only two hundred dollars. In the ebb of their fortunes, this sum was their total capital; yet they laid it unhesitatingly against Matthewson's six hundred.

The team of ten dogs was unhitched, and Buck, with his own harness, was put into the sled. He had caught the contagion of the excitement, and he felt that in some way he must do a great thing for John Thornton. Murmurs of admiration at his splendid appearance went up. He was in perfect condition, without an ounce of superfluous flesh, and the one hundred and fifty pounds that he weighed were so many pounds of grit and virility. His furry coat shone with the sheen of silk. Down the neck and across the shoulders, his mane, in repose as it was, half bristled and seemed to lift with every movement, as though excess of vigor made each particular hair alive and active. The great breast and heavy fore legs were no more than in proportion with the rest of the body, where the muscles showed in tight rolls underneath the skin. Men felt these muscles and proclaimed them hard as iron, and the odds went down to two to one.

'Gad, sir! Gad, sir!' stuttered a member of the latest dynasty, a king of the Skookum Benches. 'I offer you eight hundred for him, sir, before the test, sir; eight hundred just as he stands.'

Thornton shook his head and stepped to Buck's side.

'You must stand off from him,' Matthewson protested. 'Free play and plenty of room.'

The crowd fell silent; only could be heard the voices of the gamblers vainly offering two to one. Everybody acknowledged Buck a magnificent animal, but twenty fifty-pound sacks of flour bulked too large in their eyes for them to loosen their pouch-strings.

Thornton knelt down by Buck's side. He took his head in his two hands and rested cheek on cheek. He did not playfully shake him, as was his wont, or murmur soft love curses; but he whispered in his ear. 'As you love me, Buck. As you love me,' was what he whispered. Buck whined with suppressed eagerness.

The crowd was watching curiously. The affair was growing mysterious. It seemed like a conjuration. As Thornton got to his feet, Buck seized his mittened hand between his jaws, pressing in with his teeth and releasing slowly, half-reluctantly. It was the answer, in terms, not of speech, but of love. Thornton stepped well back.

'Now, Buck,' he said.

Buck tightened the traces, then slacked them for a matter of several inches. It was the way he had learned.

'Gee!' Thornton's voice rang out, sharp in the tense silence.

Buck swung to the right, ending the movement in a plunge that took up the slack and with a sudden jerk arrested his one hundred and fifty pounds. The load quivered, and from under the runners arose a crisp crackling.

'Haw!' Thornton commanded.

Buck duplicated the manoeuvre, this time to the left. The crackling turned into a snapping, the sled pivoting and the runners slipping and grating several inches to the side. The sled was broken out. Men were holding their breaths, intensely unconscious of the fact.

'Now, MUSH!'

Thornton's command cracked out like a pistol-shot. Buck threw himself forward, tightening the traces with a jarring lunge. His whole body was gathered compactly together in the tremendous effort, the muscles writhing and knotting like live things under the silky fur. His great chest was low to the ground, his head forward and down, while his feet were flying like mad, the claws scarring the hard-packed snow in parallel grooves. The sled swayed and trembled, half-started forward. One of his feet slipped, and one man groaned aloud. Then the sled lurched ahead in what appeared a rapid succession of jerks, though it never really came to a dead stop again ... half an inch ... an inch ... two inches ... The jerks perceptibly diminished; as the sled gained momentum, he caught them up, till it was moving steadily along.

Men gasped and began to breathe again, unaware that for a moment they had ceased to breathe. Thornton was running behind, encouraging Buck with short, cheery words. The distance had been measured off, and as he neared the pile of firewood which marked the end of the hundred yards, a cheer began to grow and grow, which burst into a roar as he passed the firewood and halted at command. Every man was tearing himself loose, even Matthewson. Hats and mittens were flying in the air. Men were shaking hands, it did not matter with whom, and bubbling over in a general incoherent babel.

But Thornton fell on his knees beside Buck. Head was against head, and he was shaking him back and forth. Those who hurried up heard him cursing Buck, and he cursed him long and fervently, and softly and lovingly.

'Gad, sir! Gad, sir!' spluttered the Skookum Bench king. 'I'll give you a thousand for him, sir, a thousand, sir – twelve hundred, sir.'

Thornton rose to his feet. His eyes were wet. The tears were streaming frankly down his cheeks. 'Sir,' he said to the Skookum Bench king, 'no, sir. You can go to hell, sir. It's the best I can do for you, sir.'

Buck seized Thornton's hand in his teeth. Thornton shook him back and forth. As though animated by a common impulse, the onlookers drew back to a respectful distance; nor were they again indiscreet enough to interrupt.

7

The Sounding of the Call

When Buck earned sixteen hundred dollars in five minutes for John Thornton, he made it possible for his master to pay off certain debts and to journey with his partners into the East after a fabled lost mine, the history of which was as old as the history of the country. Many men had sought it; few had found it; and more than a few there were who had never returned from the quest. This lost mine was steeped in tragedy and shrouded in mystery. No one knew of the first man. The oldest tradition stopped before it got back to him. From the beginning there had been an ancient and ramshackle cabin. Dying men had sworn to it, and to the mine the site of which it marked, clinching their testimony with nuggets that were unlike any known grade of gold in the Northland.

But no living man had looted this treasure house, and the dead were dead; wherefore John Thornton and Pete and Hans, with Buck and half a dozen other dogs, faced into the East on an unknown trail to achieve where men and dogs as good as themselves had failed. They sledded seventy miles up the Yukon, swung to the left into the Stewart River, passed the Mayo and the McQuestion, and held on until the Stewart itself became a streamlet, threading the upstanding peaks which marked the backbone of the continent.

John Thornton asked little of man or nature. He was unafraid of the wild. With a handful of salt and a rifle he could plunge into the wilderness and fare wherever he pleased and as long as he pleased. Being in no haste, Indian fashion, he hunted his dinner in the course of the day's travel; and if he failed to find it, like the Indian, he kept on traveling, secure in the knowledge that sooner or later he would come to it. So, on this great journey into the East, straight meat was the bill of fare, ammunition and tools principally made up the load on the sled, and the time-card was drawn upon the limitless future.

To Buck it was boundless delight, this hunting, fishing, and indefinite wandering through strange places. For weeks at a time they would hold on steadily, day after day; and for weeks upon end they would camp, here and there, the dogs loafing and the men burning holes through frozen muck and gravel and washing countless pans of dirt by the heat of the fire. Sometimes they went hungry, sometimes they feasted riotously, all according to the abundance of game and the fortune of hunting. Summer arrived, and dogs and men packed on their backs, rafted across blue mountain lakes, and descended or ascended unknown rivers in slender boats whip-sawed from the standing forest.

The months came and went, and back and forth they twisted through the uncharted vastness, where no men were and yet where men had been if the Lost Cabin were true. They went across divides in summer blizzards, shivered under the midnight sun on naked mountains between the timber line and the eternal snows, dropped into summer valleys amid swarming gnats and flies, and in the shadows of glaciers picked strawberries and flowers as ripe and fair as any the Southland could boast. In the fall of the year they penetrated a weird lake country, sad and silent, where wild-fowl had been, but where then there was no life nor sign of life – only the blowing of chill winds, the forming of ice in sheltered places, and the melancholy rippling of waves on lonely beaches.

And through another winter they wandered on the obliterated trails of men who had gone before. Once, they came upon a path blazed through the forest, an ancient path, and the Lost Cabin seemed very near. But the path began nowhere and ended nowhere, and it remained mystery, as the man who made it and the reason he made it remained mystery. Another time they chanced upon the time-graven wreckage of a hunting lodge, and amid the shreds of rotted blankets John Thornton found a long-barreled flint-lock. He knew it for a Hudson Bay Company gun of the young days in the Northwest, when such a gun was worth its height in beaver skins packed flat. And that was all – no hint as to the man who in an early day had reared the lodge and left the gun among the blankets.

Spring came on once more, and at the end of all their wandering they found, not the Lost Cabin, but a shallow placer in a broad valley where the gold showed like yellow butter across the bottom of the washing-pan. They sought no farther. Each day they worked earned them thousands of dollars in clean dust and nuggets, and they worked every day. The gold was sacked in moose-hide bags, fifty pounds to the bag, and piled like so much firewood outside the spruce-bough lodge. Like giants they toiled, days flashing on the heels of days like dreams as they heaped the treasure up.

There was nothing for the dogs to do, save the hauling in of meat now and again that Thornton killed, and Buck spent long hours musing by the fire. The vision of the short-legged hairy man came to him more frequently, now that there was little work to be done; and often, blinking by the fire, Buck wandered with him in that other world which he remembered.

The salient thing of this other world seemed fear. When he watched the hairy man sleeping by the fire, head-between his knees and hands clasped above, Buck saw that he slept restlessly, with many starts and awakenings, at which times he would peer fearfully into the darkness and fling more wood upon the fire. Did they walk by the beach of a sea, where the hairy man gathered shell-fish and ate them as he gathered, it was with eyes that roved everywhere for hidden danger and with legs prepared to run like the wind at its first appearance. Through the forest they crept noiselessly, Buck at the hairy man's heels; and they were alert and vigilant, the pair of them, ears twitching and moving and nostrils quivering, for the man heard and smelled as keenly as Buck. The hairy man could spring up into the trees and travel ahead as fast as on the ground, swinging by the arms from limb to limb, sometimes a dozen feet apart, letting go and catching, never falling, never missing his grip. In fact, he seemed as much at home among the trees as on the ground; and Buck had memories of nights of vigil spent beneath trees wherein the hairy man roosted, holding on tightly as he slept.

And closely akin to the visions of the hairy man was the call still sounding in the depths of the forest. It filled him with a great unrest and strange desires. It caused him to feel a vague, sweet gladness, and he was aware of wild yearnings and stirrings for he knew not what. Sometimes he pursued the call into the forest, looking for it as though it were a tangible thing, barking softly or defiantly, as the mood might dictate. He would thrust his nose into the cool wood moss, or into the black soil where long grasses grew, and snort with joy at the fat earth smells; or he would crouch for hours, as if in concealment, behind fungus-covered trunks of fallen trees, wide-eyed and wide-eared to all that moved and sounded about him. It might be, lying thus, that he hoped to surprise this call he could not understand. But he did not know why he did these various things. He was impelled to do them, and did not reason about them at all.

Irresistible impulses seized him. He would be lying in camp, dozing lazily in the heat of the day, when suddenly his head would lift and his ears cock up, intent and listening, and he would spring to his feet and dash away, and on and on, for hours, through the forest aisles and across the open spaces where the niggerheads bunched. He loved to run down dry watercourses, and to creep and spy upon the bird life in the woods. For a day at a time he would lie in the underbrush where he could watch the partridges drumming and strutting up and down. But especially he loved to run in the dim twilight of the summer midnights, listening to the subdued and sleepy murmurs of the forest, reading signs and sounds as man may read a book, and seeking for the mysterious something that called – called, waking or sleeping, at all times, for him to come.

One night he sprang from sleep with a start, eager-eyed, nostrils quivering and scenting, his mane bristling in recurrent waves. From the forest came the call (or one note of it, for the call was many noted), distinct and definite as never before – a long-drawn howl, like, yet unlike, any noise made by husky dog. And he knew it, in the old familiar way, as a sound heard before. He sprang through the sleeping camp and in swift silence dashed through the woods. As he drew closer to the cry he went more slowly, with caution in every movement, till he came to an open place among the trees, and looking out saw, erect on haunches, with nose pointed to the sky, a long, lean, timber wolf.

He had made no noise, yet it ceased from its howling and tried to sense his presence. Buck stalked into the open, half crouching, body gathered compactly together, tail straight and stiff, feet falling with unwonted care. Every movement advertised commingled threatening and overture of friendliness. It was the menacing truce that marks the meeting of wild beasts that prey. But the wolf fled at sight of him. He followed, with wild leapings, in a frenzy to overtake. He ran him into a blind channel, in the bed of the creek, where a timber jam barred the way. The wolf whirled about, pivoting on his hind legs after the fashion of Joe and of all cornered husky dogs, snarling and bristling, clipping his teeth together in a continuous and rapid succession of snaps.

Buck did not attack, but circled him about and hedged him in with friendly advances. The wolf was suspicious and afraid; for Buck made three of him in weight, while his head barely reached Buck's shoulder. Watching his chance, he darted away, and the chase was resumed. Time and again he was cornered, and the thing repeated, though he was in poor condition, or Buck could not so easily have overtaken him. He would run till Buck's head was even with his flank, when he would whirl around at bay, only to dash away again at the first opportunity.

But in the end Buck's pertinacity was rewarded; for the wolf, finding that no harm was intended, finally sniffed noses with him. Then they became friendly, and played about in the nervous, half-coy way with which fierce beasts belie their fierceness. After some time of this the wolf started off at an easy lope in a manner that plainly showed he was going somewhere. He made it clear to Buck that he was to come, and they ran side by side through the sombre twilight, straight up the creek bed, into the gorge from which it issued, and across the bleak divide where it took its rise.

On the opposite slope of the watershed they came down into a level country where were great stretches of forest and many streams, and through these great stretches they ran steadily, hour after hour, the sun rising higher and the day growing warmer. Buck was wildly glad. He knew he was at last answering the call, running by the side of his wood brother toward the place from where the call surely came. Old memories were coming upon him fast, and he was stirring to them as of old he stirred to the realities of which they were the shadows. He had done this thing before, somewhere in that other and dimly remembered world, and he was doing it again, now, running free in the open, the unpacked earth underfoot, the wide sky overhead.

They stopped by a running stream to drink, and, stopping, Buck remembered John Thornton. He sat down. The wolf started on toward the place from where the call surely came, then returned to him, sniffing noses and making actions as though to encourage him. But Buck turned about and started slowly on the back track. For the better part of an hour the wild brother ran by his side, whining softly. Then he sat down, pointed his nose upward, and howled. It was a mournful howl, and as Buck held steadily on his way he heard it grow faint and fainter until it was lost in the distance.

John Thornton was eating dinner when Buck dashed into camp and sprang upon him in a frenzy of affection, overturning him, scrambling upon him, licking his face, biting his hand – 'playing the general tom-fool,' as John Thornton characterized it, the while he shook Buck back and forth and cursed him lovingly.

For two days and nights Buck never left camp, never let Thornton out of his sight. He followed him about at his work, watched him while he ate, saw him into his blankets at night and out of them in the morning. But after two days the call in the forest began to sound more imperiously than ever. Buck's restlessness came back on him, and he was haunted by recollections of the wild brother, and of the smiling land beyond the divide and the run side by side through the wide forest stretches. Once again he took to wandering in the woods, but the wild brother came no more; and though he listened through long vigils, the mournful howl was never raised.

He began to sleep out at night, staying away from camp for days at a time; and once he crossed the divide at the head of the creek and went down into the land of timber and streams. There he wandered for a week, seeking vainly for fresh sign of the wild brother, killing his meat as he traveled and traveling with the long, easy lope that seems never to tire. He fished for salmon in a broad stream that emptied somewhere into the sea, and by this stream he killed a large black bear, blinded by the mosquitoes while likewise fishing, and raging through the forest helpless and terrible. Even so, it was a hard fight, and it aroused the last latent remnants of Buck's ferocity. And two days later, when he returned to his kill and found a dozen wolverenes quarreling over the spoil, he scattered them like chaff; and those that fled left two behind who would quarrel no more.

The blood-longing became stronger than ever before. He was a killer, a thing that preyed, living on the things that lived, unaided, alone, by virtue of his own strength and prowess, surviving triumphantly in a hostile environment where only the strong survived. Because of all this he became possessed of a great pride in himself, which communicated itself like a contagion to his physical being. It advertised itself in all his movements, was apparent in the play of every muscle, spoke plainly as speech in the way he carried himself, and made his glorious furry coat if anything more glorious. But for the stray brown on his muzzle and above his eyes, and for the splash of white hair that ran midmost down his chest, he might well have been mistaken for a gigantic wolf, larger than the largest of the breed. From his St Bernard father he had inherited size and weight, but it was his shepherd mother who had given shape to that size and weight. His muzzle was the long wolf muzzle, save that it was larger than the muzzle of any wolf; and his head, somewhat broader, was the wolf head on a massive scale.

His cunning was wolf cunning, and wild cunning; his intelligence, shepherd intelligence, and St Bernard intelligence; and all this, plus an experience gained in the fiercest of schools, made him as formidable a creature as any that roamed the wild. A carnivorous animal, living on a straight meat diet, he was in full flower, at the high tide of his life, overspilling with vigor and virility. When Thornton passed a caressing hand along his back, a snapping and crackling followed the hand, each hair discharging its pent magnetism at the contact. Every part, brain and body, nerve tissue and fibre, was keyed to the most exquisite pitch; and between all the parts there was a perfect equilibrium or adjustment. To sights and sounds and events which required action, he responded with lightning-like rapidity. Quickly as a husky dog could leap to defend from attack or to attack, he could leap twice as quickly. He saw the movement, or heard sound, and responded in less time than another dog required to compass the mere seeing or hearing. He perceived and determined and responded in the same instant. In point of fact the three actions of perceiving, determining, and responding were sequential; but so infinitesimal were the intervals of time between them that they appeared simultaneous. His muscles were surcharged with vitality, and snapped into play sharply, like steel springs. Life streamed through him in splendid flood, glad and rampant, until it seemed that it would burst him asunder in sheer ecstasy and pour forth generously over the world.

'Never was there such a dog,' said John Thornton one day, as the partners watched Buck marching out of camp.

'When he was made, the mould was broke,' said Pete.

'Py jingo! I t'ink so mineself,' Hans affirmed.

They saw him marching out of camp, but they did not see the instant and terrible transformation which took place as soon as he was within the secrecy of the forest. He no longer marched. At once he became a thing of the wild, stealing along softly, cat-footed, a passing shadow that appeared and disappeared among the shadows. He knew how to take advantage of every cover, to crawl on his belly like a snake, and like a snake to leap and strike. He could take a ptarmigan from its nest, kill a rabbit as it slept, and snap in mid air the little chipmunks fleeing a second too late for the trees. Fish, in open pools, were not too quick for him; nor were beaver, mending their dams, too wary. He killed to eat, not from wantonness; but he preferred to eat what he killed himself. So a lurking humor ran through his deeds, and it was his delight to steal upon the squirrels, and, when he all but had them, to let them go, chattering in mortal fear to the tree-tops.

As the fall of the year came on, the moose appeared in greater abundance, moving slowly down to meet the winter in the lower and less rigorous valleys. Buck had already dragged down a stray part-grown calf; but he wished strongly for larger and more

formidable quarry, and he came upon it one day on the divide at
the head of the creek. A band of twenty moose had crossed over
from the land of streams and timber, and chief among them was
a great bull. He was in a savage temper, and, standing over six
feet from the ground, was as formidable an antagonist as even
Buck could desire. Back and forth the bull tossed his great
palmated antlers, branching to fourteen points and embracing
seven feet within the tips. His small eyes burned with a vicious
and bitter light, while he roared with fury at sight of Buck.

From the bull's side, just forward of the flank, protruded a
feathered arrow-end, which accounted for his savageness. Guided
by that instinct which came from the old hunting days of the
primordial world, Buck proceeded to cut the bull out from the
herd. It was no slight task. He would bark and dance about in
front of the bull, just out of reach of the great antlers and of the
terrible splay hoofs which could have stamped his life out with a
single blow. Unable to turn his back on the fanged danger and go
on, the bull would be driven into paroxysms of rage. At such
moments he charged Buck, who retreated craftily, luring him on
by a simulated inability to escape. But when he was thus
separated from his fellows, two or three of the younger bulls
would charge back upon Buck and enable the wounded bull to
rejoin the herd.

There is a patience of the wild – dogged, tireless, persistent as
life itself – that holds motionless for endless hours the spider in its
web, the snake in its coils, the panther in its ambuscade; this
patience belongs peculiarly to life when it hunts its living food;
and it belonged to Buck as he clung to the flank of the herd,
retarding its march, irritating the young bulls, worrying the cows
with their half-grown calves, and driving the wounded bull mad
with helpless rage. For half a day this continued. Buck multiplied
himself, attacking from all sides, enveloping the herd in a
whirlwind of menace, cutting out his victim as fast as it could
rejoin its mates, wearing out the patience of creatures preyed
upon, which is a lesser patience than that of creatures preying.

As the day wore along and the sun dropped to its bed in the
northwest (the darkness had come back and the fall nights were
six hours long), the young bulls retraced their steps more and
more reluctantly to the aid of their beset leader. The downcoming winter was harrying them on to the lower levels, and it
seemed they could never shake off this tireless creature that held

them back. Besides, it was not the life of the herd, or of the young bulls, that was threatened. The life of only one member was demanded, which was a remoter interest than their lives, and in the end they were content to pay the toll.

As twilight fell the old bull stood with lowered head, watching his mates – the cows he had known, the calves he had fathered, the bulls he had mastered – as they shambled on at a rapid pace through the fading light. He could not follow, for before his nose leaped the merciless fanged terror that would not let him go. Three hundredweight more than half a ton he weighed; he had lived a long, strong life, full of fight and struggle, and at the end he faced death at the teeth of a creature whose head did not reach beyond his great knuckled knees.

From then on, night and day, Buck never left his prey, never gave it a moment's rest, never permitted it to browse the leaves of trees or the shoots of young birch and willow. Nor did he give the wounded bull opportunity to slake his burning thirst in the slender trickling streams they crossed. Often, in desperation, he burst into long stretches of flight. At such times Buck did not attempt to stay him, but loped easily at his heels, satisfied with the way the game was played, lying down when the moose stood still, attacking him fiercely when he strove to eat or drink.

The great head drooped more and more under its tree of horns, and the shambling trot grew weak and weaker. He took to standing for long periods, with nose to the ground and dejected ears dropped limply; and Buck found more time in which to get water for himself and in which to rest. At such moments, panting with red lolling tongue and with eyes fixed upon the big bull, it appeared to Buck that a change was coming over the face of things. He could feel a new stir in the land. As the moose were coming into the land, other kinds of life were coming in. Forest and stream and air seemed palpitant with their presence. The news of it was borne in upon him, not by sight, or sound, or smell, but by some other and subtler sense. He heard nothing, saw nothing, yet knew that the land was somehow different; that through it strange things were afoot and ranging; and he resolved to investigate after he had finished the business in hand.

At last, at the end of the fourth day, he pulled the great moose down. For a day and a night he remained by the kill, eating and sleeping, turn and turn about. Then, rested, refreshed and strong, he turned his face toward camp and John Thornton. He broke into the long easy lope, and went on, hour after hour, never at loss for the tangled way, heading straight home through strange country with a certitude of direction that put man and his magnetic needle to shame.

As he held on he became more and more conscious of the new stir in the land. There was life abroad in it different from the life which had been there throughout the summer. No longer was this fact borne in upon him in some subtle, mysterious way. The birds talked of it, the squirrels chattered about it, the very breeze whispered of it. Several times he stopped and drew in the fresh morning air in great sniffs, reading a message which made him leap on with greater speed. He was oppressed with a sense of calamity happening, if it were not calamity already happened; and as he crossed the last watershed and dropped down into the valley toward camp, he proceeded with greater caution.

Three miles away he came upon a fresh trail that sent his neck hair rippling and bristling. It led straight toward camp and John Thornton. Buck hurried on, swiftly and stealthily, every nerve straining and tense, alert to the multitudinous details which told a story – all but the end. His nose gave him a varying description of the passage of the life on the heels of which he was traveling. He remarked the pregnant silence of the forest. The bird life had flitted. The squirrels were in hiding. One only he saw – a sleek gray fellow, flattened against a gray dead limb so that he seemed a part of it, a woody excrescence upon the wood itself.

As Buck slid along with the obscureness of a gliding shadow, his nose was jerked suddenly to the side as though a positive force had gripped and pulled it. He followed the new scent into a thicket and found Nig. He was lying on his side, dead where he had dragged himself, an arrow protruding, head and feathers, from either side of his body.

A hundred yards farther on, Buck came upon one of the sled-dogs Thornton had bought in Dawson. This dog was thrashing about in a death-struggle, directly on the trail, and Buck passed around him without stopping. From the camp came the faint sound of many voices, rising and falling in a sing-song chant. Bellying forward to the edge of the clearing, he found Hans, lying on his face, feathered with arrows like a porcupine. At the same instant Buck peered out where the spruce-bough lodge had been and saw what made his hair leap straight up on his neck and shoulders. A gust of overpowering rage swept over him. He did not know that he growled, but he growled aloud with a terrible ferocity. For the last time in his life he allowed passion to usurp cunning and reason, and it was because of his great love for John Thornton that he lost his head.

The Yeehats were dancing about the wreckage of the spruce-bough lodge when they heard a fearful roaring and saw rushing upon them an animal the like of which they had never seen before. It was Buck, a live hurricane of fury, hurling himself upon them in a frenzy to destroy. He sprang at the foremost man (it was the chief of the Yeehats), ripping the throat wide open till the rent jugular spouted a fountain of blood. He did not pause to worry the victim, but ripped in passing, with the next bound tearing wide the throat of a second man. There was no withstanding him. He plunged about in their very midst, tearing, rending, destroying, in constant and terrific motion which defied the arrows they discharged at him. In fact, so inconceivably rapid were his movements, and so closely were the Indians tangled together, that they shot one another with the arrows; and one young hunter, hurling a spear at Buck in mid air, drove it through the chest of another hunter with such force that the point broke through the skin of the back and stood out beyond. Then a panic seized the Yeehats, and they fled in terror to the woods, proclaiming as they fled the advent of the Evil Spirit.

And truly Buck was the Fiend incarnate, raging at their heels and dragging them down like deer as they raced through the trees. It was a fateful day for the Yeehats. They scattered far and wide over the country, and it was not till a week later that the last of the survivors gathered together in a lower valley and counted their losses. As for Buck, wearying of the pursuit, he returned to the desolated camp. He found Pete where he had been killed in his blankets in the first moment of surprise. Thornton's desperate struggle was fresh-written on the earth, and Buck scented every detail of it down to the edge of a deep pool. By the edge, head and fore feet in the water, lay Skeet, faithful to the last. The pool itself, muddy and discolored from the sluice boxes, effectually hid what it contained, and it contained John Thornton; for Buck followed his trace into the water, from which no trace led away.

All day Buck brooded by the pool or roamed restlessly about the camp. Death, as a cessation of movement, as a passing out and away from the lives of the living, he knew, and he knew John

Thornton was dead. It left a great void in him, somewhat akin to hunger, but a void which ached and ached, and which food could not fill. At times, when he paused to contemplate the carcasses of the Yeehats, he forgot the pain of it; and at such times he was aware of a great pride in himself – a pride greater than any he had yet experienced. He had killed man, the noblest game of all, and he had killed in the face of the law of club and fang. He sniffed the bodies curiously. They had died so easily. It was harder to kill a husky dog than them. They were no match at all, were it not for their arrows and spears and clubs. Thenceforward he would be unafraid of them except when they bore in their hands their arrows, spears, and clubs.

Night came on, and a full moon rose high over the trees into the sky, lighting the land till it lay bathed in ghostly day. And with the coming of the night, brooding and mourning by the pool, Buck became alive to a stirring of the new life in the forest other than that which the Yeehats had made. He stood up, listening and scenting. From far away drifted a faint, sharp yelp, followed by a chorus of similar sharp yelps. As the moments passed the yelps grew closer and louder. Again Buck knew them as things heard in that other world which persisted in his memory. He walked to the centre of the open space and listened. It was the call, the many-noted call, sounding more luringly and compellingly than ever before. And as never before, he was ready to obey. John Thornton was dead. The last tie was broken. Man and the claims of man no longer bound him.

Hunting their living meat, as the Yeehats were hunting it, on the flanks of the migrating moose, the wolf pack had at last crossed over from the land of streams and timber and invaded Buck's valley. Into the clearing where the moonlight streamed, they poured in a silvery flood; and in the center of the clearing stood Buck, motionless as a statue, waiting their coming. They were awed, so still and large he stood, and a moment's pause fell, till the boldest one leaped straight for him. Like a flash Buck struck, breaking the neck. Then he stood, without movement, as before, the stricken wolf rolling in agony behind him. Three others tried it in sharp succession; and one after the other they drew back, streaming blood from slashed throats or shoulders.

This was sufficient to fling the whole pack forward, pell-mell, crowded together, blocked and confused by its eagerness to pull down the prey. Buck's marvelous quickness and agility stood him in good stead. Pivoting on his hind legs, and snapping and gashing, he was everywhere at once, presenting a front which was apparently unbroken so swiftly did he whirl and guard from side to side. But to prevent them from getting behind him, he was forced back, down past the pool and into the creek bed, till he brought up against a high gravel bank. He worked along to a right angle in the bank which the men had made in the course of mining, and in this angle he came to bay, protected on three sides and with nothing to do but face the front.

And so well did he face it, that at the end of half an hour the wolves drew back discomfited. The tongues of all were out and lolling, the white fangs showing cruelly white in the moonlight. Some were lying down with heads raised and ears pricked forward; others stood on their feet, watching him; and still others were lapping water from the pool. One wolf, long and lean and gray, advanced cautiously, in a friendly manner, and Buck recognized the wild brother with whom he had run for a night and a day. He was whining softly, and, as Buck whined, they touched noses.

Then an old wolf, gaunt and battle-scarred, came forward. Buck writhed his lips into the preliminary of a snarl, but sniffed noses with him. Whereupon the old wolf sat down, pointed nose at the moon, and broke out the long wolf howl. The others sat down and howled. And now the call came to Buck in unmistakable accents. He, too, sat down and howled. This over, he came out of his angle and the pack crowded around him, sniffing in half-friendly, half-savage manner. The leaders lifted the yelp of the pack and sprang away into the woods. The wolves swung in behind, yelping in chorus. And Buck ran with them, side by side with the wild brother, yelping as he ran.

And here may well end the story of Buck. The years were not many when the Yeehats noted a change in the breed of timber wolves; for some were seen with splashes of brown on head and muzzle, and with a rift of white centering down the chest. But more remarkable than this, the Yeehats tell of a Ghost Dog that runs at the head of the pack. They are afraid of this Ghost Dog, for it has cunning greater than they, stealing from their camps in fierce winters, robbing their traps, slaying their dogs, and defying their bravest hunters.

Nay, the tale grows worse. Hunters there are who fail to return to the camp, and hunters there have been whom their tribesmen found with throats slashed cruelly open and with wolf prints about them in the snow greater than the prints of any wolf. Each fall, when the Yeehats follow the movement of the moose, there is a certain valley which they never enter. And women there are who become sad when the word goes over the fire of how the Evil Spirit came to select that valley for an abiding-place.

In the summers there is one visitor, however, to that valley, of which the Yeehats do not know. It is a great, gloriously coated wolf, like, and yet unlike, all other wolves. He crosses alone from the smiling timber land and comes down into an open space among the trees. Here a yellow stream flows from rotted moose-hide sacks and sinks into the ground, with long grasses growing through it and vegetable mould overrunning it and hiding its yellow from the sun; and here he muses for a time, howling once, long and mournfully, ere he departs.

But he is not always alone. When the long winter nights come on and the wolves follow their meat into the lower valleys, he may be seen running at the head of the pack through the pale moonlight or glimmering borealis, leaping gigantic above his fellows, his great throat a-bellow as he sings a song of the younger world, which is the song of the pack.

In a Far Country (1899; 1900)

When a man journeys into a far country, he must be prepared to forget many of the things he has learned, and to acquire such customs as are inherent with existence in the new land; he must abandon the old ideals and the old gods, and oftentimes he must reverse the very codes by which his conduct has hitherto been shaped. To those who have the protean faculty of adaptability, the novelty of such change may even be a source of pleasure; but to those who happen to be hardened to the ruts in which they were created, the pressure of the altered environment is unbearable, and they chafe in body and in spirit under the new restrictions which they do not understand. This chafing is bound to act and react, producing divers evils and leading to various misfortunes. It were better for the man who cannot fit himself to the new groove to return to his own country; if he delay too long, he will surely die.

The man who turns his back upon the comforts of an elder civilization, to face the savage youth, the primordial simplicity of the North, may estimate success at an inverse ratio to the quantity and quality of his hopelessly fixed habits. He will soon discover, if he be a fit candidate, that the material habits are the less important. The exchange of such things as a dainty menu for rough fare, of the stiff leather shoe for the soft, shapeless moccasin, of the feather bed for a couch in the snow, is after all a very easy matter. But his pinch will come in learning properly to shape his mind's attitude toward all things, and especially toward his fellow man. For the courtesies of ordinary life, he must substitute unselfishness, forbearance, and tolerance. Thus, and thus only, can he gain that pearl of great price – true comradeship. He must not say 'Thank you', he must mean it without opening his mouth, and prove it by responding in kind. In short, he must substitute the deed for the word, the spirit for the letter.

When the world rang with the tale of Arctic gold, and the lure of the North gripped the heartstrings of men, Carter Weatherbee threw up his snug clerkship, turned the half of his savings over to his wife, and with the remainder bought an outfit. There was no romance in his nature – the bondage of commerce had crushed all that; he was simply tired of the ceaseless grind, and wished to risk great hazards in view of corresponding returns. Like many another fool, disdaining the old trails used by the Northland pioneers for a score of years, he hurried to Edmonton in the spring of the year; and there, unluckily for his soul's welfare, he allied himself with a party of men.

There was nothing unusual about this party, except its plans. Even its goal, like that of all other parties, was the Klondike. But the route it had mapped out to attain that goal took away the breath of the hardiest native, born and bred to the vicissitudes of the Northwest. Even Jacques Baptiste, born of a Chippewa woman and a renegade *voyageur* (having raised his first whimpers in a deerskin lodge north of the sixty-fifth parallel, and had the same hushed by blissful sucks of raw tallow), was surprised. Though he sold his services to them and agreed to travel even to the never-opening ice, he shook his head ominously whenever his advice was asked.

Percy Cuthfert's evil star must have been in the ascendant, for he, too, joined this company of argonauts. He was an ordinary man, with a bank account as deep as his culture, which is saying a good deal. He had no reason to embark on such a venture – no reason in the world, save that he suffered from an abnormal development of sentimentality. He mistook this for the true spirit of romance and adventure. Many another man has done the like, and made as fatal a mistake.

The first break-up of spring found the party following the ice-run of Elk River. It was an imposing fleet, for the outfit was large, and they were accompanied by a disreputable contingent of half-breed *voyageurs* with their women and children. Day in and day out, they labored with the bateaux and canoes, fought mosquitoes and other kindred pests, or sweated and swore at the portages. Severe toil like this lays a man naked to the very roots of his soul, and ere Lake Athabasca was lost in the south, each member of the party had hoisted his true colors.

The two shirks and chronic grumblers were Carter Weatherbee and Percy Cuthfert. The whole party complained less of its aches and pains than did either of them. Not once did they volunteer for the thousand and one petty duties of the camp. A bucket of water to be brought, an extra armful of wood to be chopped, the dishes to be washed and wiped, a search to be made through the outfit for some suddenly indispensable article – and these two effete scions of civilization discovered sprains or blisters requiring instant attention. They were the first to turn in at night, with a score of tasks yet undone; the last to turn out in the morning, when the start should be in readiness before the breakfast was begun. They were the first to fall to at meal-time, the last to have a hand in the cooking; the first to dive for a slim delicacy, the last to discover they had added to their own another man's share. If they toiled at the oars, they slyly cut the water at each stroke and allowed the boat's momentum to float up the blade. They thought nobody noticed; but their comrades swore under their breaths and grew to hate them, while Jacques Baptiste sneered openly and damned them from morning till night. But Jacques Baptiste was no gentleman.

At the Great Slave, Hudson Bay dogs were purchased, and the fleet sank to the guards with its added burden of dried fish and pemmican. Then canoe and bateau answered to the swift current of the Mackenzie, and they plunged into the Great Barren Ground. Every likely-looking 'feeder' was prospected, but the elusive 'pay-dirt' danced ever to the north. At the Great Bear, overcome by the common dread of the Unknown Lands, their *voyageurs* began to desert, and Fort of Good Hope saw the last and bravest bending to the tow-lines as they bucked the current down which they had so treacherously glided. Jacques Baptiste alone remained. Had he not sworn to travel even to the never-opening ice?

The lying charts, compiled in main from hearsay, were now constantly consulted. And they felt the need of hurry, for the sun had already passed its northern solstice and was leading the winter south again. Skirting the shores of the bay, where the Mackenzie disembogues into the Arctic Ocean, they entered the mouth of the Little Peel River. Then began the arduous upstream toil, and the two Incapables fared worse than ever. Tow-line and pole, paddle and tump-line, rapids and portages – such tortures served to give the one a deep disgust for great hazards, and printed for the other a fiery text on the true romance of adventure. One day they waxed mutinous, and being vilely cursed by Jacques Baptiste, turned, as worms sometimes will. But the half-breed thrashed the twain, and sent them, bruised and bleeding, about their work. It was the first time either had been man-handled.

Abandoning their river craft at the headwaters of the Little Peel, they consumed the rest of the summer in the great portage over the Mackenzie watershed to the West Rat. This little stream fed the Porcupine, which in turn joined the Yukon where that mighty highway of the North counter-marches on the Arctic Circle. But they had lost in the race with winter, and one day they tied their rafts to the thick eddy-ice and hurried their goods ashore. That night the river jammed and broke several times; the following morning it had fallen asleep for good.

'We can't be more 'n four hundred miles from the Yukon,' concluded Sloper, multiplying his thumb nails by the scale of the map. The council, in which the two Incapables had whined to excellent disadvantage, was drawing to a close.

'Hudson Bay Post, long time ago. No use um now.' Jacques Baptiste's father had made the trip for the Fur Company in the old days, incidentally marking the trail with a couple of frozen toes.

'Sufferin' cracky!' cried another of the party. 'No whites?'

'Nary white,' Sloper sententiously affirmed; 'but it's only five hundred more up the Yukon to Dawson. Call it a rough thousand from here.'

Weatherbee and Cuthfert groaned in chorus.

'How long'll that take, Baptiste?'

The half-breed figured for a moment. 'Workum like hell, no man play out, ten – twenty – forty – fifty days. Um babies come' (designating the Incapables), 'no can tell. Mebbe when hell freeze over; mebbe not then.'

The manufacture of snowshoes and moccasins ceased. Somebody called the name of an absent member, who came out of an ancient cabin at the edge of the camp-fire and joined them. The cabin was one of the many mysteries which lurk in the vast recesses of the North. Built when and by whom, no man could tell. Two graves in the open, piled high with stones, perhaps contained the secret of those early wanderers. But whose hand had piled the stones?

The moment had come. Jacques Baptiste paused in the fitting of a harness and pinned the struggling dog in the snow. The cook made mute protest for delay, threw a handful of bacon into a noisy pot of beans, then came to attention. Sloper rose to his feet. His body was a ludicrous contrast to the healthy physiques of the Incapables. Yellow and weak, fleeing from a South American fever-hole, he had not broken his flight across the zones, and was still able to toil with men. His weight was probably ninety pounds, with the heavy hunting-knife thrown in, and his grizzled hair told of a prime which had ceased to be. The fresh young muscles of either Weatherbee or Cuthfert were equal to ten times the endeavor of his; yet he could walk them into the earth in a day's journey. And all this day he had whipped his stronger comrades into venturing a thousand miles of the stiffest hardship man can conceive. He was the incarnation of the unrest of his race, and the old Teutonic stubbornness, dashed with the quick grasp and action of the Yankee, held the flesh in the bondage of the spirit.

'All those in favor of going on with the dogs as soon as the ice sets, say ay.'

'Ay!' rang out eight voices – voices destined to string a trail of oaths along many a hundred miles of pain.

'Contrary minded?'

'No!' For the first time the Incapables were united without some compromise of personal interests.

'And what are you going to do about it?' Weatherbee added belligerently.

'Majority rule! Majority rule!' clamored the rest of the party.

'I know the expedition is liable to fall through if you don't come,' Sloper replied sweetly; 'but I guess, if we try real hard, we can manage to do without you. What do you say, boys?'

The sentiment was cheered to the echo.

'But I say, you know,' Cuthfert ventured apprehensively; 'what's a chap like me to do?'

'Ain't you coming with us?'

'No-o.'

'Then do as you damn well please. We won't have nothing to say.'

'Kind o' calkilate yuh might settle it with that canoodlin' pardner of yourn,' suggested a heavy-going Westerner from the Dakotas, at the same time pointing out Weatherbee. 'He'll be shore to ask yuh what yur a-goin' to do when it comes to cookin' an' gatherin' the wood.'

'Then we'll consider it all arranged,' concluded Sloper. 'We'll pull out tomorrow, if we camp within five miles – just to get everything in running order and remember if we've forgotten anything.'

The sleds groaned by on their steel-shod runners, and the dogs strained low in the harnesses in which they were born to die. Jacques Baptiste paused by the side of Sloper to get a last glimpse of the cabin. The smoke curled up pathetically from the Yukon stove-pipe. The two Incapables were watching them from the doorway.

Sloper laid his hand on the other's shoulder.

'Jacques Baptiste, did you ever hear of the Kilkenny cats?'

The half-breed shook his head.

'Well, my friend and good comrade, the Kilkenny cats fought till neither hide, not hair, nor yowl, was left. You understand? – till nothing was left. Very good. Now, these two men don't like work. They won't work. We know that. They'll be all alone in that cabin all winter – a mighty long, dark winter. Kilkenny cats – well?'

The Frenchman in Baptiste shrugged his shoulders, but the Indian in him was silent. Nevertheless, it was an eloquent shrug, pregnant with prophecy.

Things prospered in the little cabin at first. The rough badinage of their comrades had made Weatherbee and Cuthfert conscious of the mutual responsibility which had devolved upon them; besides, there was not so much work after all for two healthy men. And the removal of the cruel whip-hand, or in other words the bulldozing half-breed, had brought with it a joyous reaction. At first, each strove to outdo the other, and they performed petty tasks with an unction which would have opened the eyes of their comrades who were now wearing out bodies and souls on the Long Trail.

All care was banished. The forest, which shouldered in upon them from three sides, was an inexhaustible woodyard. A few yards from their door slept the Porcupine, and a hole through its winter robe formed a bubbling spring of water, crystal clear and painfully cold. But they soon grew to find fault with even that. The hole would persist in freezing up, and thus gave them many a miserable hour of ice-chopping. The unknown builders of the cabin had extended the side-logs so as to support a cache at the rear. In this was stored the bulk of the party's provisions. Food there was, without stint, for three times the men who were fated to live upon it. But the most of it was of the kind which built up brawn and sinew, but did not tickle the palate. True, there was sugar in plenty for two ordinary men; but these two were little else than children. They early discovered the virtues of hot water judiciously saturated with sugar, and they prodigally swam their flapjacks and soaked their crusts in the rich, white syrup. Then coffee and tea, and especially the dried fruits, made disastrous inroads upon it. The first words they had were over the sugar question. And it is a really serious thing when two men, wholly dependent upon each other for company, begin to quarrel.

Weatherbee loved to discourse blatantly on politics, while Cuthfert, who had been prone to clip his coupons and let the commonwealth jog on as best it might, either ignored the subject or delivered himself of startling epigrams. But the clerk was too obtuse to appreciate the clever shaping of thought, and this waste of ammunition irritated Cuthfert. He had been used to blinding people by his brilliancy, and it worked him quite a hardship, this loss of an audience. He felt personally aggrieved and unconsciously held his mutton-head companion responsible for it.

Save existence, they had nothing in common – came in touch on no single point. Weatherbee was a clerk who had known naught but clerking all his life; Cuthfert was a master of arts, a dabbler in oils, and had written not a little. The one was a lower-class man who considered himself a gentleman, and the other was a gentleman who knew himself to be such. From this it may be remarked that a man can be a gentleman without possessing the first instinct of true comradeship. The clerk was as sensuous as the other was esthetic, and his love adventures, told at great length and chiefly coined from his imagination, affected the supersensitive master of arts in the same way as so many whiffs of sewer gas. He deemed the clerk a filthy, uncultured brute, whose place was in the muck with the swine, and told him so; and he was reciprocally informed that he was a milk-and-water sissy and a cad. Weatherbee could not have defined 'cad' for his life; but it satisfied its purpose, which after all seems the main point in life.

Weatherbee flatted every third note and sang such songs as 'The Boston Burglar' and 'The Handsome Cabin Boy', for hours at a time, while Cuthfert wept with rage, till he could stand it no longer and fled into the outer cold. But there was no escape. The intense frost could not be endured for long at a time, and the little cabin crowded them – beds, stove, table, and all – into a space of ten by twelve. The very presence of either became a personal affront to the other, and they lapsed into sullen silences which increased in length and strength as the days went by. Occasionally, the flash of an eye or the curl of a lip got the better of them, though they strove to wholly ignore each other during these mute periods. And a great wonder sprang up in the breast of each, as to how God had ever come to create the other.

With little to do, time became an intolerable burden to them. This naturally made them still lazier. They sank into a physical lethargy which there was no escaping, and which made them rebel at the performance of the smallest chore. One morning when it was his turn to cook the common breakfast, Weatherbee rolled out of his blankets, and to the snoring of his companion, lighted first the slush-lamp and then the fire. The kettles were frozen hard, and there was no water in the cabin with which to wash. But he did not mind that. Waiting for it to thaw, he sliced the bacon and plunged into the hateful task of bread-making. Cuthfert had been slyly watching through his half-closed lids. Consequently there was a scene, in which they fervently blessed each other, and agreed, thenceforth, that each do his own cooking. A week later, Cuthfert neglected his morning ablutions, but none the less complacently ate the meal which he had cooked. Weatherbee grinned. After that the foolish custom of washing passed out of their lives.

As the sugar-pile and other little luxuries dwindled, they began to be afraid they were not getting their proper shares, and in order that they might not be robbed, they fell to gorging themselves. The luxuries suffered in this gluttonous contest, as did also the men. In the absence of fresh vegetables and exercise, their blood became impoverished, and a loathsome, purplish rash crept over their bodies. Yet they refused to heed the warning. Next, their muscles and joints began to swell, the flesh turning black, while their mouths, gums, and lips took on the color of rich cream. Instead of being drawn together by their misery, each gloated over the other's symptoms as the scurvy took its course.

They lost all regard for personal appearance, and for that matter, common decency. The cabin became a pigpen, and never once were the beds made or fresh pine boughs laid underneath.

Yet they could not keep to their blankets, as they would have wished; for the frost was inexorable, and the fire box consumed much fuel. The hair of their heads and faces grew long and shaggy, while their garments would have disgusted a ragpicker. But they did not care. They were sick, and there was no one to see; besides, it was very painful to move about.

To all this was added a new trouble – the Fear of the North. This Fear was the joint child of the Great Cold and the Great Silence, and was born in the darkness of December, when the sun dipped below the southern horizon for good. It affected them according to their natures. Weatherbee fell prey to the grosser superstitions, and did his best to resurrect the spirits which slept in the forgotten graves. It was a fascinating thing, and in his dreams they came to him from out of the cold, and snuggled into his blankets, and told him of their toils and troubles ere they died. He shrank away from the clammy contact as they drew closer and twined their frozen limbs about him, and when they whispered in his ear of things to come, the cabin rang with his frightened shrieks. Cuthfert did not understand – for they no longer spoke – and when thus awakened he invariably grabbed for his revolver. Then he would sit up in bed, shivering nervously, with the weapon trained on the unconscious dreamer. Cuthfert deemed the man going mad, and so came to fear for his life.

His own malady assumed a less concrete form. The mysterious artisan who had laid the cabin, log by log, had pegged a wind-vane to the ridge-pole. Cuthfert noticed it always pointed south, and one day, irritated by its steadfastness of purpose, he turned it toward the east. He watched eagerly, but never a breath came by to disturb it. Then he turned the vane to the north, swearing never again to touch it till the wind did blow. But the air frightened him with its unearthly calm, and he often rose in the middle of the night to see if the vane had veered – ten degrees would have satisfied him. But no, it poised above him as unchangeable as fate. His imagination ran riot, till it became to him a fetich. Sometimes he followed the path it pointed across the dismal dominions, and allowed his soul to become saturated with the Fear. He dwelt upon the unseen and the unknown till the burden of eternity appeared to be crushing him. Everything in the Northland had that crushing effect – the absence of life and motion; the darkness; the infinite peace of the brooding land; the ghastly silence, which made the echo of each heart-beat a sacrilege; the solemn forest which seemed to guard an awful, inexpressible something, which neither word nor thought could compass.

The world he had so recently left, with its busy nations and great enterprises, seemed very far away. Recollections occasionally obtruded – recollections of marts and galleries and crowded thoroughfares, of evening dress and social functions, of good men and dear women he had known – but they were dim memories of a life he had lived long centuries agone, on some other planet. This phantasm was the Reality. Standing beneath the wind-vane, his eyes fixed on the polar skies, he could not bring himself to realize that the Southland really existed, that at that very moment it was a-roar with life and action. There was no Southland, no men being born of women, no giving and taking in marriage. Beyond his bleak sky-line there stretched vast solitudes, and beyond these still vaster solitudes. There were no lands of sunshine, heavy with the perfume of flowers. Such things were only old dreams of paradise. The sunlands of the West and the spicelands of the East, the smiling Arcadias and blissful Island of the Blest – ha! ha! His laughter split the void and shocked him with its unwonted sound. There was no sun. This was the Universe, dead and cold and dark, and he its only citizen. Weatherbee? At such moments Weatherbee did not count. He was a Caliban, a monstrous phantom, fettered to him for untold ages, the penalty of some forgotten crime.

He lived with Death among the dead, emasculated by the sense of his own insignificance, crushed by the passive mastery of the slumbering ages. The magnitude of all things appalled him. Everything partook of the superlative save himself – the perfect cessation of wind and motion, the immensity of the snow-covered wilderness, the height of the sky and the depth of the silence. That wind-vane – if it would only move. If a thunderbolt would fall, or the forest flare up in flame. The rolling up of the heavens as a scroll, the crash of Doom – anything, anything! But no, nothing moved; the Silence crowded in, and the Fear of the North laid icy fingers on his heart.

Once, like another Crusoe, by the edge of the river he came upon a track – the faint tracery of a snowshoe rabbit on the delicate snow-crust. It was a revelation. There was life in the Northland. He would follow it, look upon it, gloat over it. He forgot his swollen muscles, plunging through the deep snow in an ecstasy of anticipation. The forest swallowed him up, and the brief midday twilight vanished; but he pursued his quest till exhausted nature asserted itself and laid him helpless in the snow. There he groaned and cursed his folly, and knew the track to be the fancy of his brain; and late that night he dragged himself into the cabin on hands and knees, his cheeks frozen and a strange numbness about his feet. Weatherbee grinned malevolently, but made no offer to help him. He thrust needles into his toes and thawed them out by the stove. A week later mortification set in.

But the clerk had his own troubles. The dead men came out of their graves more frequently now, and rarely left him, waking or sleeping. He grew to wait and dread their coming, never passing the twin cairns without a shudder. One night they came to him in his sleep and led him forth to an appointed task. Frightened into inarticulate horror, he awoke between the heaps of stones and fled wildly to the cabin. But he had lain there for some time, for his feet and cheeks were also frozen.

Sometimes he became frantic at their insistent presence, and danced about the cabin, cutting the empty air with an axe, and smashing everything within reach. During these ghostly encounters, Cuthfert huddled into his blankets and followed the madman about with a cocked revolver, ready to shoot him if he came too near. But, recovering from one of these spells, the clerk noticed the weapon trained upon him. His suspicions were aroused, and thenceforth he, too, lived in fear of his life. They watched each other closely after that, and faced about in startled fright whenever either passed behind the other's back. This apprehensiveness became a mania which controlled them even in their sleep. Through mutual fear they tacitly let the slush-lamp burn all night, and saw to a plentiful supply of bacon-grease before retiring. The slightest movement on the part of one was sufficient to arouse the other, and many a still watch their gazes countered as they shook beneath their blankets with fingers on the trigger-guards.

What with the Fear of the North, the mental strain, and the ravages of the disease, they lost all semblance of humanity, taking on the appearance of wild beasts, hunted and desperate. Their cheeks and noses, as an aftermath of the freezing, had turned black. Their frozen toes had begun to drop away at the first and second joints. Every movement brought pain, but the fire box was insatiable, wringing a ransom of torture from their miserable bodies. Day in, day out, it demanded its food – a veritable pound of flesh – and they dragged themselves into the forest to chop wood on their knees. Once, crawling thus in search of dry sticks, unknown to each other they entered a thicket from opposite sides. Suddenly, without warning, two peering death's-heads confronted each other. Suffering had so transformed them that recognition was impossible. They sprang to their feet, shrieking with terror, and dashed away on their mangled stumps; and falling at the cabin door, they clawed and scratched like demons till they discovered their mistake.

Occasionally they lapsed normal, and during one of these sane intervals, the chief bone of contention, the sugar, had been divided equally between them. They guarded their separate sacks, stored up in the cache, with jealous eyes; for there were but a few cupfuls left, and they were totally devoid of faith in each other. But one day Cuthfert made a mistake. Hardly able to move, sick with pain, with his head swimming and eyes blinded, he crept into the cache, sugar canister in hand, and mistook Weatherbee's sack for his own.

January had been born but a few days when this occurred. The sun had some time since passed its lowest southern declination, and at meridian now threw flaunting streaks of yellow light upon the northern sky. On the day following his mistake with the sugar-bag, Cuthfert found himself feeling better, both in body and in spirit. As noontime drew near and the day brightened, he dragged himself outside to feast on the evanescent glow, which was to him an earnest of the sun's future intentions. Weatherbee was also feeling somewhat better, and crawled out beside him. They propped themselves in the snow beneath the moveless wind-vane, and waited.

The stillness of death was about them. In other climes, when nature falls into such moods, there is a subdued air of expectancy, a waiting for some small voice to take up the broken strain. Not so in the North. The two men had lived seeming aeons in this ghostly peace. They could remember no song of the past; they could conjure no song of the future. This unearthly calm had always been – the tranquil silence of eternity.

Their eyes were fixed upon the north. Unseen, behind their

backs, behind the towering mountains to the south, the sun swept toward the zenith of another sky than theirs. Sole spectators of the mighty canvas, they watched the false dawn slowly grow. A faint flame began to glow and smoulder. It deepened in intensity, ringing the changes of reddish-yellow, purple, and saffron. So bright did it become that Cuthfert thought the sun must surely be behind it – a miracle, the sun rising in the north! Suddenly, without warning and without fading, the canvas was swept clean. There was no color in the sky. The light had gone out of the day. They caught their breaths in half-sobs. But lo! the air was a-glint with particles of scintillating frost, and there, to the north, the wind-vane lay in vague outline on the snow. A shadow! A shadow! It was exactly midday. They jerked their heads hurriedly to the south. A golden rim peeped over the mountain's snowy shoulder, smiled upon them an instant, then dipped from sight again.

There were tears in their eyes as they sought each other. A strange softening came over them. They felt irresistibly drawn toward each other. The sun was coming back again. It would be with them tomorrow, and the next day, and the next. And it would stay longer every visit, and a time would come when it would ride their heaven day and night, never once dropping below the sky-line. There would be no night. The ice-locked winter would be broken; the winds would blow and the forests answer; the land would bathe in the blessed sunshine, and life renew. Hand in hand, they would quit this horrid dream and journey back to the Southland. They lurched blindly forward, and their hands met – their poor maimed hands, swollen and distorted beneath their mittens.

But the promise was destined to remain unfulfilled. The Northland is the Northland, and men work out their souls by strange rules, which other men, who have not journeyed into far countries, cannot come to understand.

An hour later, Cuthfert put a pan of bread into the oven, and fell to speculating on what the surgeons could do with his feet when he got back. Home did not seem so very far away now. Weatherbee was rummaging in the cache. Of a sudden, he raised a whirlwind of blasphemy, which in turn ceased with startling abruptness. The other man had robbed his sugar-sack. Still, things might have happened differently, had not the two dead men come out from under the stones and hushed the hot words in his throat. They led him quite gently from the cache, which he forgot to close. That consummation was reached; that something they had whispered to him in his dreams was about to happen. They guided him gently, very gently, to the woodpile, where they put the axe in his hands. Then they helped him shove open the cabin door, and he felt sure they shut it after him – at least he heard it slam and the latch fall sharply into place. And he knew they were waiting just without, waiting for him to do his task.

'Carter! I say, Carter!'

Percy Cuthfert was frightened at the look on the clerk's face, and he made haste to put the table between them.

Carter Weatherbee followed, without haste and without enthusiasm. There was neither pity nor passion in his face, but rather the patient, stolid look of one who has certain work to do and goes about it methodically.

'I say, what's the matter?'

The clerk dodged back, cutting off his retreat to the door, but never opening his mouth.

'I say, Carter, I say; let's talk. There's a good chap.'

The master of arts was thinking rapidly, now, shaping a skillful flank movement on the bed where his Smith & Wesson lay. Keeping his eyes on the madman, he rolled backward on the bunk, at the same time clutching the pistol.

'Carter!'

The powder flashed full in Weatherbee's face, but he swung his weapon and leaped forward. The axe bit deeply at the base of the spine, and Percy Cuthfert felt all consciousness of his lower limbs leave him. Then the clerk fell heavily upon him, clutching him by the throat with feeble fingers. The sharp bite of the axe had caused Cuthfert to drop the pistol, and as his lungs panted for release, he fumbled aimlessly for it among the blankets. Then he remembered. He slid a hand up the clerk's belt to the sheath-knife; and they drew very close to each other in that last clinch.

Percy Cuthfert felt his strength leave him. The lower portion of his body was useless. The inert weight of Weatherbee crushed him – crushed him and pinned him there like a bear under a trap. The cabin became filled with a familiar odor, and he knew the bread to be burning. Yet what did it matter? He would never need it. And there were all of six cupfuls of sugar in the cache – if he had foreseen this he would not have been so saving the last several days. Would the wind-vane ever move? It might even be veering now. Why not? Had he not seen the sun today? He would go and see. No; it was impossible to move. He had not thought the clerk so heavy a man.

How quickly the cabin cooled! The fire must be out. The cold was forcing in. It must be below zero already, and the ice creeping up the inside of the door. He could not see it, but his past experience enabled him to gauge its progress by the cabin's temperature. The lower hinge must be white ere now. Would the tale of this ever reach the world? How would his friends take it? They would read it over their coffee, most likely, and talk it over at the clubs. He could see them very clearly. 'Poor Old Cuthfert,' they murmured; 'not such a bad sort of a chap, after all.' He smiled at their eulogies, and passed on in search of a Turkish bath. It was the same old crowd upon the streets. Strange, they did not notice his moosehide moccasins and tattered German socks! He would take a cab. And after the bath a shave would not be bad. No; he would eat first. Steak, and potatoes, and green things – how fresh it all was! And what was that? Squares of honey, streaming liquid amber! But why did they bring so much? Ha! ha! he could never eat it all. Shine! Why certainly. He put his foot on the box. The bootblack looked curiously up at him, and he remembered his moosehide moccasins and went away hastily.

Hark! The wind-vane must be surely spinning. No; a mere singing in his ears. That was all – a mere singing. The ice must have passed the latch by now. More likely the upper hinge was covered. Between the moss-chinked roof-poles, little points of frost began to appear. How slowly they grew! No; not so slowly. There was a new one, and there another. Two – three – four; they were coming too fast to count. There were two growing together. And there, a third had joined them. Why, there were no more spots. They had run together and formed a sheet.

Well, he would have company. If Gabriel ever broke the silence of the North, they would stand together, hand in hand, before the great White Throne. And God would judge them, God would judge them!

Then Percy Cuthfert closed his eyes and dropped off to sleep.

The White Silence (1899; 1900)

'Carmen won't last more than a couple of days.' Mason spat out a chunk of ice and surveyed the poor animal carefully, then put her foot in his mouth and proceeded to bite out the ice which clustered cruelly between the toes.

'I never saw a dog with a highfalutin' name that ever was worth a rap,' he said, as he concluded his task and shoved her aside. 'They just fade away and die under the responsibility. Did ye ever see one go wrong with a sensible name like Cassiar, Siwash, or Husky? No, sir! Take a look at Shookum here, he's' –

Snap! The lean brute flashed up, the white teeth just missing Mason's throat.

'Ye will, will ye?' A shrewd clout behind the ear with the butt of the dogwhip stretched the animal in the snow, quivering softly, a yellow slaver dripping from its fangs.

'As I was saying, just look at Shookum, here – he's got the spirit. Bet ye he eats Carmen before the week's out.'

'I'll bank another proposition against that,' replied Malemute Kid, reversing the frozen bread placed before the fire to thaw. 'We'll eat Shookum before the trip is over. What d'ye say, Ruth?'

The Indian woman settled the coffee with a piece of ice, glanced from Malemute Kid to her husband, then at the dogs, but vouchsafed no reply. It was such a palpable truism that none was necessary. Two hundred miles of unbroken trail in prospect, with a scant six days' grub for themselves and none for the dogs, could admit no other alternative. The two men and the woman grouped about the fire and began their meagre meal. The dogs lay in their harnesses, for it was a midday halt, and watched each mouthful enviously.

'No more lunches after today,' said Malemute Kid. 'And we've got to keep a close eye on the dogs – they're getting vicious. They'd just as soon pull a fellow down as not, if they get a chance.'

'And I was president of an Epworth once, and taught in the Sunday school.' Having irrelevantly delivered himself of this,

Mason fell into a dreamy contemplation of his steaming moccasins, but was aroused by Ruth filling his cup. 'Thank God, we've
got slathers of tea! I've seen it growing, down in Tennessee. What
wouldn't I give for a hot corn pone just now! Never mind, Ruth;
you won't starve much longer, nor wear moccasins either.'

The woman threw off her gloom at this, and in her eyes welled
up a great love for her white lord – the first white man she had
ever seen – the first man whom she had known to treat a woman
as something better than a mere animal or beast of burden.

'Yes, Ruth,' continued her husband, having recourse to the
macaronic jargon in which it was alone possible for them to
understand each other; 'wait till we clean up and pull for the
Outside. We'll take the White Man's canoe and go to the Salt
Water. Yes, bad water, rough water – great mountains dance up
and down all the time. And so big, so far, so far away – you travel
ten sleep, twenty sleep, forty sleep' (he graphically enumerated
the days on his fingers), 'all the time water, bad water. Then you
come to great village, plenty people, just the same mosquitoes
next summer. Wigwams oh, so high – ten, twenty pines. Hi-yu
skookum!'

He paused impotently, cast an appealing glance at Malemute
Kid, then laboriously placed the twenty pines, end on end, by
sign language. Malemute Kid smiled with cheery cynicism; but
Ruth's eyes were wide with wonder, and with pleasure; for she
half believed he was joking, and such condescension pleased her
poor woman's heart.

'And then you step into a – a box, and pouf! up you go.' He
tossed his empty cup in the air by way of illustration, and as he
deftly caught it, cried: 'And biff! down you come. Oh, great
medicine-men! You go Fort Yukon, I go Arctic City – twenty-five
sleep – big string, all the time – I catch him string – I say, "Hello,
Ruth! How are ye?" – and you say, "Is that my good husband?" –
and I say "Yes," – and you say, "No can bake good bread, no
more soda," – then I say, "Look in cache, under flour; good-by."
You look and catch plenty soda. All the time you Fort Yukon, me
Arctic City. Hi-yu medicine-man!'

Ruth smiled so ingenuously at the fairy story, that both men
burst into laughter. A row among the dogs cut short the wonders
of the Outside, and by the time the snarling combatants were
separated, she had lashed the sleds and all was ready for the trail.

'Mush! Baldy! Hi! Mush on!' Mason worked his whip smartly, and as the dogs whined low in the traces, broke out the sled with the gee-pole. Ruth followed with the second team, leaving Malemute Kid, who had helped her start, to bring up the rear. Strong man, brute that he was, capable of felling an ox at a blow, he could not bear to beat the poor animals, but humored them as a dog-driver rarely does – nay, almost wept with them in their misery.

'Come, mush on there, you poor sore-footed brutes!' he murmured, after several ineffectual attempts to start the load. But his patience was at last rewarded, and though whimpering with pain, they hastened to join their fellows.

No more conversation; the toil of the trail will not permit such extravagance. And of all deadening labors, that of the Northland trail is the worst. Happy is the man who can weather a day's travel at the price of silence, and that on a beaten track.

And of all heart-breaking labors, that of breaking trail is the worst. At every step the great webbed shoe sinks till the snow is level with the knee. Then up, straight up, the deviation of a fraction of an inch being a certain precursor of disaster, the snowshoe must be lifted till the surface is cleared; then forward, down, and the other foot is raised perpendicularly for the matter of half a yard. He who tries this for the first time, if haply he avoids bringing his shoes in dangerous propinquity and measures not his length on the treacherous footing, will give up exhausted at the end of a hundred yards; he who can keep out of the way of the dogs for a whole day may well crawl into his sleeping-bag with a clear conscience and a pride which passeth all understanding; and he who travels twenty sleeps on the Long Trail is a man whom the gods may envy.

The afternoon wore on, and with the awe, born of the White Silence, the voiceless travelers bent to their work. Nature has many tricks wherewith she convinces man of his finity – the ceaseless flow of the tides, the fury of the storm, the shock of the earthquake, the long roll of heaven's artillery – but the most tremendous, the most stupefying of all, is the passive phase of the White Silence. All movement ceases, the sky clears, the heavens are as brass; the slightest whisper seems sacrilege, and man becomes timid, affrighted at the sound of his own voice. Sole speck of life journeying across the ghostly wastes of a dead world, he trembles at his audacity, realizes that his is a maggot's life, nothing more. Strange thoughts arise unsummoned, and the mystery of all things strives for utterance. And the fear of death, of God, of the universe, comes over him – the hope of the Resurrection and the Life, the yearning for immortality, the vain striving of the imprisoned essence – it is then, if ever, man walks alone with God.

So wore the day away. The river took a great bend, and Mason headed his team for the cut-off across the narrow neck of land. But the dogs balked at the high bank. Again and again, though Ruth and Malemute Kid were shoving on the sled, they slipped back. Then came the concerted effort. The miserable creatures weak from hunger, exerted their last strength. Up – up – the sled poised on the top of the bank; but the leader swung the string of dogs behind him to the right, fouling Mason's snowshoes. The result was grievous. Mason was whipped off his feet; one of the dogs fell in the traces; and the sled toppled back, dragging everything to the bottom again.

Slash! the whip fell among the dogs savagely, especially upon the one which had fallen.

'Don't, Mason,' entreated Malemute Kid; 'the poor devil's on its last legs. Wait and we'll put my team on.'

Mason deliberately withheld the whip till the last word had fallen, then out flashed the long lash, completely curling about the offending creature's body. Carmen – for it was Carmen – cowered in the snow, cried piteously, then rolled over on her side.

It was a tragic moment, a pitiful incident of the trail – a dying dog, two comrades in anger. Ruth glanced solicitously from man to man. But Malemute Kid restrained himself, though there was a world of reproach in his eyes, and bending over the dog, cut the traces. No word was spoken. The teams were double-spanned and the difficulty overcome; the sleds were under way again, the dying dog dragging herself along in the rear. As long as an animal can travel, it is not shot, and this last chance is accorded it – the crawling into camp, if it can, in the hope of a moose being killed.

Already penitent for his angry action, but too stubborn to make amends, Mason toiled on at the head of the cavalcade, little dreaming that danger hovered in the air. The timber clustered thick in the sheltered bottom, and through this they threaded their way. Fifty feet or more from the trail towered a lofty pine. For generations it had stood there, and for generations destiny had had this one end in view – perhaps the same had been decreed of Mason.

He stooped to fasten the loosened thong of his moccasin. The sleds came to a halt and the dogs lay down in the snow without a whimper. The stillness was weird; not a breath rustled the frost-encrusted forest; the cold and silence of outer space had chilled the heart and smote the trembling lips of nature. A sigh pulsed through the air – they did not seem to actually hear it, but rather felt it, like the premonition of movement in a motionless void. Then the great tree, burdened with its weight of years and snow, played its last part in the tragedy of life. He heard the warning crash and attempted to spring up, but almost erect, caught the blow squarely on the shoulder.

The sudden danger, the quick death – how often had Malemute Kid faced it! The pine needles were still quivering as he gave his commands and sprang into action. Nor did the Indian girl faint or raise her voice in idle wailing, as might many of her white sisters. At his order, she threw her weight on the end of a quickly extemporized handspike, easing the pressure and listening to her husband's groans, while Malemute Kid attacked the tree with his axe. The steel rang merrily as it bit into the frozen trunk, each stroke being accompanied by a forced, audible respiration, the 'Huh!' 'Huh!' of the woodsman.

At last the Kid laid the pitiable thing that was once a man in the snow. But worse than his comrade's pain was the dumb anguish in the woman's face, the blended look of hopeful, hopeless query. Little was said: those of the Northland are early taught the futility of words and the inestimable value of deeds. With the temperature at sixty-five below zero, a man cannot lie many minutes in the snow and live. So the sledlashings were cut, and the sufferer, rolled in furs, laid on a couch of boughs. Before him roared a fire, built of the very wood which wrought the mishap. Behind and partially over him was stretched the primitive fly – a piece of canvas, which caught the radiating heat and threw it back and down upon him – a trick which men may know who study physics at the fount.

And men who have shared their bed with death know when the call is sounded. Mason was terribly crushed. The most cursory examination revealed it. His right arm, leg, and back, were broken; his limbs were paralyzed from the hips; and the likelihood of internal injuries was large. An occasional moan was his only sign of life.

No hope; nothing to be done. The pitiless night crept slowly by – Ruth's portion, the despairing stoicism of her race, and Malemute Kid adding new lines to his face of bronze. In fact, Mason suffered least of all, for he spent his time in Eastern Tennessee, in the Great Smoky Mountains, living over the scenes of his childhood. And most pathetic was the melody of his long-forgotten Southern vernacular, as he raved of swimming-holes and coon-hunts and watermelon raids. It was as Greek to Ruth, but the Kid understood and felt – felt as only one can feel who has been shut out for years from all that civilization means.

Morning brought consciousness to the stricken man, and Malemute Kid bent closer to catch his whispers.

'You remember when we foregathered on the Tanana, four years come next ice-run? I didn't care so much for her then. It was more like she was pretty, and there was a smack of excitement about it, I think. But d'ye know, I've come to think a heap of her. She's been a good wife to me, always at my shoulder in the pitch. And when it comes to trading, you know there isn't her equal. D'ye recollect the time she shot the Moosehorn Rapids, to pull you and me off that rock, the bullets whipping the water like hailstones? – and the time of the famine at Nuklukyeto? – or when she raced the ice-run to bring the news? Yes, she's been a good wife to me, better'n that other one. Didn't know I'd been there? Never told you, eh? Well, I tried it once, down in the States. That's why I'm here. Been raised together, too. I came away to give her a chance for divorce. She got it.

'But that's got nothing to do with Ruth. I had thought of cleaning up and pulling for the Outside next year – her and I – but it's too late. Don't send her back to her people, Kid. It's beastly hard for a woman to go back. Think of it! – nearly four years on our bacon and beans and flour and dried fruit, and then to go back to her fish and cariboo. It's not good for her to have tried our ways, to come to know they're better'n her people's, and then return to them. Take care of her, Kid – why don't you – but no, you always fought shy of them – and you never told me why you came to this country. Be kind to her, and send her back to the States as soon as you can. But fix it so as she can come back – liable to get homesick, you know.

'And the youngster – it's drawn us closer, Kid. I only hope it is a boy. Think of it! – flesh of my flesh, Kid. He mustn't stop in this country. And if it's a girl, why she can't. Sell my furs; they'll fetch at least five thousand, and I've got as much more with the company. And handle my interests with yours. I think that bench claim will show up. See that he gets a good schooling; and Kid, above all, don't let him come back. This country was not made for white men.

'I'm a gone man, Kid. Three or four sleeps at the best. You've got to go on. You must go on! Remember, it's my wife, it's my boy – O God! I hope it's a boy! You can't stay by me – and I charge you, a dying man, to pull on.'

'Give me three days,' pleaded Malemute Kid. 'You may change for the better; something may turn up.'

'No.'

'Just three days.'

'You must pull on.'

'Two days.'

'It's my wife and my boy, Kid. You would not ask it.'

'One day.'

'No, no! I charge' –

'Only one day. We can shave it through on the grub, and I might knock over a moose.'

'No – all right; one day, but not a minute more. And Kid, don't – don't leave me to face it alone. Just a shot, one pull on the trigger. You understand. Think of it! Think of it! Flesh of my flesh, and I'll never live to see him!

'Send Ruth here. I want to say good-by and tell her that she must think of the boy and not wait till I'm dead. She might refuse to go with you if I didn't. Good-by, old man; good-by.

'Kid! I say – a – sink a hole above the pup, next to the slide. I panned out forty cents on my shovel there.

'And Kid!' he stooped lower to catch the last faint words, the dying man's surrender of his pride. 'I'm sorry – for – you know – Carmen.'

Leaving the girl crying softly over her man, Malemute Kid slipped into his *parka* and snowshoes, tucked his rifle under his arm, and crept away into the forest. He was no tyro in the stern sorrows of the Northland, but never had he faced so stiff a problem as this. In the abstract, it was a plain, mathematical proposition – three possible lives as against one doomed one. But now he hesitated. For five years, shoulder to shoulder, on the rivers and trails, in the camps and mines, facing death by field and flood and famine, had they knitted the bonds of their comradeship. So close was the tie, that he had often been conscious of a vague jealousy of Ruth, from the first time she had come between. And now it must be severed by his own hand.

Though he prayed for a moose, just one moose, all game seemed to have deserted the land, and nightfall found the exhausted man crawling into camp, light-handed, heavy-hearted. An uproar from the dogs and shrill cries from Ruth hastened him.

Bursting into the camp, he saw the girl in the midst of the snarling pack, laying about her with an axe. The dogs had broken the iron rule of their masters and were rushing the grub. He joined the issue with his rifle reversed, and the hoary game of natural selection was played out with all the ruthlessness of its primeval environment. Rifle and axe went up and down, hit or missed with monotonous regularity; lithe bodies flashed, with wild eyes and dripping fangs; and man and beast fought for supremacy to the bitterest conclusion. Then the beaten brutes crept to the edge of the firelight, licking their wounds, voicing their misery to the stars.

The whole stock of dried salmon had been devoured, and perhaps five pounds of flour remained to tide them over two hundred miles of wilderness. Ruth returned to her husband, while Malemute Kid cut up the warm body of one of the dogs, the skull of which had been crushed by the axe. Every portion was carefully put away, save the hide and offal, which were cast to his fellows of the moment before.

Morning brought fresh trouble. The animals were turning on each other. Carmen, who still clung to her slender thread of life, was downed by the pack. The lash fell among them unheeded. They cringed and cried under the blows, but refused to scatter till the last wretched bit had disappeared – bones, hide, hair, everything.

Malemute Kid went about his work, listening to Mason, who was back in Tennessee, delivering tangled discourses and wild exhortations to his brethren of other days.

Taking advantage of neighboring pines, he worked rapidly, and Ruth watched him make a cache similar to those sometimes used by hunters to preserve their meat from the wolverines and dogs. One after the other, he bent the tops of two small pines toward each other and nearly to the ground, making them fast with thongs of moosehide. Then he beat the dogs into submission and harnessed them to two of the sleds, loading the same with everything but the furs which enveloped Mason. These he wrapped and lashed tightly about him, fastening either end of the robes to the bent pines. A single stroke of his hunting-knife would release them and send the body high in the air.

Ruth had received her husband's last wishes and made no struggle. Poor girl, she had learned the lesson of obedience well. From a child, she had bowed, and seen all women bow, to the lords of creation, and it did not seem in the nature of things for woman to resist. The Kid permitted her one outburst of grief, as she kissed her husband – her own people had no such custom – then led her to the foremost sled and helped her into her snowshoes. Blindly, instinctively, she took the gee-pole and whip, and 'mushed' the dogs out on the trail. Then he returned to Mason, who had fallen into a coma; and long after she was out of sight, crouched by the fire, waiting, hoping, praying for his comrade to die.

It is not pleasant to be alone with painful thoughts in the White Silence. The silence of gloom is merciful, shrouding one as with protection and breathing a thousand intangible sympathies; but the bright White Silence, clear and cold, under steely skies, is pitiless.

An hour passed – two hours – but the man would not die. At high noon, the sun, without raising its rim above the southern horizon, threw a suggestion of fire athwart the heavens, then quickly drew it back. Malemute Kid roused and dragged himself to his comrade's side. He cast one glance about him. The White Silence seemed to sneer, and a great fear came upon him. There was a sharp report; Mason swung into his aerial sepulchre; and Malemute Kid lashed the dogs into a wild gallop as he fled across the snow.

The God of his Fathers (1901; 1902)

1

On every hand stretched the forest primeval – the home of noisy comedy and silent tragedy. Here the struggle for survival continued to wage with all its ancient brutality. Briton and Russian were still to overlap in the Land of the Rainbow's End – and this was the very heart of it – nor had Yankee gold yet purchased its vast domain. The wolf-pack still clung to the flank of the cariboo-herd, singling out the weak and the big with calf, and pulling them down as remorselessly as were it a thousand, thousand generations into the past. The sparse aborigines still acknowledged the rule of their chiefs and medicine men, drove out bad spirits, burned their witches, fought their neighbors, and ate their enemies with a relish which spoke well of their bellies. But it was at the moment when the stone age was drawing to a close. Already, over unknown trails and chartless wildernesses, were the harbingers of the steel arriving – fair-faced, blue-eyed, indomitable men, incarnations of the unrest of their race. By accident or design, single-handed and in twos and threes, they came from no one knew whither, and fought, or died, or passed on, no one knew whence. The priests raged against them, the chiefs called forth their fighting men, and stone clashed with steel; but to little purpose. Like water seeping from some mighty reservoir, they trickled through the dark forests and mountain passes, threading the highways in bark canoes, or with their moccasined feet breaking trail for the wolf-dogs. They came of a great breed, and their mothers were many; but the fur-clad denizens of the Northland had this yet to learn. So many an unsung wanderer fought his last and died under the cold fire of the aurora, as did his brothers in burning sands and reeking jungles, and as they shall continue to do till in the fulness of time the destiny of their race be achieved.

It was near twelve. Along the northern horizon a rosy glow, fading to the west and deepening to the east, marked the unseen dip of the midnight sun. The gloaming and the dawn were so commingled that there was no night – simply a wedding of day with day, a scarcely perceptible blending of two circles of the sun. A kildee timidly chirped good-night; the full, rich throat of a robin proclaimed good-morrow. From an island on the breast of the Yukon a colony of wild fowl voiced its interminable wrongs, while a loon laughed mockingly back across a still stretch of river.

In the foreground, against the bank of a lazy eddy, birch-bark canoes were lined two and three deep. Ivory-bladed spears, bone-barbed arrows, buckskin-thonged bows, and simple basket-woven traps bespoke the fact that in the muddy current of the river the salmon-run was on. In the background, from the tangle of skin tents and drying frames, rose the voices of the fisher folk. Bucks skylarked with bucks or flirted with the maidens, while the older squaws, shut out from this by virtue of having fulfilled the end of their existence in reproduction, gossiped as they braided rope from the green roots of trailing vines. At their feet their naked progeny played and squabbled, or rolled in the muck with the tawny wolf-dogs.

To one side of the encampment, and conspicuously apart from it, stood a second camp of two tents. But it was a white man's camp. If nothing else, the choice of position at least bore convincing evidence of this. In case of offense, it commanded the Indian quarters a hundred yards away; of defense, a rise to the ground and the cleared intervening space; and last, of defeat, the swift slope of a score of yards to the canoes below. From one of the tents came the petulant cry of a sick child and the crooning song of a mother. In the open, over the smoldering embers of a fire, two men held talk.

'Eh? I love the church like a good son. *Bien!* So great a love that my days have been spent in fleeing away from her, and my nights in dreaming dreams of reckoning. Look you!' The half-breed's voice rose to an angry snarl. 'I am Red Liver born. My father was white – as white as you. But you are Yankee, and he was British bred, and a gentleman's son. And my mother was the daughter of a chief, and I was a man. Ay, and one had to look the second time to see what manner of blood ran in my veins; for I lived with the whites, and was one of them, and my father's heart beat in me. It happened there was a maiden – white – who looked on me with kind eyes. Her father had much land and many horses, also he was a big man among his people, and his blood was the blood of the French. He said the girl knew not her own mind, and talked overmuch with her, and became wroth that such things should be.

'But she knew her mind, for we came quick before the priest. And quicker had come her father, with lying words, false promises, I know not what; so that the priest stiffened his neck and would not make us that we might live one with the other. As at the beginning it was the church which would not bless my birth, so now it was the church which refused me marriage and put the blood of men upon my hands. *Bien!* Thus have I cause to love the church. So I struck the priest on his woman's mouth, and we took swift horses, the girl and I, to Fort Pierre, where was a minister of good heart. But hot on our trail was her father, and brothers, and other men he had gathered to him. And we fought, our horses on the run, till I emptied three saddles and the rest drew off and went on to Fort Pierre. Then we took east, the girl and I, to the hills and forests, and we lived one with the other, and we were not married – the work of the good church which I love like a son.

'But mark you, for this is the strangeness of woman, the way of which no man may understand. One of the saddles I emptied was that of her father's, and the hoofs of those who came behind had pounded him into the earth. This we saw, the girl and I, and this I had forgot had she not remembered. And in the quiet of the evening, after the day's hunt were done, it came between us, and in the silence of the night when we lay beneath the stars and should have been one. It was there always. She never spoke, but it sat by our fire and held us ever apart. She tried to put it aside, but at such times it would rise up till I could read it in the look of her eyes, in the very in-take of her breath.

'So in the end she bore me a child, a woman-child, and died. Then I went among my mother's people, that it might nurse at a warm breast and live. But my hands were wet with the blood of men, look you, because of the church, wet with the blood of men. And the Riders of the North came for me, but my mother's brother, who was then chief in his own right, hid me and gave me horses and food. And we went away, my woman-child and I, even to the Hudson Bay Country, where white men were few and the questions they asked not many. And I worked for the company as a hunter, as a guide, as a driver of dogs, till my woman-child was become a woman, tall, and slender, and fair to the eye.

'You know the winter, long and lonely, breeding evil thoughts and bad deeds. The Chief Factor was a hard man, and bold. And he was not such that a woman would delight in looking upon. But he cast eyes upon my woman-child who was become a woman. Mother of God! he sent me away on a long trip with the dogs, that he might – you understand, he was a hard man and without heart. She was most white and her soul was white, and a good woman, and – well, she died.

'It was bitter cold the night of my return, and I had been away months, and the dogs were limping sore when I came to the fort. The Indians and breeds looked on me in silence, and I felt the fear of I knew not what, but I said nothing till the dogs were fed and I had eaten as a man with work before him should. Then I spoke up, demanding the word, and they shrank from me, afraid of my anger and what I should do; but the story came out, the pitiful story, word for word and act for act, and they marveled that I should be so quiet.

'When they had done I went to the Factor's house, calmer than now in the telling of it. He had been afraid and called upon the breeds to help him; but they were not pleased with the deed, and had left him to lie on the bed he had made. So he had fled to the house of the priest. Thither I followed. But when I was come to that place, the priest stood in my way, and spoke soft words, and said a man in anger should go neither to the right nor left, but straight to God. I asked by the right of a father's wrath that he give me past, but he said only over his body, and besought with me to pray. Look you, it was the church, always the church; for I passed over his body and sent the Factor to meet my woman-child before his god, which is a bad god, and the god of the white men.

'Then was there hue and cry, for word was sent to the station below, and I came away. Through the Land of the Great Slave, down the Valley of the Mackenzie to the never-opening ice, over the White Rockies, past the Great Curve of the Yukon, even to this place did I come. And from that day to this, yours is the first face of my father's people I have looked upon. May it be the last! These people, which are my people, are a simple folk, and I have been raised to honor among them. My word is their law, and their priests but do my bidding, else would I not suffer them.

When I speak for them I speak for myself. We ask to be let alone. We do not want your kind. If we permit you to sit by our fires, after you will come your church, your priests, and your gods. And know this, for each white man who comes to my village, him will I make deny his god. You are the first, and I give you grace. So it were well you go, and go quickly.'

'I am not responsible for my brothers,' the second man spoke up, filling his pipe in a meditative manner. Hay Stockard was at times as thoughtful of speech as he was wanton of action; but only at times.

'But I know your breed,' responded the other. 'Your brothers are many, and it is you and yours who break the trail for them to follow. In time they shall come to possess the land, but not in my time. Already, have I heard, are they on the head-reaches of the Great River, and far away below are the Russians.'

Hay Stockard lifted his head with a quick start. This was startling geographical information. The Hudson Bay post at Fort Yukon had other notions concerning the course of the river, believing it to flow into the Arctic.

'Then the Yukon empties into Bering Sea?' he asked.

'I do not know, but below there are Russians, many Russians. Which is neither here nor there. You may go on and see for yourself; you may go back to your brothers; but up the Koyukuk you shall not go while the priests and fighting men do my bidding. Thus do I command, I, Baptiste the Red, whose word is law and who am head man over this people.'

'And should I not go down to the Russians, or back to my brothers?'

'Then shall you go swift-footed before your god, which is a bad god, and the god of the white men.'

The red sun shot up above the northern skyline, dripping and bloody. Baptiste the Red came to his feet, nodded curtly, and went back to his camp amid the crimson shadows and the singing of the robins.

Hay Stockard finished his pipe by the fire, picturing in smoke and coal the unknown upper reaches of the Koyukuk, the strange stream which ended here its arctic travels and merged its waters with the muddy Yukon flood. Somewhere up there, if the dying words of a shipwrecked sailorman who had made the fearful overland journey were to be believed, and if the vial of golden grains in his pouch attested to anything – somewhere up there, in that home of winter, stood the Treasure House of the North. And as keeper of the gate, Baptiste the Red, English half-breed and renegade, barred the way.

'Bah!' He kicked the embers apart and rose to his full height, arms lazily outstretched, facing the flushing north with careless soul.

2

Hay Stockard swore, harshly, in the rugged monosyllables of his mother tongue. His wife lifted her gaze from the pots and pans, and followed his in a keen scrutiny of the river. She was a woman of the Teslin Country, wise in the ways of her husband's vernacular when it grew intensive. From the slipping of a snowshoe thong to the forefront of sudden death, she could gauge occasion by the pitch and volume of his blasphemy. So she knew the present occasion merited attention. A long canoe, with paddles flashing back the rays of the westering sun, was crossing the current from above and urging in for the eddy. Hay Stockard watched it intently. Three men rose and dipped, rose and dipped, in rhythmical precision; but a red bandanna, wrapped about the head of one, caught and held his eye.

'Bill!' he called. 'Oh, Bill!'

A shambling, loose-jointed giant rolled out of one of the tents, yawning and rubbing the sleep from his eyes. Then he sighted the strange canoe and was wide awake on the instant.

'By the jumping Methuselah! That damned sky-pilot!'

Hay Stockard nodded his head bitterly, half-reached for his rifle, then shrugged his shoulders.

'Pot-shot him,' Bill suggested, 'and settle the thing out of hand. He'll spoil us sure if we don't.' But the other declined this drastic measure and turned away, at the same time bidding the woman return to her work, and calling Bill back from the bank. The two Indians in the canoe moored it on the edge of the eddy, while its white occupant, conspicuous by his gorgeous head-gear, came up the bank.

'Like Paul of Tarsus, I give you greeting. Peace be unto you and grace before the Lord.'

His advances were met sullenly, and without speech.

'To you, Hay Stockard, blasphemer and Philistine, greeting. In your heart is the lust of Mammon, in your mind cunning devils, in your tent this woman whom you live with in adultery; yet of these divers sins, even here in the wilderness, I, Sturges Owen, apostle to the Lord, bid you to repent and cast from you your iniquities.'

'Save your cant! Save your cant!' Hay Stockard broke in testily. 'You'll need all you've got, and more, for Red Baptiste over yonder.'

He waved his hand toward the Indian camp, where the half-breed was looking steadily across, striving to make out the newcomers. Sturges Owen, disseminator of light and apostle to the Lord, stepped to the edge of the steep and commanded his men to bring up the camp outfit. Stockard followed him.

'Look here,' he demanded, plucking the missionary by the shoulder and twirling him about. 'Do you value your hide?'

'My life is in the Lord's keeping, and I do but work in His vineyard,' he replied solemnly.

'Oh, stow that! Are you looking for a job of martyrship?'

'If He so wills.'

'Well, you'll find it right here, but I'm going to give you some advice first. Take it or leave it. If you stop here, you'll be cut off in the midst of your labors. And not you alone, but your men, Bill, my wife –'

'Who is a daughter of Belial and hearkeneth not to the true Gospel.'

'And myself. Not only do you bring trouble upon yourself, but upon us. I was frozen in with you last winter, as you will well recollect, and I know you for a good man and a fool. If you think it your duty to strive with the heathen, well and good; but do exercise some wit in the way you go about it. This man, Red Baptiste, is no Indian. He comes of our common stock, is as bull-necked as I ever dared be, and as wild a fanatic the one way as you are the other. When you two come together, he'll be to pay, and I don't care to be mixed up in it. Understand? So take my advice and go away. If you go down-stream, you'll fall in with the Russians. There's bound to be Greek priests among them, and they'll see you safe through to Bering Sea – that's where the Yukon empties – and from there it won't be hard to get back to civilization. Take my word for it and get out of here as fast as God'll let you.'

'He who carries the Lord in his heart and the Gospel in his hand hath no fear of the machinations of man or devil,' the

missionary answered stoutly. 'I will see this man and wrestle
with him. One backslider returned to the fold is a greater victory
than a thousand heathen. He who is strong for evil can be as
mighty for good, witness Saul when he journeyed up to
Damascus to bring Christian captives to Jerusalem. And the voice
of the Savior came to him, crying, "Saul, Saul, why persecutest
thou me?" And therewith Paul arrayed himself on the side of the
Lord, and thereafter was most mighty in the saving of souls. And
even as thou, Paul of Tarsus, even so do I work in the vineyard of
the Lord, bearing trials and tribulations, scoffs and sneers, stripes
and punishments, for His dear sake.'

'Bring up the little bag with the tea and a kettle of water,' he
called the next instant to his boatmen; 'not forgetting the haunch
of cariboo and the mixing-pan.'

When his men, converts by his own hand, had gained the
bank, the trio fell to their knees, hands and backs burdened with
camp equipage, and offered up thanks for their passage through
the wilderness and their safe arrival. Hay Stockard looked upon
the function with sneering disapproval, the romance and solem-
nity of it lost to his matter-of-fact soul. Baptiste the Red, still
gazing across, recognized the familiar postures, and remembered
the girl who had shared his star-roofed couch in the hills and
forests, and the woman-child who lay somewhere by bleak
Hudson's Bay.

3

'Confound it, Baptiste, couldn't think of it. Not for a moment.
Grant that this man is a fool and of small use in the nature of
things, but still, you know, I can't give him up.'

Hay Stockard paused, striving to put into speech the rude
ethics of his heart.

'He's worried me, Baptiste, in the past and now, and caused me
all manner of troubles; but can't you see, he's my own breed –
white – and – and – why, I couldn't buy my life with his, not if he
was a nigger.'

'So be it,' Baptiste the Red made answer. 'I have given you
grace and choice. I shall come presently, with my priests and
fighting men, and either shall I kill you, or you deny your god.
Give up the priest to my pleasure, and you shall depart in peace.
Otherwise your trail ends here. My people are against you to the

babies. Even now have the children stolen away your canoes.' He pointed down to the river. Naked boys had slipped down the water from the point above, cast loose the canoes, and by then had worked them into the current. When they had drifted out of rifle-shot they clambered over the sides and paddled ashore.

'Give me the priest, and you may have them back again. Come! Speak your mind, but without haste.'

Stockard shook his head. His glance dropped to the woman of the Teslin Country with his boy at her breast, and he would have wavered had he not lifted his eyes to the men before him.

'I am not afraid,' Sturges Owen spoke up. 'The Lord bears me in his right hand, and alone am I ready to go into the camp of the unbeliever. It is not too late. Faith may move mountains. Even in the eleventh hour may I win his soul to the true righteousness.'

'Trip the beggar up and make him fast,' Bill whispered hoarsely in the ear of his leader, while the missionary kept the floor and wrestled with the heathen. 'Make him hostage, and bore him if they get ugly.'

'No,' Stockard answered. 'I gave him my word that he could speak with us unmolested. Rules of warfare, Bill; rules of warfare. He's been on the square, given us warning, and all that, and – why, damn it, man, I can't break my word!'

'He'll keep his, never fear.'

'Don't doubt it, but I won't let a half-breed outdo me in fair dealing. Why not do what he wants – give him the missionary and be done with it?'

'N-no,' Bill hesitated doubtfully.

'Shoe pinches, eh?'

Bill flushed a little and dropped the discussion. Baptiste the Red was still waiting the final decision. Stockard went up to him.

'It's this way, Baptiste. I came to your village minded to go up the Koyukuk. I intended no wrong. My heart was clean of evil. It is still clean. Along comes this priest, as you call him. I didn't bring him here. He'd have come whether I was here or not. But now that he is here, being of my people, I've got to stand by him. And I'm going to. Further, it will be no child's play. When you have done, your village will be silent and empty, your people wasted as after a famine. True, we will be gone; likewise the pick of your fighting men –'

'But those who remain shall be in peace, nor shall the word of strange gods and the tongues of strange priests be buzzing in their ears.'

Both men shrugged their shoulders and turned away, the half-breed going back to his own camp. The missionary called his two men to him, and they fell into prayer. Stockard and Bill attacked the few standing pines with their axes, felling them into convenient breastworks. The child had fallen asleep, so the woman placed it on a heap of furs and lent a hand in fortifying the camp. Three sides were thus defended, the steep declivity at the rear precluding attack from that direction. When these arrangements had been completed, the two men stalked into the open, clearing away, here and there, the scattered underbrush. From the opposing camp came the booming of war-drums and the voices of the priests stirring the people to anger.

'Worst of it is they'll come in rushes,' Bill complained as they walked back with shouldered axes.

'And wait till midnight, when the light gets dim for shooting.'

'Can't start the ball a-rolling too early, then.' Bill exchanged the axe for a rifle, and took a careful rest. One of the medicine-men, towering above his tribesmen, stood out distinctly. Bill drew a bead on him.

'All ready?' he asked.

Stockard opened the ammunition box, placed the woman where she could reload in safety, and gave the word. The medicine-man dropped. For a moment there was silence, then a wild howl went up and a flight of bone arrows fell short.

'I'd like to take a look at the beggar,' Bill remarked, throwing a fresh shell into place. 'I'll swear I drilled him clean between the eyes.'

'Didn't work.' Stockard shook his head gloomily. Baptiste had evidently quelled the more warlike of his followers, and instead of precipitating an attack in the bright light of day, the shot had caused a hasty exodus, the Indians drawing out of the village beyond the zone of fire.

In the full tide of his proselyting fervor, borne along by the hand of God, Sturges Owen would have ventured alone into the camp of the unbeliever, equally prepared for miracle or martyr-dom; but in the waiting which ensued, the fever of conviction died away gradually, as the natural man asserted itself. Physical fear replaced spiritual hope; the love of life, the love of God. It was no new experience. He could feel his weakness coming on, and knew it of old time. He had struggled against it and been overcome by it before.

He remembered when the other men had driven their paddles like mad in the van of a roaring ice-flood, how, at the critical moment, in a panic of worldly terror, he had dropped his paddle and besought wildly with his God for pity. And there were other times. The recollection was not pleasant. It brought shame to him that his spirit should be so weak and his flesh so strong. But the love of life! the love of life! He could not strip it from him. Because of it had his dim ancestors perpetuated their line; because of it was he destined to perpetuate his. His courage, if courage it might be called, was bred of fanaticism. The courage of Stockard and Bill was the adherence to deep-rooted ideals. Not that the love of life was less, but the love of race tradition more; not that they were unafraid to die, but that they were brave enough not to live at the price of shame.

The missionary rose, for the moment swayed by the mood of sacrifice. He half crawled over the barricade to proceed to the other camp, but sank back, a trembling mass, wailing: 'As the spirit moves! As the spirit moves! Who am I that I should set aside the judgments of God? Before the foundations of the world were all things written in the book of life. Worm that I am, shall I erase the page or any portion thereof? As God wills, so shall the spirit move!'

Bill reached over, plucked him to his feet, and shook him, fiercely, silently. Then he dropped the bundle of quivering nerves and turned his attention to the two converts. But they showed little fright and a cheerful alacrity in preparing for the coming passage at arms.

Stockard, who had been talking in undertones with the Teslin woman, now turned to the missionary.

'Fetch him over here,' he commanded of Bill.

'Now,' he ordered, when Sturges Owen had been duly deposited before him, 'make us man and wife, and be lively about it.' Then he added apologetically to Bill: 'No telling how it's to end, so I just thought I'd get my affairs straightened up.'

The woman obeyed the behest of her white lord. To her the ceremony was meaningless. By her lights she was his wife, and had been from the day they first foregathered. The converts served as witnesses. Bill stood over the missionary, prompting him when he stumbled. Stockard put the responses in the woman's mouth, and when the time came, for want of better, ringed her finger with thumb and forefinger of his own.

'Kiss the bride!' Bill thundered, and Sturges Owen was too weak to disobey.

'Now baptize the child!'

'Neat and tidy,' Bill commented.

'Gathering the proper outfit for a new trail,' the father explained, taking the boy from the mother's arms. 'I was grub-staked, once, into the Cascades, and had everything in the kit except salt. Never shall forget it. And if the woman and the kid cross the divide tonight they might as well be prepared for pot-luck. A long shot, Bill, between ourselves, but nothing lost if it misses.'

A cup of water served the purpose, and the child was laid away in a secure corner of the barricade. The men built the fire, and the evening meal was cooked.

The sun hurried round to the north, sinking closer to the horizon. The heavens in that quarter grew red and bloody. The shadows lengthened, the light dimmed, and in the somber recesses of the forest life slowly died away. Even the wild fowl in the river softened their raucous chatter and feigned the nightly farce of going to bed. Only the tribesmen increased their clamor, war-drums booming and voices raised in savage folk songs. But as the sun dipped they ceased their tumult. The rounded hush of midnight was complete. Stockard rose to his knees and peered over the logs. Once the child wailed in pain and disconcerted him. The mother bent over it, but it slept again. The silence was interminable, profound. Then, of a sudden, the robins burst into full-throated song. The night had passed.

A flood of dark figures boiled across the open. Arrows whistled and bow-thongs sang. The shrill-tongued rifles answered back. A spear, and a mighty cast, transfixed the Teslin woman as she hovered above the child. A spent arrow, diving between the logs, lodged in the missionary's arm.

There was no stopping the rush. The middle distance was cumbered with bodies, but the rest surged on, breaking against and over the barricade like an ocean wave. Sturges Owen fled to the tent, while the men were swept from their feet, buried beneath the human tide. Hay Stockard alone regained the surface, flinging the tribesmen aside like yelping curs. He had managed to seize an axe. A dark hand grasped the child by a naked foot, and drew it from beneath its mother. At arm's length its puny body circled through the air, dashing to death against the logs. Stockard clove the man to the chin and fell to clearing space. The ring of savage faces closed in, raining upon him spear-thrusts and bone-barbed arrows. The sun shot up, and they swayed back and forth in the crimson shadows. Twice, with his axe blocked by too deep a blow, they rushed him; but each time he flung them clear. They fell underfoot and he trampled dead and dying, the way slippery with blood. And still the day brightened and the robins sang. Then they drew back from him in awe, and he leaned breathless upon his axe.

'Blood of my soul!' cried Baptiste the Red. 'But thou art a man. Deny thy god, and thou shalt yet live.'

Stockard swore his refusal, feebly but with grace.

'Behold! A woman!' Sturges Owen had been brought before the half-breed.

Beyond a scratch on the arm, he was uninjured, but his eyes roved about him in an ecstasy of fear. The heroic figure of the blasphemer, bristling with wounds and arrows, leaning defiantly upon his axe, indifferent, indomitable, superb, caught his wavering vision. And he felt a great envy of the man who could go down serenely to the dark gates of death. Surely Christ, and not he, Sturges Owen, had been moulded in such manner. And why not he? He felt dimly the curse of ancestry, the feebleness of spirit which had come down to him out of the past, and he felt an anger at the creative force, symbolize it as he would, which had formed him, its servant, so weakly. For even a stronger man, this anger and the stress of circumstance were sufficient to breed apostasy, and for Sturges Owen it was inevitable. In the fear of man's anger he would dare the wrath of God. He had been raised up to serve the Lord only that he might be cast down. He had been given faith without the strength of faith; he had been given spirit without the power of spirit. It was unjust.

'Where now is thy god?' the half-breed demanded.

'I do not know.' He stood straight and rigid, like a child repeating a catechism.

'Hast thou then a god at all?'

'I had.'

'And now?'

'No.'

Hay Stockard swept the blood from his eyes and laughed. The

missionary looked at him curiously, as in a dream. A feeling of infinite distance came over him, as though of a great remove. In that which had transpired, and which was to transpire, he had no part. He was a spectator – at a distance, yes, at a distance. The words of Baptiste came to him faintly:

'Very good. See that this man go free, and that no harm befall him. Let him depart in peace. Give him a canoe and food. Set his face toward the Russians, that he may tell their priests of Baptiste the Red, in whose country there is no god.'

They led him to the edge of the steep, where they paused to witness the final tragedy. The half-breed turned to Hay Stockard.

'There is no god,' he prompted.

The man laughed in reply. One of the young men poised a war-spear for the cast.

'Hast thou a god?'

'Ay, the God of my fathers.'

He shifted the axe for a better grip. Baptiste the Red gave the sign, and the spear hurtled full against his breast. Sturges Owen saw the ivory head stand out beyond his back, saw the man sway, laughing, and snap the shaft short as he fell upon it. Then he went down to the river, that he might carry to the Russians the message of Baptiste the Red, in whose country there was no god.

To Build a Fire (1902)

For land travel or seafaring, the world over, a companion is usually considered desirable. In the Klondike, as Tom Vincent found out, such a companion is absolutely essential. But he found it out, not by precept, but through bitter experience.

'Never travel alone,' is a precept of the north. He had heard it many times and laughed; for he was a strapping young fellow, big-boned and big-muscled, with faith in himself and in the strength of his head and hands.

It was on a bleak January day when the experience came that taught him respect for the frost, and for the wisdom of the men who had battled with it.

He had left Calumet Camp on the Yukon with a light pack on his back, to go up Paul Creek to the divide between it and Cherry Creek, where his party was prospecting and hunting moose.

The frost was sixty degrees below zero, and he had thirty miles of lonely trail to cover, but he did not mind. In fact, he enjoyed it, swinging along through the silence, his blood pounding warmly through his veins, and his mind carefree and happy. For he and his comrades were certain they had struck 'pay' up there on the Cherry Creek Divide; and, further, he was returning to them from Dawson with cheery home letters from the States.

At seven o'clock, when he turned the heels of his moccasins toward Calumet Camp, it was still black night. And when day broke at half past nine he had made the four-mile cut-off across the flats and was six miles up Paul Creek. The trail, which had seen little travel, followed the bed of the creek, and there was no possibility of his getting lost. He had gone to Dawson by way of Cherry Creek and Indian River, so Paul Creek was new and strange. By half past eleven he was at the forks, which had been described to him, and he knew he had covered fifteen miles, half the distance.

He knew that in the nature of things the trail was bound to grow worse from there on, and thought that, considering the good time he had made, he merited lunch. Casting off his pack and taking a seat on a fallen tree, he unmittened his right hand, reached inside his shirt next to the skin, and fished out a couple of biscuits sandwiched with sliced bacon and wrapped in a handkerchief – the only way they could be carried without freezing solid.

He had barely chewed the first mouthful when his numbing fingers warned him to put his mitten on again. This he did, not without surprise at the bitter swiftness with which the frost bit in. Undoubtedly it was the coldest snap he had ever experienced, he thought.

He spat upon the snow – a favorite northland trick – and the sharp crackle of the instantly congealed spittle startled him. The spirit thermometer at Calumet had registered sixty below when he left, but he was certain it had grown much colder, how much colder he could not imagine.

Half of the first biscuit was yet untouched, but he could feel himself beginning to chill – a thing most unusual for him. This would never do, he decided, and slipping the pack-straps across his shoulders, he leaped to his feet and ran briskly up the trail.

A few minutes of this made him warm again, and he settled down to a steady stride, munching the biscuits as he went along. The moisture that exhaled with his breath crusted his lips and mustache with pendent ice and formed a miniature glacier on his chin. Now and again sensation forsook his nose and cheeks, and he rubbed them till they burned with the returning blood.

Most men wore nose-straps; his partners did, but he had scorned such 'feminine contraptions', and till now had never felt the need of them. Now he did feel the need, for he was rubbing constantly.

Nevertheless he was aware of a thrill of joy, of exultation. He was doing something, achieving something, mastering the elements. Once he laughed aloud in sheer strength of life, and with his clenched fist defied the frost. He was its master. What he did he did in spite of it. It could not stop him. He was going on to the Cherry Creek Divide.

Strong as were the elements, he was stronger. At such times animals crawled away into their holes and remained in hiding. But he did not hide. He was out in it, facing it, fighting it. He was a man, a master of things.

In such fashion, rejoicing proudly, he tramped on. After half an hour he rounded a bend, where the creek ran close to the mountainside, and came upon one of the most insignificant-appearing but most formidable dangers in northern travel.

The creek itself was frozen solid to its rocky bottom, but from the mountain came the outflow of several springs. These springs never froze, and the only effect of the severest cold snaps was to lessen their discharge. Protected from the frost by the blanket of snow, the water of these springs seeped down into the creek, and, on top of the creek ice, formed shallow pools.

The surface of these pools, in turn, took on a skin of ice which grew thicker and thicker, until the water overran, and so formed a second ice-skinned pool above the first.

Thus at the bottom was the solid creek ice, then probably six to eight inches of water, then a thin ice-skin, then another six inches of water and another ice-skin. And on top of this last skin was about an inch of recent snow to make the trap complete.

To Tom Vincent's eye the unbroken snow surface gave no warning of the lurking danger. As the crust was thicker at the edge, he was well toward the middle before he broke through.

In itself it was a very insignificant mishap – a man does not drown in twelve inches of water – but in its consequences as serious an accident as could possibly befall him.

At the instant he broke through he felt the cold water strike his feet and ankles, and with half a dozen lunges he made the bank. He was quite cool and collected. The thing to do, and the only thing to do, was to build a fire. For another precept of the north runs: *Travel with wet socks down to twenty below zero; after that build a fire.* And it was three times twenty below and colder, and he knew it.

He knew, further, that great care must be exercised; that with failure at the first attempt, the chance was made greater for failure at the second attempt. In short, he knew that there must be no failure. The moment before a strong, exulting man, boastful of his mastery of the elements, he was now fighting for his life against those same elements – such was the difference caused by the injection of a quart of water into a northland traveler's calculations.

In a clump of pines on the rim of the bank the spring high-water had lodged many twigs and small branches. Thoroughly dried by the summer sun, they now waited the match.

It is impossible to build a fire with heavy Alaskan mittens on one's hands, so Vincent bared his, gathered a sufficient number of twigs, and knocking the snow from them, knelt down to kindle his fire. From an inside pocket he drew out his matches and a strip of thin birch bark. The matches were of the Klondike kind, sulphur matches, one hundred in a bunch.

He noticed how quickly his fingers had chilled as he separated one match from the bunch and scratched it on his trousers. The birch bark, like the dryest of paper, burst into bright flame. This he carefully fed with the smallest twigs and finest débris, cherishing the flame with the utmost care. It did not do to hurry things, as he well knew, and although his fingers were now quite stiff, he did not hurry.

After the first quick, biting sensation of cold, his feet had ached with a heavy, dull ache and were rapidly growing numb. But the fire, although a very young one, was now a success, and he knew that a little snow, briskly rubbed, would speedily cure his feet.

But at the moment he was adding the first thick twigs to the fire a grievous thing happened. The pine boughs above his head were burdened with a four months' snowfall, and so finely adjusted were the burdens that his slight movements in collecting the twigs had been sufficient to disturb the balance.

The snow from the topmost bough was the first to fall, striking and dislodging the snow on the boughs beneath. And all this snow, accumulating as it fell, smote Tom Vincent's head and shoulders and blotted out his fire.

He still kept his presence of mind, for he knew how great his danger was. He started at once to rebuild the fire, but his fingers were now so cold that he could not bend them, and he was forced to pick up each twig and splinter between the tips of the fingers of either hand.

When he came to the match he encountered great difficulty in separating one from the bunch. This he succeeded in managing, however, and also, by a great effort, in clutching the match between his thumb and forefinger. But in scratching it, he dropped it in the snow and could not pick it up again.

He stood up, desperate. He could not feel even his weight on his feet, although the ankles were aching painfully. Putting on his mittens, he stepped to one side, so that the snow would not fall upon the new fire he was to build, and beat his hands violently against a tree-trunk.

This enabled him to separate and strike a second match and to set fire to the remaining fragment of birch bark. But his body had now begun to chill and he was shivering, so that when he tried to add the first twigs his hand shook and the tiny flame was quenched.

The frost had beaten him. His hands were worthless. But he had the foresight to drop the bunch of matches into his wide-mouthed outside pocket before he slipped on his mittens in despair, and started to run up the trail. One cannot run the frost out of wet feet at sixty below and colder, however, as he quickly discovered.

He came round a sharp turn of the creek to where he could look ahead for a mile. But there was no help, no sign of help, only the white trees and the white hills, the quiet cold and the brazen silence! If only he had a comrade whose feet were not freezing, he thought, only such a comrade to start the fire that could save him!

Then his eyes chanced upon another high-water lodgment of twigs and leaves and branches. If he could strike a match, all might yet be well. With stiff fingers which he could not bend, he got out a bunch of matches, but found it impossible to separate them.

He sat down and awkwardly shuffled the bunch about on his knees, until he got it resting on his palm with the sulphur ends projecting, somewhat in the manner the blade of a hunting-knife would project when clutched in the fist.

But his fingers stood straight out. They could not clutch. This he overcame by pressing the wrist of the other hand against them, and so forcing them down upon the bunch. Time and again, holding thus by both hands, he scratched the bunch on his leg and finally ignited it. But the flame burned into the flesh of his hand, and he involuntarily relaxed his hold. The bunch fell into the snow, and while he tried vainly to pick it up, sizzled and went out.

Again he ran, by this time badly frightened. His feet were utterly devoid of sensation. He stubbed his toes once on a buried log, but beyond pitching him into the snow and wrenching his back, it gave him no feelings.

His fingers were helpless and his wrists were beginning to grow numb. His nose and cheeks he knew were freezing, but they did not count. It was his feet and hands that were to save him, if he was to be saved.

He recollected being told of a camp of moose-hunters some-where above the forks of Paul Creek. He must be somewhere near it, he thought, and if he could find it he yet might be saved. Five minutes later he came upon it, lone and deserted, with drifted snow sprinkled inside the pine-bough shelter in which the hunters had slept. He sank down, sobbing. All was over. In an hour at best, in that terrific temperature, he would be an icy corpse.

But the love of life was strong in him, and he sprang again to his feet. He was thinking quickly. What if the matches did burn his hands? Burned hands were better than dead hands. No hands at all were better than death. He floundered along the trail till he came upon another high-water lodgement. There were twigs and branches, leaves and grasses, all dry and waiting the fire.

Again he sat down and shuffled the bunch of matches on his knees, got it into place on his palm, with the wrist of his other hand forced the nerveless fingers down against the bunch, and with the wrist kept them there. At the second scratch the bunch caught fire, and he knew that if he could stand the pain he was saved. He choked with the sulphur fumes, and the blue flame licked the flesh of his hands.

At first he could not feel it, but it burned quickly in through the frosted surface. The odor of the burning flesh – his flesh – was strong in his nostrils. He writhed about in his torment, yet held on. He set his teeth and swayed back and forth, until the clear white flame of the burning match shot up, and he had applied that flame to the leaves and grasses.

An anxious five minutes followed, but the fire gained steadily. Then he set to work to save himself. Heroic measures were necessary, such was his extremity, and he took them.

Alternately rubbing his hands with snow and thrusting them into the flames, and now and again beating them against the hard trees, he restored their circulation sufficiently for them to be of use to him. With his hunting-knife he slashed the straps from his pack, unrolled his blanket, and got out dry socks and foot-gear.

Then he cut away his moccasins and bared his feet. But while he had taken liberties with his hands, he kept his feet fairly away from the fire and rubbed them with snow. He rubbed till his hands grew numb, when he would cover his feet with the blanket, warm his hands by the fire, and return to the rubbing.

For three hours he worked, till the worst effects of the freezing had been counteracted. All that night he stayed by the fire, and it was late the next day when he limped pitifully into the camp on the Cherry Creek Divide.

In a month's time he was able to be about on his feet, although the toes were destined always after that to be very sensitive to frost. But the scars on his hands he knows he will carry to the grave. And – *'Never travel alone!'* he now lays down the precept of the north.

The League of the Old Men (1902)

At the Barracks a man was being tried for his life. He was an old man, a native from the Whitefish River, which empties into the Yukon below Lake Le Barge. All Dawson was wrought up over the affair, and likewise the Yukon-dwellers for a thousand miles up and down. It has been the custom of the land-robbing and sea-robbing Anglo-Saxon to give the law to conquered peoples, and ofttimes this law is harsh. But in the case of Imber the law for once seemed inadequate and weak. In the mathematical nature of things, equity did not reside in the punishment to be accorded him. The punishment was a foregone conclusion, there could be no doubt of that; and though it was capital, Imber had but one life, while the tale against him was one of scores.

In fact, the blood of so many was upon his hands that the killings attributed to him did not permit of precise enumeration. Smoking a pipe by the trailside or lounging around the stove, men made rough estimates of the numbers that had perished at his hand. They had been whites, all of them, these poor murdered people, and they had been slain singly, in pairs, and in parties. And so purposeless and wanton had been these killings, that they had long been a mystery to the mounted police, even in the time of the captains, and later, when the creeks realized, and a governor came from the Dominion to make the land pay for its prosperity.

But more mysterious still was the coming of Imber to Dawson to give himself up. It was in the late spring, when the Yukon was growling and writhing under its ice, that the old Indian climbed painfully up the bank from the river trail and stood blinking on the main street. Men who had witnessed his advent, noted that he was weak and tottery, and that he staggered over to a heap of cabin-logs and sat down. He sat there a full day, staring straight before him at the unceasing tide of white men that flooded past. Many a head jerked curiously to the side to meet his stare, and more than one remark was dropped anent the old Siwash with so strange a look upon his face. No end of men remembered afterward that they had been struck by his extraordinary figure, and forever afterward prided themselves upon their swift discernment of the unusual.

But it remained for Dickensen, Little Dickensen, to be the hero of the occasion. Little Dickensen had come into the land with great dreams and a pocketful of cash; but with the cash the dreams vanished, and to earn his passage back to the States he had accepted a clerical position with the brokerage firm of Holbrook and Mason. Across the street from the office of Holbrook and Mason was the heap of cabin-logs upon which Imber sat. Dickensen looked out of the window at him before he went to lunch; and when he came back from lunch he looked out of the window, and the old Siwash was still there.

Dickensen continued to look out of the window, and he, too, forever afterward prided himself upon his swiftness of discernment. He was a romantic little chap, and he likened the immobile old heathen to the genius of the Siwash race, gazing calm-eyed upon the hosts of the invading Saxon. The hours swept along, but Imber did not vary his posture, did not by a hair's-breadth move a muscle; and Dickensen remembered the man who once sat upright on a sled in the main street where men passed to and fro. They thought the man was resting, but later, when they touched him, they found him stiff and cold, frozen to death in the midst of the busy street. To undouble him, that he might fit into a coffin, they had been forced to lug him to a fire and thaw him out a bit. Dickensen shivered at the recollection.

Later on, Dickensen went out on the sidewalk to smoke a cigar and cool off; and a little later Emily Travis happened along. Emily Travis was dainty and delicate and rare, and whether in London or Klondike she gowned herself as befitted the daughter of a millionnaire mining engineer. Little Dickensen deposited his cigar on an outside window ledge where he could find it again, and lifted his hat.

They chatted for ten minutes or so, when Emily Travis, glancing past Dickensen's shoulder, gave a startled little scream. Dickensen turned about to see, and was startled, too. Imber had crossed the street and was standing there, a gaunt and hungry-looking shadow, his gaze riveted upon the girl.

'What do you want?' Little Dickensen demanded, tremulously plucky.

Imber grunted and stalked up to Emily Travis. He looked her over, keenly and carefully, every square inch of her. Especially did he appear interested in her silky brown hair, and in the color of her cheek, faintly sprayed and soft, like the downy bloom of a butterfly wing. He walked around her, surveying her with the calculating eye of a man who studies the lines upon which a horse or a boat is builded. In the course of his circuit the pink shell of her ear came between his eye and the westering sun, and he stopped to contemplate its rosy transparency. Then he returned to her face and looked long and intently into her blue eyes. He grunted and laid a hand on her arm midway between the shoulder and elbow. With his other hand he lifted her forearm and doubled it back. Disgust and wonder showed in his face, and he dropped her arm with a contemptuous grunt. Then he muttered a few guttural syllables, turned his back upon her, and addressed himself to Dickensen.

Dickensen could not understand his speech, and Emily Travis laughed. Imber turned from one to the other, frowning, but both shook their heads. He was about to go away, when she called out:

'Oh, Jimmy! Come here!'

Jimmy came from the other side of the street. He was a big, hulking Indian clad in approved white-man style, with an Eldorado king's sombrero on his head. He talked with Imber, haltingly, with throaty spasms. Jimmy was a Sitkan, possessed of no more than a passing knowledge of the interior dialects.

'Him Whitefish man,' he said to Emily Travis. 'Me savve um talk no very much. Him want to look see chief white man.'

'The Governor,' suggested Dickensen.

Jimmy talked some more with the Whitefish man, and his face went grave and puzzled.

'I t'ink um want Cap'n Alexander,' he explained. 'Him say um kill white man, white woman, white boy, plenty kill um white people. Him want to die.'

'Insane, I guess,' said Dickensen.

'What you call dat?' queried Jimmy.

Dickensen thrust a finger figuratively inside his head and imparted a rotary motion thereto.

'Mebbe so, mebbe so,' said Jimmy, returning to Imber, who still demanded the chief man of the white men.

A mounted policeman (unmounted for Klondike service) joined the group and heard Imber's wish repeated. He was a stalwart young fellow, broad-shouldered, deep-chested, legs cleanly built and stretched wide apart, and tall though Imber was, he towered above him by half a head. His eyes were cool, and gray, and steady, and he carried himself with the peculiar confidence of power that is bred of blood and tradition. His splendid masculinity was emphasized by his excessive boyishness – he was a mere lad – and his smooth cheek promised a blush as willingly as the cheek of a maid.

Imber was drawn to him at once. The fire leaped into his eyes at sight of a sabre slash that scarred his cheek. He ran a withered hand down the young fellow's leg and caressed the swelling thew. He smote the broad chest with his knuckles, and pressed and prodded the thick muscle-pads that covered the shoulders like a cuirass. The group had been added to by curious passers-by – husky miners, mountaineers, and frontiersmen, sons of the long-legged and broad-shouldered generations. Imber glanced from one to another, then he spoke aloud in the Whitefish tongue.

'What did he say?' asked Dickensen.

'Him say um all the same one man, dat p'liceman,' Jimmy interpreted.

Little Dickensen was little, and what of Miss Travis, he felt sorry for having asked the question.

The policeman was sorry for him and stepped into the breach. 'I fancy there may be something in his story. I'll take him up to the captain for examination. Tell him to come along with me, Jimmy.'

Jimmy indulged in more throaty spasms, and Imber grunted and looked satisfied.

'But ask him what he said, Jimmy, and what he meant when he took hold of my arm.'

So spoke Emily Travis, and Jimmy put the question and received the answer.

'Him say you no afraid,' said Jimmy.

Emily Travis looked pleased.

'Him say you no *skookum*, no strong, all the same very soft like little baby. Him break you, in um two hands, to little pieces. Him t'ink much funny, very strange, how you can be mother of men so big, so strong, like dat p'liceman.'

Emily Travers kept her eyes up and unfaltering, but her cheeks were sprayed with scarlet. Little Dickensen blushed and was quite embarrassed. The policeman's face blazed with his boy's blood.

'Come along, you,' he said gruffly, setting his shoulder to the crowd and forcing a way.

Thus it was that Imber found his way to the Barracks, where he made full and voluntary confession, and from the precincts of which he never emerged.

Imber looked very tired. The fatigue of hopelessness and age was in his face. His shoulders drooped depressingly, and his eyes were lack-lustre. His mop of hair should have been white, but sun and weatherbeat had burned and bitten it so that it hung limp and lifeless and colorless. He took no interest in what went on around him. The courtroom was jammed with the men of the creeks and trails, and there was an ominous note in the rumble and grumble of their low-pitched voices, which came to his ears like the growl of the sea from deep caverns.

He sat close by a window, and his apathetic eyes rested now and again on the dreary scene without. The sky was overcast, and a gray drizzle was falling. It was flood-time on the Yukon. The ice was gone, and the river was up in the town. Back and forth on the main street, in canoes and poling-boats, passed the people that never rested. Often he saw these boats turn aside from the street and enter the flooded square that marked the Barracks' parade-ground. Sometimes they disappeared beneath him, and he heard them jar against the house-logs and their occupants scramble in through the window. After that came the slush of water against men's legs as they waded across the lower room and mounted the stairs. Then they appeared in the doorway, with doffed hats and dripping sea-boots, and added themselves to the waiting crowd.

And while they centered their looks on him, and in grim anticipation enjoyed the penalty he was to pay, Imber looked at them, and mused on their ways, and on their Law that never slept, but went on unceasing, in good times and bad, in flood and famine, through trouble and terror and death, and which would go on unceasing, it seemed to him, to the end of time.

A man rapped sharply on a table, and the conversation droned away into silence. Imber looked at the man. He seemed one in authority, yet Imber divined the square-browed man who sat by a desk farther back to be the one chief over them all and over the man who had rapped. Another man by the same table uprose and began to read aloud from many fine sheets of paper. At the top of each sheet he cleared his throat, at the bottom moistened his fingers. Imber did not understand his speech, but the others did, and he knew that it made them angry. Sometimes it made them very angry, and once a man cursed him, in single syllables, stinging and tense, till a man at the table rapped him to silence.

For an interminable period the man read. His monotonous, sing-song utterance lured Imber to dreaming, and he was dreaming deeply when the man ceased. A voice spoke to him in his own Whitefish tongue, and he roused up, without surprise, to look upon the face of his sister's son, a young man who had wandered away years agone to make his dwelling with the whites.

'Thou dost not remember me,' he said by way of greeting.

'Nay,' Imber answered. 'Thou art Howkan who went away. Thy mother be dead.'

'She was an old woman,' said Howkan.

But Imber did not hear, and Howkan, with hand upon his shoulder, roused him again.

'I shall speak to thee what the man has spoken, which is the tale of the troubles thou hast done and which thou hast told, O fool, to the Captain Alexander. And thou shalt understand and say if it be true talk or talk not true. It is so commanded.'

Howkan had fallen among the mission folk and been taught by them to read and write. In his hands he held the many fine sheets from which the man had read aloud, and which had been taken down by a clerk when Imber first made confession, through the mouth of Jimmy, to Captain Alexander. Howkan began to read. Imber listened for a space, when a wonderment rose up in his face and he broke in abruptly.

'That be my talk, Howkan. Yet from thy lips it comes when thy ears have not heard.'

Howkan smirked with self-appreciation. His hair was parted in the middle. 'Nay, from the paper it comes, O Imber. Never have my ears heard. From the paper it comes, through my eyes, into my head, and out of my mouth to thee. Thus it comes.'

'Thus it comes? It be there in the paper?' Imber's voice sank in whisperful awe as he crackled the sheets 'twixt thumb and finger and stared at the charactery scrawled thereon. 'It be a great medicine, Howkan, and thou art a worker of wonders.'

'It be nothing, it be nothing,' the young man responded carelessly and pridefully. He read at hazard from the document:

'*In that year, before the break of the ice, came an old man, and a boy who was lame of one foot. These also did I kill, and the old man made much noise –*'

'It be true,' Imber interrupted breathlessly. 'He made much noise and would not die for a long time. But how dost thou know, Howkan? The chief man of the white men told thee, mayhap? No one beheld me, and him alone have I told.'

Howkan shook his head with impatience. 'Have I not told thee it be there in the paper, O fool?'

Imber stared hard at the ink-scrawled surface. 'As the hunter looks upon the snow and says, Here but yesterday there passed a rabbit; and here by the willow scrub it stood and listened, and heard, and was afraid; and here it turned upon its trail; and here it went with great swiftness, leaping wide; and here, with greater swiftness and wider leapings, came a lynx; and here, where the claws cut deep into the snow, the lynx made a very great leap; and here it struck, with the rabbit under and rolling belly up; and here leads off the trail of the lynx alone, and there is no more rabbit – as the hunter looks upon the markings of the snow and says thus and so and here, dost thou, too, look upon the paper and say thus and so and here be the things old Imber hath done?'

'Even so,' said Howkan. 'And now do thou listen, and keep thy woman's tongue between thy teeth till thou art called upon for speech.'

Thereafter, and for a long time, Howkan read to him the confession, and Imber remained musing and silent. At the end, he said:

'It be my talk, and true talk, but I am grown old, Howkan, and forgotten things come back to me which were well for the head man there to know. First, there was the man who came over the Ice Mountains, with cunning traps made of iron, who sought the beaver of the Whitefish. Him I slew. And there were three men seeking gold on the Whitefish long ago. Them also I slew, and left them to the wolverines. And at the Five Fingers there was a man with a raft and much meat.'

At the moments when Imber paused to remember, Howkan translated and a clerk reduced to writing. The courtroom listened stolidly to each unadorned little tragedy, till Imber told of a red-haired man whose eyes were crossed and whom he had killed with a remarkably long shot.

'Hell,' said a man in the forefront of the onlookers. He said it soulfully and sorrowfully. He was red-haired. 'Hell,' he repeated. 'That was my brother Bill.' And at regular intervals throughout the session, his solemn 'Hell' was heard in the courtroom; nor did his comrades check him, nor did the man at the table rap him to order.

Imber's head drooped once more, and his eyes went dull, as though a film rose up and covered them from the world. And he dreamed as only age can dream upon the colossal futility of youth.

Later, Howkan roused him again, saying: 'Stand up, O Imber. It be commanded that thou tellest why you did these troubles, and slew these people, and at the end journeyed here seeking the Law.'

Imber rose feebly to his feet and swayed back and forth. He began to speak in a low and faintly rumbling voice, but Howkan interrupted him.

'This old man, he is damn crazy,' he said in English to the square-browed man. 'His talk is foolish and like that of a child.'

'We will hear his talk which is like that of a child,' said the square-browed man. 'And we will hear it, word for word, as he speaks it. Do you understand?'

Howkan understood, and Imber's eyes flashed, for he had witnessed the play between his sister's son and the man in authority. And then began the story, the epic of a bronze patriot which might well itself be wrought into bronze for the generations unborn. The crowd fell strangely silent, and the square-browed judge leaned head on hand and pondered his soul and the soul of his race. Only was heard the deep tones of Imber, rhythmically alternating with the shrill voice of the interpreter, and now and again, like the bell of the Lord, the wondering and meditative 'Hell' of the red-haired man.

'I am Imber of the Whitefish people.' So ran the interpretation of Howkan, whose inherent barbarism gripped hold of him, and who lost his mission culture and veneered civilization as he caught the savage ring and rhythm of old Imber's tale. 'My father was Otsbaok, a strong man. The land was warm with sunshine and gladness when I was a boy. The people did not hunger after strange things, nor hearken to new voices, and the ways of their fathers were their ways. The women found favor in the eyes of the young men, and the young men looked upon them with content. Babes hung at the breasts of the women, and they were heavy-hipped with increase of the tribe. Men were men in those days. In peace and plenty, and in war and famine, they were men.

'At that time there was more fish in the water than now, and more meat in the forest. Our dogs were wolves, warm with thick hides and hard to the frost and storm. And as with our dogs so with us, for we were likewise hard to the frost and storm. And when the Pellys came into our land we slew them and were slain. For we were men, we Whitefish, and our fathers and our fathers' fathers had fought against the Pellys and determined the bounds of the land.

'As I say, with our dogs, so with us. And one day came the first white man. He dragged himself, so, on hand and knee, in the snow. And his skin was stretched tight, and his bones were sharp beneath. Never was such a man, we thought, and we wondered of what strange tribe he was, and of its land. And he was weak, most weak, like a little child, so that we gave him a place by the fire, and warm furs to lie upon, and we gave him food as little children are given food.

'And with him was a dog, large as three of our dogs, and very weak. The hair of this dog was short, and not warm, and the tail was frozen so that the end fell off. And this strange dog we fed, and bedded by the fire, and fought from it our dogs, which else would have killed him. And what of the moose meat and the sun-dried salmon, the man and dog took strength to themselves; and what of the strength they became big and unafraid. And the man spoke loud words and laughed at the old men and young men, and looked boldly upon the maidens. And the dog fought with our dogs, and for all of his short hair and softness slew three of them in one day.

'When we asked the man concerning his people, he said, "I have many brothers," and laughed in a way that was not good. And when he was in his full strength he went away, and with him went Noda, daughter to the chief. First, after that, was one of our bitches brought to pup. And never was there such a breed of dogs – big-headed, thick-jawed, and short-haired, and helpless. Well do I remember my father, Otsbaok, a strong man. His face was black with anger at such helplessness, and he took a stone, so, and so, and there was no more helplessness. And two summers after that came Noda back to us with a man-child in the hollow of her arm.

'And that was the beginning. Came a second white man, with short-haired dogs, which he left behind him when he went. And with him went six of our strongest dogs, for which, in trade, he had given Koo-So-Tee, my mother's brother, a wonderful pistol that fired with great swiftness six times. And Koo-So-Tee was very big, what of the pistol, and laughed at our bows and arrows. "Woman's things," he called them, and went forth against the bald-face grizzly, with the pistol in his hand. Now it be known that it is not good to hunt the bald-face with a pistol, but how were we to know? and how was Koo-So-Tee to know? So he went against the bald-face, very brave, and fired the pistol with great swiftness six times; and the bald-face but grunted and broke in his breast like it were an egg, and like honey from a bee's nest dripped the brains of Koo-So-Tee upon the ground. He was a good hunter, and there was no one to bring meat to his squaw and children. And we were bitter, and we said, "That which for the white men is well, is for us not well." And this be true. There be many white men and fat, but their ways have made us few and lean.

'Came the third white man, with great wealth of all manner of wonderful foods and things. And twenty of our strongest dogs he took from us in trade. Also, what of presents and great promises, ten of our young hunters did he take with him on a journey which fared no man knew where. It is said they died in the snow of the Ice Mountains where man has never been, or in the Hills of Silence which are beyond the edge of the earth. Be that as it may, dogs and young hunters were seen never again by the Whitefish people.

'And more white men came with the years, and ever, with pay and presents, they led the young men away with them. And sometimes the young men came back with strange tales of dangers and toils in the lands beyond the Pellys, and sometimes they did not come back. And we said, "If they be unafraid of life, these white men, it is because they have many lives; but we be few by the Whitefish, and the young men shall go away no more." But the young men did go away; and the young women went also; and we were very wroth.

'It be true, we ate flour, and salt pork, and drank tea which was a great delight; only, when we could not get tea, it was very bad and we became short of speech and quick of anger. So we grew to hunger for the things the white men brought in trade.

Trade! trade! all the time was it trade! One winter we sold our meat for clocks that would not go, and watches with broken guts, and files worn smooth, and pistols without cartridges and worthless. And then came famine, and we were without meat, and two score died ere the break of spring.

'"Now are we grown weak," we said; "and the Pellys will fall upon us, and our bounds be overthrown." But as it fared with us, so had it fared with the Pellys, and they were too weak to come against us.

'My father, Otsboak, a strong man, was now old and very wise. And he spoke to the chief, saying: "Behold, our dogs be worthless. No longer are they thick-furred and strong, and they die in the frost and harness. Let us go into the village and kill them, saving only the wolf ones, and these let us tie out in the night that they may mate with the wild wolves of the forest. Thus shall we have dogs warm and strong again."

'And his word was harkened to, and we Whitefish became known for our dogs, which were the best in the land. But known we were not for ourselves. The best of our young men and women had gone away with the white men to wander on trail and river to far places. And the young women came back old and broken, as Noda had come, or they came not at all. And the young men came back to sit by our fires for a time, full of ill speech and rough ways, drinking evil drinks and gambling through long nights and days, with a great unrest always in their hearts, till the call of the white men came to them and they went away again to the unknown places. And they were without honor and respect, jeering the old-time customs and laughing in the faces of chief and shamans.

'As I say, we were become a weak breed, we Whitefish. We sold our warm skins and furs for tobacco and whiskey and thin cotton things that left us shivering in the cold. And the coughing sickness came upon us, and men and women coughed and sweated through the long nights, and the hunters on trail spat blood upon the snow. And now one, and now another, bled swiftly from the mouth and died. And the women bore few children, and those they bore were weak and given to sickness. And other sicknesses came to us from the white men, the like of which we had never known and could not understand. Smallpox, likewise measles, have I heard these sicknesses named, and we died of them as die the salmon in the still eddies when in the fall

their eggs are spawned and there is no longer need for them to
live.

'And yet, and here be the strangeness of it, the white men
come as the breath of death; all their ways lead to death, their
nostrils are filled with it; and yet they do not die. Theirs the
whiskey, and tobacco, and short-haired dogs; theirs the many
sicknesses, the smallpox and measles, the coughing and mouth-
bleeding; theirs the white skin, and softness to the frost and
storm; and theirs the pistols that shoot six times very swift and
are worthless. And yet they grow fat on their many ills, and
prosper, and lay a heavy hand over all the world and tread
mightily upon its peoples. And their women, too, are soft as little
babes, most breakable and never broken, the mothers of men.
And out of all this softness, and sickness, and weakness, come
strength, and power, and authority. They be gods, or devils, as
the case may be. I do not know. What do I know, I, old Imber of
the Whitefish? Only do I know that they are past understanding,
these white men, far-wanderers and fighters over the earth that
they be.

'As I say, the meat in the forest became less and less. It be true,
the white man's gun is most excellent and kills a long way off;
but of what worth the gun, when there is no meat to kill? When I
was a boy on the Whitefish there was moose on every hill, and
each year came the caribou uncountable. But now the hunter
may take the trail ten days and not one moose gladden his eyes,
while the caribou uncountable come no more at all. Small worth
the gun, I say, killing a long way off, when there be nothing to
kill.

'And I, Imber, pondered upon these things, watching the while
the Whitefish, and the Pellys, and all the tribes of the land,
perishing as perished the meat of the forest. Long I pondered. I
talked with the shamans and the old men who were wise. I went
apart that the sounds of the village might not disturb me, and I
ate no meat so that my belly should not press upon me and make
me slow of eye and ear. I sat long and sleepless in the forest,
wide-eyed for the sign, my ears patient and keen for the word
that was to come. And I wandered alone in the blackness of night
to the river bank, where was wind-moaning and sobbing of
water, and where I sought wisdom from the ghosts of old
shamans in the trees and dead and gone.

'And in the end, as in a vision, came to me the short-haired and detestable dogs, and the way seemed plain. By the wisdom of Otsbaok, my father and a strong man, had the blood of our own wolf-dogs been kept clean, wherefore had they remained warm of hide and strong in the harness. So I returned to my village and made oration to the men. "This be a tribe, these white men," I said. "A very large tribe, and doubtless there is no longer meat in their land, and they are come among us to make a new land for themselves. But they weaken us, and we die. They are a very hungry folk. Already has our meat gone from us, and it were well, if we would live, that we deal by them as we have dealt by their dogs."

'And further oration I made, counselling fight. And the men of the Whitefish listened, and some said one thing, and some spoke of other and worthless things, and no man made brave talk of deeds and war. But while the young men were weak as water and afraid, I watched that the old men sat silent, and that in their eyes fires came and went. And later, when the village slept and no one knew, I drew the old men away into the forest and made more talk. And now we were agreed, and we remembered the good young days, and the free land, and the times of plenty, and the gladness and sunshine; and we called ourselves brothers, and swore great secrecy, and a mighty oath to cleanse the land of the evil breed that had come upon it. It be plain we were fools, but how were we to know, we old men of the Whitefish?

'And to hearten the others, I did the first deed. I kept guard upon the Yukon till the first canoe came down. In it were two white men, and when I stood upright upon the bank and raised my hand they changed their course and drove in to me. And as the man in the bow lifted his head, so, that he might know wherefore I wanted him, my arrow sang through the air straight to his throat, and he knew. The second man, who held paddle in the stern, had his rifle half to his shoulder when the first of my three spear-casts smote him.

'"These be the first," I said, when the old men had gathered to me. "Later we will bind together all the old men of all the tribes, and after that the young men who remain strong, and the work will become easy."

'And then the two dead white men we cast into the river. And of the canoe, which was a very good canoe, we made a fire, and a fire, also, of the things within the canoe. But first we looked at the things, and they were pouches of leather which we cut open with our knives. And inside these pouches were many papers, like that from which thou hast read, O Howkan, with markings on them which we marveled at and could not understand. Now, I am become wise, and I know them for the speech of men as thou hast told me.'

A whisper and buzz went around the courtroom when Howkan finished interpreting the affair of the canoe, and one man's voice spoke up: 'That was the lost '91 mail, Peter James and Delaney bringing it in and last spoken at Le Barge by Matthews going out.' The clerk scratched steadily away, and another paragraph was added to the history of the North.

'There be little more,' Imber went on slowly. 'It be there on the paper, the things we did. We were old men, and we did not understand. Even I, Imber, do not understand. Secretly we slew, and continued to slay, for with our years we were crafty and we had learned the swiftness of going without haste. When white men came among us with black looks and rough words, and took away six of the young men with irons binding them helpless, we knew we must slay wider and farther. And one by one we old men departed up river and down to the unknown lands. It was a brave thing. Old we were, and unafraid, but the fear of far places is a terrible fear to men who are old.

'So we slew, without haste and craftily. On the Chilcoot and in the Delta we slew, from the passes to the sea, wherever the white men camped or broke their trails. It be true, they died, but it was without worth. Ever did they come over the mountains, ever did they grow and grow, while we, being old, became less and less. I remember, by the Caribou Crossing, the camp of a white man. He was a very little white man, and three of the old men came upon him in his sleep. And the next day I came upon the four of them. The white man alone still breathed, and there was breath in him to curse me once and well before he died.

'And so it went, now one old man, and now another. Sometimes the word reached us long after of how they died, and sometimes it did not reach us. And the old men of the other tribes were weak and afraid, and would not join with us. As I say, one by one, till I alone was left. I am Imber, of the Whitefish people. My father was Otsbaok, a strong man. There are no Whitefish now. Of the old men I am the last. The young men and young women are gone away, some to live with the Pellys, some with the Salmons, and more with the white men. I am very old, and very tired, and it being vain fighting the Law, as thou sayest, Howkan, I am come seeking the Law.'

'O Imber, thou art indeed a fool,' said Howkan.

But Imber was dreaming. The square-browed judge likewise dreamed, and all his race rose up before him in a mighty phantasmagoria – his steel-shod, mail-clad race, the lawgiver and world-maker among the families of men. He saw it dawn red-flickering across the dark forests and sullen seas; he saw it blaze, bloody and red, to full and triumphant noon; and down the shaded slope he saw the blood-red sands dropping into night. And through it all he observed the Law, pitiless and potent, ever unswerving and ever ordaining, greater than the motes of men who fulfilled it or were crushed by it, even as it was greater than he, his heart speaking for softness.

Love of Life (1905; 1907)

'This out of all will remain –
They have lived and have tossed:
So much of the game will be gain,
Though the gold of the dice has been lost.'

They limped painfully down the bank, and once the foremost of the two men staggered among the rough-strewn rocks. They were tired and weak, and their faces had the drawn expression of patience which comes of hardship long endured. They were heavily burdened with blanket packs which were strapped to their shoulders. Head-straps, passing across the forehead, helped support these packs. Each man carried a rifle. They walked in a stooped posture, the shoulders well forward, the head still farther forward, the eyes bent upon the ground.

'I wish we had just about two of them cartridges that's layin' in that cache of ourn,' said the second man.

His voice was utterly and drearily expressionless. He spoke without enthusiasm; and the first man, limping into the milky stream that foamed over the rocks, vouchsafed no reply.

The other man followed at his heels. They did not remove their footgear, though the water was icy cold – so cold that their ankles ached and their feet went numb. In places the water dashed against their knees, and both men staggered for footing.

The man who followed slipped on a smooth boulder, nearly fell, but recovered himself with a violent effort, at the same time uttering a sharp exclamation of pain. He seemed faint and dizzy and put out his free hand while he reeled, as though seeking support against the air. When he had steadied himself he stepped forward, but reeled again and nearly fell. Then he stood still and looked at the other man, who had never turned his head.

The man stood still for fully a minute, as though debating with himself. Then he called out:

'I say, Bill, I've sprained my ankle.'

Bill staggered on through the milky water. He did not look around. The man watched him go, and though his face was expressionless as ever, his eyes were like the eyes of a wounded deer.

The other man limped up the farther bank and continued straight on without looking back. The man in the stream watched him. His lips trembled a little, so that the rough thatch of brown hair which covered them was visibly agitated. His tongue even strayed out to moisten them.

'Bill!' he cried out.

It was the pleading cry of a strong man in distress, but Bill's head did not turn. The man watched him go, limping grotesquely and lurching forward with stammering gait up the slow slope toward the soft sky-line of the low-lying hill. He watched him go till he passed over the crest and disappeared. Then he turned his gaze and slowly took in the circle of the world that remained to him now that Bill was gone.

Near the horizon the sun was smoldering dimly, almost obscured by formless mists and vapors, which gave an impression of mass and density without outline or tangibility. The man pulled out his watch, the while resting his weight on one leg. It was four o'clock, and as the season was near the last of July or first of August – he did not know the precise date within a week or two – he knew that the sun roughly marked the northwest. He looked to the south and knew that somewhere beyond those bleak hills lay the Great Bear Lake; also, he knew that in that direction the Arctic Circle cut its forbidding way across the Canadian Barrens. This stream in which he stood was a feeder to the Coppermine River, which in turn flowed north and emptied into Coronation Gulf and the Arctic Ocean. He had never been there, but he had seen it, once, on a Hudson Bay Company chart.

Again his gaze completed the circle of the world about him. It was not a heartening spectacle. Everywhere was soft sky-line. The hills were all low-lying. There were no trees, no shrubs, no grasses – naught but a tremendous and terrible desolation that sent fear swiftly dawning into his eyes.

'Bill!' he whispered, once and twice; 'Bill!'

He cowered in the midst of the milky water, as though the vastness were pressing in upon him with overwhelming force, brutally crushing him with its complacent awfulness. He began to shake as with an ague-fit, till the gun fell from his hand with a splash. This served to rouse him. He fought with his fear and pulled himself together, groping in the water and recovering the weapon. He hitched his pack farther over on his left shoulder, so as to take a portion of its weight from off the injured ankle. Then he proceeded, slowly and carefully, wincing with pain, to the bank.

He did not stop. With a desperation that was madness, unmindful of the pain, he hurried up the slope to the crest of the hill over which his comrade had disappeared – more grotesque and comical by far than that limping, jerking comrade. But at the crest he saw a shallow valley, empty of life. He fought with his fear again, overcame it, hitched the pack still farther over on his left shoulder, and lurched on down the slope.

The bottom of the valley was soggy with water, which the thick moss held, spongelike, close to the surface. This water squirted out from under his feet at every step, and each time he lifted a foot the action culminated in a sucking sound as the wet moss reluctantly released its grip. He picked his way from muskeg to muskeg, and followed the other man's footsteps along and across the rocky ledges which thrust like islets through the sea of moss.

Though alone, he was not lost. Farther on he knew he would come to where dead spruce and fir, very small and weazened, bordered the shore of a little lake, the *titchin-nichilie*, in the tongue of the country, the 'land of little stick'. And into that lake flowed a small stream, the water of which was not milky. There was rush-grass on that stream – this he remembered well – but no timber, and he would follow it till its first trickle ceased at a divide. He would cross this divide to the first trickle of another stream, flowing to the west, which he would follow until it emptied into the river Dease, and here he would find a cache under an upturned canoe and piled over with many rocks. And in this cache would be ammunition for his empty gun, fish-hooks and lines, a small net – all the utilities for the killing and snaring of food. Also, he would find flour – not much – a piece of bacon, and some beans.

Bill would be waiting for him there, and they would paddle away south down the Dease to the Great Bear Lake. And south across the lake they would go, ever south, till they gained the Mackenzie. And south, still south, they would go, while the winter raced vainly after them, and the ice formed in the eddies, and the days grew chill and crisp, south to some warm Hudson

Bay Company post, where timber grew tall and generous and there was grub without end.

These were the thoughts of the man as he strove onward. But hard as he strove with his body, he strove equally hard with his mind, trying to think that Bill had not deserted him, that Bill would surely wait for him at the cache. He was compelled to think this thought, or else there would not be any use to strive, and he would have lain down and died. And as the dim ball of the sun sank slowly into the northwest he covered every inch – and many times – of his and Bill's flight south before the downcoming winter. And he conned the grub of the cache and the grub of the Hudson Bay Company post over and over again. He had not eaten for two days; for a far longer time he had not had all he wanted to eat. Often he stooped and picked pale muskeg berries, put them into his mouth, and chewed and swallowed them. A muskeg berry is a bit of seed enclosed in a bit of water. In the mouth the water melts away and the seed chews sharp and bitter. The man knew there was no nourishment in the berries, but he chewed them patiently with a hope greater than knowledge and defying experience.

At nine o'clock he stubbed his toe on a rocky ledge, and from sheer weariness and weakness staggered and fell. He lay for some time, without movement, on his side. Then he slipped out of the pack-straps and clumsily dragged himself into a sitting posture. It was not yet dark, and in the lingering twilight he groped about among the rocks for shreds of dry moss. When he had gathered a heap he built a fire – a smouldering, smudgy fire – and put a tin pot of water on to boil.

He unwrapped his pack and the first thing he did was to count his matches. There were sixty-seven. He counted them three times to make sure. He divided them into several portions, wrapping them in oil paper, disposing of one bunch in his empty tobacco pouch, of another bunch in the inside band of his battered hat, of a third bunch under his shirt on the chest. This accomplished, a panic came upon him, and he unwrapped them all and counted them again. There were still sixty-seven.

He dried his wet foot-gear by the fire. The moccasins were in soggy shreds. The blanket socks were worn through in places, and his feet were raw and bleeding. His ankle was throbbing, and he gave it an examination. It had swollen to the size of his knee. He tore a long strip from one of his two blankets and bound the ankle tightly. He tore other strips and bound them about his feet to serve for both moccasins and socks. Then he drank the pot of water, steaming hot, wound his watch, and crawled between his blankets.

He slept like a dead man. The brief darkness around midnight came and went. The sun arose in the northeast – at least the day dawned in that quarter, for the sun was hidden by gray clouds.

At six o'clock he awoke, quietly lying on his back. He gazed straight up into the gray sky and knew that he was hungry. As he rolled over on his elbow he was startled by a loud snort, and saw a bull caribou regarding him with alert curiosity. The animal was not more than fifty feet away, and instantly into the man's mind leaped the vision and the savor of a caribou steak sizzling and frying over a fire. Mechanically he reached for the empty gun, drew a bead, and pulled the trigger. The bull snorted and leaped away, his hoofs rattling and clattering as he fled across the ledges.

The man cursed and flung the empty gun from him. He groaned aloud as he started to drag himself to his feet. It was a slow and arduous task. His joints were like rusty hinges. They worked harshly in their sockets, with much friction, and each bending or unbending was accomplished only through a sheer exertion of will. When he finally gained his feet, another minute or so was consumed in straightening up, so that he could stand erect as a man should stand.

He crawled up a small knoll and surveyed the prospect. There were no trees, no bushes, nothing but a gray sea of moss scarcely diversified by gray rocks, gray lakelets, and gray streamlets. The sky was gray. There was no sun nor hint of sun. He had no idea of north, and he had forgotten the way he had come to this spot the night before. But he was not lost. He knew that. Soon he would come to the land of the little sticks. He felt that it lay off to the left somewhere, not far – possibly just over the next low hill.

He went back to put his pack into shape for traveling. He assured himself of the existence of his three separate parcels of matches, though he did not stop to count them. But he did linger, debating, over a squat moose-hide sack. It was not large. He could hide it under his two hands. He knew that it weighed fifteen pounds – as much as all the rest of the pack – and it worried him. He finally set it to one side and proceeded to roll the pack. He paused to gaze at the squat moose-hide sack. He picked it up hastily with a defiant glance about him, as though the desolation were trying to rob him of it; and when he rose to his feet to stagger on into the day, it was included in the pack on his back.

He bore away to the left, stopping now and again to eat muskeg berries. His ankle had stiffened, his limp was more pronounced, but the pain of it was as nothing compared with the pain of his stomach. The hunger pangs were sharp. They gnawed and gnawed until he could not keep his mind steady on the course he must pursue to gain the land of little sticks. The muskeg berries did not allay this gnawing, while they made his tongue and the roof of his mouth sore with their irritating bite.

He came upon a valley where rock ptarmigan rose on whirring wings from the ledges and muskegs. Ker–ker–ker was the cry they made. He threw stones at them, but could not hit them. He placed his pack on the ground and stalked them as a cat stalks a sparrow. The sharp rocks cut through his pants' legs till his knees left a trail of blood; but the hurt was lost in the hurt of his hunger. He squirmed over the wet moss, saturating his clothes and chilling his body; but he was not aware of it, so great was his fever for food. And always the ptarmigan rose, whirring, before him, till their ker–ker–ker became a mock to him, and he cursed them and cried aloud at them with their own cry.

Once he crawled upon one that must have been asleep. He did not see it till it shot up in his face from its rocky nook. He made a clutch as startled as was the rise of the ptarmigan, and there remained in his hand three tail-feathers. As he watched its flight he hated it, as though it had done him some terrible wrong. Then he returned and shouldered his pack.

As the day wore along he came into valleys or swales where game was more plentiful. A band of caribou passed by, twenty and odd animals, tantalizingly within rifle range. He felt a wild desire to run after them, a certitude that he could run them down. A black fox came toward him, carrying a ptarmigan in his mouth. The man shouted. It was a fearful cry, but the fox, leaping away in fright, did not drop the ptarmigan.

Late in the afternoon he followed a stream, milky with lime, which ran through sparse patches of rush-grass. Grasping these rushes firmly near the root, he pulled up what resembled a young onion-sprout no larger than a shingle-nail. It was tender, and his teeth sank into it with a crunch that promised deliciously of food.

But its fibers were tough. It was composed of stringy filaments saturated with water, like the berries, and devoid of nourishment. He threw off his pack and went into the rush-grass on hands and knees, crunching and munching, like some bovine creature.

He was very weary and often wished to rest – to lie down and sleep; but he was continually driven on – not so much by his desire to gain the land of little sticks as by his hunger. He searched little ponds for frogs and dug up the earth with his nails for worms, though he knew in spite that neither frogs nor worms existed so far north.

He looked into every pool of water vainly, until, as the long twilight came on, he discovered a solitary fish, the size of a minnow, in such a pool. He plunged his arm in up to the shoulder, but it eluded him. He reached for it with both hands and stirred up the milky mud at the bottom. In his excitement he fell in, wetting himself to the waist. Then the water was too muddy to admit of his seeing the fish, and he was compelled to wait until the sediment had settled.

The pursuit was renewed, till the water was again muddied. But he could not wait. He unstrapped the tin bucket and began to bale the pool. He baled wildly at first, splashing himself and flinging the water so short a distance that it ran back into the pool. He worked more carefully, striving to be cool, though his heart was pounding against his chest and his hands were trembling. At the end of half an hour the pool was nearly dry. Not a cupful of water remained. And there was no fish. He found a hidden crevice among the stones through which it had escaped to the adjoining and larger pool – a pool which he could not empty in a night and a day. Had he known of the crevice, he could have closed it with a rock at the beginning and the fish would have been his.

Thus he thought, and crumpled up and sank down upon the wet earth. At first he cried softly to himself, then he cried loudly to the pitiless desolation that ringed him around; and for a long time after he was shaken by great dry sobs.

He built a fire and warmed himself by drinking quarts of hot water, and made camp on a rocky ledge in the same fashion he had the night before. The last thing he did was to see that his matches were dry and to wind his watch. The blankets were wet and clammy. His ankle pulsed with pain. But he knew only that he was hungry, and through his restless sleep he dreamed of feasts and banquets and of food served and spread in all imaginable ways.

He awoke chilled and sick. There was no sun. The gray of earth and sky had become deeper, more profound. A raw wind was blowing, and the first flurries of snow were whitening the hilltops. The air about him thickened and grew white while he made a fire and boiled more water. It was wet snow, half rain, and the flakes were large and soggy. At first they melted as soon as they came in contact with the earth, but ever more fell, covering the ground, putting out the fire, spoiling his supply of moss-fuel.

This was a signal for him to strap on his pack and stumble onward, he knew not where. He was not concerned with the land of little sticks, nor with Bill and the cache under the upturned canoe by the river Dease. He was mastered by the verb 'to eat'. He was hunger-mad. He took no heed of the course he pursued, so long as that course led him through the swale bottoms. He felt his way through the wet snow to the watery muskeg berries, and went by feel as he pulled up the rush-grass by the roots. But it was tasteless stuff and did not satisfy. He found a weed that tasted sour and he ate all he could find of it, which was not much, for it was a creeping growth, easily hidden under the several inches of snow.

He had no fire that night, nor hot water, and crawled under his blanket to sleep the broken hunger-sleep. The snow turned into a cold rain. He awakened many times to feel it falling on his upturned face. Day came – a gray day and no sun. It had ceased raining. The keenness of his hunger had departed. Sensibility, as far as concerned the yearning for food, had been exhausted. There was a dull, heavy ache in his stomach, but it did not bother him so much. He was more rational, and once more he was chiefly interested in the land of little sticks and the cache by the river Dease.

He ripped the remnant of one of his blankets into strips and bound his bleeding feet. Also, he recinched the injured ankle and prepared himself for a day of travel. When he came to his pack, he paused long over the squat moose-hide sack, but in the end it went with him.

The snow had melted under the rain, and only the hilltops showed white. The sun came out, and he succeeded in locating the points of the compass, though he knew now that he was lost.

Perhaps, in his previous days' wanderings, he had edged away too far to the left. He now bore off to the right to counteract the possible deviation from his true course.

Though the hunger pangs were no longer so exquisite, he realized that he was weak. He was compelled to pause for frequent rests, when he attacked the muskeg berries and rush-grass patches. His tongue felt dry and large, as though covered with a fine hairy growth, and it tasted bitter in his mouth. His heart gave him a great deal of trouble. When he had travelled a few minutes it would begin a remorseless thump, thump, thump, and then leap up and away in a painful flutter of beats that choked him and made him go faint and dizzy.

In the middle of the day he found two minnows in a large pool. It was impossible to bale it, but he was calmer now and managed to catch them in his tin bucket. They were no longer than his little finger, but he was not particularly hungry. The dull ache in his stomach had been growing duller and fainter. It seemed almost that his stomach was dozing. He ate the fish raw, masticating with painstaking care, for the eating was an act of pure reason. While he had no desire to eat, he knew that he must eat to live.

In the evening he caught three more minnows, eating two and saving the third for breakfast. The sun had dried stray shreds of moss, and he was able to warm himself with hot water. He had not covered more than ten miles that day; and the next day, travelling whenever his heart permitted him, he covered no more than five miles. But his stomach did not give him the slightest uneasiness. It had gone to sleep. He was in a strange country, too, and the caribou were growing more plentiful, also the wolves. Often their yelps drifted across the desolation, and once he saw three of them slinking away before his path.

Another night; and in the morning, being more rational, he untied the leather string that fastened the squat moose-hide sack. From its open mouth poured a yellow stream of coarse gold-dust and nuggets. He roughly divided the gold in halves, caching one half on a prominent ledge, wrapped in a piece of blanket, and returning the other half to the sack. He also began to use strips of the one remaining blanket for his feet. He still clung to his gun, for there were cartridges in that cache by the river Dease.

This was a day of fog, and this day hunger awoke in him again. He was very weak and was afflicted with a giddiness which at times blinded him. It was no uncommon thing now for him to stumble and fall; and stumbling once, he fell squarely into a ptarmigan nest. There were four newly hatched chicks, a day old – little specks of pulsating life no more than a mouthful; and he ate them ravenously, thrusting them alive into his mouth and crunching them like egg-shells between his teeth. The mother ptarmigan beat about him with great outcry. He used his gun as a club with which to knock her over, but she dodged out of reach. He threw stones at her and with one chance shot broke a wing. Then she fluttered away, running, trailing the broken wing, with him in pursuit.

The little chicks had no more than whetted his appetite. He hopped and bobbed clumsily along on his injured ankle, throwing stones and screaming hoarsely at times; at other times hopping and bobbing silently along, picking himself up grimly and patiently when he fell, or rubbing his eyes with his hand when the giddiness threatened to overpower him.

The chase led him across swampy ground in the bottom of the valley, and he came upon footprints in the soggy moss. They were not his own – he could see that. They must be Bill's. But he could not stop, for the mother ptarmigan was running on. He would catch her first, then he would return and investigate.

He exhausted the mother ptarmigan; but he exhausted himself. She lay panting on her side. He lay panting on his side, a dozen feet away, unable to crawl to her. And as he recovered she recovered, fluttering out of reach as his hungry hand went out to her. The chase was resumed. Night settled down and she escaped. He stumbled from weakness and pitched head foremost on his face, cutting his cheek, his pack upon his back. He did not move for a long while; then he rolled over on his side, wound his watch, and lay there until morning.

Another day of fog. Half of his last blanket had gone into foot-wrappings. He failed to pick up Bill's trail. It did not matter. His hunger was driving him too compellingly – only – only he wondered if Bill, too, were lost. By midday the irk of his pack became too oppressive. Again he divided the gold, this time merely spilling half of it on the ground. In the afternoon he threw the rest of it away, there remaining to him only the half-blanket, the tin bucket, and the rifle.

An hallucination began to trouble him. He felt confident that one cartridge remained to him. It was in the chamber of the rifle and he had overlooked it. On the other hand, he knew all the time that the chamber was empty. But the hallucination persisted. He fought it off for hours, then threw his rifle open and was confronted with emptiness. The disappointment was as bitter as though he had really expected to find the cartridge.

He plodded on for half an hour, when the hallucination arose again. Again he fought it, and still it persisted, till for very relief he opened his rifle to unconvince himself. At times his mind wandered farther afield, and he plodded on, a mere automaton, strange conceits and whimsicalities gnawing at his brain like worms. But these excursions out of the real were of brief duration, for ever the pangs of the hungerbite called him back. He was jerked back abruptly once from such an excursion by a sight that caused him nearly to faint. He reeled and swayed, doddering like a drunken man to keep from falling. Before him stood a horse. A horse! He could not believe his eyes. A thick mist was in them, intershot with sparkling points of light. He rubbed his eyes savagely to clear his vision, and beheld, not a horse, but a great brown bear. The animal was studying him with bellicose curiosity.

The man had brought his gun halfway to his shoulder before he realized. He lowered it and drew his hunting-knife from its beaded sheath at his hip. Before him was meat and life. He ran his thumb along the edge of his knife. It was sharp. The point was sharp. He would fling himself upon the bear and kill it. But his heart began its warning thump, thump, thump. Then followed the wild upward leap and tattoo of flutters, the pressing as of an iron band about his forehead, the creeping of the dizziness into his brain.

His desperate courage was evicted by a great surge of fear. In his weakness, what if the animal attacked him? He drew himself up to his most imposing stature, gripping the knife and staring hard at the bear. The bear advanced clumsily a couple of steps, reared up, and gave vent to a tentative growl. If the man ran, he would run after him; but the man did not run. He was animated now with the courage of fear. He, too, growled, savagely, terribly, voicing the fear that is to life germane and that lies twisted about life's deepest roots.

The bear edged away to one side, growling menacingly, himself appalled by this mysterious creature that appeared upright and unafraid. But the man did not move. He stood like a statue till the danger was past, when he yielded to a fit of trembling and sank down into the wet moss.

He pulled himself together and went on, afraid now in a new way. It was not the fear that he should die passively from lack of food, but that he should be destroyed violently before starvation had exhausted the last particle of the endeavor in him that made toward surviving. There were the wolves. Back and forth across the desolation drifted their howls, weaving the very air into a fabric of menace that was so tangible that he found himself, arms in the air, pressing it back from him as it might be the walls of a wind-blown tent.

Now and again the wolves, in packs of two and three, crossed his path. But they sheered clear of him. They were not in sufficient numbers, and besides they were hunting the caribou, which did not battle, while this strange creature that walked erect might scratch and bite.

In the late afternoon he came upon scattered bones where the wolves had made a kill. The débris had been a caribou calf an hour before, squawking and running and very much alive. He contemplated the bones, clean-picked and polished, pink with the cell-life in them which had not yet died. Could it possibly be that he might be that ere the day was done! Such was life, eh? A vain and fleeting thing. It was only life that pained. There was no hurt in death. To die was to sleep. It meant cessation, rest. Then why was he not content to die?

But he did not moralize long. He was squatting in the moss, a bone in his mouth, sucking at the shreds of life that still dyed it faintly pink. The sweet meaty taste, thin and elusive almost as a memory, maddened him. He closed his jaws on the bones and crunched. Sometimes it was the bone that broke, sometimes his teeth. Then he crushed the bones between rocks, pounded them to a pulp, and swallowed them. He pounded his fingers, too, in his haste, and yet found a moment in which to feel surprise at the fact that his fingers did not hurt much when caught under the descending rock.

Came frightful days of snow and rain. He did not know when he made camp, when he broke camp. He travelled in the night as much as in the day. He rested wherever he fell, crawled on whenever the dying life in him flickered up and burned less dimly. He, as a man, no longer strove. It was the life in him, unwilling to die, that drove him on. He did not suffer. His nerves had become blunted, numb, while his mind was filled with weird visions and delicious dreams.

But ever he sucked and chewed on the crushed bones of the caribou calf, the least remnants of which he had gathered up and carried with him. He crossed no more hills or divides, but automatically followed a large stream which flowed through a wide and shallow valley. He did not see this stream nor this valley. He saw nothing save visions. Soul and body walked or crawled side by side, yet apart, so slender was the thread that bound them.

He awoke in his right mind, lying on his back on a rocky ledge. The sun was shining bright and warm. Afar off he heard the squawking of caribou calves. He was aware of vague memories of rain and wind and snow, but whether he had been beaten by the storm for two days or two weeks he did not know.

For some time he lay without movement, the genial sunshine pouring upon him and saturating his miserable body with its warmth. A fine day, he thought. Perhaps he could manage to locate himself. By a painful effort he rolled over on his side. Below him flowed a wide and sluggish river. Its unfamiliarity puzzled him. Slowly he followed it with his eyes, winding in wide sweeps among the bleak, bare hills, bleaker and barer and lower-lying than any hills he had yet encountered. Slowly, deliberately, without excitement or more than the most casual interest, he followed the course of the strange stream toward the sky-line and saw it emptying into a bright and shining sea. He was still unexcited. Most unusual, he thought, a vision or a mirage – more likely a vision, a trick of his disordered mind. He was confirmed in this by sight of a ship lying at anchor in the midst of the shining sea. He closed his eyes for a while, then opened them. Strange how the vision persisted! Yet not strange. He knew there were no seas or ships in the heart of the barren lands, just as he had known there was no cartridge in the empty rifle.

He heard a snuffle behind him – a half-choking gasp or cough. Very slowly, because of his exceeding weakness and stiffness, he rolled over on his other side. He could see nothing near at hand, but he waited patiently. Again came the snuffle and cough, and outlined between two jagged rocks not a score of feet away he made out the gray head of a wolf. The sharp ears were not pricked so sharply as he had seen them on other wolves; the eyes were bleared and bloodshot, the head seemed to droop limply and forlornly. The animal blinked continually in the sunshine. It seemed sick. As he looked it snuffled and coughed again.

This, at least, was real, he thought, and turned on the other side so that he might see the reality of the world which had been veiled from him before by the vision. But the sea still shone in the distance and the ship was plainly discernible. Was it reality, after all? He closed his eyes for a long while and thought, and then it came to him. He had been making north by east, away from the Dease Divide and into the Coppermine Valley. This wide and sluggish river was the Coppermine. That shining sea was the Arctic Ocean. That ship was a whaler, strayed east, far east, from the mouth of the Mackenzie, and it was lying at anchor in Coronation Gulf. He remembered the Hudson Bay Company chart he had seen long ago, and it was all clear and reasonable to him.

He sat up and turned his attention to immediate affairs. He had worn through the blanket-wrappings, and his feet were shapeless lumps of raw meat. His last blanket was gone. Rifle and knife were both missing. He had lost his hat somewhere, with the bunch of matches in the band, but the matches against his chest were safe and dry inside the tobacco pouch and oil paper. He looked at his watch. It marked eleven o'clock and was still running. Evidently he had kept it wound.

He was calm and collected. Though extremely weak, he had no sensation of pain. He was not hungry. The thought of food was not even pleasant to him, and whatever he did was done by his reason alone. He ripped off his pants' legs to the knees and bound them about his feet. Somehow he had succeeded in retaining the tin bucket. He would have some hot water before he began what he foresaw was to be a terrible journey to the ship.

His movements were slow. He shook as with a palsy. When he started to collect dry moss, he found he could not rise to his feet. He tried again and again, then contented himself with crawling about on hands and knees. Once he crawled near to the sick wolf. The animal dragged itself reluctantly out of his way, licking its chops with a tongue which seemed hardly to have the strength to curl. The man noticed that the tongue was not the customary healthy red. It was a yellowish brown and seemed coated with a rough and half-dry mucus.

After he had drunk a quart of hot water the man found he was able to stand, and even to walk as well as a dying man might be supposed to walk. Every minute or so he was compelled to rest. His steps were feeble and uncertain, just as the wolf's that trailed him were feeble and uncertain; and that night, when the shining sea was blotted out by blackness, he knew he was nearer to it by no more than four miles.

Throughout the night he heard the cough of the sick wolf, and now and then the squawking of the caribou calves. There was life all around him, but it was strong life, very much alive and well, and he knew the sick wolf clung to the sick man's trail in the hope that the man would die first. In the morning, on opening his eyes, he beheld it regarding him with a wistful and hungry stare. It stood crouched, with tail between its legs, like a miserable and woe-begone dog. It shivered in the chill morning wind, and grinned dispiritedly when the man spoke to it in a voice that achieved no more than a hoarse whisper.

The sun rose brightly, and all morning the man tottered and fell toward the ship on the shining sea. The weather was perfect. It was the brief Indian Summer of the high latitudes. It might last a week. Tomorrow or next day it might be gone.

In the afternoon the man came upon a trail. It was of another man, who did not walk, but who dragged himself on all fours. The man thought it might be Bill, but he thought in a dull, uninterested way. He had no curiosity. In fact, sensation and emotion had left him. He was no longer susceptible to pain. Stomach and nerves had gone to sleep. Yet the life that was in him drove him on. He was very weary, but it refused to die. It was because it refused to die that he still ate muskeg berries and minnows, drank his hot water, and kept a wary eye on the sick wolf.

He followed the trail of the other man who dragged himself along, and soon came to the end of it – a few fresh-picked bones where the soggy moss was marked by the foot-pads of many wolves. He saw a squat moose-hide sack, mate to his own, which had been torn by sharp teeth. He picked it up, though its weight was almost too much for his feeble fingers. Bill had carried it to the last. Ha! ha! He would have the laugh on Bill. He would survive and carry it to the ship in the shining sea. His mirth was hoarse and ghastly, like a raven's croak, and the sick wolf joined him, howling lugubriously. The man ceased suddenly. How could he have the laugh on Bill if that were Bill; if those bones, so pinky-white and clean, were Bill?

He turned away. Well, Bill had deserted him; but he would not take the gold, nor would he suck Bill's bones. Bill would have, though, had it been the other way around, he mused as he staggered on.

He came to a pool of water. Stooping over in quest of minnows, he jerked his head back as though he had been stung. He had caught sight of his reflected face. So horrible was it that sensibility awoke long enough to be shocked. There were three minnows in the pool, which was too large to drain; and after several ineffectual attempts to catch them in the tin bucket he forbore. He was afraid, because of his great weakness, that he might fall in and drown. It was for this reason that he did not trust himself to the river astride one of the many drift-logs which lined its sand-spits.

That day he decreased the distance between him and the ship by three miles; the next day by two – for he was crawling now as Bill had crawled; and the end of the fifth day found the ship still seven miles away and him unable to make even a mile a day. Still the Indian Summer held on, and he continued to crawl and faint, turn and turn about; and even the sick wolf coughed and wheezed at his heels. His knees had become raw meat like his feet, and though he padded them with the shirt from his back it was a red track he left behind him on the moss and stones. Once, glancing back, he saw the wolf licking hungrily his bleeding trail, and he saw sharply what his own end might be – unless – unless he could get the wolf. Then began as grim a tragedy of existence as was ever played – a sick man that crawled, a sick wolf that limped, two creatures dragging their dying carcasses across the desolation and hunting each other's lives.

Had it been a well wolf, it would not have mattered so much to the man; but the thought of going to feed the maw of that loathsome and all but dead thing was repugnant to him. He was finicky. His mind had begun to wander again, and to be perplexed by hallucinations, while his lucid intervals grew rarer and shorter.

He was awakened once from a faint by a wheeze close in his ear. The wolf leaped lamely back, losing its footing and falling in its weakness. It was ludicrous, but he was not amused. Nor was he even afraid. He was too far gone for that. But his mind was for the moment clear, and he lay and considered. The ship was no more than four miles away. He could see it quite distinctly when he rubbed the mists out of his eyes, and he could see the white sail of a small boat cutting the water of the shining sea. But he could never crawl those four miles. He knew that, and was very calm in the knowledge. He knew that he could not crawl half a mile. And yet he wanted to live. It was unreasonable that he should die after all he had undergone. Fate asked too much of him. And, dying, he declined to die. It was stark madness, perhaps, but in the very grip of Death he defied Death and refused to die.

He closed his eyes and composed himself with infinite precaution. He steeled himself to keep above the suffocating languor that lapped like a rising tide through all the wells of his being. It was very like a sea, this deadly languor, that rose and rose and drowned his consciousness bit by bit. Sometimes he was all but submerged, swimming through oblivion with a faltering stroke; and again, by some strange alchemy of soul, he would find another shred of will and strike out more strongly.

Without movement he lay on his back, and he could hear, slowly drawing near and nearer, the wheezing intake and output of the sick wolf's breath. It drew closer, ever closer, through an infinitude of time, and he did not move. It was at his ear. The harsh dry tongue grated like sandpaper against his cheek. His hands shot out – or at least he willed them to shoot out. The fingers were curved like talons, but they closed on empty air. Swiftness and certitude require strength, and the man had not this strength.

The patience of the wolf was terrible. The man's patience was no less terrible. For half a day he lay motionless, fighting off unconsciousness and waiting for the thing that was to feed upon him and upon which he wished to feed. Sometimes the languid sea rose over him and he dreamed long dreams; but ever through it all, waking and dreaming, he waited for the wheezing breath and the harsh caress of the tongue.

He did not hear the breath, and he slipped slowly from some dream to the feel of the tongue along his hand. He waited. The fangs pressed softly; the pressure increased; the wolf was exerting its last strength in an effort to sink teeth in the food for which it had waited so long. But the man had waited long, and the lacerated hand closed on the jaw. Slowly, while the wolf struggled feebly and the hand clutched feebly, the other hand crept across to a grip. Five minutes later the whole weight of the man's body was on top of the wolf. The hands had not sufficient strength to choke the wolf, but the face of the man was pressed close to the throat of the wolf and the mouth of the man was full of hair. At the end of half an hour the man was aware of a warm trickle in his throat. It was not pleasant. It was like molten lead being forced into his stomach, and it was forced by his will alone. Later the man rolled over on his back and slept.

There were some members of a scientific expedition on the whale-ship *Bedford*. From the deck they remarked a strange object on the shore. It was moving down the beach toward the water. They were unable to classify it, and, being scientific men, they climbed into the whale-boat alongside and went ashore to see. And they saw something that was alive but which could hardly be called a man. It was blind, unconscious. It squirmed along the ground like some monstrous worm. Most of its efforts were ineffectual, but it was persistent, and it writhed and twisted and went ahead perhaps a score of feet an hour.

Three weeks afterward the man lay in a bunk on the whale-ship *Bedford*, and with tears streaming down his wasted cheeks told who he was and what he had undergone. He also babbled incoherently of his mother, of sunny Southern California, and a home among the orange groves and flowers.

The days were not many after that when he sat at table with the scientific men and ship's officers. He gloated over the spectacle of so much food, watching it anxiously as it went into the mouths of others. With the disappearance of each mouthful an expression of deep regret came into his eyes. He was quite sane, yet he hated those men at meal-time. He was haunted by a fear that the food would not last. He inquired of the cook, the cabin-boy, the captain, concerning the food stores. They reassured him countless times; but he could not believe them, and pried cunningly about the lazarette to see with his own eyes.

It was noticed that the man was getting fat. He grew stouter with each day. The scientific men shook their heads and theorized. They limited the man at his meals, but still his girth increased and he swelled prodigiously under his shirt.

The sailors grinned. They knew. And when the scientific men set a watch on the man, they knew too. They saw him slouch for'ard after breakfast, and, like a mendicant, with outstretched palm, accost a sailor. The sailor grinned and passed him a fragment of sea biscuit. He clutched it avariciously, looked at it as a miser looks at gold, and thrust it into his shirt bosom. Similar were the donations from other grinning sailors.

The scientific men were discreet. They let him alone. But they privily examined his bunk. It was lined with hardtack; the mattress was stuffed with hardtack; every nook and cranny was filled with hardtack. Yet he was sane. He was taking precautions against another possible famine – that was all. He would recover from it, the scientific men said; and he did, ere the *Bedford's* anchor rumbled down in San Francisco Bay.

A Piece of Steak (1909; 1911)

With the last morsel of bread Tom King wiped his plate clean of the last particle of flour gravy and chewed the resulting mouthful in a slow and meditative way. When he arose from the table, he was oppressed by the feeling that he was distinctly hungry. Yet he alone had eaten. The two children in the other room had been sent early to bed in order that in sleep they might forget they had gone supperless. His wife had touched nothing, and had sat silently and watched him with solicitous eyes. She was a thin, worn woman of the working-class, though signs of an earlier prettiness were not wanting in her face. The flour for the gravy she had borrowed from the neighbor across the hall. The last two ha'pennies had gone to buy the bread.

He sat down by the window on a rickety chair that protested under his weight, and quite mechanically he put his pipe in his mouth and dipped into the side pocket of his coat. The absence of any tobacco made him aware of his action, and, with a scowl for his forgetfulness, he put the pipe away. His movements were slow, almost hulking, as though he were burdened by the heavy weight of his muscles. He was a solid-bodied, stolid-looking man, and his appearance did not suffer from being overprepossessing. His rough clothes were old and slouchy. The uppers of his shoes were too weak to carry the heavy resoling that was itself of no recent date. And his cotton shirt, a cheap, two-shilling affair, showed a frayed collar and ineradicable paint stains.

But it was Tom King's face that advertised him unmistakably for what he was. It was the face of a typical prize-fighter; of one who had put in long years of service in the squared ring and, by that means, developed and emphasized all the marks of the fighting beast. It was distinctly a lowering countenance, and, that no feature of it might escape notice, it was clean-shaven. The lips were shapeless, and constituted a mouth harsh to excess, that was like a gash in his face. The jaw was aggressive, brutal, heavy. The eyes, slow of movement and heavy-lidded, were almost expressionless under the shaggy, indrawn brows. Sheer animal that he was, the eyes were the most animal-like feature about him. They were sleepy, lion-like – the eyes of a fighting animal. The forehead slanted quickly back to the hair, which, clipped close, showed every bump of a villainous-looking head. A nose, twice broken and moulded variously by countless blows, and a cauliflower ear, permanently swollen and distorted to twice its size, completed his adornment, while the beard, fresh-shaven as it was, sprouted in the skin and gave the face a blue-black stain.

All together, it was the face of a man to be afraid of in a dark alley or lonely place. And yet Tom King was not a criminal, nor had he ever done anything criminal. Outside of brawls, common to his walk in life, he had harmed no one. Nor had he ever been known to pick a quarrel. He was a professional, and all the fighting brutishness of him was reserved for his professional appearances. Outside the ring he was slow-going, easy-natured, and, in his younger days, when money was flush, too open-handed for his own good. He bore no grudges and had few enemies. Fighting was a business with him. In the ring he struck to hurt, struck to maim, struck to destroy; but there was no animus in it. It was a plain business proposition. Audiences assembled and paid for the spectacle of men knocking each other out. The winner took the big end of the purse. When Tom King faced the Woolloomoolloo Gouger, twenty years before, he knew that the Gouger's jaw was only four months healed after having been broken in a Newcastle bout. And he had played for that jaw and broken it again in the ninth round, not because he bore the Gouger any ill-will, but because that was the surest way to put the Gouger out and win the big end of the purse. Nor had the Gouger borne him any ill-will for it. It was the game, and both knew the game and played it.

Tom King had never been a talker, and he sat by the window, morosely silent, staring at his hands. The veins stood out on the backs of the hands, large and swollen; and the knuckles, smashed and battered and malformed, testified to the use to which they had been put. He had never heard that a man's life was the life of his arteries, but well he knew the meaning of those big, upstanding veins. His heart had pumped too much blood through them at top pressure. They no longer did the work. He had stretched the elasticity out of them, and with their distention had passed his endurance. He tired easily now. No longer could he do a fast twenty rounds, hammer and tongs, fight, fight, fight, from gong to gong, with fierce rally on top of fierce rally, beaten to the ropes and in turn beating his opponent to the ropes, and rallying fiercest and fastest of all in that last, twentieth round, with the house on its feet and yelling, himself rushing, striking, ducking, raining showers of blows upon showers of blows and receiving showers of blows in return, and all the time the heart faithfully pumping the surging blood through the adequate veins. The veins, swollen at the time, had always shrunk down again, though not quite – each time, imperceptibly at first, remaining just a trifle larger than before. He stared at them and at his battered knuckles, and, for the moment, caught a vision of the youthful excellence of those hands before the first knuckle had been smashed on the head of Benny Jones, otherwise known as the Welsh Terror.

The impression of his hunger came back on him.

'Blimey, but couldn't I go a piece of steak!' he muttered aloud, clenching his huge fists and spitting out a smothered oath.

'I tried both Burke's an' Sawley's,' his wife said half apologetically.

'An' they wouldn't?' he demanded.

'Not a ha'penny. Burke said –' She faltered.

'G'wan! Wot'd he say?'

'As how 'e was thinkin' Sandel ud do ye tonight, an' as how yer score was comfortable big as it was.'

Tom King grunted, but did not reply. He was busy thinking of the bull terrier he had kept in his younger days to which he had fed steaks without end. Burke would have given him credit for a thousand steaks – then. But times had changed. Tom King was getting old; and old men, fighting before second-rate clubs, couldn't expect to run bills of any size with the tradesmen.

He had got up in the morning with a longing for a piece of steak, and the longing had not abated. He had not had a fair training for this fight. It was a drought year in Australia, times were hard, and even the most irregular work was difficult to find. He had had no sparring partner; and his food had not been of the best nor always sufficient. He had done a few days' navvy work when he could get it, and he had run around the Domain in the early mornings to get his legs in shape. But it was hard, training without a partner and with a wife and two kiddies that must be fed. Credit with the tradesmen had undergone very slight expansion when he was matched with Sandel. The secretary of

the Gayety Club had advanced him three pounds – the loser's end
of the purse – and beyond that had refused to go. Now and again
he had managed to borrow a few shillings from old pals, who
would have lent more only that it was a drought year and they
were hard put themselves. No – and there was no use in
disguising the fact – his training had not been satisfactory. He
should have had better food and no worries. Besides, when a man
is forty, it is harder to get into condition than when he is twenty.

'What time is it, Lizzie?' he asked.

His wife went across the hall to inquire, and came back.

'Quarter before eight.'

'They'll be startin' the first bout in a few minutes,' he said.
'Only a try-out. Then there's a four-round spar 'tween Dealer
Wells an' Gridley, an' a ten-round go 'tween Starlight an' some
sailor bloke. I don't come on for over an hour.'

At the end of another silent ten minutes, he rose to his feet.

'Truth is, Lizzie, I ain't had proper trainin'.'

He reached for his hat and started for the door. He did not offer
to kiss her – he never did on going out – but on this night she
dared to kiss him, throwing her arms around him and compelling
him to bend down to her face. She looked quite small against the
massive bulk of the man.

'Good luck, Tom,' she said. 'You gotter do 'im.'

'Ay, I gotter do 'im,' he repeated. 'That's all there is to it. I jus'
gotter do 'im.'

He laughed with an attempt at heartiness, while she pressed
more closely against him. Across her shoulders he looked around
the bare room. It was all he had in the world, with the rent
overdue, and her and the kiddies. And he was leaving it to go out
into the night to get meat for his mate and cubs – not like a
modern working-man going to his machine grind, but in the old,
primitive, royal, animal way, by fighting for it.

'I gotter do 'im,' he repeated, this time a hint of desperation in
his voice. 'If it's a win, it's thirty quid – an' I can pay all that's
owin', with a lump o' money left over. If it's a lose, I get naught –
not even a penny for me to ride home on the tram. The
secretary's give all that's comin' from a loser's end. Good-by, old
woman. I'll come straight home if it's a win.'

'An' I'll be waitin' up,' she called to him along the hall.

It was full two miles to the Gayety, and as he walked along he
remembered how in his palmy days – he had once been the

heavyweight champion of New South Wales – he would have ridden in a cab to the fight, and how, most likely, some heavy backer would have paid for the cab and ridden with him. There were Tommy Burns and that Yankee nigger, Jack Johnson – they rode about in motor-cars. And he walked! And, as any man knew, a hard two miles was not the best preliminary to a fight. He was an old un, and the world did not wag well with old uns. He was good for nothing now except navvy work, and his broken nose and swollen ear were against him even in that. He found himself wishing that he had learned a trade. It would have been better in the long run. But no one had told him, and he knew, deep down in his heart, that he would not have listened if they had. It had been so easy. Big money – sharp, glorious fights – periods of rest and loafing in between – a following of eager flatterers, the slaps on the back, the shakes of the hand, the toffs glad to buy him a drink for the privilege of five minutes' talk – and the glory of it, the yelling houses, the whirlwind finish, the referee's 'King wins!' and his name in the sporting columns next day.

Those had been times! But he realized now, in his slow, ruminating way, that it was the old uns he had been putting away. He was Youth, rising; and they were Age, sinking. No wonder it had been easy – they with their swollen veins and battered knuckles and weary in the bones of them from the long battles they had already fought. He remembered the time he put out old Stowsher Bill, at Rush-Cutters Bay, in the eighteenth round, and how old Bill had cried afterward in the dressing-room like a baby. Perhaps old Bill's rent had been overdue. Perhaps he'd had at home a missus an' a couple of kiddies. And perhaps Bill, that very day of the fight, had had a hungering for a piece of steak. Bill had fought game and taken incredible punishment. He could see now, after he had gone through the mill himself, that Stowsher Bill had fought for a bigger stake, that night twenty years ago, than had young Tom King, who had fought for glory and easy money. No wonder Stowsher Bill had cried afterward in the dressing-room.

Well, a man had only so many fights in him, to begin with. It was the iron law of the game. One man might have a hundred hard fights in him, another man only twenty; each, according to the make of him and the quality of his fiber, had a definite number, and, when he had fought them, he was done. Yes, he had had more fights in him than most of them, and he had had far more than his share of the hard, gruelling fights – the kind that worked the heart and lungs to bursting, that took the elastic out of the arteries and made hard knots of muscle out of Youth's sleek suppleness, that wore out nerve and stamina and made brain and bones weary from excess of effort and endurance overwrought. Yes, he had done better than all of them. There was none of his old fighting partners left. He was the last of the old guard. He had seen them all finished, and he had had a hand in finishing some of them.

They had tried him out against the old uns, and one after another he had put them away – laughing when, like old Stowsher Bill, they cried in the dressing-room. And now he was an old un, and they tried out the youngsters on him. There was that bloke, Sandel. He had come over from New Zealand with a record behind him. But nobody in Australia knew anything about him, so they put him up against old Tom King. If Sandel made a showing, he would be given better men to fight, with bigger purses to win; so it was to be depended upon that he would put up a fierce battle. He had everything to win by it – money and glory and career; and Tom King was the grizzled old chopping-block that guarded the highway to fame and fortune. And he had nothing to win except thirty quid, to pay to the landlord and the tradesmen. And, as Tom King thus ruminated, there came to his stolid vision the form of Youth, glorious Youth, rising exultant and invincible, supple of muscle and silken of skin, with heart and lungs that had never been tired and torn and that laughed at limitation of effort. Yes, Youth was the Nemesis. It destroyed the old uns and recked not that, in so doing, it destroyed itself. It enlarged its arteries and smashed its knuckles, and was in turn destroyed by Youth. For Youth was ever youthful. It was only Age that grew old.

At Castlereagh Street he turned to the left, and three blocks along came to the Gayety. A crowd of young larrikins hanging outside the door made respectful way for him, and he heard one say to another: 'That's 'im! That's Tom King!'

Inside, on the way to his dressing-room, he encountered the secretary, a keen-eyed, shrewd-faced young man, who shook his hand.

'How are you feelin', Tom?' he asked.

'Fit as a fiddle,' King answered, though he knew that he lied, and that if he had a quid, he would give it right there for a good piece of steak.

When he emerged from the dressing-room, his seconds behind him, and came down the aisle to the squared ring in the centre of the hall, a burst of greeting and applause went up from the waiting crowd. He acknowledged salutations right and left, though few of the faces did he know. Most of them were the faces of kiddies unborn when he was winning his first laurels in the squared ring. He leaped lightly to the raised platform and ducked through the ropes to his corner, where he sat down on a folding stool. Jack Ball, the referee, came over and shook his hand. Ball was a broken-down pugilist who for over ten years had not entered the ring as a principal. King was glad that he had him for referee. They were both old uns. If he should rough it with Sandel a bit beyond the rules, he knew Ball could be depended upon to pass it by.

Aspiring young heavyweights, one after another, were climbing into the ring and being presented to the audience by the referee. Also, he issued their challenges for them.

'Young Pronto,' Bill announced, 'from North Sydney, challenges the winner for fifty pounds side bet.'

The audience applauded, and applauded again as Sandel himself sprang through the ropes and sat down in his corner. Tom King looked across the ring at him curiously, for in a few minutes they would be locked together in merciless combat, each trying with all the force of him to knock the other into unconsciousness. But little could he see, for Sandel, like himself, had trousers and sweater on over his ring costume. His face was strongly handsome, crowned with a curly mop of yellow hair, while his thick, muscular neck hinted at bodily magnificence.

Young Pronto went to one corner and then the other, shaking hands with the principals and dropping down out of the ring. The challenges went on. Ever Youth climbed through the ropes – Youth unknown, but insatiable – crying out to mankind that with strength and skill it would match issues with the winner. A few years before, in his own heyday of invincibleness, Tom King would have been amused and bored by these preliminaries. But now he sat fascinated, unable to shake the vision of Youth from his eyes. Always were these youngsters rising up in the boxing game, springing through the ropes and shouting their defiance; and always were the old uns going down before them. They climbed to success over the bodies of the old uns. And ever they came, more and more youngsters – Youth unquenchable and irresistible – and ever they put the old uns away, themselves becoming old uns and travelling the same downward path, while behind them, ever pressing on them, was Youth eternal – the new babies, grown lusty and dragging their elders down, with behind them more babies to the end of time – Youth that must have its will and that will never die.

King glanced over to the press box and nodded to Morgan, of the *Sportsman*, and Corbett, of the *Referee*. Then he held out his hands, while Sid Sullivan and Charley Bates, his seconds, slipped on his gloves and laced them tight, closely watched by one of Sandel's seconds, who first examined critically the tapes on King's knuckles. A second of his own was in Sandel's corner, performing a like office. Sandel's trousers were pulled off, and, as he stood up, his sweater was skinned off over his head. And Tom King, looking, saw Youth incarnate, deep-chested, heavy-thewed, with muscles that slipped and slid like live things under the white satin skin. The whole body was acrawl with life, and Tom King knew that it was a life that had never oozed its freshness out through the aching pores during the long fights wherein Youth paid its toll and departed not quite so young as when it entered.

The two men advanced to meet each other, and, as the gong sounded and the seconds clattered out of the ring with the folding stools, they shook hands and instantly took their fighting attitudes. And instantly, like a mechanism of steel and springs balanced on a hair trigger, Sandel was in and out and in again, landing a left to the eyes, a right to the ribs, ducking a counter, dancing lightly away and dancing menacingly back again. He was swift and clever. It was a dazzling exhibition. The house yelled its approbation. But King was not dazzled. He had fought too many fights and too many youngsters. He knew the blows for what they were – too quick and too deft to be dangerous. Evidently Sandel was going to rush things from the start. It was to be expected. It was the way of Youth, expending its splendor and excellence in wild insurgence and furious onslaught, over-whelming opposition with its own unlimited glory of strength and desire.

Sandel was in and out, here, there, and everywhere, light-footed and eager-hearted, a living wonder of white flesh and stinging muscle that wove itself into a dazzling fabric of attack, slipping and leaping like a flying shuttle from action to action through a thousand actions, all of them centered upon the destruction of Tom King, who stood between him and fortune. And Tom King patiently endured. He knew his business, and he knew Youth now that Youth was no longer his. There was nothing to do till the other lost some of his steam, was his thought, and he grinned to himself as he deliberately ducked so as to receive a heavy blow on the top of his head. It was a wicked thing to do, yet eminently fair according to the rules of the boxing game. A man was supposed to take care of his own knuckles, and, if he insisted on hitting an opponent on the top of the head, he did so at his own peril. King could have ducked lower and let the blow whiz harmlessly past, but he remembered his own early fights and how he smashed his first knuckle on the head of the Welsh Terror. He was but playing the game. That duck had accounted for one of Sandel's knuckles. Not that Sandel would mind it now. He would go on, superbly regardless, hitting as hard as ever throughout the fight. But later on, when the long ring battles had begun to tell, he would regret that knuckle and look back and remember how he smashed it on Tom King's head.

The first round was all Sandel's, and he had the house yelling with the rapidity of his whirlwind rushes. He overwhelmed King with avalanches of punches, and King did nothing. He never struck once, contenting himself with covering up, blocking and ducking and clinching to avoid punishment. He occasionally feinted, shook his head when the weight of a punch landed, and moved stolidly about, never leaping or springing or wasting an ounce of strength. Sandel must foam the froth of Youth away before discreet Age could dare to retaliate. All King's movements were slow and methodical, and his heavy-lidded, slow-moving eyes gave him the appearance of being half asleep or dazed. Yet they were eyes that saw everything, that had been trained to see everything through all his twenty years and odd in the ring. They were eyes that did not blink or waver before an impending blow, but that coolly saw and measured distance.

Seated in his corner for the minute's rest at the end of the round, he lay back with outstretched legs, his arms resting on the right angle of the ropes, his chest and abdomen heaving frankly and deeply as he gulped down the air driven by the towels of his seconds. He listened with closed eyes to the voices of the house,

'Why don't yeh fight, Tom?' many were crying. 'Yeh ain't afraid of 'im, are yeh?'

'Muscle-bound,' he heard a man on a front seat comment. 'He can't move quicker. Two to one on Sandel, in quids.'

The gong struck and the two men advanced from their corners. Sandel came forward fully three-quarters of the distance, eager to begin again; but King was content to advance the shorter distance. It was in line with his policy of economy. He had not been well trained, and he had not had enough to eat, and every step counted. Besides, he had already walked two miles to the ringside. It was a repetition of the first round, with Sandel attacking like a whirlwind and with the audience indignantly demanding why King did not fight. Beyond feinting and several slowly delivered and ineffectual blows he did nothing save block and stall and clinch. Sandel wanted to make the pace fast, while King, out of his wisdom, refused to accommodate him. He grinned with a certain wistful pathos in his ring-battered countenance, and went on cherishing his strength with the jealousy of which only Age is capable. Sandel was Youth, and he threw his strength away with the munificent abandon of Youth. To King belonged the ring generalship, the wisdom bred of long, aching fights. He watched with cool eyes and head, moving slowly and waiting for Sandel's froth to foam away. To the majority of the onlookers it seemed as though King was hopelessly outclassed, and they voiced their opinion in offers of three to one on Sandel. But there were wise ones, a few, who knew King of old time, and who covered what they considered easy money.

The third round began as usual, one-sided, with Sandel doing all the leading and delivering all the punishment. A half-minute had passed when Sandel, overconfident, left an opening. King's eyes and right arm flashed in the same instant. It was his first real blow – a hook, with the twisted arch of the arm to make it rigid, and with all the weight of the half-pivoted body behind it. It was like a sleepy-seeming lion suddenly thrusting out a lightning paw. Sandel, caught on the side of the jaw, was felled like a bullock. The audience gasped and murmured awe-stricken applause. The man was not muscle-bound, after all, and he could drive a blow like a trip-hammer.

Sandel was shaken. He rolled over and attempted to rise, but the sharp yells from his seconds to take the count restrained him.

He knelt on one knee, ready to rise, and waited, while the referee stood over him, counting the seconds loudly in his ear. At the ninth he rose in fighting attitude, and Tom King, facing him, knew regret that the blow had not been an inch nearer the point of the jaw. That would have been a knockout, and he could have carried the thirty quid home to the missus and the kiddies.

The round continued to the end of its three minutes, Sandel for the first time respectful of his opponent and King slow of movement and sleepy-eyed as ever. As the round neared its close, King, warned of the fact by sight of the seconds crouching outside ready for the spring in through the ropes, worked the fight around to his own corner. And when the gong struck, he sat down immediately on the waiting stool, while Sandel had to walk all the way across the diagonal of the square to his own corner. It was a little thing, but it was the sum of little things that counted. Sandel was compelled to walk that many more steps, to give up that much energy, and to lose a part of the precious minute of rest. At the beginning of every round King loafed slowly out from his corner, forcing his opponent to advance the greater distance. The end of every round found the fight maneuvered by King into his own corner so that he could immediately sit down.

Two more rounds went by, in which King was parsimonious of effort and Sandel prodigal. The latter's attempt to force a fast pace made King uncomfortable, for a fair percentage of the multitudinous blows showered upon him went home. Yet King persisted in his dogged slowness, despite the crying of the young hotheads for him to go in and fight. Again, in the sixth round, Sandel was careless, again Tom King's fearful right flashed out to the jaw, and again Sandel took the nine seconds count.

By the seventh round Sandel's pink of condition was gone, and he settled down to what he knew was to be the hardest fight in his experience. Tom King was an old un, but a better old un than he had ever encountered – an old un who never lost his head, who was remarkably able at defense, whose blows had the impact of a knotted club, and who had a knockout in either hand. Nevertheless, Tom King dared not hit often. He never forgot his battered knuckles, and knew that every hit must count if the knuckles were to last out the fight. As he sat in his corner, glancing across at his opponent, the thought came to him that the sum of his wisdom and Sandel's youth would constitute a

world's champion heavyweight. But that was the trouble. Sandel
would never become a world champion. He lacked the wisdom,
and the only way for him to get it was to buy it with Youth; and
when wisdom was his, Youth would have been spent in buying
it.

King took every advantage he knew. He never missed an
opportunity to clinch, and in effecting most of the clinches his
shoulder drove stiffly into the other's ribs. In the philosophy of
the ring a shoulder was as good as a punch so far as damage was
concerned, and a great deal better so far as concerned expendi-
ture of effort. Also, in the clinches King rested his weight on his
opponent, and was loath to let go. This compelled the interfer-
ence of the referee, who tore them apart, always assisted by
Sandel, who had not yet learned to rest. He could not refrain
from using those glorious flying arms and writhing muscles of
his, and when the other rushed into a clinch, striking shoulder
against ribs, and with head resting under Sandel's left arm,
Sandel almost invariably swung his right behind his own back
and into the projecting face. It was a clever stroke, much admired
by the audience, but it was not dangerous, and was, therefore,
just that much wasted strength. But Sandel was tireless and
unaware of limitations, and King grinned and doggedly endured.

Sandel developed a fierce right to the body, which made it
appear that King was taking an enormous amount of punishment, and it was only the old ringsters who appreciated the deft
touch of King's left glove to the other's biceps just before the
impact of the blow. It was true, the blow landed each time; but
each time it was robbed of its power by that touch on the biceps.
In the ninth round, three times inside a minute, King's right
hooked its twisted arch to the jaw; and three times Sandel's body,
heavy as it was, was levelled to the mat. Each time he took the
nine seconds allowed him and rose to his feet, shaken and jarred,
but still strong. He had lost much of his speed, and he wasted less
effort. He was fighting grimly; but he continued to draw upon his
chief asset, which was Youth. King's chief asset was experience.
As his vitality had dimmed and his vigor abated, he had replaced
them with cunning, with wisdom born of the long fights and with
a careful shepherding of strength. Not alone had he learned
never to make a superfluous movement, but he had learned how
to seduce an opponent into throwing his strength away. Again
and again, by feint of foot and hand and body he continued to

inveigle Sandel into leaping back, ducking, or countering. King rested, but he never permitted Sandel to rest. It was the strategy of Age.

Early in the tenth round King began stopping the other's rushes with straight lefts to the face, and Sandel, grown wary, responded by drawing the left, then by ducking it and delivering his right in a swinging hook to the side of the head. It was too high up to be vitally effective; but when first it landed, King knew the old, familiar descent of the black veil of unconsciousness across his mind. For the instant, or for the slightest fraction of an instant, rather, he ceased. In the one moment he saw his opponent ducking out of his field of vision and the background of white, watching faces; in the next moment he again saw his opponent and the background of faces. It was as if he had slept for a time and just opened his eyes again, and yet the interval of unconsciousness was so microscopically short that there had been no time for him to fall. The audience saw him totter and his knees give, and then saw him recover and tuck his chin deeper into the shelter of his left shoulder.

Several times Sandel repeated the blow, keeping King partially dazed, and then the latter worked out his defence, which was also a counter. Feinting with his left he took a half-step backward, at the same time upper cutting with the whole strength of his right. So accurately was it timed that it landed squarely on Sandel's face in the full, downward sweep of the duck, and Sandel lifted in the air and curled backward, striking the mat on his head and shoulders. Twice King achieved this, then turned loose and hammered his opponent to the ropes. He gave Sandel no chance to rest or to set himself, but smashed blow in upon blow till the house rose to its feet and the air was filled with an unbroken roar of applause. But Sandel's strength and endurance were superb, and he continued to stay on his feet. A knockout seemed certain, and a captain of police, appalled at the dreadful punishment, arose by the ringside to stop the fight. The gong struck for the end of the round and Sandel staggered to his corner, protesting to the captain that he was sound and strong. To prove it, he threw two back air-springs, and the police captain gave in.

Tom King, leaning back in his corner and breathing hard, was disappointed. If the fight had been stopped, the referee, perforce, would have rendered him the decision and the purse would have been his. Unlike Sandel, he was not fighting for glory or career, but for thirty quid. And now Sandel would recuperate in the minute of rest.

Youth will be served – this saying flashed into King's mind, and he remembered the first time he had heard it, the night when he had put away Stowsher Bill. The toff who had bought him a drink after the fight and patted him on the shoulder had used those words. Youth will be served! The toff was right. And on that night in the long ago he had been Youth. Tonight Youth sat in the opposite corner. As for himself, he had been fighting for half an hour now, and he was an old man. Had he fought like Sandel, he would not have lasted fifteen minutes. But the point was that he did not recuperate. Those upstanding arteries and that sorely tried heart would not enable him to gather strength in the intervals between the rounds. And he had not had sufficient strength in him to begin with. His legs were heavy under him and beginning to cramp. He should not have walked those two miles to the fight. And there was the steak which he had got up longing for that morning. A great and terrible hatred rose up in him for the butchers who had refused him credit. It was hard for an old man to go into a fight without enough to eat. And a piece of steak was such a little thing, a few pennies at best; yet it meant thirty quid to him.

With the gong that opened the eleventh round, Sandel rushed, making a show of freshness which he did not really possess. King knew it for what it was – a bluff as old as the game itself. He clinched to save himself, then, going free, allowed Sandel to get set. This was what King desired. He feinted with his left, drew the answering duck and swinging upward hook, then made the half-step backward, delivered the upper cut full to the face and crumpled Sandel over to the mat. After that he never let him rest, receiving punishment himself, but inflicting far more, smashing Sandel to the ropes, hooking and driving all manner of blows into him, tearing away from his clinches or punching him out of attempted clinches, and ever when Sandel would have fallen, catching him with one uplifting hand and with the other immediately smashing him into the ropes where he could not fall.

The house by this time had gone mad, and it was his house, nearly every voice yelling: 'Go it, Tom!' 'Get 'im! Get 'im!' 'You've got 'im, Tom! You've got 'im!' It was to be a whirlwind finish, and that was what a ringside audience paid to see.

And Tom King, who for half an hour had conserved his

strength, now expended it prodigally in the one great effort he knew he had in him. It was his one chance – now or not at all. His strength was waning fast, and his hope was that before the last of it ebbed out of him he would have beaten his opponent down for the count. And as he continued to strike and force, coolly estimating the weight of his blows and the quality of the damage wrought, he realized how hard a man Sandel was to knock out. Stamina and endurance were his to an extreme degree, and they were the virgin stamina and endurance of Youth. Sandel was certainly a coming man. He had it in him. Only out of such rugged fiber were successful fighters fashioned.

Sandel was reeling and staggering, but Tom King's legs were cramping and his knuckles going back on him. Yet he steeled himself to strike the fierce blows, every one of which brought anguish to his tortured hands. Though now he was receiving practically no punishment, he was weakening as rapidly as the other. His blows went home, but there was no longer the weight behind them, and each blow was the result of a severe effort of will. His legs were like lead, and they dragged visibly under him; while Sandel's backers, cheered by this symptom, began calling encouragement to their man.

King was spurred to a burst of effort. He delivered two blows in succession – a left, a trifle too high, to the solar plexus, and a right cross to the jaw. They were not heavy blows, yet so weak and dazed was Sandel that he went down and lay quivering. The referee stood over him, shouting the count of the fatal seconds in his ear. If before the tenth second was called, he did not rise, the fight was lost. The house stood in hushed silence. King rested on trembling legs. A mortal dizziness was upon him, and before his eyes the sea of faces sagged and swayed, while to his ears, as from a remote distance, came the count of the referee. Yet he looked upon the fight as his. It was impossible that a man so punished could rise.

Only Youth could rise, and Sandel rose. At the fourth second he rolled over on his face and groped blindly for the ropes. By the seventh second he had dragged himself to his knee, where he rested, his head rolling groggily on his shoulders. As the referee cried 'Nine!' Sandel stood upright, in proper stalling position, his left arm wrapped about his face, his right wrapped about his stomach. Thus were his vital points guarded, while he lurched forward toward King in the hope of effecting a clinch and gaining more time.

At the instant Sandel arose, King was at him, but the two blows he delivered were muffled on the stalled arms. The next moment Sandel was in the clinch and holding on desperately while the referee strove to drag the two men apart. King helped to force himself free. He knew the rapidity with which Youth recovered, and he knew that Sandel was his if he could prevent that recovery. One stiff punch would do it. Sandel was his, indubitably his. He had outgeneraled him, outfought him, outpointed him. Sandel reeled out of the clinch, balanced on the hair line between defeat or survival. One good blow would topple him over and down and out. And Tom King, in a flash of bitterness, remembered the piece of steak and wished that he had it then behind that necessary punch he must deliver. He nerved himself for the blow, but it was not heavy enough nor swift enough. Sandel swayed, but did not fall, staggering back to the ropes and holding on. King staggered after him, and, with a pang like that of dissolution, delivered another blow. But his body had deserted him. All that was left of him was a fighting intelligence that was dimmed and clouded from exhaustion. The blow that was aimed for the jaw struck no higher than the shoulder. He had willed the blow higher, but the tired muscles had not been able to obey. And, from the impact of the blow, Tom King himself reeled back and nearly fell. Once again he strove. This time his punch missed altogether, and, from absolute weakness, he fell against Sandel and clinched, holding on to him to save himself from sinking to the floor.

King did not attempt to free himself. He had shot his bolt. He was gone. And Youth had been served. Even in the clinch he could feel Sandel growing stronger against him. When the referee thrust them apart, there, before his eyes, he saw Youth recuperate. From instant to instant Sandel grew stronger. His punches, weak and futile at first, became stiff and accurate. Tom King's bleared eyes saw the gloved fist driving at his jaw, and he willed to guard it by interposing his arm. He saw the danger, willed the act; but the arm was too heavy. It seemed burdened with a hundredweight of lead. It would not lift itself, and he strove to lift it with his soul. Then the gloved fist landed home. He experienced a sharp snap that was like an electric spark, and, simultaneously, the veil of blackness enveloped him.

When he opened his eyes again he was in his corner, and he heard the yelling of the audience like the roar of the surf at Bondi Beach. A wet sponge was being pressed against the base of his brain, and Sid Sullivan was blowing cold water in a refreshing spray over his face and chest. His gloves had already been removed, and Sandel, bending over him, was shaking his hand. He bore no ill-will toward the man who had put him out, and he returned the grip with a heartiness that made his battered knuckles protest. Then Sandel stepped to the center of the ring and the audience hushed its pandemonium to hear him accept young Pronto's challenge and offer to increase the side bet to one hundred pounds. King looked on apathetically while his seconds mopped the streaming water from him, dried his face, and prepared him to leave the ring. He felt hungry. It was not the ordinary, gnawing kind, but a great faintness, a palpitation at the pit of the stomach that communicated itself to all his body. He remembered back into the fight to the moment when he had Sandel swaying and tottering on the hair-line balance of defeat. Ah, that piece of steak would have done it! He had lacked just that for the decisive blow, and he had lost. It was all because of the piece of steak.

His seconds were half-supporting him as they helped him through the ropes. He tore free from them, ducked through the ropes unaided, and leaped heavily to the floor, following on their heels as they forced a passage for him down the crowded center aisle. Leaving the dressing-room for the street, in the entrance to the hall, some young fellow spoke to him.

'W'y didn't yuh go in an' get 'im when yuh 'ad 'im?' the young fellow asked.

'Aw, go to hell!' said Tom King, and passed down the steps to the sidewalk.

The doors of the public house at the corner were swinging wide, and he saw the lights and the smiling barmaids, heard the many voices discussing the fight and the prosperous chink of money on the bar. Somebody called to him to have a drink. He hesitated perceptibly, then refused and went on his way.

He had not a copper in his pocket, and the two-mile walk home seemed very long. He was certainly getting old. Crossing the Domain, he sat down suddenly on a bench, unnerved by the thought of the missus sitting up for him, waiting to learn the outcome of the fight. That was harder than any knockout, and it seemed almost impossible to face.

He felt weak and sore, and the pain of his smashed knuckles warned him that, even if he could find a job at navvy work, it would be a week before he could grip a pick handle or a shovel. The hunger palpitation at the pit of the stomach was sickening. His wretchedness overwhelmed him, and into his eyes came an unwonted moisture. He covered his face with his hands, and, as he cried, he remembered Stowsher Bill and how he had served him that night in the long ago. Poor old Stowsher Bill! He could understand now why Bill had cried in the dressing-room.

Koolau the Leper (1909; 1912)

'Because we are sick they take away our liberty. We have obeyed the law. We have done no wrong. And yet they would put us in prison. Molokai is a prison. That you know. Niuli, there, his sister was sent to Molokai seven years ago. He has not seen her since. Nor will he ever see her. She must stay there until she dies. This is not her will. It is not Niuli's will. It is the will of the white men who rule the land. And who are these white men?

'We know. We have it from our fathers and our fathers' fathers. They came like lambs, speaking softly. Well might they speak softly, for we were many and strong, and all the islands were ours. As I say, they spoke softly. They were of two kinds. The one kind asked our permission, our gracious permission, to preach to us the word of God. The other kind asked our permission, our gracious permission, to trade with us. That was the beginning. Today all the islands are theirs, all the land, all the cattle – everything is theirs. They that preached the word of God and they that preached the word of Rum have foregathered and become great chiefs. They live like kings in houses of many rooms, with multitudes of servants to care for them. They who had nothing have everything, and if you, or I, or any Kanaka be hungry, they sneer and say, "Well, why don't you work? There are the plantations." '

Koolau paused. He raised one hand, and with gnarled and twisted fingers lifted up the blazing wreath of hibiscus that crowned his black hair. The moonlight bathed the scene in silver. It was a night of peace, though those who sat about him and listened had all the seeming of battle-wrecks. Their faces were leonine. Here a space yawned in a face where should have been a nose, and there an arm-stump showed where a hand had rotted off. They were men and women beyond the pale, the thirty of them, for upon them had been placed the mark of the beast.

They sat, flower-garlanded, in the perfumed, luminous night, and their lips made uncouth noises and their throats rasped approval of Koolau's speech. They were creatures who once had been men and women. But they were men and women no longer. They were monsters – in face and form grotesque caricatures of everything human. They were hideously maimed and distorted, and had the seeming of creatures that had been racked in millenniums of hell. Their hands, when they possessed them, were like harpy-claws. Their faces were the misfits and slips, crushed and bruised by some mad god at play in the machinery of life. Here and there were features which the mad god had smeared half away, and one woman wept scalding tears from twin pits of horror, where her eyes once had been. Some were in pain and groaned from their chests. Others coughed, making sounds like the tearing of tissue. Two were idiots, more like huge apes marred in the making, until even an ape were an angel. They mowed and gibbered in the moonlight, under crowns of drooping, golden blossoms. One, whose bloated ear-lobe flapped like a fan upon his shoulder, caught up a gorgeous flower of orange and scarlet and with it decorated the monstrous ear that flip-flapped with his every movement.

And over these things Koolau was king. And this was his kingdom – a flower-throttled gorge, with beetling cliffs and crags, from which floated the blattings of wild goats. On three sides the grim walls rose, festooned in fantastic draperies of tropic vegetation and pierced by cave-entrances – the rocky lairs of Koolau's subjects. On the fourth side the earth fell away into a tremendous abyss, and, far below, could be seen the summits of lesser peaks and crags, at whose bases foamed and rumbled the Pacific surge. In fine weather a boat could land on the rocky beach that marked the entrance of Kalalau Valley, but the weather must be very fine. And a cool-headed mountaineer might climb from the beach to the head of Kalalau Valley, to this pocket among the peaks where Koolau ruled; but such a mountaineer must be very cool of head, and he must know the wild-goat trails as well. The marvel was that the mass of human wreckage that constituted Koolau's people should have been able to drag its helpless misery over the giddy goat-trails to this inaccessible spot.

'Brothers,' Koolau began.

But one of the mowing, apelike travesties emitted a wild shriek of madness, and Koolau waited while the shrill cachinnation was tossed back and forth among the rocky walls and echoed distantly through the pulseless night.

'Brothers, is it not strange? Ours was the land, and behold, the land is not ours. What did these preachers of the word of God and the word of Rum give us for the land? Have you received one dollar, as much as one dollar, any one of you, for the land? Yet it is theirs, and in return they tell us we can go to work on the land, their land, and that what we produce by our toil shall be theirs. Yet in the old days we did not have to work. Also, when we are sick, they take away our freedom.'

'Who brought the sickness, Koolau?' demanded Kiloliana, a lean and wiry man with a face so like a laughing faun's that one might expect to see the cloven hoofs under him. They were cloven, it was true, but the cleavages were great ulcers and livid putrefactions. Yet this was Kiloliana, the most daring climber of them all, the man who knew every goat-trail and who had led Koolau and his wretched followers into the recesses of Kalalau.

'Ay, well questioned,' Koolau answered. 'Because we would not work the miles of sugar-cane where once our horses pastured, they brought the Chinese slaves from over seas. And with them came the Chinese sickness – that which we suffer from and because of which they would imprison us on Molokai. We were born on Kauai. We have been to the other islands, some here and some there, to Oahu, to Maui, to Hawaii, to Honolulu. Yet always did we come back to Kauai. Why did we come back? There must be a reason. Because we love Kauai. We were born here. Here we have lived. And here shall we die – unless – unless – there be weak hearts amongst us. Such we do not want. They are fit for Molokai. And if there be such, let them not remain. Tomorrow the soldiers land on the shore. Let the weak hearts go down to them. They will be sent swiftly to Molokai. As for us, we shall stay and fight. But know that we will not die. We have rifles. You know the narrow trails where men must creep, one by one. I, alone, Koolau, who was once a cowboy on Niihau, can hold the trail against a thousand men. Here is Kapahei, who was once a judge over men and a man with honor, but who is now a hunted rat, like you and me. Hear him. He is wise.'

Kapahei arose. Once he had been a judge. He had gone to college at Punahou. He had sat at meat with lords and chiefs and the high representatives of alien powers who protected the interests of traders and missionaries. Such had been Kapahei. But now, as Koolau had said, he was a hunted rat, a creature outside the law, sunk so deep in the mire of human horror that he was above the law as well as beneath it. His face was featureless, save for gaping orifices and for the lidless eyes that burned under hairless brows.

'Let us not make trouble,' he began. 'We ask to be left alone.

But if they do not leave us alone, then is the trouble theirs, and the penalty. My fingers are gone, as you see.' He held up his stumps of hands that all might see. 'Yet have I the joint of one thumb left, and it can pull a trigger as firmly as did its lost neighbor in the old days. We love Kauai. Let us live here, or die here, but do not let us go to the prison of Molokai. The sickness is not ours. We have not sinned. The men who preached the word of God and the word of Rum brought the sickness with the coolie slaves who work the stolen land. I have been a judge. I know the law and the justice, and I say to you it is unjust to steal a man's land, to make that man sick with the Chinese sickness, and then to put that man in prison for life.'

'Life is short, and the days are filled with pain,' said Koolau. 'Let us drink and dance and be happy as we can.'

From one of the rocky lairs calabashes were produced and passed around. The calabashes were filled with the fierce distillation of the root of the *ti*-plant; and as the liquid fire coursed through them and mounted to their brains, they forgot that they had once been men and women, for they were men and women once more. The woman who wept scalding tears from open eye-pits was indeed a woman apulse with life as she plucked the strings of an *ukulele* and lifted her voice in a barbaric love-call such as might have come from the dark forest-depths of the primeval world. The air tingled with her cry, softly imperious and seductive. Upon a mat, timing his rhythm to the woman's song, Kiloliana danced. It was unmistakable. Love danced in all his movements, and next, dancing with him on the mat, was a woman whose heavy hips and generous breast gave the lie to her disease-corroded face. It was a dance of the living dead, for in their disintegrating bodies life still loved and longed. Ever the woman whose sightless eyes ran scalding tears chanted her love-cry, ever the dancers danced of love in the warm night, and ever the calabashes went around till in all their brains were maggots crawling of memory and desire. And with the woman on the mat danced a slender maid whose face was beautiful and unmarred, but whose twisted arms that rose and fell marked the disease's ravage. And the two idiots, gibbering and mouthing strange noises, danced apart, grotesque, fantastic, travestying love as they themselves had been travestied by life.

But the woman's love-cry broke midway, the calabashes were lowered, and the dancers ceased, as all gazed into the abyss above the sea, where a rocket flared like a wan phantom through the moonlit air.

'It is the soldiers,' said Koolau. 'Tomorrow there will be fighting. It is well to sleep and be prepared.'

The lepers obeyed, crawling away to their lairs in the cliff, until only Koolau remained, sitting motionless in the moonlight, his rifle across his knees, as he gazed far down to the boats landing on the beach.

The far head of Kalalau Valley had been well chosen as a refuge. Except Kiloliana, who knew back-trails up the precipitous walls, no man could win to the gorge save by advancing across a knife-edged ridge. This passage was a hundred yards in length. At best, it was a scant twelve inches wide. On either side yawned the abyss. A slip, and to right or left the man would fall to his death. But once across he would find himself in an earthly paradise. A sea of vegetation laved the landscape, pouring its green billows from wall to wall, dripping from the cliff-lips in great vine-masses, and flinging a spray of ferns and air-plants into the multitudinous crevices. During the many months of Koolau's rule, he and his followers had fought with this vegetable sea. The choking jungle, with its riot of blossoms, had been driven back from the bananas, oranges, and mangoes that grew wild. In little clearings grew the wild arrowroot; on stone terraces, filled with soil scrapings, were the *taro* patches and the melons; and in every open space where the sunshine penetrated, were *papaia* trees burdened with their golden fruit.

Koolau had been driven to this refuge from the lower valley by the beach. And if he were driven from it in turn, he knew of gorges among the jumbled peaks of the inner fastnesses where he could lead his subjects and live. And now he lay with his rifle beside him, peering down through a tangled screen of foliage at the soldiers on the beach. He noted that they had large guns with them, from which the sunshine flashed as from mirrors. The knife-edged passage lay directly before him. Crawling upward along the trail that led to it he could see tiny specks of men. He knew they were not the soldiers, but the police. When they failed, then the soldiers would enter the game.

He affectionately rubbed a twisted hand along his rifle barrel and made sure that the sights were clean. He had learned to shoot as a wild-cattle hunter on Niihau, and on that island his skill as a marksman was unforgotten. As the toiling specks of men grew nearer and larger, he estimated the range, judged the deflection of the wind that swept at right angles across the line of fire, and calculated the chances of overshooting marks that were so far below his level. But he did not shoot. Not until they reached the beginning of the passage did he make his presence known. He did not disclose himself, but spoke from the thicket.

'What do you want?' he demanded.

'We want Koolau, the leper,' answered the man who led the native police, himself a blue-eyed American.

'You must go back,' Koolau said.

He knew the man, a deputy sheriff, for it was by him that he had been harried out of Niihau, across Kauai, to Kalalau Valley, and out of the valley to the gorge.

'Who are you?' the sheriff asked.

'I am Koolau, the leper,' was the reply.

'Then come out. We want you. Dead or alive, there is a thousand dollars on your head. You cannot escape.'

Koolau laughed aloud in the thicket.

'Come out!' the sheriff commanded, and was answered by silence.

He conferred with the police, and Koolau saw that they were preparing to rush him.

'Koolau,' the sheriff called. 'Koolau, I am coming across to get you.'

'Then look first and well about you at the sun and sea and sky, for it will be the last time you behold them.'

'That's all right, Koolau,' the sheriff said soothingly. 'I know you're a dead shot. But you won't shoot me. I have never done you any wrong.'

Koolau grunted in the thicket.

'I say, you know, I've never done you any wrong, have I?' the sheriff persisted.

'You do me wrong when you try to put me in prison,' was the reply. 'And you do me wrong when you try for the thousand dollars on my head. If you will live, stay where you are.'

'I've got to come across and get you. I'm sorry. But it is my duty.'

'You will die before you get across.'

The sheriff was no coward. Yet was he undecided. He gazed into the gulf on either side, and ran his eyes along the knife-edge he must travel. Then he made up his mind.

'Koolau,' he called.

But the thicket remained silent.

'Koolau, don't shoot. I am coming.'

The sheriff turned, gave some orders to the police, then started on his perilous way. He advanced slowly. It was like walking a tight rope. He had nothing to lean upon but the air. The lava rock crumbled under his feet, and on either side the dislodged fragments pitched downward through the depths. The sun blazed upon him, and his face was wet with sweat. Still he advanced, until the halfway point was reached.

'Stop!' Koolau commanded from the thicket. 'One more step and I shoot.'

The sheriff halted, swaying for balance as he stood poised above the void. His face was pale, but his eyes were determined. He licked his dry lips before he spoke.

'Koolau, you won't shoot me. I know you won't.'

He started once more. The bullet whirled him half about. On his face was an expression of querulous surprise as he reeled to the fall. He tried to save himself by throwing his body across the knife-edge; but at that moment he knew death. The next moment the knife-edge was vacant. Then came the rush, five policemen, in single file, with superb steadiness, running along the knife-edge. At the same instant the rest of the posse opened fire on the thicket. It was madness. Five times Koolau pulled the trigger, so rapidly that his shots constituted a rattle. Changing his position and crouching low under the bullets that were biting and singing through the bushes, he peered out. Four of the police had followed the sheriff. The fifth lay across the knife-edge, still alive. On the farther side, no longer firing, were the surviving police. On the naked rock there was no hope for them. Before they could clamber down Koolau could have picked off the last man. But he did not fire, and, after a conference, one of them took off a white undershirt and waved it as a flag. Followed by another, he advanced along the knife-edge to their wounded comrade. Koolau gave no sign, but watched them slowly withdraw and become specks as they descended into the lower valley.

Two hours later, from another thicket, Koolau watched a body of police trying to make the ascent from the opposite side of the valley. He saw the wild goats flee before them as they climbed higher and higher, until he doubted his judgment and sent for Kiloliana who crawled in beside him.

'No, there is no way,' said Kiloliana.

'The goats?' Koolau questioned.

'They come over from the next valley, but they cannot pass to this. There is no way. Those men are not wiser than goats. They may fall to their deaths. Let us watch.'

'They are brave men,' said Koolau. 'Let us watch.'

Side by side they lay among the morning-glories, with the yellow blossoms of the *hau* dropping upon them from overhead, watching the motes of men toil upward, till the thing happened, and three of them, slipping, rolling, sliding, dashed over a cliff-lip and fell sheer half a thousand feet.

Kiloliana chuckled.

'We will be bothered no more,' he said.

'They have war guns,' Koolau made answer. 'The soldiers have not yet spoken.'

In the drowsy afternoon, most of the lepers lay in their rock dens asleep. Koolau, his rifle on his knees, fresh-cleaned and ready, dozed in the entrance to his own den. The maid with the twisted arm lay below in the thicket and kept watch on the knife-edge passage. Suddenly Koolau was startled wide awake by the sound of an explosion on the beach. The next instant the atmosphere was incredibly rent asunder. The terrible sound frightened him. It was as if all the gods had caught the envelope of the sky in their hands and were ripping it apart as a woman rips apart a sheet of cotton cloth. But it was such an immense ripping, growing swiftly nearer. Koolau glanced up apprehensively, as if expecting to see the thing. Then high up on the cliff overhead the shell burst in a fountain of black smoke. The rock was shattered, the fragments falling to the foot of the cliff.

Koolau passed his hand across his sweaty brow. He was terribly shaken. He had had no experience with shell-fire, and this was more dreadful than anything he had imagined.

'One,' said Kapahei, suddenly bethinking himself to keep count.

A second and a third shell flew screaming over the top of the wall, bursting beyond view. Kapahei methodically kept the count. The lepers crowded into the open space before the caves. At first they were frightened, but as the shells continued their flight overhead the leper folk became reassured and began to admire the spectacle. The two idiots shrieked with delight, prancing wild antics as each air-tormenting shell went by.

Koolau began to recover his confidence. No damage was being done. Evidently they could not aim such large missiles at such long range with the precision of a rifle.

But a change came over the situation. The shells began to fall short. One burst below in the thicket by the knife-edge. Koolau remembered the maid who lay there on watch, and ran down to see. The smoke was still rising from the bushes when he crawled in. He was astounded. The branches were splintered and broken. Where the girl had lain was a hole in the ground. The girl herself was in shattered fragments. The shell had burst right on her.

First peering out to make sure no soldiers were attempting the passage, Koolau started back on the run for the caves. All the time the shells were moaning, whining, screaming by, and the valley was rumbling and reverberating with the explosions. As he came in sight of the caves, he saw the two idiots cavorting about, clutching each other's hands with their stumps of fingers. Even as he ran, Koolau saw a spout of black smoke rise from the ground, near to the idiots. They were flung apart bodily by the explosion. One lay motionless, but the other was dragging himself by his hands toward the cave. His legs trailed out helplessly behind him, while the blood was pouring from his body. He seemed bathed in blood, and as he crawled he cried like a little dog. The rest of the lepers, with the exception of Kapahei, had fled into the caves.

'Seventeen,' said Kapahei. 'Eighteen,' he added.

This last shell had fairly entered into one of the caves. The explosion caused all the caves to empty. But from the particular cave no one emerged. Koolau crept in through the pungent, acrid smoke. Four bodies, frightfully mangled, lay about. One of them was the sightless woman whose tears till now had never ceased.

Outside, Koolau found his people in a panic and already beginning to climb the goat trail that led out of the gorge and on among the jumbled heights and chasms. The wounded idiot, whining feebly and dragging himself along on the ground by his hands, was trying to follow. But at the first pitch of the wall his helplessness overcame him and he fell back.

'It would be better to kill him,' said Koolau to Kapalei, who still sat in the same place.

'Twenty-two,' Kapahei answered. 'Yes, it would be a wise thing to kill him. Twenty-three – twenty-four.'

The idiot whined sharply when he saw the rifle leveled at him. Koolau hesitated, then lowered the gun.

'It is a hard thing to do,' he said.

'You are a fool, twenty-six, twenty-seven,' said Kapahei. 'Let me show you.'

He arose and, with a heavy fragment of rock in his hand, approached the wounded thing. As he lifted his arm to strike, a shell burst full upon him, relieving him of the necessity of the act and at the same time putting an end to his count.

Koolau was alone in the gorge. He watched the last of his people drag their crippled bodies over the brow of the height and disappear. Then he turned and went down to the thicket where the maid had been killed. The shell-fire still continued, but he remained; for far below he could see the soldiers climbing up. A shell burst twenty feet away. Flattening himself into the earth, he heard the rush of the fragments above his body. A shower of *hau* blossoms rained upon him. He lifted his head to peer down the trail, and sighed. He was very much afraid. Bullets from rifles would not have worried him, but this shell-fire was abominable. Each time a shell shrieked by he shivered and crouched; but each time he lifted his head again to watch the trail.

At last the shells ceased. This, he reasoned, was because the soldiers were drawing near. They crept along the trail in single file, and he tried to count them until he lost track. At any rate, there were a hundred or so of them – all come after Koolau the leper. He felt a fleeting prod of pride. With war guns and rifles, police and soldiers, they came for him, and he was only one man, a crippled wreck of a man at that. They offered a thousand dollars for him, dead or alive. In all his life he had never possessed that much money. The thought was a bitter one. Kapahei had been right. He, Koolau, had done no wrong. Because the *haoles* wanted labor with which to work the stolen land, they had brought in the Chinese coolies, and with them had come the sickness. And now, because he had caught the sickness, he was worth a thousand dollars – but not to himself. It was his worthless carcass, rotten with disease or dead from a bursting shell, that was worth all that money.

When the soldiers reached the knife-edged passage, he was prompted to warn them. But his gaze fell upon the body of the murdered maid, and he kept silent. When six had ventured on the knife-edge, he opened fire. Nor did he cease when the knife-

edge was bare. He emptied his magazine, reloaded, and emptied it
again. He kept on shooting. All his wrongs were blazing in his
brain, and he was in a fury of vengeance. All down the goat trail
the soldiers were firing, and though they lay flat and sought to
shelter themselves in the shallow inequalities of the surface, they
were exposed marks to him. Bullets whistled and thudded about
him, and an occasional ricochet sang sharply through the air.
One bullet ploughed a crease through his scalp, and a second
burned across his shoulder-blade without breaking the skin.

It was a massacre, in which one man did the killing. The
soldiers began to retreat, helping along their wounded. As
Koolau picked them off he became aware of the smell of burnt
meat. He glanced about him at first, and then discovered that it
was his own hands. The heat of the rifle was doing it. The leprosy
had destroyed most of the nerves in his hands. Though his flesh
burned and he smelled it, there was no sensation.

He lay in the thicket, smiling, until he remembered the war
guns. Without doubt they would open up on him again, and this
time upon the very thicket from which he had inflicted the
damage. Scarcely had he changed his position to a nook behind a
small shoulder of the wall where he had noted that no shells fell,
than the bombardment recommenced. He counted the shells.
Sixty more were thrown into the gorge before the war-guns
ceased. The tiny area was pitted with their explosions, until it
seemed impossible that any creature could have survived. So the
soldiers thought, for, under the burning afternoon sun, they
climbed the goat trail again. And again the knife-edged passage
was disputed, and again they fell back to the beach.

For two days longer Koolau held the passage, though the
soldiers contented themselves with flinging shells into his retreat.
Then Pahau, a leper boy, came to the top of the wall at the back
of the gorge and shouted down to him that Kiloliana, hunting
goats that they might eat, had been killed by a fall, and that the
women were frightened and knew not what to do. Koolau called
the boy down and left him with a spare gun with which to guard
the passage. Koolau found his people disheartened. The majority
of them were too helpless to forage food for themselves under
such forbidding circumstances, and all were starving. He selected
two women and a man who were not too far gone with the
disease, and sent them back to the gorge to bring up food and

mats. The rest he cheered and consoled until even the weakest took a hand in building rough shelters for themselves.

But those he had dispatched for food did not return, and he started back for the gorge. As he came out on the brow of the wall, half a dozen rifles cracked. A bullet tore through the fleshy part of his shoulder, and his cheek was cut by a sliver of rock where a second bullet smashed against the cliff. In the moment that this happened, and he leaped back, he saw that the gorge was alive with soldiers. His own people had betrayed him. The shell-fire had been too terrible, and they had preferred the prison of Molokai.

Koolau dropped back and unslung one of his heavy cartridge-belts. Lying among the rocks, he allowed the head and shoulders of the first soldier to rise clearly into view before pulling trigger. Twice this happened, and then, after some delay, in place of a head and shoulders a white flag was thrust above the edge of the wall.

'What do you want?' he demanded.

'I want you, if you are Koolau the leper,' came the answer.

Koolau forgot where he was, forgot everything, as he lay and marveled at the strange persistence of these *haoles* who would have their will though the sky fell in. Aye, they would have their will over all men and all things, even though they died in getting it. He could not but admire them, too, what of that will in them that was stronger than life and that bent all things to their bidding. He was convinced of the hopelessness of his struggle. There was no gainsaying that terrible will of the *haoles*. Though he killed a thousand, yet would they rise like the sands of the sea and come upon him, ever more and more. They never knew when they were beaten. That was their fault and their virtue. It was where his own kind lacked. He could see, now, how the handful of the preachers of God and the preachers of Rum had conquered the land. It was because –

'Well, what have you got to say? Will you come with me?'

It was the voice of the invisible man under the white flag. There he was, like any *haole*, driving straight toward the end determined.

'Let us talk,' said Koolau.

The man's head and shoulders arose, then his whole body. He was a smooth-faced, blue-eyed youngster of twenty-five, slender and natty in his captain's uniform. He advanced until halted, then seated himself a dozen feet away:

'You are a brave man,' said Koolau wonderingly. 'I could kill
you like a fly.'

'No, you couldn't,' was the answer.

'Why not?'

'Because you are a man, Koolau, though a bad one. I know
your story. You kill fairly.'

Koolau grunted, but was secretly pleased. 'What have you
done with my people?' he demanded. 'The boy, the two women,
and the man?'

'They gave themselves up, as I have now come for you to do.'

Koolau laughed incredulously.

'I am a free man,' he announced. 'I have done no wrong. All I
ask is to be left alone. I have lived free, and I shall die free. I will
never give myself up.'

'Then your people are wiser than you,' answered the young
captain. 'Look – they are coming now.'

Koolau turned and watched the remnant of his band approach.
Groaning and sighing, a ghastly procession, it dragged its
wretchedness past. It was given to Koolau to taste a deeper
bitterness, for they hurled imprecations and insults at him as
they went by; and the panting hag who brought up the rear
halted, and with skinny, harpy-claws extended, shaking her
snarling death's head from side to side, she laid a curse upon him.
One by one they dropped over the lip-edge and surrendered to the
hiding soldiers.

'You can go now,' said Koolau to the captain. 'I will never give
myself up. That is my last word. Good-by.'

The captain slipped over the cliff to his soldiers. The next
moment, and without a flag of truce, he hoisted his hat on his
scabbard, and Koolau's bullet tore through it. That afternoon
they shelled him out from the beach, and as he retreated into the
high inaccessible pockets beyond, the soldiers followed him.

For six weeks they hunted him from pocket to pocket, over the
volcanic peaks and along the goat trails. When he hid in the
lantana jungle, they formed lines of beaters, and through lantana
jungle and guava scrub they drove him like a rabbit. But ever he
turned and doubled and eluded. There was no cornering him.
When pressed too closely, his sure rifle held them back and they
carried their wounded down the goat trails to the beach. There
were times when they did the shooting as his brown body
showed for a moment through the underbrush. Once, five of

them caught him on an exposed goat trail between pockets. They emptied their rifles at him as he limped and climbed along his dizzy way. Afterward they found blood-stains and knew that he was wounded. At the end of six weeks they gave up. The soldiers and police returned to Honolulu, and Kalalau Valley was left to him for his own, though head-hunters ventured after him from time to time and to their own undoing.

Two years later, and for the last time, Koolau crawled unto a thicket and lay down among the ti-leaves and wild ginger blossoms. Free he had lived, and free he was dying. A slight drizzle of rain began to fall, and he drew a ragged blanket about the distorted wreck of his limbs. His body was covered with an oilskin coat. Across his chest he laid his Mauser rifle, lingering affectionately for a moment to wipe the dampness from the barrel. The hand with which he wiped had no fingers left upon it with which to pull the trigger.

He closed his eyes, for, from the weakness in his body and the fuzzy turmoil in his brain, he knew that his end was near. Like a wild animal he had crept into hiding to die. Half-conscious, aimless and wandering, he lived back in his life to his early manhood on Niihau. As life faded and the drip of the rain grew dim in his ears, it seemed to him that he was once more in the thick of the horse-breaking, with raw colts rearing and bucking under him, his stirrups tied together beneath, or charging madly about the breaking corral and driving the helping cowboys over the rails. The next instant, and with seeming naturalness, he found himself pursuing the wild bulls of the upland pastures, roping them and leading them down to the valleys. Again the sweat and dust of the branding pen stung his eyes and bit his nostrils.

All his lusty, whole-bodied youth was his, until the sharp pangs of impending dissolution brought him back. He lifted his monstrous hands and gazed at them in wonder. But how? Why? Why should the wholeness of that wild youth of his change to this? Then he remembered, and once again, and for a moment, he was Koolau, the leper. His eyelids fluttered wearily down and the drip of the rain ceased in his ears. A prolonged trembling set up in his body. This, too, ceased. He half-lifted his head, but it fell back. Then his eyes opened, and did not close. His last thought was of his Mauser, and he pressed it against his chest with his folded, fingerless hands.

War (1911; 1913)

1

He was a young man, not more than twenty-four or five, and he might have sat his horse with the careless grace of his youth had he not been so catlike and tense. His black eyes roved everywhere, catching the movements of twigs and branches where small birds hopped, questing ever onward through the changing vistas of trees and brush, and returning always to the clumps of undergrowth on either side. And as he watched, so did he listen, though he rode on in silence, save for the boom of heavy guns from far to the west. This had been sounding monotonously in his ears for hours, and only its cessation would have aroused his notice. For he had business closer to hand. Across his saddle-bow was balanced a carbine.

So tensely was he strung, that a bunch of quail, exploding into flight from under his horse's nose, startled him to such an extent that automatically, instantly, he had reined in and fetched the carbine halfway to his shoulder. He grinned sheepishly, recovered himself, and rode on. So tense was he, so bent upon the work he had to do, that the sweat stung his eyes unwiped, and unheeded rolled down his nose and spattered his saddle pommel. The band of his cavalryman's hat was fresh-stained with sweat. The roan horse under him was likewise wet. It was high noon of a breathless day of heat. Even the birds and squirrels did not dare the sun, but sheltered in shady hiding places among the trees.

Man and horse were littered with leaves and dusted with yellow pollen, for the open was ventured no more than was compulsory. They kept to the brush and trees, and invariably the man halted and peered out before crossing a dry glade or naked stretch of upland pasturage. He worked always to the north, though his way was devious, and it was from the north that he seemed most to apprehend that for which he was looking. He was no coward, but his courage was only that of the average civilized man, and he was looking to live, not die.

Up a small hillside he followed a cowpath through such dense scrub that he was forced to dismount and lead his horse. But

when the path swung around to the west, he abandoned it and
headed to the north again along the oak-covered top of the ridge.

The ridge ended in a steep descent – steep that he zigzagged back
and forth across the face of the slope, sliding and stumbling among
the dead leaves and matted vines and keeping a watchful eye on
the horse above that threatened to fall down upon him. The sweat
ran from him, and the pollendust, settling pungently in mouth and
nostrils, increased his thirst. Try as he would, nevertheless the
descent was noisy, and frequently he stopped, panting in the dry
heat and listening for any warning from beneath.

At the bottom he came out on a flat, so densely forested that he
could not make out its extent. Here the character of the woods
changed, and he was able to remount. Instead of the twisted
hillside oaks, tall straight trees, big-trunked and prosperous, rose
from the damp fat soil. Only here and there were thickets, easily
avoided, while he encountered winding, park-like glades where
the cattle had pastured in the days before war had run them off.

His progress was more rapid now, as he came down into the
valley, and at the end of half an hour he halted at an ancient rail
fence on the edge of a clearing. He did not like the openness of it,
yet his path lay across to the fringe of trees that marked the banks
of the stream. It was a mere quarter of a mile across that open, but
the thought of venturing out in it was repugnant. A rifle, a score of
them, a thousand, might lurk in that fringe by the stream.

Twice he essayed to start, and twice he paused. He was
appalled by his own loneliness. The pulse of war that beat from
the West suggested the companionship of battling thousands;
here was naught but silence, and himself, and possible death-
dealing bullets from a myriad ambushes. And yet his task was to
find what he feared to find. He must go on, and on, till
somewhere, some time, he encountered another man, or other
men, from the other side, scouting, as he was scouting, to make
report, as he must make report, of having come in touch.

Changing his mind, he skirted inside the woods for a distance,
and again peeped forth. This time, in the middle of the clearing,
he saw a small farmhouse. There were no signs of life. No smoke
curled from the chimney, not a barnyard fowl clucked and
strutted. The kitchen door stood open, and he gazed so long and
hard into the black aperture that it seemed almost that a farmer's
wife must emerge at any moment.

He licked the pollen and dust from his dry lips, stiffened

himself, mind and body, and rode out into the blazing sunshine. Nothing stirred. He went on past the house, and approached the wall of trees and bushes by the river's bank. One thought persisted maddeningly. It was of the crash into his body of a high-velocity bullet. It made him feel very fragile and defenseless, and he crouched lower in the saddle.

Tethering his horse in the edge of the wood, he continued a hundred yards on foot till he came to the stream. Twenty feet wide it was, without perceptible current, cool and inviting, and he was very thirsty. But he waited inside his screen of leafage, his eyes fixed on the screen on the opposite side. To make the wait endurable, he sat down, his carbine resting on his knees. The minutes passed, and slowly his tenseness relaxed. At last he decided there was no danger; but just as he prepared to part the bushes and bend down to the water, a movement among the opposite bushes caught his eye.

It might be a bird. But he waited. Again there was an agitation of the bushes, and then, so suddenly that it almost startled a cry from him, the bushes parted and a face peered out. It was a face covered with several weeks' growth of ginger-colored beard. The eyes were blue and wide apart, with laughter-wrinkles in the corners that showed despite the tired and anxious expression of the whole face.

All this he could see with microscopic clearness, for the distance was no more than twenty feet. And all this he saw in such brief time, that he saw it as he lifted his carbine to his shoulder. He glanced along the sights, and knew that he was gazing upon a man who was as good as dead. It was impossible to miss at such point blank range.

But he did not shoot. Slowly he lowered the carbine and watched. A hand, clutching a water-bottle, became visible and the ginger beard bent downward to fill the bottle. He could hear the gurgle of the water. Then arm and bottle and ginger beard disappeared behind the closing bushes. A long time he waited, when, with thirst unslaked, he crept back to his horse, rode slowly across the sun-washed clearing, and passed into the shelter of the woods beyond.

2

Another day, hot and breathless. A deserted farmhouse, large, with many outbuildings and an orchard, standing in a clearing.

From the woods, on a roan horse, carbine across pommel, rode the young man with the quick black eyes. He breathed with relief as he gained the house. That a fight had taken place here earlier in the season was evident. Clips and empty cartridges, tarnished with verdigris, lay on the ground, which, while wet, had been torn up by the hoofs of horses. Hard by the kitchen garden were graves, tagged and numbered. From the oak tree by the kitchen door, in tattered, weather-beaten garments, hung the bodies of two men. The faces, shriveled and defaced, bore no likeness to the faces of men. The roan horse snorted beneath them, and the rider caressed and soothed it and tied it farther away.

Entering the house, he found the interior a wreck. He trod on empty cartridges as he walked from room to room to reconnoiter from the windows. Men had camped and slept everywhere, and on the floor of one room he came upon stains unmistakable where the wounded had been laid down.

Again outside, he led the horse around behind the barn and invaded the orchard. A dozen trees were burdened with ripe apples. He filled his pockets, eating while he picked. Then a thought came to him, and he glanced at the sun, calculating the time of his return to camp. He pulled off his shirt, tying the sleeves and making a bag. This he proceeded to fill with apples.

As he was about to mount his horse, the animal suddenly pricked up its ears. The man, too, listened, and heard, faintly, the thud of hoofs on soft earth. He crept to the corner of the barn and peered out. A dozen mounted men, strung out loosely, approaching from the opposite side of the clearing, were only a matter of a hundred yards or so away. They rode on to the house. Some dismounted, while others remained in the saddle as an earnest that their stay would be short. They seemed to be holding a council, for he could hear them talking excitedly in the detested tongue of the alien invader. The time passed, but they seemed unable to reach a decision. He put the carbine away in its boot, mounted, and waited impatiently, balancing the shirt of apples on the pommel.

He heard footsteps approaching, and drove his spurs so fiercely into the roan as to force a surprised groan from the animal as it leaped forward. At the corner of the barn he saw the intruder, a mere boy of nineteen or twenty for all of his uniform, jump back to escape being run down. At the same moment the roan swerved, and its rider caught a glimpse of the aroused men by the house. Some were springing from their horses, and he could see the rifles going to their shoulders. He passed the kitchen door and the dried corpses swinging in the shade, compelling his foes to run around the front of the house. A rifle cracked, and a second, but he was going fast, leaning forward, low in the saddle, one hand clutching the shirt of apples, the other guiding the horse.

The top bar of the fence was four feet high, but he knew his roan and leaped it at full career to the accompaniment of several scattered shots. Eight hundred yards straight away were the woods, and the roan was covering the distance with mighty strides. Every man was now firing. They were pumping their guns so rapidly that he no longer heard individual shots. A bullet went through his hat, but he was unaware, though he did know when another tore through the apples on the pommel. And he winced and ducked even lower when a third bullet, fired low, struck a stone between his horse's legs and ricochetted off through the air, buzzing and humming like some incredible insect.

The shots died down as the magazines were emptied, until, quickly, there was no more shooting. The young man was elated. Through that astonishing fusillade he had come unscathed. He glanced back. Yes, they had emptied their magazines. He could see several reloading. Others were running back behind the house for their horses. As he looked, two already mounted, came back into view around the corner, riding hard. And at the same moment, he saw the man with the unmistakable ginger beard kneel down on the ground, level his gun, and coolly take his time for the long shot.

The young man threw his spurs into the horse, crouched very low, and swerved in his flight in order to distract the other's aim. And still the shot did not come. With each jump of the horse, the woods sprang nearer. They were only two hundred yards away, and still the shot was delayed.

And then he heard it, the last thing he was to hear, for he was dead ere he hit the ground in the long crashing fall from the saddle. And they, watching at the house, saw him fall, saw his body bounce when it struck the earth, and saw the burst of red-cheeked apples that rolled about him. They laughed at the unexpected eruption of apples, and clapped their hands in applause of the long shot by the man with the ginger beard.

The Mexican (1911; 1913)

1

Nobody knew his history – they of the Junta least of all. He was their 'little mystery', their 'big patriot', and in his way he worked as hard for the coming Mexican Revolution as did they. They were tardy in recognizing this, for not one of the Junta liked him. The day he first drifted into their crowded, busy rooms, they all suspected him of being a spy – one of the bought tools of the Diaz secret service. Too many of the comrades were in civil and military prisons scattered over the United States, and others of them, in irons, were even then being taken across the border to be lined up against adobe walls and shot.

At the first sight the boy did not impress them favorably. Boy he was, not more than eighteen and not over large for his years. He announced that he was Felipe Rivera, and that it was his wish to work for the Revolution. That was all – not a wasted word, no further explanation. He stood waiting. There was no smile on his lips, no geniality in his eyes. Big dashing Paulino Vera felt an inward shudder. Here was something forbidding, terrible, inscrutable. There was something venomous and snakelike in the boy's black eyes. They burned like cold fire, as with a vast, concentrated bitterness. He flashed them from the faces of the conspirators to the typewriter which little Mrs Sethby was industriously operating. His eyes rested on hers but an instant – she had chanced to look up – and she, too, sensed the nameless something that made her pause. She was compelled to read back in order to regain the swing of the letter she was writing.

Paulino Vera looked questioningly at Arrellano and Ramos, and questioningly they looked back and to each other. The indecision of doubt brooded in their eyes. This slender boy was the Unknown, vested with all the menace of the Unknown. He was unrecognizable, something quite beyond the ken of honest, ordinary revolutionists whose fiercest hatred for Diaz and his tyranny after all was only that of honest and ordinary patriots.

Here was something else, they knew not what. But Vera, always the most impulsive, the quickest to act, stepped into the breach.

'Very well,' he said coldly. 'You say you want to work for the Revolution. Take off your coat. Hang it over there. I will show you – come – where are the buckets and cloths. The floor is dirty. You will begin by scrubbing it, and by scrubbing the floors of the other rooms. The spittoons need to be cleaned. Then there are the windows.'

'Is it for the Revolution?' the boy asked.

'It is for the Revolution,' Vera answered.

Rivera looked cold suspicion at all of them, then proceeded to take off his coat.

'It is well,' he said.

And nothing more. Day after day he came to his work – sweeping, scrubbing, cleaning. He emptied the ashes from the stoves, brought up the coal and kindling, and lighted the fires before the most energetic one of them was at his desk.

'Can I sleep here?' he asked once.

Ah, ha! So that was it – the hand of Diaz showing through! To sleep in the rooms of the Junta meant access to their secrets, to the lists of names, to the addresses of comrades down on Mexican soil. The request was denied, and Rivera never spoke of it again. He slept they knew not where, and ate they knew not where nor how. Once, Arrellano offered him a couple of dollars. Rivera declined the money with a shake of the head. When Vera joined in and tried to press it upon him, he said:

'I am working for the Revolution.'

It takes money to raise a modern revolution, and always the Junta was pressed. The members starved and toiled, and the longest day was none too long, and yet there were times when it appeared as if the Revolution stood or fell on no more than the matter of a few dollars. Once, the first time, when the rent of the house was two months behind and the landlord was threatening dispossession, it was Felipe Rivera, the scrub-boy in the poor, cheap clothes, worn and threadbare, who laid sixty dollars in gold on May Sethby's desk. There were other times. Three hundred letters, clicked out on the busy typewriters (appeals for assistance, for sanctions from the organized labor groups, requests for square news deals to the editors of newspapers, protests against the high-handed treatment of revolutionists by the United States courts), lay unmailed, awaiting postage. Vera's watch had disappeared – the old-fashioned gold repeater that had been his father's. Likewise had gone the plain gold band from May Sethby's third finger. Things were desperate. Ramos and Arrellano pulled their long mustaches in despair. The letters must go off, and the Post Office allowed no credit to purchasers of stamps. Then it was that Rivera put on his hat and went out. When he came back he laid a thousand two-cent stamps on May Sethby's desk.

'I wonder if it is the cursed gold of Diaz?' said Vera to the comrades.

They elevated their brows and could not decide. And Felipe Rivera, the scrubber for the Revolution, continued, as occasion arose, to lay down gold and silver for the Junta's use.

And still they could not bring themselves to like him. They did not know him. His ways were not theirs. He gave no confidences. He repelled all probing. Youth that he was, they could never nerve themselves to dare to question him.

'A great and lonely spirit, perhaps, I do not know, I do not know,' Arrellano said helplessly.

'He is not human,' said Ramos.

'His soul has been seared,' said May Sethby. 'Light and laughter have been burned out of him. He is like one dead, and yet he is fearfully alive.'

'He has been through hell,' said Vera. 'No man could look like that who has not been through hell – and he is only a boy.'

Yet they could not like him. He never talked, never inquired, never suggested. He would stand listening, expressionless, a thing dead, save for his eyes, coldly burning, while their talk of the Revolution ran high and warm. From face to face and speaker to speaker his eyes would turn, boring like gimlets of incandescent ice, disconcerting and perturbing.

'He is no spy,' Vera confided to May Sethby. 'He is a patriot – mark me, the greatest patriot of us all. I know it, I feel it, here in my heart and head I feel it. But him I know not at all.'

'He has a bad temper,' said May Sethby.

'I know,' said Vera, with a shudder. 'He has looked at me with those eyes of his. They do not love; they threaten; they are savage as a wild tiger's. I know, if I should prove unfaithful to the Cause, that he would kill me. He has no heart. He is pitiless as steel, keen and cold as frost. He is like moonshine in a winter night when a man freezes to death on some lonely mountain top. I am not afraid of Diaz and all his killers; but this boy, of him am I afraid. I tell you true. I am afraid. He is the breath of death.'

Yet Vera it was who persuaded the others to give the first trust to Rivera. The line of communication between Los Angeles and Lower California had broken down. Three of the comrades had dug their own graves and been shot into them. Two more were United States prisoners in Los Angeles. Juan Alvarado, the Federal commander, was a monster. All their plans did he checkmate. They could no longer gain access to the active revolutionists, and the incipient ones, in Lower California.

Young Rivera was given his instructions and dispatched south. When he returned, the line of communication was re-established, and Juan Alvarado was dead. He had been found in bed, a knife hilt-deep in his breast. This had exceeded Rivera's instructions, but they of the Junta knew the times of his movements. They did not ask him. He said nothing. But they looked at one another and conjectured.

'I have told you,' said Vera. 'Diaz has more to fear from this youth than from any man. He is implacable. He is the hand of God.'

The bad temper, mentioned by May Sethby, and sensed by them all, was evidenced by physical proofs. Now he appeared with a cut lip, a blackened cheek, or a swollen ear. It was patent that he brawled, somewhere in that outside world where he ate and slept, gained money, and moved in ways unknown to them. As the time passed, he had come to set type for the little revolutionary sheet they published weekly. There were occasions when he was unable to set type, when his knuckles were bruised and battered, when his thumbs were injured and helpless, when one arm or the other hung wearily at his side while his face was drawn with unspoken pain.

'A wastrel,' said Arrellano.

'A frequenter of low places,' said Ramos.

'But where does he get the money?' Vera demanded. 'Only today, just now, have I learned that he paid the bill for white paper – one hundred and forty dollars.'

'There are his absences,' said May Sethby. 'He never explains them.'

'We should set a spy upon him,' Ramos propounded.

'I should not care to be that spy,' said Vera. 'I fear you would never see me again, save to bury me. He has a terrible passion.

Not even God would he permit to stand between him and the way of his passion.'

'I feel like a child before him,' Ramos confessed.

'To me he is power – he is the primitive, the wild wolf – the striking rattlesnake, the stinging centipede,' said Arrellano.

'He is the Revolution incarnate,' said Vera. 'He is the flame and the spirit of it, the insatiable cry for vengeance that makes no cry but that slays noiselessly. He is a destroying angel moving through the still watches of the night.'

'I could weep over him,' said May Sethby. 'He knows nobody. He hates all people. Us he tolerates, for we are the way of his desire. He is alone . . . lonely.' Her voice broke in a half sob and there was dimness in her eyes.

Rivera's ways and times were truly mysterious. There were periods when they did not see him for a week at a time. Once, he was away a month. These occasions were always capped by his return, when, without advertisement or speech, he laid gold coins on May Sethby's desk. Again, for days and weeks, he spent all his time with the Junta. And yet again, for irregular periods, he would disappear through the heart of each day, from early morning until late afternoon. At such times he came early and remained late. Arrellano had found him at midnight, setting type with fresh swollen knuckles, or mayhap it was his lip, new-split, that still bled.

2

The time of the crisis approached. Whether or not the Revolution would be depended upon the Junta, and the Junta was hard-pressed. The need for money was greater than ever before, while money was harder to get. Patriots had given their last cent and now could give no more. Section gang laborers – fugitive peons from Mexico – were contributing half their scanty wages. But more than that was needed. The heart-breaking, conspiring, undermining toil of years approached fruition. The time was ripe. The Revolution hung on the balance. One shove more, one last heroic effort, and it would tremble across the scales to victory. They knew their Mexico. Once started, the Revolution would take care of itself. The whole Diaz machine would go down like a house of cards. The border was ready to rise. One Yankee, with a hundred IWW men, waited the word to cross over the border and begin the conquest of Lower California. But he needed guns. And clear across to the Atlantic, the Junta in touch with them all and all of them needing guns, mere adventurers, soldiers of fortune, bandits, disgruntled American union men, socialists, anarchists, rough-necks, Mexican exiles, peons escaped from bondage, whipped miners from the bull-pens of Coeur d'Alene and Colorado who desired only the more vindictively to fight – all the flotsam and jetsam of wild spirits from the madly complicated modern world. And it was guns and ammunition, ammunition and guns – the unceasing and eternal cry.

Fling this heterogeneous, bankrupt, vindictive mass across the border, and the Revolution was on. The custom house, the northern ports of entry, would be captured. Diaz could not resist. He dared not throw the weight of his armies against them, for he must hold the south. And through the south the flame would spread despite. The people would rise. The defenses of city after city would crumple up. State after state would totter down. And at last, from every side, the victorious armies of the Revolution would close in on the City of Mexico itself, Diaz's last stronghold.

But the money. They had the men, impatient and urgent, who would use the guns. They knew the traders who would sell and deliver the guns. But to culture the Revolution thus far had exhausted the Junta. The last dollar had been spent, the last resource and the last starving patriot milked dry, and the great adventure still trembled on the scales. Guns and ammunition! The ragged battalions must be armed. But how? Ramos lamented his confiscated estates. Arrellano wailed the spendthriftness of his youth. May Sethby wondered if it would have been different had they of the Junta been more economical in the past.

'To think that the freedom of Mexico should stand or fall on a few paltry thousands of dollars,' said Paulino Vera.

Despair was in all their faces. José Amarillo, their last hope, a recent convert, who had promised money, had been apprehended at his hacienda in Chihuahua and shot against his own stable wall. The news had just come through.

Rivera, on his knees, scrubbing, looked up, with suspended brush, his bare arms flecked with soapy, dirty water.

'Will five thousand do it?' he asked.

They looked their amazement. Vera nodded and swallowed. He could not speak, but he was on the instant invested with a vast faith.

'Order the guns,' Rivera said, and thereupon was guilty of the longest flow of words they had ever heard him utter. 'The time is short. In three weeks I shall bring you the five thousand. It is well. The weather will be warmer for those who fight. Also, it is the best I can do.'

Vera fought his faith. It was incredible. Too many fond hopes had been shattered since he had begun to play the revolution game. He believed this threadbare scrubber of the Revolution, and yet he dared not believe.

'You are crazy,' he said.

'In three weeks,' said Rivera. 'Order the guns.'

He got up, rolled down his sleeves, and put on his coat.

'Order the guns,' he said. 'I am going now.'

3

After hurrying and scurrying, much telephoning and bad language, a night session was had in Kelly's office. Kelly was rushed with business; also, he was unlucky. He had brought Danny Ward out from New York, arranged the fight for him with Billy Carthey, the date was three weeks away, and for two days now, carefully concealed from the sporting writers, Carthey had been lying up, badly injured. There was no one to take his place. Kelly had been burning the wires East to every eligible lightweight, but they were tied up with dates and contracts. And now hope had revived, though faintly.

'You've got a hell of a nerve,' Kelly addressed Rivera, after one look, as soon as they got together.

Hate that was malignant was in Rivera's eyes, but his face remained impassive.

'I can lick Ward,' was all he said.

'How do you know? Ever see him fight?'

Rivera shook his head.

'He can beat you up with one hand and both eyes closed.'

Rivera shrugged his shoulders.

'Haven't you got anything to say?' the fight promoter snarled.

'I can lick him.'

'Who'd you ever fight, anyway?' Michael Kelly demanded. Michael was the promoter's brother, and ran the Yellowstone pool rooms where he made goodly sums on the fight game.

Rivera favored him with a bitter, unanswering stare.

The promoter's secretary, a distinctively sporty young man, sneered audibly.

'Well, you know Roberts,' Kelly broke the hostile silence. 'He ought to be here. I've sent for him. Sit down and wait, though from the looks of you, you haven't got a chance. I can't throw the public down with a bum fight. Ringside seats are selling at fifteen dollars, you know that.'

When Roberts arrived, it was patent that he was mildly drunk. He was a tall, lean, slack-jointed individual, and his walk, like his talk, was a smooth and languid drawl.

Kelly went straight to the point.

'Look here, Roberts, you've been braggin' you discovered this little Mexican. You know Carthey's broke his arm. Well, this little yellow streak has the gall to blow in today and say he'll take Carthey's place. What about it?'

'It's all right, Kelly,' came the slow response. 'He can put up a fight.'

'I suppose you'll be sayin' next that he can lick Ward,' Kelly snapped.

Roberts considered judicially.

'No, I won't say that. Ward's a top-notcher and a ring general. But he can't hashhouse Rivera in short order. I know Rivera. Nobody can get his goat. He ain't got a goat that I could ever discover. And he's a two-handed fighter. He can throw in the sleep-makers from any position.'

'Never mind that. What kind of a show can he put up? You've been conditioning and training fighters all your life. I take off my hat to your judgment. Can he give the public a run for its money?'

'He sure can, and he'll worry Ward a mighty heap on top of it. You don't know that boy. I do. I discovered him. He ain't got a goat. He's a devil. He's a wizzy-wooz if anybody should ask you. He'll make Ward sit up with a show of local talent that'll make the rest of you sit up. I won't say he'll lick Ward, but he'll put up such a show that you'll all know he's a comer.'

'All right.' Kelly turned to his secretary. 'Ring up Ward. I warned him to show up if I thought it worth while. He's right across at the Yellowstone, throwin' chests and doing the popular.' Kelly turned back to the conditioner. 'Have a drink?'

Roberts sipped his highball and unburdened himself.

'Never told you how I discovered the little cuss. It was a couple

of years ago he showed up out at the quarters. I was getting
Prayne ready for his fight with Delaney. Prayne's wicked. He
ain't got a tickle of mercy in his make-up. He'd chopped up his
pardner's something cruel, and I couldn't find a willing boy
that'd work with him. I'd noticed this little starved Mexican kid
hanging around, and I was desperate. So I grabbed him, slammed
on the gloves, and put him in. He was tougher'n rawhide, but
weak. And he didn't know the first letter in the alphabet of
boxing. Prayne chopped him to ribbons. But he hung on for two
sickening rounds, when he fainted. Starvation, that was all.
Battered? You couldn't have recognized him. I gave him half a
dollar and a square meal. You oughta seen him wolf it down. He
hadn't had a bite for a couple of days. That's the end of him,
thinks I. But next day he showed up, stiff an'sore, ready for
another half and a square meal. And he done better as time went
by. Just a born fighter, and tough beyond belief. He hasn't a
heart. He's a piece of ice. And he never talked eleven words in a
string since I know him. He saws wood and does his work.'

'I've seen 'm,' the secretary said. 'He's worked a lot for you.'

'All the big little fellows has tried out on him,' Roberts
answered. 'And he's learned from 'em. I've seen some of them he
could lick. But his heart wasn't in it. I reckoned he never liked
the game. He seemed to act that way.'

'He's been fighting some before the little clubs the last few
months,' Kelly said.

'Sure. But I don't know what struck 'm. All of a sudden his
heart got into it. He just went out like a streak and cleaned up all
the little local fellows. Seemed to want the money, and he's won
a bit, though his clothes don't look it. He's peculiar. Nobody
knows his business. Nobody knows how he spends his time. Even
when he's on the job, he plumb up and disappears most of each
day soon as his work is done. Sometimes he just blows away for
weeks at a time. But he don't take advice. There's a fortune in it
for the fellow that gets the job of managin' him, only he won't
consider it. And you watch him hold out for the cash money
when you get down to terms.'

It was at this stage that Danny Ward arrived. Quite a party it
was. His manager and trainer were with him, and he breezed in
like a gusty draught of geniality, good-nature, and all-conquer-
ingness. Greetings flew about, a joke here, a retort there, a smile
or a laugh for everybody. Yet it was his way, and only partly

sincere. He was a good actor, and he had found geniality a most valuable asset in the game of getting on in the world. But down underneath he was the deliberate, cold-blooded fighter and business man. The rest was a mask. Those who knew him or trafficked with him said that when it came to brass tacks he was Danny-on-the-Spot. He was invariably present at all business discussions, and it was urged by some that his manager was a blind whose only function was to serve as Danny's mouth-piece.

Rivera's way was different. Indian blood, as well as Spanish, was in his veins, and he sat back in a corner, silent, immobile, only his black eyes passing from face to face and noting everything.

'So that's the guy,' Danny said, running an appraising eye over his proposed antagonist. 'How de do, old chap.'

Rivera's eyes burned venomously, but he made no sign of acknowledgment. He disliked all Gringos, but this Gringo he hated with an immediacy that was unusual even in him.

'Gawd!' Danny protested facetiously to the promoter. 'You ain't expectin' me to fight a deef mute.' When the laughter subsided, he made another hit. 'Los Angeles must be on the dink when this is the best you can scare up. What kindergarten did you get 'm from?'

'He's a good little boy, Danny, take it from me,' Roberts defended. 'Not as easy as he looks.'

'And half the house is sold already,' Kelly pleaded. 'You'll have to take 'm on, Danny. It's the best we can do.'

Danny ran another careless and unflattering glance over Rivera and sighed.

'I gotta be easy with 'm, I guess. If only he don't blow up.'

Roberts snorted.

'You gotta be careful,' Danny's manager warned. 'No taking chances with a dub that's likely to sneak a lucky one across.'

'Oh, I'll be careful all right, all right,' Danny smiled. 'I'll get 'm at the start an' nurse 'm along for the dear public's sake. What d' ye say to fifteen rounds, Kelly – An' then the hay for him?'

'That'll do,' was the answer. 'As long as you make it realistic.'

'Then let's get down to biz.' Danny paused and calculated. 'Of course, sixty-five per cent of gate receipts, same as with Carthey. But the split'll be different. Eighty will just about suit me.' And to his manager, 'That right?'

The manager nodded.

'Here, you, did you get that?' Kelly asked Rivera.

Rivera shook his head.

'Well, it's this way,' Kelly exposited. 'The purse'll be sixty-five per cent of the gate receipts. You're a dub, and an unknown. You and Danny split, twenty per cent goin' to you, an' eighty to Danny. That's fair, isn't it, Roberts?'

'Very fair, Rivera,' Roberts agreed. 'You see, you ain't got a reputation yet.'

'What will sixty-five per cent of the gate receipts be?' Rivera demanded.

'Oh, maybe five thousand, maybe as high as eight thousand,' Danny broke in to explain. 'Something like that. Your share'll come to something like a thousand or sixteen hundred. Pretty good for takin' a licking from a guy with my reputation. What d' ye say?'

Then Rivera took their breaths away.

'Winner takes all,' he said with finality.

A dead silence prevailed.

'It's like candy from a baby,' Danny's manager proclaimed.

Danny shook his head.

'I've been in the game too long,' he explained. 'I'm not casting reflections on the referee, or the present company. I'm not sayin' nothing about book-makers an' frame-ups that sometimes happen. But what I do say is that it's poor business for a fighter like me. I play safe. There's no tellin'. Mebbe I break my arm, eh? Or some guy slips me a bunch of dope?' He shook his head solemnly. 'Win or lose, eighty is my split. What d' ye say, Mexican?'

Rivera shook his head.

Danny exploded. He was getting down to brass tacks now.

'Why, you dirty little greaser! I've a mind to knock your block off right now.'

Roberts drawled his body to interposition between hostilities.

'Winner takes all,' Rivera repeated sullenly.

'Why do you stand out that way?' Danny asked.

'I can lick you,' was the straight answer.

Danny half started to take off his coat. But, as his manager knew, it was a grand stand play. The coat did not come off, and Danny allowed himself to be placated by the group. Everybody sympathized with him. Rivera stood alone.

'Look here, you little fool,' Kelly took up the argument. 'You're nobody. We know what you've been doing the last few months –

putting away little local fighters. But Danny is class. His next fight after this will be for the championship. And you're unknown. Nobody ever heard of you out of Los Angeles.'

'They will,' Rivera answered with a shrug, 'after this fight.'

'You think for a second you can lick me?' Danny blurted in. Rivera nodded.

'Oh, come; listen to reason,' Kelly pleaded. 'Think of the advertising.'

'I want the money,' was Rivera's answer.

'You couldn't win from me in a thousand years,' Danny assured him.

'Then what are you holding out for?' Rivera countered. 'If the money's that easy, why don't you go after it?'

'I will, so help me!' Danny cried with abrupt conviction. 'I'll beat you to death in the ring, my boy – you monkeyin' with me this way. Make out the articles, Kelly. Winner take all. Play it up in the sportin' columns. Tell 'em it's a grudge fight. I'll show this fresh kid a few.'

Kelly's secretary had begun to write, when Danny interrupted.

'Hold on!' He turned to Rivera. 'Weights?'

'Ringside,' came the answer.

'Not on your life, Fresh Kid. If winner takes all, we weigh in at ten a.m.'

'And winner takes all?' Rivera queried.

Danny nodded. That settled it. He would enter the ring in his full ripeness of strength.

'Weigh in at ten,' Rivera said.

The secretary's pen went on scratching.

'It means five pounds,' Roberts complained to Rivera. 'You've given too much away. You've thrown the fight right there. Danny'll be as strong as a bull. You're a fool. He'll lick you sure. You ain't got the chance of a dewdrop in hell.'

Rivera's answer was a calculated look of hatred. Even this Gringo he despised, and him had he found the whitest Gringo of them all.

4

Barely noticed was Rivera as he entered the ring. Only a very slight and very scattering ripple of half-hearted handclapping greeted him. The house did not believe in him. He was the lamb led to slaughter at the hands of the great Danny. Besides, the house was disappointed. It had expected a rushing battle between Danny Ward and Billy Carthey, and here it must put up with this poor little tyro. Still further, it had manifested its disapproval of the change by betting two, and even three, to one on Danny. And where a betting audience's money is, there is its heart.

The Mexican boy sat down in his corner and waited. The slow minutes lagged by. Danny was making him wait. It was an old trick, but ever it worked on the young, new fighters. They grew frightened, sitting thus and facing their own apprehensions and a callous, tobacco-smoking audience. But for once the trick failed. Roberts was right. Rivera had no goat. He, who was more delicately coordinated, more finely nerved and strung than any of them, had no nerves of this sort. The atmosphere of foredoomed defeat in his own corner had no effect on him. His handlers were Gringos and strangers. Also they were scrubs – the dirty driftage of the fight game, without honor, without efficiency. And they were chilled, as well, with certitude that theirs was the losing corner.

'Now you gotta be careful,' Spider Hagerty warned him. Spider was his chief second. 'Make it last as long as you can – them's my instructions from Kelly. If you don't, the papers'll call it another bum fight and give the game a bigger black eye in Los Angeles.'

All of which was not encouraging. But Rivera took no notice. He despised prizefighting. It was the hated game of the hated Gringo. He had taken up with it, as a chopping block for others in the training quarters, solely because he was starving. The fact that he was marvelously made for it, had meant nothing. He hated it. Not until he had come in to the Junta, had he fought for money, and he had found the money easy. Not first among the sons of men had he been to find himself successful at a despised vocation.

He did not analyze. He merely knew that he must win this fight. There could be no other outcome. For behind him, nerving him to this belief, were profounder forces than any the crowded house dreamed. Danny Ward fought for money, and for the easy ways of life that money would bring. But the things Rivera fought for burned in his brain – blazing and terrible visions, that, with eyes wide open, sitting lonely in the corner of the ring and waiting for his tricky antagonist, he saw as clearly as he had lived them.

He saw the white-walled, water-power factories of Rio Blanco. He saw the six thousand workers, starved and wan, and the little children, seven and eight years of age, who toiled long shifts for ten cents a day. He saw the perambulating corpses, the ghastly death's heads of men who labored in the dye-rooms. He remembered that he had heard his father call the dye-rooms the 'suicide-holes', where a year was death. He saw the little patio, and his mother cooking and moiling at crude housekeeping and finding time to caress and love him. And his father he saw, large, big-mustached and deep-chested, kindly above all men, who loved all men and whose heart was so large that there was love to overflowing still left for the mother and the little muchacho playing in the corner of the patio. In those days his name had not been Felipe Rivera. It had been Fernandez, his father's and mother's name. Him had they called Juan. Later, he had changed it himself, for he had found the name of Fernandez hated by prefects of police, *jefes politicos*, and *rurales*.

Big, hearty Joaquin Fernandez! A large place he occupied in Rivera's visions. He had not understood at the time, but looking back he could understand. He could see him setting type in the little printery, or scribbling endless hasty, nervous lines on the much-cluttered desk. And he could see strange evenings, when workmen, coming secretly in the dark like men who did ill deeds, met with his father and talked long hours where he, the muchacho, lay not always asleep in the corner.

As from a remote distance he could hear Spider Hagerty saying to him: 'No layin' down at the start. Them's instructions. Take a beatin' an' earn your dough.'

Ten minutes had passed, and he still sat in his corner. There were no signs of Danny, who was evidently playing the trick to the limit.

But more visions burned before the eye of Rivera's memory. The strike, or, rather, the lockout, because the workers of Rio Blanco had helped their striking brothers of Puebla. The hunger, the expeditions in the hills for berries, the roots and herbs that all ate and that twisted and pained the stomachs of all of them. And then, the nightmare; the waste of ground before the company's store; the thousands of starving workers; General Rosalio Martinez and the soldiers of Porfirio Diaz; and the death-spitting rifles that seemed never to cease spitting, while the workers' wrongs were washed and washed again in their own blood. And that night! He saw the flat cars, piled high with the bodies of the slain, consigned to Vera Cruz, food for the sharks of the bay. Again he crawled over the grisly heaps, seeking and finding, stripped and mangled, his father and his mother. His mother he especially remembered – only her face projecting, her body burdened by the weight of dozens of bodies. Again the rifles of the soldiers of Porfirio Diaz cracked, and again he dropped to the ground and slunk away like some hunted coyote of the hills.

To his ears came a great roar, as of the sea, and he saw Danny Ward, leading his retinue of trainers and seconds, coming down the center aisle. The house was in wild uproar for the popular hero who was bound to win. Everybody proclaimed him. Everybody was for him. Even Rivera's own seconds warmed to something akin to cheerfulness when Danny ducked jauntily through the ropes and entered the ring. His face continually spread to an unending succession of smiles, and when Danny smiled he smiled in every feature, even to the laughter-wrinkles of the corners of the eyes and into the depths of the eyes themselves. Never was there so genial a fighter. His face was a running advertisement of good feeling, of good fellowship. He knew everybody. He joked, and laughed, and greeted his friends through the ropes. Those farther away, unable to suppress their admiration, cried loudly: 'Oh, you Danny!' It was a joyous ovation of affection that lasted a full five minutes.

Rivera was disregarded. For all that the audience noticed, he did not exist. Spider Hagerty's bloated face bent down close to his.

'No gettin' scared,' the Spider warned. 'An' remember instructions. You gotta last. No layin' down. If you lay down, we got instructions to beat you up in the dressing-rooms. Savve? You just gotta fight.'

The house began to applaud. Danny was crossing the ring to him. Danny bent over, caught Rivera's right hand in both his own and shook it with impulsive heartiness. Danny's smile-wreathed face was close to his. The audience yelled its appreciation of Danny's display of sporting spirit. He was greeting his opponent with the fondness of a brother. Danny's lips moved, and the audience, interpreting the unheard words to be those of a kindly-natured sport, yelled again. Only Rivera heard the low words.

'You little Mexican rat,' hissed from between Danny's gaily smiling lips, 'I'll fetch the yellow outa you.'

Rivera made no move. He did not rise. He merely hated with his eyes.

'Get up, you dog!' some man yelled through the ropes from behind.

The crowd began to hiss and boo him for his unsportsmanlike conduct, but he sat unmoved. Another great outburst of applause was Danny's as he walked back across the ring.

When Danny stripped, there was ohs! and ahs! of delight. His body was perfect, alive with easy suppleness and health and strength. The skin was white as a woman's, and as smooth. All grace, and resilience, and power resided therein. He had proved it in scores of battles. His photographs were in all the physical culture magazines.

A groan went up as Spider Hagerty peeled Rivera's sweater over his head. His body seemed leaner, because of the swarthiness of the skin. He had muscles, but they made no display like his opponent's. What the audience neglected to see was the deep chest. Nor could it guess the toughness of the fiber of the flesh, the instantaneousness of the cell explosions of the muscles, the fineness of the nerves that wired every part of him into a splendid fighting mechanism. All the audience saw was a brown-skinned boy of eighteen with what seemed the body of a boy. With Danny it was different. Danny was a man of twenty-four, and his body was a man's body. The contrast was still more striking as they stood together in the center of the ring receiving the referee's last instructions.

Rivera noticed Roberts sitting directly behind the newspaper men. He was drunker than usual, and his speech was correspondingly slower.

'Take it easy, Rivera,' Roberts drawled. 'He can't kill you, remember that. He'll rush you at the go-off, but don't get rattled. You just cover up, and stall, and clinch. He can't hurt you much. Just make believe to yourself that he's choppin' out on you at the trainin' quarters.'

Rivera made no sign that he had heard.

'Sullen little devil,' Roberts muttered to the man next to him. 'He always was that way.'

But Rivera forgot to look his usual hatred. A vision of countless rifles blinded his eyes. Every face in the audience, far as he could see, to the high dollar-seats, was transformed into a rifle. And he saw the long Mexican border arid and sun-washed and aching, and along it he saw the ragged bands that delayed only for the guns.

Back in his corner he waited, standing up. His seconds had crawled out through the ropes, taking the canvas stool with them. Diagonally across the squared ring, Danny faced him. The gong struck, and the battle was on. The audience howled its delight. Never had it seen a battle open more convincingly. The papers were right. It was a grudge fight. Three-quarters of the distance Danny covered in the rush to get together, his intention to eat up the Mexican lad plainly advertised. He assailed with not one blow, nor two, nor a dozen. He was a gyroscope of blows, a whirlwind of destruction. Rivera was nowhere. He was overwhelmed, buried beneath avalanches of punches delivered from every angle and position by a past master in the art. He was overborne, swept back against the ropes, separated by the referee, and swept back against the ropes again.

It was not a fight. It was a slaughter, a massacre. Any audience, save a prizefighting one, would have exhausted its emotions in that first minute. Danny was certainly showing what he could do – a splendid exhibition. Such was the certainty of the audience, as well as its excitement and favoritism, that it failed to take notice that the Mexican still stayed on his feet. It forgot Rivera. It rarely saw him, so closely was he enveloped in Danny's man-eating attack. A minute of this went by, and two minutes. Then, in a separation, it caught a clear glimpse of the Mexican. His lip was cut, his nose was bleeding. As he turned and staggered into a clinch, the welts of oozing blood, from his contacts with the ropes, showed in red bars across his back. But what the audience did not notice was that his chest was not heaving and that his eyes were coldly burning as ever. Too many aspiring champions, in the cruel welter of the training camps, had practiced this man-eating attack on him. He had learned to live through for a compensation of from half a dollar a go up to fifteen dollars a week – a hard school, and he was schooled hard.

Then happened the amazing thing. The whirling, blurring mixup ceased suddenly. Rivera stood alone. Danny, the redoubtable Danny, lay on his back. His body quivered as consciousness strove to return to it. He had not staggered and sunk down, nor had he gone over in a long slumping fall. The right hook of Rivera had dropped him in midair with the abruptness of death. The referee shoved Rivera back with one hand, and stood over the fallen gladiator counting the seconds. It is the custom of prizefighting audiences to cheer a clean knock-down blow. But this audience did not cheer. The thing had been too unexpected. It watched the toll of the seconds in tense silence, and through this silence the voice of Roberts rose exultantly:

'I told you he was a two-handed fighter!'

By the fifth second, Danny was rolling over on his face, and when seven was counted, he rested on one knee, ready to rise after the count of nine and before the count of ten. If his knee still touched the floor at 'ten', he was considered 'down', and also 'out'. The instant his knee left the floor, he was considered 'up', and in that instant it was Rivera's right to try and put him down again. Rivera took no chances. The moment that knee left the floor he would strike again. He circled around, but the referee circled in between, and Rivera knew that the seconds he counted were very slow. All Gringos were against him, even the referee.

At 'nine' the referee gave Rivera a sharp thrust back. It was unfair, but it enabled Danny to rise, the smile back on his lips. Doubled partly over, with arms wrapped about face and abdomen, he cleverly stumbled into a clinch. By all the rules of the game the referee should have broken it, but he did not, and Danny clung on like a surf-battered barnacle and moment by moment recuperated. The last minute of the round was going fast. If he could live to the end, he would have a full minute in his corner to revive. And live to the end he did, smiling through all desperateness and extremity.

'The smile that won't come off!' somebody yelled, and the audience laughed loudly in its relief.

'The kick that Greaser's got is something God-awful,' Danny gasped in his corner to his adviser while his handlers worked frantically over him.

The second and third rounds were tame. Danny, a tricky and consummate ring general, stalled and blocked and held on, devoting himself to recovering from that dazing first-round blow. In the fourth round he was himself again. Jarred and shaken, nevertheless his good condition had enabled him to regain his vigor. But he tried no man-eating tactics. The Mexican had proved a tartar. Instead, he brought to bear his best fighting powers. In tricks and skill and experience he was the master, and though he could land nothing vital, he proceeded scientifically to chop and wear down his opponent. He landed three blows to

Rivera's one, but they were punishing blows only, and not deadly. It was the sum of many of them that constituted deadliness. He was respectful of this two-handed dub with the amazing short-arm kicks in both his fists.

In defense, Rivera developed a disconcerting straight-left. Again and again, attack after attack he straight-lefted away from him with accumulated damage to Danny's mouth and nose. But Danny was protean. That was why he was the coming champion. He could change from style to style of fighting at will. He now devoted himself to infighting. In this he was particularly wicked, and it enabled him to avoid the other's straight-left. Here he set the house wild repeatedly, capping it with a marvelous lock-break and lift of an inside upper-cut that raised the Mexican in the air and dropped him to the mat. Rivera rested on one knee, making the most of the count, and in the soul of him he knew the referee was counting short seconds on him.

Again, in the seventh, Danny achieved the diabolical inside uppercut. He succeeded only in staggering Rivera, but, in the ensuing moment of defenseless helplessness, he smashed him with another blow through the ropes. Rivera's body bounced on the heads of the newspaper men below, and they boosted him back to the edge of the platform outside the ropes. Here he rested on one knee, while the referee raced off the seconds. Inside the ropes, through which he must duck to enter the ring, Danny waited for him. Nor did the referee intervene or thrust Danny back.

The house was beside itself with delight.

'Kill 'm, Danny, kill 'm!' was the cry.

Scores of voices took it up until it was like a war-chant of wolves.

Danny did his best, but Rivera, at the count of eight, instead of nine, came unexpectedly through the ropes and safely into a clinch. Now the referee worked, tearing him away so that he could be hit, giving Danny every advantage that an unfair referee can give.

But Rivera lived, and the daze cleared from his brain. It was all of a piece. They were the hated Gringos and they were all unfair. And in the worst of it visions continued to flash and sparkle in his brain – long lines of railroad track that simmered across the desert; *rurales* and American constables; prisons and calabooses; tramps at water tanks – all the squalid and painful panorama of his odyssey after Rio Blanca and the strike. And, resplendent and glorious, he saw the great, red Revolution sweeping across his land. The guns were there before him. Every hated face was a gun. It was for the guns he fought. He was the guns. He was the Revolution. He fought for all Mexico.

The audience began to grow incensed with Rivera. Why didn't he take the licking that was appointed him? Of course he was going to be licked, but why should he be so obstinate about it? Very few were interested in him, and they were the certain, definite percentage of a gambling crowd that plays long shots. Believing Danny to be the winner, nevertheless they had put their money on the Mexican at four to ten and one to three. More than a trifle was up on the point of how many rounds Rivera could last. Wild money had appeared at the ringside proclaiming that he could not last seven rounds, or even six. The winners of this, now that their cash risk was happily settled, had joined in cheering on the favorite.

Rivera refused to be licked. Through the eighth round his opponent strove vainly to repeat the uppercut. In the ninth, Rivera stunned the house again. In the midst of a clinch he broke the lock with a quick, lithe movement, and in the narrow space between their bodies his right lifted from the waist. Danny went to the floor and took the safety of the count. The crowd was appalled. He was being bested at his own game. His famous right-uppercut had been worked back on him. Rivera made no attempt to catch him as he arose at 'nine'. The referee was openly blocking that play, though he stood clear when the situation was reversed and it was Rivera who desired to rise.

Twice in the tenth, Rivera put through the right-uppercut, lifted from waist to opponent's chin. Danny grew desperate. The smile never left his face, but he went back to his man-eating rushes. Whirlwind as he would, he could not damage Rivera, while Rivera, through the blur and whirl, dropped him to the mat three times in succession. Danny did not recuperate so quickly now, and by the eleventh round he was in a serious way. But from then till the fourteenth he put up the gamest exhibition of his career. He stalled and blocked, fought parsimoniously, and strove to gather strength. Also, he fought as foully as a successful fighter knows how. Every trick and device he employed, butting in the clinches with the seeming of accident, pinioning Rivera's glove between arm and body, heeling his glove on Rivera's mouth to clog his breathing. Often, in the clinches, through his cut and smiling lips he snarled insults unspeakable and vile in Rivera's ear. Everybody, from the referee to the house, was with Danny and was helping Danny. And they knew what he had in mind. Bested by this surprise-box of an unknown, he was pinning all on a single punch. He offered himself for punishment, fished, and feinted, and drew, for that one opening that would enable him to whip a blow through with all his strength and turn the tide. As another and greater fighter had done before him, he might do – a right and left, to solar plexus and across the jaw. He could do it, for he was noted for the strength of punch that remained in his arms as long as he could keep his feet.

Rivera's seconds were not half-caring for him in the intervals between rounds. Their towels made a showing, but drove little air into his panting lungs. Spider Hagerty talked advice to him, but Rivera knew it was wrong advice. Everybody was against him. He was surrounded by treachery. In the fourteenth round he put Danny down again, and himself stood resting, hands dropped at side, while the referee counted. In the other corner Rivera had been noting suspicious whisperings. He saw Michael Kelly make his way to Roberts and bend and whisper. Rivera's ears were a cat's, desert-trained, and he caught snatches of what was said. He wanted to hear more, and when his opponent arose he maneuvered the fight into a clinch over against the ropes.

'Got to,' he could hear Michael, while Roberts nodded. 'Danny's got to win – I stand to lose a mint – I've got a ton of money covered – my own – If he lasts the fifteenth I'm bust – The boy'll mind you. Put something across.'

And thereafter Rivera saw no more visions. They were trying to job him. Once again he dropped Danny and stood resting, his hands at his side. Roberts stood up.

'That settled him,' he said. 'Go to your corner.'

He spoke with authority, as he had often spoken to Rivera at the training quarters. But Rivera looked hatred at him and waited for Danny to rise. Back in his corner in the minute interval, Kelly, the promoter, came and talked to Rivera.

'Throw it, damn you,' he rasped in a harsh low voice. 'You gotta lay down, Rivera. Stick with me and I'll make your future. I'll let you lick Danny next time. But here's where you lay down.'

Rivera showed with his eyes that he heard, but he made neither sign of assent nor dissent.

'Why don't you speak?' Kelly demanded angrily.

'You lose, anyway,' Spider Hagerty supplemented. 'The referee'll take it away from you. Listen to Kelly, and lay down.'

'Lay down, kid,' Kelly pleaded, 'and I'll help you to the championship.'

Rivera did not answer.

'I will, so help me, kid.'

At the strike of the gong Rivera sensed something impending. The house did not. Whatever it was it was there inside the ring with him and very close. Danny's earlier surety seemed returned to him. The confidence of his advance frightened Rivera. Some trick was about to be worked. Danny rushed, but Rivera refused the encounter. He side-stepped away into safety. What the other wanted was a clinch. It was in some way necessary to the trick. Rivera backed and circled away, yet he knew, sooner or later, the clinch and the trick would come. Desperately he resolved to draw it. He made as if to effect the clinch with Danny's next rush. Instead, at the last instant, just as their bodies should have come together, Rivera darted nimbly back. And in the same instant Danny's corner raised a cry of foul. Rivera had fooled them. The referee paused irresolutely. The decision that trembled on his lips was never uttered, for a shrill, boy's voice from the gallery piped, 'Raw work!'

Danny cursed Rivera openly, and forced him, while Rivera danced away. Also, Rivera made up his mind to strike no more blows at the body. In this he threw away half his chance of winning, but he knew if he was to win at all it was with the outfighting that remained to him. Given the least opportunity, they would lie a foul on him. Danny threw all caution to the winds. For two rounds he tore after and into the boy who dared not meet him at close quarters. Rivera was struck again and again; he took blows by the dozens to avoid the perilous clinch. During this supreme final rally of Danny's the audience rose to its feet and went mad. It did not understand. All it could see was that its favorite was winning after all.

'Why don't you fight?' it demanded wrathfully of Rivera. 'You're yellow! You're yellow!' 'Open up, you cur! Open up!' 'Kill 'm, Danny! Kill 'm!' 'You sure got 'm! Kill 'm!'

In all the house, bar none, Rivera was the only cold man. By temperament and blood he was the hottest-passioned there; but he had gone through such vastly greater heats that this collective passion of ten thousand throats, rising surge on surge, was to his brain no more than the velvet cool of a summer twilight.

Into the seventeenth round Danny carried his rally. Rivera, under a heavy blow, drooped and sagged. His hands dropped helplessly as he reeled backward. Danny thought it was his chance. The boy was at his mercy. Thus Rivera, feigning, caught him off his guard, lashing out a clean drive to the mouth. Danny went down. When he arose, Rivera felled him with a down-chop of the right on neck and jaw. Three times he repeated this. It was impossible for any referee to call these blows foul.

'Oh, Bill! Bill!' Kelly pleaded to the referee.

'I can't,' that official lamented back. 'He won't give me a chance.'

Danny, battered and heroic, still kept coming up. Kelly and others near to the ring began to cry out to the police to stop it, though Danny's corner refused to throw in the towel. Rivera saw the fat police captain starting awkwardly to climb through the ropes, and was not sure what it meant. There were so many ways of cheating in this game of the Gringos. Danny, on his feet, tottered groggily and helplessly before him. The referee and the captain were both reaching for Rivera when he struck the last blow. There was no need to stop the fight, for Danny did not rise.

'Count!' Rivera cried hoarsely to the referee.

And when the count was finished, Danny's seconds gathered him up and carried him to his corner.

'Who wins?' Rivera demanded.

Reluctantly, the referee caught his gloved hand and held it aloft.

There were no congratulations for Rivera. He walked to his corner unattended, where his seconds had not yet placed his stool. He leaned backward on the ropes and looked his hatred at them, swept it on and about him till the whole ten thousand Gringos were included. His knees trembled under him, and he was sobbing from exhaustion. Before his eyes the hated faces swayed back and forth in the giddiness of nausea. Then he remembered they were the guns. The guns were his. The Revolution could go on.

The Strength of the Strong (1911; 1914)

> 'Parables don't lie, but liars will parable.'
> – Lip-King

Old Long Beard paused in his narrative, licked his greasy fingers, and wiped them on his naked sides where his one piece of ragged bearskin failed to cover him. Crouched around him, on their hams, were three young men, his grandsons, Deer-Runner, Yellow-Head, and Afraid-of-the-Dark. In appearance they were much the same. Skins of wild animals partly covered them. They were lean and meager of build, narrow-hipped and crooked-legged, and at the same time deep-chested, with heavy arms and enormous hands. There was much hair on their chests and shoulders, and on the outsides of their arms and legs. Their heads were matted with uncut hair, long locks of which often strayed before their eyes, beady and black and glittering like the eyes of birds. They were narrow between the eyes and broad between the cheeks, while their lower jaws were projecting and massive.

It was a night of clear starlight, and below them, stretching away remotely, lay range on range of forest-covered hills. In the distance the heavens were red from the glow of a volcano. At their backs yawned the black mouth of a cave, out of which, from time to time, blew draughty gusts of wind. Immediately in front of them blazed a fire. At one side, partly devoured, lay the carcass of a bear, with about it, at a respectable distance, several large dogs, shaggy and wolf-like. Beside each man lay his bow and arrows and a huge club. In the cave-mouth a number of rude spears leaned against the rock.

'So that was how we moved from the cave to the tree,' old Long Beard spoke up.

They laughed boisterously, like big children, at recollection of a previous story his words called up. Long Beard laughed, too, the five-inch bodkin of bone, thrust midway through the cartilage of his nose, leaping and dancing and adding to his ferocious appearance. He did not exactly say the words recorded, but he made animal-like sounds with his mouth that meant the same thing.

'And that is the first I remember of the Sea Valley,' Long Beard went on. 'We were a very foolish crowd. We did not know the secret of strength. For, behold, each family lived by itself, and took care of itself. There were thirty families, but we got no strength from one another. We were in fear of each other all the time. No one ever paid visits. In the top of our tree we built a grass house, and on the platform outside was a pile of rocks, which were for the heads of any that might chance to try to visit us. Also, we had our spears and arrows. We never walked under the trees of the other families, either. My brother did, once, under old Boo-oogh's tree, and he got his head broken and that was the end of him.

'Old Boo-oogh was very strong. It was said he could pull a grown man's head right off. I never heard of him doing it, because no man would give him a chance. Father wouldn't. One day, when father was down on the beach, Boo-oogh took after mother. She couldn't run fast, for the day before she had got her leg clawed by a bear when she was up on the mountain gathering berries. So Boo-oogh caught her and carried her up into his tree. Father never got her back. He was afraid. Old Boo-oogh made faces at him.

'But father did not mind. Strong-Arm was another strong man. He was one of the best fishermen. But one day, climbing after seagull eggs, he had a fall from the cliff. He was never strong after that. He coughed a great deal, and his shoulders drew near to each other. So father took Strong-Arm's wife. When he came around and coughed under our tree, father laughed at him and threw rocks at him. It was our way in those days. We did not know how to add strength together and become strong.'

'Would a brother take a brother's wife?' Deer-Runner demanded.

'Yes, if he had gone to live in another tree by himself.'

'But we do not do such things now,' Afraid-of-the-Dark objected.

'It is because I have taught your fathers better.' Long Beard thrust his hairy paw into the bear meat and drew out a handful of suet, which he sucked with a meditative air. Again he wiped his hands on his naked sides and went on. 'What I am telling you happened in the long ago, before we knew any better.'

'You must have been fools not to know better,' was Deer-Runner's comment, Yellow-Head grunting approval.

'So we were, but we became bigger fools, as you shall see. Still, we did learn better, and this was the way of it. We Fish-Eaters had not learned to add our strength until our strength was the strength of all of us. But the Meat-Eaters, who lived across the divide in the Big Valley, stood together, hunted together, fished together, and fought together. One day they came into our valley. Each family of us got into its own cave and tree. There were only ten Meat-Eaters, but they fought together, and we fought each family by itself.'

Long Beard counted long and perplexedly on his fingers.

'There were sixty men of us,' was what he managed to say with fingers and lips combined. 'And we were very strong, only we did not know it. So we watched the ten men attack Boo-oogh's tree. He made a good fight, but he had no chance. We looked on. When some of the Meat-Eaters tried to climb the tree, Boo-oogh had to show himself in order to drop stones on their heads, whereupon the other Meat-Eaters, who were waiting for that very thing, shot him full of arrows. And that was the end of Boo-oogh.

'Next, the Meat-Eaters got One-Eye and his family in his cave. They built a fire in the mouth and smoked him out, like we smoked out the bear there today. Then they went after Six-Fingers, up his tree, and, while they were killing him and his grown son, the rest of us ran away. They caught some of our women, and killed two old men who could not run fast and several children. The women they carried away with them to the Big Valley.

'After that the rest of us crept back, and, somehow, perhaps because we were in fear and felt the need for one another, we talked the thing over. It was our first council – our first real council. And in that council we formed our first tribe. For we had learned the lesson. Of the ten Meat-Eaters, each man had had the strength of ten, for the ten had fought as one man. They had added their strength together. But of the thirty families and the sixty men of us, we had had the strength of but one man, for each had fought alone.

'It was a great talk we had, and it was hard talk, for we did not have the words then as now with which to talk. The Bug made some of the words long afterward, and so did others of us make words from time to time. But in the end we agreed to add our strength together and to be as one man when the Meat-Eaters came over the divide to steal our women. And that was the tribe.

'We set two men on the divide, one for the day and one for the night, to watch if the Meat-Eaters came. These were the eyes of the tribe. Then, also, day and night, there were to be ten men awake with their clubs and spears and arrows in their hands, ready to fight. Before, when a man went after fish, or clams, or gull-eggs, he carried his weapons with him, and half the time he was getting food and half the time watching for fear some other man would get him. Now that was all changed. The men went out without their weapons and spent all their time getting food. Likewise, when the women went into the mountains after roots and berries, five of the ten men went with them to guard them. While all the time, day and night, the eyes of the tribe watched from the top of the divide.

'But troubles came. As usual, it was about the women. Men without wives wanted other men's wives, and there was much fighting between men, and now and again one got his head smashed or a spear through his body. While one of the watchers was on top the divide, another man stole his wife, and he came down to fight. Then the other watcher was in fear that someone would take his wife, and he came down likewise. Also, there was trouble among the ten men who carried always their weapons, and they fought five against five, till some ran away down the coast and the others ran after them.

'So it was that the tribe was left without eyes or guards. We had not the strength of sixty. We had no strength at all. So we held a council and made our first laws. I was but a cub at the time, but I remember. We said that, in order to be strong, we must not fight one another, and we made a law that when a man killed another him would the tribe kill. We made another law that whoso stole another man's wife him would the tribe kill. We said that whatever man had too great strength, and by that strength hurt his brothers in the tribe, him would we kill that his strength might hurt no more. For, if we let his strength hurt, the brothers would become afraid and the tribe would fall apart, and we would be as weak as when the Meat-Eaters first came upon us and killed Boo-oogh.

'Knuckle-Bone was a strong man, a very strong man, and he knew not law. He knew only his own strength, and in the fullness thereof he went forth and took the wife of Three-Clams. Three-Clams tried to fight, but Knuckle-Bone clubbed out his brains. Yet had Knuckle-Bone forgotten that all the men of us had added our strength to keep the law among us, and him we killed, at the foot of his tree, and hung his body on a branch as a warning that the law was stronger than any man. For we were the law, all of us, and no man was greater than the law.

'Then there were other troubles, for know, O Deer-Runner, and Yellow-Head, and Afraid-of-the-Dark, that it is not easy to make a tribe. There were many things, little things, that it was a great trouble to call all the men together to have a council about. We were having councils morning, noon, and night, and in the middle of the night. We could find little time to go out and get food, what of the councils, for there was always some little thing to be settled, such as naming two new watchers to take the place of the old ones on the hill, or naming how much food should fall to the share of the men who kept their weapons always in their hands and got no food for themselves.

'We stood in need of a chief man to do these things, who would be the voice of the council, and who would account to the council for the things he did. So we named Fith-Fith the chief man. He was a strong man, too, and very cunning, and when he was angry he made noises just like that, *fith-fith*, like a wildcat.

'The ten men who guarded the tribe were set to work making a wall of stones across the narrow part of the valley. The women and large children helped, as did other men, until the wall was strong. After that, all the families came down out of their caves and trees and built grass houses behind the shelter of the wall. These houses were large and much better than the caves and trees, and everybody had a better time of it because the men had added their strength together and become a tribe. Because of the wall and the guards and the watchers, there was more time to hunt and fish and pick roots and berries; there was more food, and better food, and no one went hungry. And Three-Legs, so named because his legs had been smashed when a boy and who walked with a stick – Three-Legs got the seed of the wild corn and planted it in the ground in the valley near his house. Also, he tried planting fat roots and other things he found in the mountain valleys.

'Because of the safety in the Sea Valley, which was because of the wall and the watchers and the guards, and because there was food in plenty for all without having to fight for it, many families came in from the coast valleys on both sides and from the high back mountains where they had lived more like wild animals than men. And it was not long before the Sea Valley filled up, and in it were countless families. But, before this happened, the land, which had been free to all and belonged to all, was divided up. Three-Legs began it when he planted corn. But most of us did not care about the land. We thought the marking of the boundaries with fences of stone was a foolishness. We had plenty to eat, and what more did we want? I remember that my father and I built stone fences for Three-Legs and were given corn in return.

'So only a few got all the land, and Three-Legs got most of it. Also, others that had taken land gave it to the few that held on, being paid in return with corn and fat roots, and bearskins, and fishes which the farmers got from the fishermen in exchange for corn. And, the first thing we knew, all the land was gone.

'It was about this time that Fith-Fith died and Dog-Tooth, his son, was made chief. He demanded to be made chief anyway, because his father had been chief before him. Also, he looked upon himself as a greater chief than his father. He was a good chief at first, and worked hard, so that the council had less and less to do. Then arose a new voice in the Sea Valley. It was Twisted-Lip. We had never thought much of him, until he began to talk with the spirits of the dead. Later we called him Big-Fat, because he ate over-much, and did no work, and grew round and large. One day Big-Fat told us that the secrets of the dead were his, and that he was the voice of God. He became great friends with Dog-Tooth, who commanded that we build Big-Fat a grass house. And Big-Fat put taboos all around this house and kept God inside.

'More and more Dog-Tooth became greater than the council, and when the council grumbled and said it would name a new chief, Big-Fat spoke with the voice of God and said no. Also, Three-Legs and the others who held the land stood behind Dog-Tooth. Moreover, the strongest man in the council was Sea-Lion, and him the land-owners gave land to secretly, along with many bearskins and baskets of corn. So Sea-Lion said that Big-Fat's voice was truly the voice of God and must be obeyed. And soon afterward Sea-Lion was named the voice of Dog-Tooth and did most of his talking for him.

'Then there was Little-Belly, a little man, so thin in the middle that he looked as if he had never had enough to eat. Inside the mouth of the river, after the sand-bar had combed the strength of the breakers, he built a big fish-trap. No man had ever seen or dreamed a fish-trap before. He worked weeks on it, with his son and his wife, while the rest of us laughed at their labors. But, when it was done, the first day he caught more fish in it than could the whole tribe in a week, whereat there was great rejoicing. There was only one other place in the river for a fish-trap, but, when my father and I and a dozen other men started to make a very large trap, the guards came from the big grass-house we had built for Dog-Tooth. And the guards poked us with their spears and told us begone, because Little-Belly was going to build a trap there himself on the word of Sea-Lion, who was the voice of Dog-Tooth.

'There was much grumbling, and my father called a council. But, when he rose to speak, him the Sea-Lion thrust through the throat with a spear and he died. And Dog-Tooth and Little-Belly, and Three-Legs and all that held land said it was good. And Big-Fat said it was the will of God. And after that all men were afraid to stand up in the council, and there was no more council.

'Another man, Pig-Jaw, began to keep goats. He had heard about it as among the Meat-Eaters, and it was not long before he had many flocks. Other men, who had no land and no fish-traps, and who else would have gone hungry, were glad to work for Pig-Jaw, caring for his goats, guarding them from wild dogs and tigers, and driving them to the feeding pastures in the mountains. In return, Pig-Jaw gave them goat-meat to eat and goat-skins to wear, and sometimes they traded the goat-meat for fish and corn and fat roots.

'It was this time that money came to be. Sea-Lion was the man who first thought of it, and he talked it over with Dog-Tooth and Big-Fat. You see, these three were the ones that got a share of everything in the Sea Valley. One basket out of every three of corn was theirs, one fish out of every three, one goat out of every three. In return, they fed the guards and the watchers, and kept the rest for themselves. Sometimes, when a big haul of fish was made, they did not know what to do with all their share. So Sea-Lion set the women to making money out of shell — little round pieces, with a hole in each one, and all made smooth and fine. These were strung on strings, and the strings were called money.

'Each string was of the value of thirty fish, or forty fish, but the women, who made a string a day, were given two fish each. The fish came out of the shares of Dog-Tooth, Big-Fat, and Sea-Lion, which they three did not eat. So all the money belonged to them. Then they told Three-Legs and the other land owners that they would take their share of corn and roots in money, Little-Belly that they would take their share of fish in money, the Pig-Jaw that they would take their share of goats and cheese in money. Thus, a man who had nothing, worked for one who had, and was paid in money. With this money he bought corn, and fish, and meat, and cheese. And Three-Legs and all owners of things paid Dog-Tooth and Sea-Lion and Big-Fat their share in money. And they paid the guards and watchers in money, and the guards and watchers bought their food with the money. And, because money was cheap, Dog-Tooth made many more men into guards. And, because money was cheap to make, a number of men began to make money out of shell themselves. But the guards stuck spears in them and shot them full of arrows, because they were trying to break up the tribe. It was bad to break up the tribe, for then the Meat-Eaters would come over the divide and kill them all.

'Big-Fat was the voice of God, but he took Broken-Rib and made him into a priest, so that he became the voice of Big-Fat and did most of his talking for him. And both had other men to be servants to them. So, also, did Little-Belly and Three-Legs and Pig-Jaw have other men to lie in the sun about their grass houses and carry messages for them and give commands. And more and more were men taken away from work, so that those that were left worked harder than ever before. It seemed that men desired to do no work and strove to seek out other ways whereby men should work for them. Crooked-Eyes found such a way. He made the first fire-brew out of corn. And thereafter he worked no more, for he talked secretly with Dog-Tooth and Big-Fat and the other masters, and it was agreed that he should be the only one to make fire-brew. But Crooked-Eyes did no work himself. Men made the brew for him, and he paid them in money. Then he sold the fire-brew for money, and all men bought. And many strings of money did he give Dog-Tooth and Sea-Lion and all of them.

'Big-Fat and Broken-Rib stood by Dog-Tooth when he took his second wife, and his third wife. They said Dog-Tooth was different from other men and second only to God that Big-Fat kept in his taboo house, and Dog-Tooth said so, too, and wanted to know who were they to grumble about how many wives he took. Dog-Tooth had a big canoe made, and many more men he took from work, who did nothing and lay in the sun, save only when Dog-Tooth went in the canoe, when they paddled for him. And he made Tiger-Face head man over all the guards, so that Tiger-Face became his right arm, and when he did not like a man Tiger-Face killed that man for him. And Tiger-Face, also, made another man to be his right arm, and to give commands, and to kill for him.

'But this was the strange thing: as the days went by we who were left worked harder and harder, and yet did we get less and less to eat.'

'But what of the goats and the corn and the fat roots and the fish-trap,' spoke up Afraid-of-the-Dark, 'what of all this? Was there not more food to be gained by man's work?'

'It is so,' Long-Beard agreed. 'Three men on the fish-trap got more fish than the whole tribe before there was a fish-trap. But have I not said we were fools? The more food we were able to get, the less food did we have to eat.'

'But was it not plain that the many men who did not work ate it all up?' Yellow-Head demanded.

Long-Beard nodded his head sadly. 'Dog-Tooth's dogs were stuffed with meat, and the men who lay in the sun and did no work were rolling in fat, and, at the same time, there were little children crying themselves to sleep with hunger biting them with every wail.'

Deer-Runner was spurred by the recital of famine to tear out a chunk of bear-meat and broil it on a stick over the coals. This he devoured with smacking lips, while Long-Beard went on:

'When we grumbled Big-Fat arose, and with the voice of God said that God had chosen the wise men to own the land and the goats and the fish-trap and the fire-brew, and that without these wise men we would all be animals, as in the days when we lived in trees.

'And there arose one who became a singer of songs for the king. Him they called the Bug, because he was small and ungainly of face and limb and excelled not in work or deed. He loved the fattest marrow bones, the choicest fish, the milk warm from the goats, the first corn that was ripe, and the snug place by the fire. And thus, becoming singer of songs to the king, he found a way to do nothing and be fat. And when the people grumbled more and more, and some threw stones at the king's grass house, the Bug sang a song of how good it was to be a Fish-Eater. In his song he told that the Fish-Eaters were the chosen of God and the finest men God had made. He sang of the Meat-Eaters as pigs and crows, and sang how fine and good it was for the Fish-Eater to fight and die doing God's work, which was the killing of Meat-Eaters. The words of his song were like fire in us, and we clamored to be led against the Meat-Eaters. And we forgot that we were hungry, and why we had grumbled, and were glad to be led by Tiger-Face over the divide, where we killed many Meat-Eaters and were content.

'But things were no better in the Sea Valley. The only way to get food was to work for Three-Legs or Little-Belly or Pig-Jaw; for there was no land that a man might plant with corn for himself. And often there were more men than Three-Legs and the others had work for. So these men went hungry, and so did their wives and children and their old mothers. Tiger-Face said they could become guards if they wanted to, and many of them did, and thereafter they did no work except to poke spears in the men who did work and who grumbled at feeding so many idlers.

'And when we grumbled, ever the Bug sang new songs. He said that Three-Legs and Pig-Jaw and the rest were strong men, and that that was why they had so much. He said that we should be glad to have strong men with us, else would we perish of our own worthlessness and the Meat-Eaters. Therefore, we should be glad to let such strong men have all they could lay hands on. And Big-Fat and Pig-Jaw and Tiger-Face and all the rest said it was true.

'"All right," said Long-Fang, "then will I, too, be a strong man."' And he got himself corn and began to make fire-brew and sell it for strings of money. And, when Crooked-Eyes complained, Long-Fang said that he was himself a strong man, and that if Crooked-Eyes made any more noise he would bash his brains out for him. Whereat Crooked-Eyes was afraid and went and talked with Three-Legs and Pig-Jaw. And all three went and talked to Dog-Tooth. And Dog-Tooth spoke to Sea-Lion, and Sea-Lion sent a runner with a message to Tiger-Face. And Tiger-Face sent his guards, who burned Long-Fang's house along with the fire-brew he had made. Also, they killed him and all his family. And Big-Fat said it was good, and the Bug sang another song about how

good it was to observe the law, and what a fine land the Sea
Valley was, and how every man who loved the Sea Valley should
go forth and kill the bad Meat-Eaters. And again his song was as
fire to us, and we forgot to grumble.

'It was very strange. When Little-Belly caught too many fish,
so that it took a great many to sell for a little money, he threw
many of the fish back into the sea, so that more money would be
paid for what was left. And Three-Legs often let many large fields
lie idle so as to get more money for his corn. And the women,
making so much money out of shell that much money was
needed to buy with, Dog-Tooth stopped the making of money.
And the women had no work, so they took the places of the men.
I worked on the fish-trap, getting a string of money every five
days. But my sister now did my work, getting a string of money
for every ten days. The women worked cheaper, and there was
less food, and Tiger-Face said for us to become guards. Only I
could not become a guard because I was lame of one leg and
Tiger-Face would not have me. And there were many like me.
We were broken men and only fit to beg for work or to take care
of the babies while the women worked.'

Yellow-Head, too, was made hungry by the recital and broiled
a piece of bear-meat on the coals.

'But why didn't you rise up, all of you, and kill Three-Legs and
Pig-Jaw and Big-Fat and the rest and get enough to eat?' Afraid-
in-the-Dark demanded.

'Because we could not understand,' Long-Beard answered.
'There was too much to think about, and, also, there were the
guards sticking spears into us, and Big-Fat talking about God,
and the Bug singing new songs. And when any man did think
right, and said so, Tiger-Face and the guards got him, and he was
tied out to the rocks at low tide so that the rising waters drowned
him.

'It was a strange thing – the money. It was like the Bug's
songs. It seemed all right, but it wasn't, and we were slow to
understand. Dog-Tooth began to gather the money in. He put it
in a big pile, in a grass house, with guards to watch it day and
night. And the more money he piled in the house the dearer
money became, so that a man worked a longer time for a string
of money than before. Then, too, there was always talk of war
with the Meat-Eaters, and Dog-Tooth and Tiger-Face filled many
houses with corn, and dried fish, and smoked goat-meat, and

cheese. And with the food piled there in mountains the people had not enough to eat. But what did it matter? Whenever the people grumbled too loudly the Bug sang a new song, and Big-Fat said it was God's word that we should kill Meat-Eaters, and Tiger-Face led us over the divide to kill and be killed. I was not good enough to be a guard and lie fat in the sun, but, when we made war, Tiger-Face was glad to take me along. And when we had eaten all the food stored in the houses we stopped fighting and went back to work to pile up more food.'

'Then were you all crazy,' commented Deer-Runner.

'Then were we indeed all crazy,' Long-Beard agreed. 'It was strange, all of it. There was Split-Nose. He said everything was wrong. He said it was true that we grew strong by adding our strength together. And he said that, when we first formed the tribe, it was right that the men whose strength hurt the tribe should be shorn of their strength – men who bashed their brothers' heads and stole their brothers' wives. And now, he said, the tribe was not getting stronger, but was getting weaker, because there were men with another kind of strength that were hurting the tribe – men who had the strength of the land, like Three-Legs; who had the strength of the fish-trap, like Little-Belly; who had the strength of all the goat meat, like Pig-Jaw. The thing to do, Split-Nose said, was to shear these men of their evil strength; to make them go to work, all of them, and to let no man eat who did not work.

'And the Bug sang another song about men like Split-Nose, who wanted to go back and live in trees.

'Yet Split-Nose said no; that he did not want to go back, but ahead; that they grew strong only as they added their strength together; and that, if the Fish-Eaters would add their strength to the Meat-Eaters, there would be no more fighting and no more watchers and no more guards, and that, with all men working, there would be so much food that each man would have to work not more than two hours a day.

'Then the Bug sang again, and he sang that Split-Nose was lazy, and he sang also the "Song of the Bees". It was a strange song, and those who listened were made mad, as from the drinking of strong fire-brew. The song was of a swarm of bees, and of a robber wasp who had come in to live with the bees and who was stealing all their honey. The wasp was lazy and told them there was no need to work; also, he told them to make friends with the bears, who were not honey-stealers but only very good friends. And the Bug sang in crooked words, so that those who listened knew that the swarm was the Sea Valley tribe, that the bears were the Meat-Eaters, and that the lazy wasp was Split-Nose. And, when the Bug sang that the bees listened to the wasp till the swarm was near to perishing, the people growled and snarled, and when the Bug sang that at last the good bees arose and stung the wasp to death, the people picked up stones from the ground and stoned Split-Nose to death till there was naught to be seen of him but the heap of stones they had flung on top of him. And there were many poor people who worked long and hard and had not enough to eat that helped throw the stones on Split-Nose.

'And, after the death of Split-Nose, there was but one other man that dared rise up and speak his mind, and that man was Hair-Face. "Where is the strength of the strong?" he asked. "We are the strong, all of us, and we are stronger than Dog-Tooth and Tiger-Face and Three-Legs and Pig-Jaw and all the rest who do nothing and eat much and weaken us by the hurt of their strength which is bad strength. Men who are slaves are not strong. If the man who first found the virtue and use of fire had used his strength we would have been his slaves, as we are the slaves today of Little-Belly, who found the virtue and use of the fish-trap; and of the men who found the virtue and use of the land, and the goats, and the fire-brew. Before, we lived in trees, my brothers, and no man was safe. But we fight no more with one another. We have added our strength together. Then let us fight no more with the Meat-Eaters. Let us add our strength and their strength together. Then will we be indeed strong. And then we will go out together, the Fish-Eaters and the Meat-Eaters, and we will kill the tigers and the lions and the wolves and the wild dogs, and we will pasture our goats on all the hillsides and plant our corn and fat roots in all the high mountain valleys. In that day we will be so strong that all the wild animals will flee before us and perish. And nothing will withstand us, for the strength of each man will be the strength of all men in the world."

'So said Hair-Face, and they killed him, because, they said, he was a wild man and wanted to go back and live in a tree. It was very strange. Whenever a man arose and wanted to go forward all those that stood still said he went backward and should be killed. And the poor people helped stone him, and were fools. We were all fools, except those who were fat and did not work. The fools were called wise, and the wise were stoned. Men who worked did not get enough to eat, and the men who did not work ate too much.

'And the tribe went on losing strength. The children were weak and sickly. And, because we ate not enough, strange sicknesses came among us and we died like flies. And then the Meat-Eaters came upon us. We had followed Tiger-Face too often over the divide and killed them. And now they came to repay in blood. We were too weak and sick to man the big wall. And they killed us, all of us, except some of the women, which they took away with them. The Bug and I escaped, and I hid in the wildest places, and became a hunter of meat and went hungry no more. I stole a wife from the Meat-Eaters, and went to live in the caves of the high mountains where they could not find me. And we had three sons, and each son stole a wife from the Meat-Eaters. And the rest you know, for are you not the sons of my sons?'

'But the Bug?' queried Deer-Runner. 'What became of him?'

'He went to live with the Meat-Eaters and to be a singer of songs to the king. He is an old man now, but he sings the same old songs; and, when a man rises up to go forward, he sings that that man is walking backward to live in a tree.'

Long Beard dipped into the bear-carcass and sucked with toothless gums at a fist of suet.

'Some day,' he said, wiping his hands on his sides, 'all the fools will be dead and then all live men will go forward. The strength of the strong will be theirs, and they will add their strength together, so that, of all the men in the world, not one will fight with another. There will be no guards nor watchers on the walls. And all the hunting animals will be killed, and, as Hair-Face said, all the hillsides will be pastured with goats and all the high mountain valleys will be planted with corn and fat roots. And all men will be brothers, and no man will lie idle in the sun and be fed by his fellows. And all that will come to pass in the time when the fools are dead, and when there will be no more singers to stand still and sing the "Song of the Bees". Bees are not men.'

The Dream of Debs (1909; 1914)

I awoke fully an hour before my customary time. This in itself was remarkable, and I lay very wide awake, pondering over it. Something was the matter, something was wrong – I knew not what. I was oppressed by a premonition of something terrible that had happened or was about to happen. But what was it? I strove to orient myself. I remembered that at the time of the Great Earthquake of 1906 many claimed they awakened some moments before the first shock and that during these moments they experienced strange feelings of dread. Was San Francisco again to be visited by earthquake?

I lay for a full minute, numbly expectant, but there occurred no reeling of walls nor shock and grind of falling masonry. All was quiet. That was it! The silence! No wonder I had been perturbed. The hum of the great live city was strangely absent. The surface cars passed along my street, at that time of day, on an average of one every three minutes; but in the ten succeeding minutes not a car passed. Perhaps it was a street railway strike, was my thought; or perhaps there had been an accident and the power was shut off. But no, the silence was too profound. I heard no jar and rattle of wagon wheels, nor stamp of iron-shod hoofs straining up the steep cobble-stones.

Pressing the push-button beside my bed, I strove to hear the sound of the bell, though I well knew it was impossible for the sound to rise three stories to me even if the bell did ring. It rang all right, for a few minutes later Brown entered with the tray and morning paper. Though his features were impassive as ever, I noted a startled, apprehensive light in his eyes. I noted, also, that there was no cream on the tray.

'The Creamery did not deliver this morning,' he explained; 'nor did the bakery.'

I glanced again at the tray. There were no fresh French rolls – only slices of stale graham bread from yesterday, the most detestable of bread so far as I was concerned.

'Nothing was delivered this morning, sir,' Brown started to explain apologetically; but I interrupted him.

'The paper?'

'Yes, sir, it was delivered, but it was the only thing, and it is the last time, too. There won't be any paper tomorrow. The paper says so. Can I send out and get you some condensed milk?'

I shook my head, accepted the coffee black, and spread open the paper. The headlines explained everything – explained too much, in fact, for the lengths of pessimism to which the journal went were ridiculous. A general strike, it said, had been called all over the United States; and most foreboding anxieties were expressed concerning the provisioning of the great cities.

I read on hastily, skimming much and remembering much of labor troubles in the past. For a generation the general strike had been the dream of organized labor, which dream had arisen originally in the mind of Debs, one of the great labor leaders of thirty years before. I recollected that in my young college-settlement days I had even written an article on the subject for one of the magazines and that I had entitled it, 'The Dream of Debs'. And I must confess that I had treated the idea very cavalierly and academically as a dream and nothing more. Time and the world had rolled on, Gompers was gone, the American Federation of Labor was gone, and gone was Debs with all his wild revolutionary ideas; but the dream had persisted, and here it was at last realized in fact. But I laughed, as I read, at the journal's gloomy outlook. I knew better. I had seen organized labor worsted in too many conflicts. It would be a matter only of days when the thing would be settled. This was a national strike, and it wouldn't take the government long to break it.

I threw the paper down and proceeded to dress. It would certainly be interesting to be out in the streets of San Francisco when not a wheel was turning and the whole city was taking an enforced vacation.

'I beg your pardon, sir,' Brown said, as he handed me my cigar case, 'but Mr Harmmed has asked to see you before you go out.'

'Send him in right away,' I answered.

Harmmed was the butler. When he entered I could see he was laboring under controlled excitement. He came at once to the point.

'What shall I do, sir? There will be needed provisions, and the delivery drivers are on strike. And the electricity is shut off – I guess they're on strike, too.'

'Are the shops open?' I asked.

'Only the small ones, sir. The retail clerks are out, and the big ones can't open; but the owners and their families are running the little ones themselves.'

'Then take the machine,' I said, 'and go the rounds and make your purchases. Buy plenty of everything you need or may need. Get a box of candles – no, get half a dozen boxes. And, when you're done, tell Harrison to bring the machine around to the club for me – not later than eleven.'

Harmmed shook his head gravely. 'Mr Harrison has struck along with the Chauffeurs' Union, and I don't know how to run the machine myself.'

'Oh, ho, he has, has he?' I said. 'Well, when next *Mister* Harrison happens around you tell him that he can look elsewhere for a position.'

'Yes, sir.'

'You don't happen to belong to a Butlers' Union, do you, Harmmed?'

'No, sir,' was the answer. 'And even if I did I'd not desert my employer in a crisis like this. No, sir, I would –'

'All right, thank you,' I said. 'Now you get ready to accompany me. I'll run the machine myself, and we'll lay in a stock of provisions to stand a siege.'

It was a beautiful first of May, even as May days go. The sky was cloudless, there was no wind, and the air was warm – almost balmy. Many autos were out, but the owners were driving them themselves. The streets were crowded but quiet. The working class, dressed in its Sunday best, was out taking the air and observing the effects of the strike. It was all so unusual, and withal so peaceful, that I found myself enjoying it. My nerves were tingling with mild excitement. It was a sort of placid adventure. I passed Miss Chickering. She was at the helm of her little runabout. She swung around and came after me, catching me at the corner.

'Oh, Mr Corf!' she hailed. 'Do you know where I can buy candles? I've been to a dozen shops, and they're all sold out. It's dreadfully awful, isn't it?'

But her sparkling eyes gave the lie to her words. Like the rest of us, she was enjoying it hugely. Quite an adventure it was, getting those candles. It was not until we went across the city and down into the working-class quarter south of Market Street that we found small corner groceries that had not yet sold out. Miss Chickering thought one box was sufficient, but I persuaded her into taking four. My car was large, and I laid in a dozen boxes. There was no telling what delays might arise in the settlement of the strike. Also, I filled the car with sacks of flour, baking-powder, tinned goods, and all the ordinary necessaries of life suggested by Harmmed, who fussed around and clucked over the purchases like an anxious old hen.

The remarkable thing, that first day of the strike, was that no one really apprehended anything serious. The announcement of organized labor in the morning papers that it was prepared to stay out a month or three months was laughed at. And yet that very first day we might have guessed as much from the fact that the working class took practically no part in the great rush to buy provisions. Of course not. For weeks and months, craftily and secretly, the whole working class had been laying in private stocks of provisions. That was why we were permitted to go down and buy out the little groceries in the working-class neighborhoods.

It was not until I arrived at the Club that afternoon that I began to feel the first alarm. Everything was in confusion. There were no olives for the cocktails, and the service was by hitches and jerks. Most of the men were angry, and all were worried. A babel of voices greeted me as I entered. General Folsom, nursing his capacious paunch in a window seat in the smoking-room was defending himself against half a dozen excited gentlemen who were demanding that he do something.

'What can I do more than I have done?' he was saying. 'There are no orders from Washington. If you gentlemen will get a wire through I'll do anything I am commanded to do. But I don't see what can be done. The first thing I did this morning, as soon as I learned of the strike, was to order in the troops from the Presidio – three thousand of them. They're guarding the banks, the Mint, the post office, and all the public buildings. There is no disorder whatever. The strikers are keeping the peace perfectly. You can't expect me to shoot them down as they walk along the streets with wives and children all in their best bib and tucker.'

'I'd like to know what's happening on Wall Street,' I heard Jimmy Wombold say as I passed along. I could imagine his anxiety, for I knew that he was deep in the big Consolidated-Western deal.

'Say, Corf,' Atkinson bustled up to me, 'is your machine running?'

'Yes,' I answered, 'but what's the matter with your own?'

'Broken down, and the garages are all closed. And my wife's somewhere around Truckee, I think, stalled on the overland. Can't get a wire to her for love or money. She should have arrived this evening. She may be starving. Lend me your machine.'

'Can't get it across the bay,' Halstead spoke up. 'The ferries aren't running. But I tell you what you can do. There's Rollinson – oh, Rollinson, come here a moment. Atkinson wants to get a machine across the bay. His wife is stuck on the overland at Truckee. Can't you bring the *Lurlette* across from Tiburon and carry the machine over for him?'

The *Lurlette* was a two-hundred-ton, ocean-going, schooner-yacht.

Rollinson shook his head. 'You couldn't get a longshoreman to land the machine on board, even if I could get the *Lurlette* over, which I can't, for the crew are members of the Coast Seamen's Union, and they're on strike along with the rest.'

'But my wife may be starving,' I could hear Atkinson wailing as I moved on.

At the other end of the smoking-room I ran into a group of men bunched excitedly and angrily around Bertie Messener. And Bertie was stirring them up and prodding them in his cool, cynical way. Bertie didn't care about the strike. He didn't care much about anything. He was blasé – at least in all the clean things of life; the nasty things had no attraction for him. He was worth twenty millions, all of it in safe investments, and he had never done a tap of productive work in his life – inherited it all from his father and two uncles. He had been everywhere, seen everything, and done everything but get married, and this last in the face of the grim and determined attack of a few hundred ambitious mammas. For years he had been the greatest catch, and as yet he had avoided being caught. He was disgracefully eligible. On top of his wealth he was young, handsome, and, as I said before, clean. He was a great athlete, a young blond god that did everything perfectly and admirably with the solitary exception of matrimony. And he didn't care about anything, had no ambitions, no passions, no desire to do the very things he did so much better than other men.

'This is sedition!' one man in the group was crying. Another called it revolt and revolution, and another called it anarchy.

'I can't see it,' Bertie said. 'I have been out in the streets all morning. Perfect order reigns. I never saw a more law-abiding populace. There's no use calling it names. It's not any of those things. It's just what it claims to be, a general strike, and it's your turn to play, gentlemen.'

'And we'll play all right!' cried Garfield, one of the traction millionaires. 'We'll show this dirt where its place is – the beasts! Wait till the government takes a hand.'

'But where is the government?' Bertie interposed. 'It might as well be at the bottom of the sea so far as you're concerned. You don't know what's happening at Washington. You don't know whether you've got a government or not.'

'Don't you worry about that!' Garfield blurted out.

'I assure you I'm not worrying,' Bertie smiled languidly. 'But it seems to me it's what you fellows are doing. Look in the glass, Garfield.'

Garfield did not look, but had he looked he would have seen a very excited gentleman with rumpled, iron-gray hair, a flushed face, mouth sullen and vindictive, and eyes wildly gleaming.

'It's not right, I tell you,' little Hanover said; and from his tone I was sure that he had already said it a number of times.

'Now that's going too far, Hanover,' Bertie replied. 'You fellows make me tired. You're all open-shop men. You've eroded my eardrums with your endless gabble for the open shop and the right of a man to work. You've harangued along those lines for years. Labor is doing nothing wrong in going out on this general strike. It is violating no law of God nor man. Don't you talk, Hanover. You've been ringing the changes too long on the God-given right to work ... or not to work; you can't escape the corollary. It's a dirty little sordid scrap, that's all the whole thing is. You've got labor down and gouged it, and now labor's got you down and is gouging you, that's all, and you're squealing.'

Every man in the group broke out in indignant denials that labor had ever been gouged.

'No sir!' Garfield was shouting. 'We've done the best for labor. Instead of gouging it, we've given it a chance to live. We've made work for it. Where would labor be if it hadn't been for us?'

'A whole lot better off,' Bertie sneered. 'You've got labor down and gouged it every time you got a chance, and you went out of your way to make chances.'

'No! No!' were the cries.

'There was the teamsters' strike, right here in San Francisco,' Bertie went on imperturbably. 'The Employers' Association precipitated that strike. You know that. And you know I know it, too, for I've sat in these very rooms and heard the inside talk and news of the fight. First you precipitated the strike, then you bought the Mayor and the Chief of Police and broke the strike. A pretty spectacle, you philanthropists getting the teamsters down and gouging them.

'Hold on, I'm not through with you. It's only last year that the labor ticket of Colorado elected a governor. He was never seated. You know why. You know how your brother philanthropists and capitalists of Colorado worked it. It was a case of getting labor down and gouging it. You kept the President of the Southwestern Amalgamated Association of Miners in jail for three years on trumped-up murder charges, and with him out of the way you broke up the association. That was gouging labor, you'll admit. The third time the graduated income tax was declared unconstitutional was a gouge. So was the Eight-hour Bill you killed in the last Congress.

'And of all unmitigated immoral gouges, your destruction of the closed-shop principle was the limit. You know how it was done. You bought out Farburg, the last president of the old American Federation of Labor. He was your creature – or the creature of all the trusts and employers' associations, which is the same thing. You precipitated the big closed-shop strike. Farburg betrayed that strike. You won, and the old American Federation of Labor crumbled to pieces. You fellows destroyed it, and by so doing undid yourselves; for right on top of it began the organization of the ILW – the biggest and solidest organization of labor the United States has ever seen, and you are responsible for its existence and for the present general strike. You smashed all the old federations and drove labor into the ILW, and the ILW called the general strike – still fighting for the closed shop. And then you have the effrontery to stand here face to face and tell me that you never got labor down and gouged it. Bah!'

This time there were no denials. Garfield broke out in self-defense:

'We've done nothing we were not compelled to do, if we were to win.'

'I'm not saying anything about that,' Bertie answered. 'What I am complaining about is your squealing now that you're getting a taste of your own medicine. How many strikes have you won by starving labor into submission? Well, labor's worked out a scheme whereby to starve you into submission. It wants the closed shop, and, if it can get it by starving you, why starve you shall.'

'I notice that you have profited in the past by those very labor-gouges you mention,' insinuated Brentwood, one of the wiliest and most astute of our corporation lawyers. 'The receiver is as bad as the thief,' he sneered. 'You had no hand in the gouging, but you took your whack out of the gouge.'

'That is quite beside the question, Brentwood,' Bertie drawled. 'You're as bad as Hanover, intruding the moral element. I haven't said that anything is right or wrong. It's all a rotten game, I know; and my sole kick is that you fellows are squealing now that you're down and labor's taking a gouge out of you. Of course I've taken the profits from the gouging and, thanks to you, gentlemen, without having personally to do the dirty work. You did that for me – oh, believe me, not because I am more virtuous than you, but because my good father and his various brothers left me a lot of money with which to pay for the dirty work.'

'If you mean to insinuate –' Brentwood began hotly.

'Hold on, don't get all – ruffled up,' Bertie interposed insolently. 'There's no use in playing hypocrites in this thieves' den. The high and lofty is all right for the newspapers, boys' clubs, and Sunday schools – that's part of the game; but for heaven's sake don't let's play it on one another. You know, and you know that I know, just what jobbery was done in the building trades strike last fall, who put up the money, who did the work, and who profited by it.' (Brentwood flushed darkly.) 'But we are all tarred with the same brush, and the best thing for us to do is to leave morality out of it. Again I repeat, play the game, play it to the last finish, but for goodness' sake don't squeal when you get hurt.'

When I left the group Bertie was off on a new tack tormenting them with the more serious aspects of the situation, pointing out the shortage of supplies that was already making itself felt, and asking them what they were going to do about it. A little later I met him in the cloak room, leaving, and gave him a lift home in my machine.

'It's a great stroke, this general strike,' he said, as we bowled along through the crowded, but orderly, streets. 'It's a smashing body-blow. Labor caught us napping and struck at our weakest place, the stomach. I'm going to get out of San Francisco, Corf. Take my advice and get out, too. Head for the country, anywhere. You'll have more chance. Buy up a stock of supplies and get into a tent or a cabin somewhere. Soon there'll be nothing but starvation in this city for such as we.'

How correct Bertie Messener was I never dreamed. I decided that he was an alarmist. As for myself, I was content to remain and watch the fun. After I dropped him, instead of going directly home, I went on in a hunt for more food. To my surprise, I learned that the small groceries where I had bought in the morning were sold out. I extended my search to the Potrero, and by good luck managed to pick up another box of candles, two sacks of wheat flour, ten pounds of graham flour (which would do for the servants), a case of tinned corn, and two cases of tinned tomatoes. It did look as though there was going to be at least a temporary food shortage, and I hugged myself over the goodly stock of provisions I had laid in.

The next morning I had my coffee in bed as usual, and, more than the cream, I missed the daily paper. It was this absence of knowledge of what was going on in the world that I found the chiefest hardship. Down at the club there was little news. Rider had crossed from Oakland in his launch, and Halstead had been down to San Jose and back in his machine. They reported the same conditions in those places as in San Francisco. Everything was tied up by the strike. All grocery stocks had been bought out by the upper classes. And perfect order reigned. But what was happening over the rest of the country – in Chicago? New York? Washington? Most probably the same things that were happening with us, we concluded; but the fact that we did not know with absolute surety was irritating.

General Folsom had a bit of news. An attempt had been made to place army telegraphers in the telegraph offices, but the wires had been cut in every direction. This was, so far, the one unlawful act committed by labor, and that it was a concerted act he was fully convinced. He had communicated by wireless with the army post at Benicia, the telegraph lines were even then being patroled by soldiers all the way to Sacramento. Once, for one short instant, they had got the Sacramento call, then the wires, somewhere, were cut again. General Folsom reasoned that similar attempts to open communication were being made by the authorities all the way across the continent, but he was non-committal as to whether or not he thought the attempt would succeed. What worried him was the wire-cutting; he could not but believe that it was an important part of the deep-laid labor conspiracy. Also, he regretted that the government had not long since established its projected chain of wireless stations.

The days came and went, and for a while it was a humdrum time. Nothing happened. The edge of excitement had become blunted. The streets were not so crowded. The working class did not come uptown any more to see how we were taking the strike. And there were not so many automobiles running around. The repair shops and garages were closed, and whenever a machine broke down it went out of commission. The clutch on mine broke, and love nor money could not get it repaired. Like the rest, I now was walking. San Francisco lay dead, and we did not know what was happening over the rest of the country. But from the very fact that we did not know we could conclude only that the rest of the country lay as dead as San Francisco. From time to time the city was placarded with the proclamations of organized labor – these had been printed months before, and evidenced how thoroughly the ILW had prepared for the strike. Every detail had been worked out long in advance. No violence had occurred as yet, with the exception of the shooting of a few wire-cutters by the soldiers, but the people of the slums were starving and growing ominously restless.

The business men, the millionaires, and the professional class held meetings and passed resolutions, but there was no way of making the proclamations public. They could not even get them printed. One result of these meetings, however, was that General Folsom was persuaded into taking military possession of the wholesale houses and of all the flour, grain, and food warehouses. It was high time, for suffering was becoming acute in the homes of the rich, and bread-lines were necessary. I knew that my servants were beginning to draw long faces, and it was amazing – the hole they made in my stock of provisions. In fact, as I afterward surmised, each servant was stealing from me and secreting a private stock of provisions for himself.

But with the formation of the bread-lines came new troubles. There was only so much of a food reserve in San Francisco, and at the best it could not last long. Organized labor, we knew, had its private supplies; nevertheless, the whole working class joined the bread-lines. As a result, the provisions General Folsom had taken possession of diminished with perilous rapidity. How were the soldiers to distinguish between a shabby middle-class man, a member of the ILW, or a slum dweller? The first and the last had to

be fed, but the soldiers did not know all the ILW men in the city,
much less the wives and sons and daughters of the ILW men. The
employers helping, a few of the known union men were flung out
of the bread-lines; but that amounted to nothing. To make matters
worse, the government tugs that had been hauling food from the
army depots on Mare Island to Angel Island found no more food to
haul. The soldiers now received their rations from the confiscated
provisions, and they received them first.

The beginning of the end was in sight. Violence was beginning
to show its face. Law and order were passing away, and passing
away, I must confess, among the slum people and the upper
classes. Organized labor still maintained perfect order. It could
well afford to – it had plenty to eat. I remember the afternoon at
the club when I caught Halstead and Brentwood whispering in a
corner. They took me in on the venture. Brentwood's machine
was still in running order, and they were going out cow-stealing.
Halstead had a long butcher knife and a cleaver. We went out to
the outskirts of the city. Here and there were cows grazing, but
always they were guarded by their owners. We pursued our
quest, following along the fringe of the city to the east, and on
the hills near Hunter's Point we came upon a cow guarded by a
little girl. There was also a young calf with the cow. We wasted
no time on preliminaries. The little girl ran away screaming,
while we slaughtered the cow. I omit the details, for they are not
nice – we were unaccustomed to such work, and we bungled it.

But in the midst of it, working with the haste of fear, we heard
cries, and we saw a number of men running toward us. We
abandoned the spoils and took to our heels. To our surprise we
were not pursued. Looking back, we saw the men hurriedly
cutting up the cow. They had been on the same lay as ourselves.
We argued that there was plenty for all, and ran back. The scene
that followed beggars description. We fought and squabbled over
the division like savages. Brentwood, I remember, was a perfect
brute, snarling and snapping and threatening that murder would
be done if we did not get our proper share.

And we were getting our share when there occurred a new
irruption on the scene. This time it was the dreaded peace officers
of the ILW. The little girl had brought them. They were armed
with whips and clubs, and there were a score of them. The little
girl danced up and down in anger, the tears streaming down her
cheeks, crying: 'Give it to 'em! Give it to 'em! That guy with the

specs – he did it! Mash his face for him! Mash his face!' That guy with the specs was I, and I got my face mashed, too, though I had the presence of mind to take off my glasses at the first. My! but we did receive a trouncing as we scattered in all directions. Brentwood, Halstead and I fled away for the machine. Brentwood's nose was bleeding, while Halstead's cheek was cut across with the scarlet slash of a black-snake whip.

And, lo, when the pursuit ceased and we had gained the machine, there, hiding behind it, was the frightened calf. Brentwood warned us to be cautious, and crept up on it like a wolf or a tiger. Knife and cleaver had been left behind, but Brentwood still had his hands, and over and over on the ground he rolled with the poor little calf as he throttled it. We threw the carcass into the machine, covered it over with a robe, and started for home. But our misfortunes had only begun. We blew out a tire. There was no way of fixing it, and twilight was coming on. We abandoned the machine, Brentwood puffing and staggering along in advance, the calf, covered by the robe, slung across his shoulders. We took turn about carrying that calf, and it nearly killed us. Also, we lost our way. And then, after hours of wandering and toil, we encountered a gang of hoodlums. They were not ILW men, and I guess they were as hungry as we. At any rate, they got the calf and we got the thrashing. Brentwood raged like a madman the rest of the way home, and he looked like one, what of his torn clothes, swollen nose, and blackened eyes.

There wasn't any more cow-stealing after that. General Folsom sent his troopers out and confiscated all the cows, and his troopers, aided by the militia, ate most of the meat. General Folsom was not to be blamed; it was his duty to maintain law and order, and he maintained it by means of the soldiers, wherefore he was compelled to feed them first of all.

It was about this time that the great panic occurred. The wealthy classes precipitated the flight, and then the slum people caught the contagion and stampeded wildly out of the city. General Folsom was pleased. It was estimated that at least 200,000 had deserted San Francisco, and by that much was his food problem solved. Well do I remember that day. In the morning I had eaten a crust of bread. Half of the afternoon I had stood in the bread-line; and after dark I returned home, tired and miserable, carrying a quart of rice and a slice of bacon. Brown met me at the door. His face was worn and terrified. All the servants had fled, he informed me. He alone remained. I was touched by his faithfulness and, when I learned that he had eaten nothing all day, I divided my food with him. We cooked half the rice and half the bacon, sharing it equally and reserving the other half for morning. I went to bed with my hunger, and tossed restlessly all night. In the morning I found Brown had deserted me, and, greater misfortune still, he had stolen what remained of the rice and bacon.

It was a gloomy handful of men that came together at the Club that morning. There was no service at all. The last servant was gone. I noticed, too, that the silver was gone, and I learned where it had gone. The servants had not taken it, for the reason, I presume, that the club members got to it first. Their method of disposing of it was simple. Down south of Market Street, in the dwellings of the ILW, the housewives had given square meals in exchange for it. I went back to my house. Yes, my silver was gone – all but a massive pitcher. This I wrapped up and carried down south of Market.

I felt better after the meal, and returned to the Club to learn if there was anything new in the situation. Hanover, Collins, and Dakon were just leaving. There was no one inside, they told me, and they invited me to come along with them. They were leaving the city, they said, on Dakon's horses, and there was a spare one for me. Dakon had four magnificent carriage horses that he wanted to save, and General Folsom had given him the tip that next morning all the horses that remained in the city were to be confiscated for food. There were not many horses left, for tens of thousands of them had been turned loose into the country when the hay and grain gave out during the first days. Birdall, I remember, who had great draying interests, had turned loose three hundred dray horses. At an average value of five hundred dollars, this had amounted to $150,000. He had hoped, at first, to recover most of the horses after the strike was over, but in the end he never recovered one of them. They were all eaten by the people that fled from San Francisco. For that matter, the killing of the army mules and horses for food had already begun.

Fortunately for Dakon, he had had a plentiful supply of hay and grain stored in his stable. We managed to raise four saddles, and we found the animals in good condition and spirited, withal unused to being ridden. I remembered the San Francisco of the great earthquake as we rode through the streets, but this San

Francisco was vastly more pitiable. No cataclysm of nature had caused this, but, rather, the tyranny of the labor unions. We rode down past Union Square and through the theater, hotel, and shopping districts. The streets were deserted. Here and there stood automobiles, abandoned where they had broken down or when the gasolene had given out. There was no sign of life, save for the occasional policemen and the soldiers guarding the banks and public buildings. Once we came upon an ILW man pasting up the latest proclamation. We stopped to read. 'We have maintained an orderly strike,' it ran; 'and we shall maintain order to the end. The end will come when our demands are satisfied, and our demands will be satisfied when we have starved our employers into submission, as we ourselves in the past have often been starved into submission.'

'Messener's very words,' Collins said. 'And I, for one, am ready to submit, only they won't give me a chance to submit. I haven't had a full meal in an age. I wonder what horse meat tastes like?'

We stopped to read another proclamation: 'When we think our employers are ready to submit we shall open up the telegraphs and place the employers' associations of the United States in communication. But only messages relating to peace terms shall be permitted over the wires.'

We rode on, crossed Market Street, and a little later were passing through the working-class district. Here the streets were not deserted. Leaning over gates or standing in groups were the ILW men. Happy, well-fed children were playing games, and stout housewives sat on the front steps gossiping. One and all cast amused glances at us. Little children ran after us, crying: 'Hey, mister, ain't you hungry?' And one woman, a nursing child at her breast, called to Dakon: 'Say, Fatty, I'll give you a meal for your skate – ham and potatoes, currant jelly, white bread, canned butter, and two cups of coffee.'

'Have you noticed, the last few days,' Hanover remarked to me, 'that there's not been a stray dog in the streets?'

I had noticed, but I had not thought about it before. It was high time to leave the unfortunate city. We at last managed to connect with the San Bruno Road, along which we headed south. I had a country place near Menlo, and it was our objective. But soon we began to discover that the country was worse off and far more dangerous than the city. There the soldiers and the ILW kept order; but the country had been turned over to anarchy. Two hundred thousand people had fled from San Francisco, and we had countless evidences that their flight had been like that of an army of locusts. They had swept everything clean. There had been robbery and fighting. Here and there we passed bodies by the roadside and saw the blackened ruins of farmhouses. The fences were down, and the crops had been trampled by the feet of a multitude. All the vegetable patches had been rooted up by the famished hordes. All the chickens and farm animals had been slaughtered. This was true of all the main roads that led out of San Francisco. Here and there, away from the roads, farmers had held their own with shotguns and revolvers, and were still holding their own. They warned us away and refused to parley with us. And all the destruction and violence had been done by the slum dwellers and the upper classes. The ILW men, with plentiful food supplies, remained quietly in their homes in the cities.

Early in the ride we received concrete proof of how desperate was the situation. To the right of us we heard cries and rifle shots. Bullets whistled dangerously near. There was a crashing in the underbrush; then a magnificent black truck-horse broke across the road in front of us and was gone. We had barely time to notice that he was bleeding and lame. He was followed by three soldiers. The chase went on among the trees on the left. We could hear the soldiers calling to one another. A fourth soldier limped out upon the road from the right, sat down on a boulder, and mopped the sweat from his face.

'Militia,' Dakon whispered. 'Deserters.'

The man grinned up at us and asked for a match. In reply to Dakon's 'What's the word?' he informed us that the militiamen were deserting. 'No grub,' he explained. 'They're feedin' it all to the regulars.' We also learned from him that the military prisoners had been released from Alcatraz Island because they could no longer be fed.

I shall never forget the next sight we encountered. We came upon it abruptly, around a turn of the road. Overhead arched the trees. The sunshine was filtering down through the branches. Butterflies were fluttering by, and from the fields came the song of larks. And there it stood, a powerful touring car. About it and in it lay a number of corpses. It told its own tale. Its occupants, fleeing from the city, had been attacked and dragged down by a gang of slum dwellers – hoodlums. The thing had occurred within twenty-four hours. Freshly opened meat and fruit tins explained the reason for the attack. Dakon examined the bodies.

'I thought so,' he reported. 'I've ridden in that car. It was Perriton – the whole family. We've got to watch out for ourselves from now on.'

'But we have no food with which to invite attack,' I objected.

Dakon pointed to the horse I rode, and I understood.

Early in the day Dakon's horse had cast a shoe. The delicate hoof had split, and by noon the animal was limping. Dakon refused to ride it farther, and refused to desert it. So, on his solicitation, we went on. He would lead the horse and join us at my place. That was the last we saw of him; nor did we ever learn his end.

By one o'clock we arrived at the town of Menlo, or, rather, at the site of Menlo, for it was in ruins. Corpses lay everywhere. The business part of the town, as well as part of the residences, had been gutted by fire. Here and there a residence still held out; but there was no getting near them. When we approached too closely we were fired upon. We met a woman who was poking about in the smoking ruins of her cottage. The first attack, she told us, had been on the stores, and as she talked we could picture that raging, roaring, hungry mob flinging itself on the handful of townspeople. Millionaires and paupers had fought side by side for the food, and then fought with one another after they got it. The town of Palo Alto and Stanford University had been sacked in similar fashion, we learned. Ahead of us lay a desolate, wasted land; and we thought we were wise in turning off to my place. It lay three miles to the west, snuggling among the first rolling swells of the foothills.

But as we rode along we saw that the devastation was not confined to the main roads. The van of the flight had kept to the roads, sacking the small towns as it went; while those that followed had scattered out and swept the whole countryside like a great broom. My place was built of concrete, masonry, and tiles, and so had escaped being burned, but it was gutted clean. We found the gardener's body in the windmill, littered around with empty shotgun shells. He had put up a good fight. But no trace could we find of the two Italian laborers, nor of the housekeeper and her husband. Not a live thing remained. The calves, the colts, all the fancy poultry and thoroughbred stock, everything, was gone. The kitchen and the fireplaces, where the mob had cooked, were a mess, while many camp-fires outside bore witness to the large number that had fed and spent the night. What they had not eaten they had carried away. There was not a bite for us.

We spent the rest of the night vainly waiting for Dakon, and in the morning, with our revolvers, fought off half a dozen marauders. Then we killed one of Dakon's horses, hiding for the future what meat we did not immediately eat. In the afternoon Collins went out for a walk, but failed to return. This was the last straw to Hanover. He was for flight there and then, and I had great difficulty in persuading him to wait for daylight. As for myself, I was convinced that the end of the general strike was near, and I was resolved to return to San Francisco. So, in the morning, we parted company, Hanover heading south, fifty pounds of horse meat strapped to his saddle, while I, similarly loaded, headed north. Little Hanover pulled through all right, and to the end of his life he will persist, I know, in boring everybody with the narrative of his subsequent adventures.

I got as far as Belmont, on the main road back, when I was robbed of my horse meat by three militiamen. There was no change in the situation, they said, except that it was going from bad to worse. The ILW had plenty of provisions hidden away and could last out for months. I managed to get as far as Baden, when my horse was taken away from me by a dozen men. Two of them were San Francisco policemen, and the remainder were regular soldiers. This was ominous. The situation was certainly extreme when the regulars were beginning to desert. When I continued my way on foot, they already had the fire started, and the last of Dakon's horses lay slaughtered on the ground.

As luck would have it, I sprained my ankle, and succeeded in getting no farther than South San Francisco. I lay there that night in an outhouse, shivering with the cold and at the same time burning with fever. Two days I lay there, too sick to move, and on the third, reeling and giddy, supporting myself on an extemporized crutch, I tottered on toward San Francisco. I was weak as well, for it was the third day since food had passed my lips. It was a day of nightmare and torment. As in a dream I passed hundreds of regular soldiers drifting along in the opposite direction, and many policemen, with their families, organized in large groups for mutual protection.

As I entered the city I remembered the workman's house at which I had traded the silver pitcher, and in that direction my hunger drove me. Twilight was falling when I came to the place. I passed around by the alleyway and crawled up the back steps, on which I collapsed. I managed to reach out with the crutch and knock on the door. Then I must have fainted, for I came to in the kitchen, my face wet with water and whisky being poured down my throat. I choked and spluttered and tried to talk. I began saying something about not having any more silver pitchers, but that I would make it up to them afterward if they would only give me something to eat. But the housewife interrupted me.

'Why you poor man!' she said. 'Haven't you heard? The strike was called off this afternoon. Of course we'll give you something to eat.'

She bustled around, opening a tin of breakfast bacon and preparing to fry it.

'Let me have some now, please,' I begged; and I ate the raw bacon on a slice of bread, while her husband explained that the demands of the ILW had been granted. The wires had been opened up in the early afternoon, and everywhere the employers' associations had given in. There hadn't been any employers left in San Francisco, but General Folsom had spoken for them. The trains and steamers would start running in the morning, and so would everything else just as soon as system could be established.

And that was the end of the general strike. I never want to see another one. It was worse than a war. A general strike is a cruel and immoral thing, and the brain of man should be capable of running industry in a more rational way. Harrison is still my chauffeur. It was part of the conditions of the ILW that all of its members should be reinstated in their old positions. Brown never came back, but the rest of the servants are with me. I hadn't the heart to discharge them – poor creatures, they were pretty hard-pressed when they deserted with the food and silver. And now I can't discharge them. They have all been unionized by the ILW. The tyranny of organized labor is getting beyond human endurance. Something must be done.